Lost Children
PROTECTORS

Stories To Benefit PROTECT

This collection was published to benefit PROTECT and The National Association to Protect Children. This is an independently organized project, not officially sponsored by PROTECT. If you enjoyed it, please consider becoming a member. http://www.protect.org/

Your support matters.

You can see the donation record for the Protectors anthology at our website: http://the-lost-children.blogspot.com/

PROTECT lobbies for legislation that protects children from physical, sexual, and emotional abuse. Among their victories are the Protect Our Children Act of 2008, which mandated that the Justice Department change course and design a new national nerve center for law enforcement to wage a war on child exploitation.

Find more about PROTECT and join the fight at http://www.protect.org/

Thank you.

Table of Contents

FOREWORD

Dave Marsh

"I have a tale to tell
Sometimes it gets so hard to hide it well"
—Madonna, *"Live to Tell"*

The stories in this book are about children in jeopardy. They're made up, works of the imagination, all with coherent beginning, middle and end. One thing leads to another, believably but never quite predictably. I'd pay good money to read more of them, any time.

PROTECT, and its parent organization, the National Association to Protect Children, is in the business of telling stories too. They're real, about works nobody untouched by evil would imagine, and they often have to be sifted from an inchoate web of occurrences, although sometimes their outcomes are all too predictable. Everybody involved in PROTECT would pay in blood, sweat and tears to keep such stories from happening again, at least someday.

Unlike the writers in this book, PROTECT has a very specific audience in mind for the tales it tells. Mainly, that audience consists of lawmakers who hold the power to change the ways in which abusers of children are defined, captured and punished. It also speaks to the public, those who are interested in learning about the prevalence of child abuse, the numerous forms it takes, the difference between abuse in real life and the sort portrayed on television. The NAPC is a nonprofit membership organization. It was founded on the premise that the most important and sacred obligation of humans—let alone citizens and parents—is to keep children safe from harm. Its programs include the creation and circulation of technologies which make it more possible to identify both sex predators and the distributors of child pornography, which is both the profit center and the bait of the child abuse culture; the adoption and effective use of "sunshine" laws that make those bureaucracies charged with taking care of children more accountable and effective; and grassroots campaigns such as Not One More Child.

PROTECT is a lobby (and thus can't be a nonprofit), which works in both the United States Congress and in the legislatures of the 50 states to help write and pass laws on deterrence and punishment, and perhaps more importantly, to make sure that the laws already existing receive adequate financial support and are kept a high priority.

I became a life member the minute I heard about PROTECT, because I know from experience, both as a kid and as a writer, that abuse is one of the most powerful forces shaping our lives. For the most part, as the stories here reflect, that abuse isn't the dramatic sort you see on the screen. For every child abducted, more than a hundred are abused by people they know and see virtually every day. Many are abused in their own homes. And abused kids aren't just those who are sexually violated. Some are battered, some are bullied, some are subjected to physical and verbal humiliation, some are tortured in other ways.

You can look up the statistics for yourself. But there's only two numbers that really matter: One and zero. One kid abused is too many. Zero is the only reasonable goal.

Of course, I am exaggerating about the numbers, though not about the varieties of abuse, the nature of the problem and the goals. Some other numbers that matter are the number of votes legislators cast in favor of the things that protect kids. And that number is directly derived from the number of citizens who make taking care of our most vulnerable children a priority. Which is reflected in the membership numbers of PROTECT and the National Association to Protect Children.

In NAPC and PROTECT these issues bring together cops, death metal bands, lawyers, clergy, social workers, liberals, conservatives and old '60s radicals. All of us know the same thing: Abused kids can't solve their problems all by themselves. The help they're receiving isn't enough. And anyway, no amount of help is too much because it's a lousy reflection on all of us that these kids are abused in the first place.

What happens to our kids—all of them, not just some of them—tells yet another story. This one's about how much America really values its children. Not just how much the politicians and the courts and the "child protective services" bureaucracies care. About how much the rest of us care, too. Everybody in the rest of the world can read that one.

The authors of the stories in *Protectors* have made their stand.

Now it's up to the rest of us.

Lost Children

PRO TEC TORS

Stories To Benefit **PROTECT**

The Search for Michael

Patricia Abbott

Michael had been gone nearly ten years when my father looked out the window at a San Francisco restaurant and spotted him on a crowded pier.

Instinctively, Dad climbed on his chair and began to rap on the thick glass, arousing the interest of nearby patrons, the staff, and a few tourists outside. By the time Dad made his way down the three flights of stairs and found the right piling, Michael was gone.

"Sure it was him, Max?" one of his colleagues asked after Dad returned breathless and shaken. They had watched horrified as Michael, or the boy Max identified as his son, slung a backpack over his shoulder and disappeared. "I never knew him but that kid looked awfully young. More like seventeen."

"You only saw him from the rear, Max," another friend reminded him. "Could have been anyone."

"No, it was Michael. There was something about the tilt of his head, the way he propped his leg on the post," Dad told them, ignoring their looks of skepticism. "And that backpack—I recognized it immediately."

"Same backpack, huh? How long has it been now?" the third colleague said.

Women would've known not to pursue it, but these men, used to solving problems, were determined to make Dad see it didn't make sense. That the boy on the pier was not Michael—that Michael would no longer be a boy with a backpack.

"Ten years." Dad's voice had grown small.

"And he'd be how old now?"

When Dad remained silent, the one who knew him best answered for him. "Thirty. Michael would be thirty by now."

• • •

"I could never mistake someone else for Michael," he told my mother and me later. We nodded, believing that to be true. Or believing that he believed it.

Within a month, Dad accepted a retirement package with the idea of devoting himself to the search for Michael. He cashed in a portion of their stocks, down-sized the house, and used the money to travel the country, following any lead, however small, offered to him.

Mom, of course, went along with all of it.

• • •

It was Mom's offhand remark that had sent Michael into the streets ten years earlier.

"Lynnie, what was it you said to him again?"

It was a cold March night and the furnace ran steadily in our Michigan home. Dad's hands rotated a bottle of Michael's prescription on the kitchen table. I edged out of the room, anxious to get back to my anatomy text, knowing what my mother had said.

"I told him he'd do better in school if he were more like Beth."

Despite the wall separating us, I felt their two heads swivel in my direction. And with it came the familiar discomfort I had for being Beth and not Michael. What was easy for me came harder for my brother. My almost inaudible sigh was heard in the next room.

"I know I shouldn't have said it, but it popped out. Day after day, year after year . . ." Mom's voice grew low as she reminded Dad that his son was floundering, had always floundered.

But it was Dad who decided Michael could manage a residential college.

We helped him move into a dorm room in September, only to bring him home again in November. He'd stopped going to classes and seldom left his room. His roommate filled us in by phone. "I think you better come up."

And we arrived to find Michael buried under piles of pilfered blankets in his narrow bed. His hair uncombed, his glasses lost, he looked more fragile than ever.

More than one person warned us Michael couldn't handle the demands of such a competitive college. That any success would only come with a family on-hand to lend support. But we didn't listen, convinced he should go to Ann Arbor after his high SATs, making good on the dream of the Wolverine pennants on his wall.

Delusional, we chose handsome luggage, a new computer, a green glass reading lamp—everything necessary to furnish his room handsomely.

Later—when we put our minds to it, encouraged by the clinic where Michael spent the next two months—we were able to pinpoint signs of his illness as early as sixth grade.

"Remember the time he urinated in the water fountain—after his teacher told him he had to wait till recess to use the boys' room."

Mom cleared her throat. "He didn't have any memory of it a few seconds later."

I had heard this story before, of course, Word traveled fast in a suburban school system, and if I were asked to identify the first signs of illness,

I would mention incidents my parents never knew about: Michael staring into a mirror for an hour at a time, Michael out-cold for sixteen hours and still craving more sleep, Michael, hiding on a closet shelf when he was nine. Keeping silent when the rest of us had grown frantic trying to find him. It was as if he inhabited the wrong world—that the one he was meant to live in was galaxies away.

Mom's remarks that day seemed almost insignificant given the years of harsher pronouncements doled out by relatives, friends, social workers, doctors, teachers, principles, and on more than one occasion, a police officer. But it sent him to his room, where he stuffed what he could into his book bag and left the house when our heads were turned.

Despite several documented incidents of his illness, it was difficult to get much help from the police. He'd left on his own accord, packed a bag even. The fact that underwear and socks were missing from his drawer seemed to make their case—that he was in control of himself.

They tracked him as far as the bus station in Detroit, ascertained he'd traveled to New York. Then the trail went cold. Just one of the thousands of college-age students who arrive in New York every day.

Ten years passed. Now and then, we made stabs at trying to find him. Certain leads would present themselves and Dad followed up on them. I finished medical school, interned at Detroit Receiving, began a residency at Henry Ford Hospital in pediatrics, joined a practice in Plymouth, married, had a pair of twin boys.

Mom worked as a docent at the art museum and Dad continued to teach at the Ed. School at the University. He collected coins and campaign buttons; he walked the beagles: first Fanny and later, Fred.

But none of us ever went to bed with a clear mind, nor celebrated a holiday with total joy, never answered an unexpected phone call without hope. Michael knew how to keep his silence—if he was still alive.

Dad's search lasted less than a year. The eulogies at his memorial service all called attention to the search for his son. It became the defining characteristic of his life. If Dad's cross-country, hands-on search suited his gregarious, peripatetic nature, Mom found a different method to suit hers after Dad died. Not liking to travel, nor being particularly independent, Mom began to look for Michael through psychics and mediums, through tarot cards, tea leaves, channelers and Ouija boards.

Six months passed before I discovered her secret. It never occurred to me until a bill for services from a psychic in Saginaw was misdirected to my office.

"Mom," I said, placing the bill on the hall table, "what's this about?" It never occurred to me it had anything to do with Michael. She's always been somewhat interested in the occult. I could remember her watching *IN SEARCH OF...* when I was a teenager. Clinging to the words that Leonard Nimoy intoned.

Mom's hand shot to her mouth and her eyes widened.

"I've been looking for Michael. Now don't look at me that way, Beth. Your father would've wanted it."

"He would have wanted you to throw money at someone called Madame Rouschenko?" I said, reading the name from the invoice. "You've been driving all the way to Saginaw to see her?" The bill was for $700.

"Do we need the money?" Mom asked. She shifted cagily to the offensive then. "Is the practice suffering? Do the kids need braces?"

"At least Dad," I began to say.

"At least Dad what! This may not have occurred to you but some of those endless trips he took were probably to get away from me. To get away from the one he blamed, the one he shared the blame with." She paused and pulled herself together. "Well, I hope you never have to find out what something like this does to a marriage. How all you can see is the missing child when you look at each other."

"Or the missing brother?"

My mother blanched—as if this hadn't quite occurred to her.

"So finding something out about Michael now would change all that—those last years?"

She shrugged. "I'd be fulfilling his mission. Our mission."

· · ·

Six months and several clairvoyants later, Mom located a woman in Buffalo who convinced her Michael was indeed alive and living near water in a warm place, which seemed like something the psychic might wish for herself amid an upstate New York winter.

"How about driving out there with me?" Mom suggested on the phone, pulling me from an examining room to suggest this.

"Can we talk about this later?" I asked, smiling at a shy teenager standing on the scale three feet from me.

"I have to let her know if we're coming."

"I'd think she'd know that already."

"Beth! Mother said. "She's a caterer and works antique shows if no one's coming."

"Does that tell you anything, Mom?" I sighed, picturing the woman handing out steamed hotdogs at a VFW Hall in Tonawanda. I had scheduled the weekend off, planning vaguely for some time at home.

Mom had her excuses ready, and before I knew it, I'd agreed to her plan, made the necessary arrangements and was driving across Canada.

The woman's house was northeast of Buffalo.

"Why didn't I pull a map off the Internet," I said, looking futilely for a Highway #207 sign on the road ahead. "Mrs. Quinn's mapmaking skills don't bode well for how she'll navigate the beyond."

Mom laughed weakly, fanning out the page of directions on her lap. Included were markers like "the gas station with the crates of Hires Root Beer near the air hose" and "the insurance agency with dented blue Civic by the side door."

"There it is," Mom shouted, spotting the road sign for #207. Let's give her a chance, Beth. Your skepticism will just make things more difficult."

"Maybe I should wait outside."

"No, no, I need you to hear what she says. I might go all funny."

"I think it's more likely she will."

"Can you ever pass up the opportunity to make a joke out of things? Humor is worrisome in a physician. Look," she said, waving a white sheet of paper. "She has a good resume. The Buffalo police have used her extensively."

I nodded, not having the energy to remind her that we only had the woman's word for that.

"Anyway, isn't it nice being together for a few days." She gave me an indefatigable smile and applied another coat of lipstick to it.

From the look of it, the tea leaf reading business must have hit hard times in Buffalo. The small house keeled bravely toward the right, its hopeful ochre paint peeling in the October winds, the shingles on the roof trembling in accompaniment. The sparse lawn was decorated for the next's week Halloween celebration with a dozen plastic tombstones, RIP painted in blood red. A witch rode saucily on a rope strung between two trees.

Mom looked at it grim-faced. "Ready," she said finally, picking up her purse.

We picked our way to the door along a pathway littered with abandoned objects, mostly, but not solely, toys. It might have been easier to see into the future than into her yard.

Mrs. Quinn, a tiny woman, clad in the ubiquitous get-up of jeans, a sweatshirt, and white running shoes, opened the door before Mom's finger was off the bell button.

Holding a cell to her ear, she waved us in. We sat in the living room while she finished a hushed conversation in the kitchen.

After a few minutes, when we had picked up on a few mumbled words, it became clear to us that Mrs. Quinn had a 900 number and was with another client. At some point, Mom began to lose her nerve. And when Mrs.

Quinn finally made her entrance sans cell, Mom looked ready to bolt. Her torso had sunk into her lap and her face began to collapse too. I didn't know what to expect from a tea-leaf reader and saw nothing in particular to alarm me, but clearly Mom was a veteran of superior performances elsewhere.

Mrs. Quinn's prognostication closed with the words, "Matthew,"

"Michael." I corrected her before Mom could. "Michael Bright."

"Michael, yes, of course, Michael, Well, I can tell you he's leading a productive life despite his problems."

Mrs. Quinn's words were heartening, full of descriptions of his house (split level), his car, (a newish Toyota), his new life in a warm, watery setting. I got the impression of sandy sheets, exotic drinks and spectacular sunsets. A postcard on her fridge, when I followed her to the kitchen to pay her, presented just such a vista.

As Mom grew more agitated with what she heard, Mrs. Quinn saw her chances for a long-term lucrative relationship wilting and began to offer less measured, more specific predictions, even suggesting at one point, Matthew (no, Michael) was living in a motel with a flamingo theme, was involved with a croupier at a casino, and was a skilled surfer. She tapped every cliché of Floridian life one could imagine.

Mom bought none of it, and she was soon out the door, with me fumbling for my checkbook. Mrs. Quinn took the check silently, seemingly expectant of just such a finish.

"That's it," Mom said when we had pulled away from the curb. "I've put enough heart into this search. It's your turn now." Struggling to hold back tears, she added, "I'm too old for cross-country trips anyway."

"My turn?" I pictured travels, accompanied only by my faithful dog, Blue, my practice left in the care of the personable Bappaditya from Bombay, who was interning in the office this year. "When did she lose you?"

"Lose me. Oh, you mean Mrs. Quinn. I guess when I heard her telling her 900 call that she had a vision of a body of water."

"Didn't catch that," I said, pulling back onto the highway. "Perhaps her proximity to the Falls interferes with her accuracy."

"You were too busy eyeballing the mold on the walls. Yes, water does seem to haunt her."

"Rising damp, the English call it." I glanced over. "So the handoff is official."

"What? Oh, yes, you'll find your own way to look for Michael. Doesn't have to be mine or your father's." She blew her nose.

"Tears or mold?"

"Both I'm afraid."

• • •

When I began my search, I started where the police left off—fifteen years before, surmising that most people never left New York once they'd arrived, especially a person looking for cutting-edge medical treatment. If Michael were still alive—which I doubted—he was probably still in Manhattan. I also forced myself to go back over the months preceding his departure. Surely there were things other than my parents' grousing that propelled his apparently abrupt decision to leave. What had been different that week?

Mom and I tried to reconstruct the months preceding his exodus. Recovering from a small stroke, she sat pale and fragile on a lounge chair in her tiny backyard, facing a surfeit of lemon lilies along the graying picket fence. The stroke had twisted the left side of her face a bit and I found it hard not to fuss over her. When had her fingers grown so thin?

"The worst time for all of us was when he developed tardive dyskinesia from the Thorazine," Mom remembered, tripping over the difficult words. She shaded her eyes from the sun while she looked through the careful records Dad had kept. I was impressed by Dad's innate ability to be concise yet thorough in his notes.

"Michael was so ashamed. He couldn't control the drooling and the lip-smacking. Remember how his arms flailed?"

I remembered only vaguely because I was in medical school by then. I barely had time to shave my legs much less observe my kid brother's reaction to the drugs he was trying out. "He was used to feeling odd, but not looking it. I think he ran into some old friends down at school."

I remember him telling us about it—a boy he'd played tennis with in high school—before he got so sick. "I remember him saying 'You could drown in the slobber. Like I'm on drugs.' He laughed in the odd way he had—almost hiccupping. "And, of course, I am.'"

"Look at this," Mom said, passing me a treatment chart Dad had prepared. The chart seemed like a medieval artifact fifteen years later, the bright blue ink fading to blackish, the ruled lines childish now that computer could produce high-quality charts in seconds. "He tried insulin therapy, electroshock and two new drugs in this short time period."

I shook my head. "None of this first generation of drugs helped him at all. And frankly, I'm surprised the protocol allowed him to sign up for so many trial treatments in such a short time."

"What does that mean?" Mom asked. "The first generation?"

"Around the time Michael took off, they came out with a second generation of drugs. A drug called Clozapine was especially effective." I looked up. "It was the most important drug for treating treatment-refractory patients for years. Of course, there are newer ones now."

"Treatment-refractory? You mean patients who weren't helped by Thorazine."

"Or suffered such debilitating side-effects, for another."

She shook her head. "Oh, if only he waited."

"For the Clozapine?"

"No, for you."

• • •

For me? That took me back, too.

Michael had come to me for help. It was minutes after Mom had made that callous remark—the one comparing us. Michael sidled into my bedroom. I was getting ready for a date, probably with the man I'd eventually marry. He poked his head in the door, looking pointedly at the books on my desk. I never studied there, preferring the roominess of the dining room table, but I kept my books there when I wasn't using them.

"Found anyone like me in there yet?" he asked. He yawned the kind of yawn he used to lighten a dark topic.

"What?" I probably said, more interested in finding a pair of leather gloves I'd misplaced. Or perhaps it was my purse. I was in the closet by then, my voice muffled by the thick robe on the hook on the door.

"I asked if there was any help for your brother in any of these tomes." He was paging through the top one when I stepped out of the closet. I couldn't help but notice how handsome he was with the desk light flooding up on him. His hands on the book were as delicate and graceful as a pianist's. His dark hair curled across his brow, his blue eyes luminous. Why had I grown Dad's face and he Mom's?

"I don't think we get to cases like yours until the third year," I joked, looking under the bed for my shoes, not thinking about Michael's problems for once.

"Well, if I'm still around, I'll stop by for your diagnosis then." His voice, and it was the last time I ever heard it, trailed off as the book fell shut and he stepped out of my room.

He left that day, and later that night, I let Mom take all the blame—never mentioning he'd come to me for help and been turned away.

Physicians have considerable access to hospital records and various other medical documents. But I found my brother on the Internet. Medical journals had begun to put articles online—even ones from the past. When I came across the case of Vincent Dark I knew I had found Michael. The name he was assigned in the article was easy to decipher. Vincent Van Gogh was one of the most famous victims of schizophrenia. And change the name Bright to Dark—Vincent Dark.

Vincent Dark was a twenty year old man with a history of refractory schizophrenia who was not responding to conventional antipsychotic therapy when he was administered Clozapine, the drug of choice for schizophrenia after the late eighties, at an outpatient clinic at Bellevue Hospital in Manhattan. A baseline electrocardiogram (ECG) was administered and the result was within normal limits. In six weeks' time, Mr. Dark's illness had improved dramatically and he was stabilized on a moderate dosage of Clozapine. Within a few weeks of that notation, however, "Vincent" was unable to climb a flight of stairs and he was diagnosed with myocarditis with congestive heart failure. There was also evidence of pulmonary edema. Although Clozapine was discontinued immediately and he was treated with antibiotics, steroids and diuretics, Vincent died a few days later, one of a few dozen patients to suffer this reaction and die from the drug.

If this was Michael, and I thought it was, he'd died within a few months of leaving Detroit. There were other similarities in the article. An incident of urination in a water fountain was mentioned. His family history mentioned an older sister, a father in education.

• • •

"Beth, can you come here straight from work?"

I hurried through the sore throat in Exam Room 1 and the sprained ankle that followed it, arriving two hours later.

"I got it in the mail today," my mother said excitedly. She picked up a post-card and handed it to me. It was an aerial shot of the beach in Miami. It was mostly ocean but you could also make out a few inches of sandy beach and a beachfront hotel.

"Look closer," she said when I didn't react.

Finally I saw the inked blue arrow pointing at a hotel window. "Me," it said at the other end of the arrow.

"It has to be Michael." Her voice trembled. "Who else?"

I turned the postcard over, looking for another clue. Nothing. I looked at the postmark and it was three days earlier. A chill went up my spine. Could I have misread the file on Vincent Dark? Had Michael really spent the last ten years as a surfer, a beach bum, a world traveler? Mom's name and address were typed on a label—nothing there.

"Why wouldn't he have written something? I asked.

"Maybe he just wants us to know he's alive."

My mind raced. Should I mention the incongruities in her reasoning?

Should I tell her the story of Vincent Dark? I hadn't yet. Had that woman in Buffalo decided to vindicate herself?

Mom's face was serene as she examined the card. "Even if I never hear from him again, I feel at peace. Florida's a nice place for him."

I swallowed all the nay-saying my head wanted me to air. All the data that proved this scenario wrong. The idea that a charlatan had stepped in.

"Let's go out for dinner, Mom," I finally said. "A little celebration seems called for."

The Drowning
Of Jeremiah Fishfinger

Ian Ayris

Jeremiah Fishfinger began life between the wars, the youngest of six, three boys and three girls, a strain on their parents, every one. His father—a boatman and a bully—worked all day on the Royal Victoria Dock. He would come home from work, drunk and loud, and beat the children with a bicycle chain. And as he did so, Jeremiah's mother kept to the kitchen, scrubbing the sink till her hands bled.

When Jeremiah's father would eventually pass out in the armchair, his own tears blinding him to the barbarity of his actions, Jeremiah's mother would gather the children to her breast and salve their pain with buttered crumpets and assurances that their father really loved them very much indeed.

But Jeremiah knew different, and fought back with spiteful words, sneering and snarling, until he felt the back of his mother's hand on more than one occasion. As he lay awake at night, his father's snoring filling the house, his mother's sobs breaking his heart, Jeremiah would dream of what it would be like to be blind, to live in a world of complete darkness. And then, when he felt himself right on the edge of comfort, he would close his eyes, ever so slowly, and dream of colours.

It is a wonder Jeremiah survived to his eighth birthday, but he did. September the seventh, nineteen-forty. And on that day, young Jeremiah looked to the skies, planes like birds, rising and falling, bursting asunder like the colours in his dreams.

Jeremiah's brother Charlie, the eldest Fishfinger, was sent away with the soldiers to fight in North Africa, Ernie, the next along, to Burma. The two eldest girls, Sophie and Mary, turned lathes in a munitions factory on the Commercial Road, and little Annie found herself in a sweet factory in Limehouse making Blackjacks.

Being on the docks, Mr Fishfinger carried on his important work, loading and unloading, moving things here and moving things there. He volunteered as a fireman from the first days of the war, carrying a small child from a burning building in Custom House, and gaining a reputation as a man reckless and brave. He was the last to leave the exploded munitions factory on the Commercial Road where Sophie and Mary worked, his face streaked with grease and black and blood—his daughters lost.

The funeral of Sophie and Mary took place in the drizzling rain at St. Margaret's and All Saints Church, on the Barking Road. Mrs Fishfinger sobbed into the shoulder of her husband, and Jeremiah looked on from behind a tree as his sisters were buried, wondering what it would be like to suffocate under so much earth.

Mr Fishfinger had lost a piece of his heart the day the munitions factory went up—he said so—and from that moment on, he ceased to beat little Annie. Indeed, it seemed as if a part of him had softened. He would hold Annie close, open himself to her tentative advances, and whisper into her ear she was his special girl. In his work as a wartime fire-fighter he became ever more fearless. Flames dare not touch him and huge lumps of masonry fell about him as if the grief he suffered shielded him from further pain.

Still he beat Jeremiah with the bicycle chain, but it was with a heavy heart and a stilled tongue.

Jeremiah jumped off the Southwark Bridge just short of his tenth birthday whilst playing with Johnny Cottle from across the street. Johnny jumped in to save Jeremiah, and was drowned. Mr Smithson, the haberdasher, pulled Jeremiah out and pumped the water from his lungs with big iron fists. And Jeremiah hated him for it.

The young Jeremiah continued to spend his days alone, spotting aeroplanes and sifting through the London debris for something he could make sense of.

Mrs Fishfinger was killed in forty-four when the Woolworths on the Bethnal Green Road took a direct hit from a V2. Jeremiah was twelve years old. Mr Fishfinger broke down at the death of his wife, and laid aside his bicycle chain for good. He continued his fire-fighting work until a concrete slab of street ripped his legs apart when a hitherto unexploded bomb went off on the East India Dock Road.

So, with little Annie working in the sweet factory in Limehouse ten hours a day, Jeremiah was left alone with the father he hated, the father he had to care for, to wash, to cook for, to clean.

Day after day.

Day after day.

And the fire burned.

Jeremiah was able to quell his hatred by locking himself into the day to day duties of his life—boiling the potatoes and peeling the carrots for dinner, scrubbing the front step, keeping the windows gleaming and bright. If not for this, Jeremiah would not have been able to block out the disgust that overwhelmed him as he washed his father in the tin bath in the kitchen. Even the occasional incontinence, though he felt his father's shame, could be dealt with, mechanically, without fuss. But by far the worst were the drunken penitent looks from his father, one slurred word of tearful remorse about the beatings and the treatment meted out in days gone by, and Jeremiah would feel his blood begin to rise, the walls that kept him together begin to shudder and shake.

Charlie Fishfinger returned to the family home in March of forty-five, exhilarated by his wartime exploits at El Alamein and Monte Cassino. Ernie arrived back a few months later, a victim of the Japanese prison camps, his body and mind too badly broken ever to recover.

Charlie was a local hero. He had medals, and a mop of hair and a shoulders-back steady gait the girls swooned over. But he couldn't stand to be in this house of misery. Meanwhile, Ernie sat in his mother's old armchair, opposite his broken father, and spent his hours wide-eyed and mumbling.

And so the war ended. A new-found sense of hope filled the streets. A new day had begun.

But not for Jeremiah Fishfinger. Not for him. For him the scars would not heal, his heart was too ravaged, the cracks too deep. Charlie soon left to train the Hottentots in Botswana, whilst Ernie slept safe and sound behind the asylum walls.

• • •

It had been six years almost to the day since Jeremiah jumped from the Southwark Bridge. Six years of a life shattered beyond hope.

Jeremiah's father faltered and stumbled from the front room—the place he'd bedded down in since the night his legs were ripped off by the flying slab of concrete—his whole weight bearing down on two wooden crutches, pain carved into his face. When he neared the table, he swung himself into his chair, and laid the crutches down, his entire face oozing sweat.

'Morning, Jeremiah,' he said, stern and functional.

Jeremiah continued to stir the porridge on the stove, his back to his father, his knuckles screaming white around the wooden spoon.

'I said, morning, Jeremiah.'

Jeremiah inclined his head slightly to view his father from the corner of his eye, making sure he continued the same rhythmic stirring of the porridge.

'Morning,' Jeremiah said.

Satisfied the order of things had been set for the day, Jeremiah's father settled himself at the table, and fell into a reverie, his head lowered to his chest.

And the porridge steamed and the porridge bubbled.

Jeremiah thought of little Johnny Cottle, all those years ago, struggling for breath in the water. And he remembered his eyes as they remained open, pleading, scared and unseeing, as little Johnny sank to the bottom of the river.

'Don't let that porridge burn, boy,' Jeremiah's father said.

Burn like the streets. Burn like the planes that fell from the sky. Burn like Mary and Sophie. Burn like Mum.

'Did you hear me, boy? Did you hear me?'

Burn. Like. Mum.

Johnny Cottle Johnny Cottle Johnny Cottle Johnny Cottle.

Jeremiah scraped the wooden spoon one last time around the inside of the pot, and turned off the gas.

'That's it, boy. Now hurry yourself before it gets cold.'

Hurry? Hurry? There was all the time in the world. For what is time but the passing of days? Days in which your loved ones perish, your heart breaks, and your dreams shatter. Time, time means nothing when you are watching fragments of the world go by through the eyes of a grief-torn child.

Jeremiah poured the porridge into the three bowls set out beside the stove. He watched as the porridge glooped into place, until it glooped no more. He watched as the steam rose from the bowls in dancing pirouettes then disappear forever.

Jeremiah knew the time was not long.

'Boy? Boy?'

Not long, Dad. Father. Oh father of mine.

Little Annie pranced into the room, hair tied back, the same old life-giving smile upon her face. A one of a kind, Annie. A beauty. An angel from on high.

'Morning, Dad,' she said, giving her father a kiss on the top of his head, taking her place at the table next to him.

And the darkness that was upon that man gently lifted in the presence of his only daughter, as if blown by a summer breeze.

'Morning, my darling,' he said.

Jeremiah set the bowls on the table, and sat opposite his father.

Boil and bubble. Toil and trouble.

Jeremiah scooped spoonful after spoonful of porridge into his mouth, not swallowing, not tasting, just filling the empty space.

'Eat your porridge properly boy, or I'll ram it down your throat.'

Jeremiah wanted to laugh. The stupid man. The stupid, evil man.

Jeremiah ate faster, filling his mouth entirely before looking up at his father and slowly swallowing the pain.

'Boy!'

Little Annie jumped, her spoon tumbling onto the table. She picked it up, and carried on eating, her head down, dreading what was to come.

But those days were no more. Her father had no legs. The bicycle chain hung limp in the shed from a rusting nail. Little Annie spooned her porridge mechanically into her little mouth, the delight of the day now shadowed in fear.

Jeremiah finished first, his face red with pain, his throat burnt.

'Come round here, boy,' his father said.

But Jeremiah did not.

Little Annie took her bowl to the kitchen sink, tears cutting tracks down her cheeks, her heart pounding. And then left the two broken souls to themselves, for she could feel their pain no longer.

Alone in the house, sitting across the table—a table once filled with loved ones now gone—sat but two.

Son stared at father, father at son, neither one a word left to speak.

Jeremiah's father cried inside for his wife and his two girls, and for not being able to love his youngest son. Jeremiah stared at his father blank, and felt nothing.

• • •

The first time Jeremiah Fishfinger had been swallowed up by the dark waters of the Thames, he'd been nine years old. He'd been dragged home by his father, and beaten to within an inch of his life. And now, six years later, he placed a note gently on the kitchen table for little Annie, left the house quietly, and headed for the Southwark Bridge, the bicycle chain trailing behind him, scraping red in his wake.

The Kindness Of Strangers

Ray Banks

There are few things as obnoxiously loud as a gymnasium full of children. It's a strange, unearthly din, a combination of roar and shriek punctuated with high-pitched giggles, sudden shouts and the ongoing impatient swinging and shuffling of feet. Even when they're just chattering amongst themselves, a couple of hundred kids will generate enough noise to drown out a 747, and it's not something you can comfortably endure without blowing an eardrum first. I mean, I suppose if you taught the buggers on a daily basis, you'd get used to it, but for a visitor, even one as regular as I was, it could be excruciating. So when Miss Morgan asked me something, I had to ask her to repeat it.

She smiled. "You asked if they were ready?"

"Ah." I matched her smile and raised her a couple of teeth. "Yes."

She nodded towards the mass of children off to my right, all sat on benches. "They're arranged by year in alphabetical order. Is that okay?"

I gave her the thumbs-up. "Brilliant."

"You need anything else?"

"Sorry?"

"Do-you-need-anything-else."

"No, I don't think so. Who's my sheepdog?"

Miss Morgan smiled again. When her face was in repose, she could've passed for a porcelain doll, and when she smiled she looked younger than many of the pupils in her Year Ten class. She wore grey and brown, tried to hide her bony little body in the folds of her clothes, but she had strong teeth and that smile meant that she was comfortable with me, which was a step in the right direction.

"Mr Grant," she said, and pointed at a wide-shouldered, heavy-stomached man with a full beard. Mr Grant wore a tracksuit that made him look like a refugee from *The Krypton Factor* circa 1986.

He was my sheepdog, charged with arranging the children as well as pushing them through at a fair clip. From the look on his face, he knew what kind of hellish chore it was going to be, and he'd obviously already decided that I was the one to blame.

"He's a PE teacher, isn't he?"

Miss Morgan's smile became a grin, and she arched an eyebrow. "What gave you that idea?"

"He looks like Bullet Baxter."

She laughed. I waved a hand at Mr Grant and he snapped into action. He arranged the Year Sevens into a line. The first kid—a tubby boy with a mop of blonde hair and cut lip named Michael Adler—was sent forward. He pulled himself up onto the seat in front of me and gave his best photo smile.

"Just look at the camera there, Michael."

I pointed at the webcam. When he looked at my finger, I clicked the mouse, took the picture, and then signalled for the next child. Miss Morgan sent Michael on his way. A little pigtailed girl named Andrea Barker dropped into the seat. She gave me a gummy, wet smile and I clicked the mouse again.

That was my job. When I told people I took pictures of children for a living, they normally did a bit of a double-take and then looked around the room until I told them that, hey, it really wasn't as creepy as it sounded. Sometimes I didn't tell them for a while, though, just to torture them. After all, people's minds did tend to go to the darkest places, and sometimes I wanted to see them think of me like that, just to see what it looked like, before I explained myself and that look of mild alarm was replaced by one of mild guilt.

The truth of the matter was that I worked for a large multinational corporation that specialised in access control and cashless payment systems, which is about as rock 'n' roll as it sounds. In layman's terms, if you've ever had to use a plastic card on an electronic reader to pay for something, enter a building, or even prove you were who you said you were, the chances are both card and reader came from us. Right then, the biggest market was education. Some universities and colleges, but mostly schools, because if there was one thing parents cared about, it was their child's attendance. And if there was something *else* they care about, it was their child's diet. So what the large multinational corporation did was make a series of deals with local authorities and schools up and down the country. We supplied each child with his or her own triple-function plastic card. The children used the embedded chip to enter the school and log their attendance. There was also a mag stripe on the card which could be loaded with money by the parent to spend on school dinners. The beauty of this was that the parent could specify the kind of food their child was allowed to purchase, so no more kets for chunky Michael Adler. Finally, the card itself was printed with the child's vital information and his or her photograph.

And that was where I came in.

Now, you might not have thought there was much work involved with something like that, but when each kid needed a new photo each year, and there was a good two-three thousand of them in one school alone, then that was quite the to-do list. Throw in the fact that I was covering pretty much every school in the North East, from Berwick down to the arse end of Teesside, with occasional jaunts into the No Man's Land of Cumbria, where the men were men and so were the women, and you could be forgiven for thinking that there weren't enough hours in the day.

Tell you, sometimes, it certainly felt that way. But then, I took a great deal of pride in my work, and if there was ever a photo that didn't immediately resemble the child in front of me, I'd take it again. Sometimes I might have even taken an extra moment to make sure my subject looked their best, but only in those rare cases when the boy or girl in question looked as if they'd rather chew off their own fingers than have their photo taken. The way I saw it—the way I remembered it from my own school days—is that those kids were going to have a battered, frightened year ahead of them anyway, so why remind them of their physical faults every time they swipe for a Mars Bar?

Case in poInt: last year, over at Benton Manor School, there was a girl named Mary Yanoulis who was the last of the Year Tens and nicknamed Virgin Mary by her giggling classmates. She was fourteen, taller than the rest of her class. She carried herself in a kind of round-shouldered forward lean, as if she'd been shoved out of the house that morning and hadn't quite caught her balance yet. She was an ugly duckling who was destined to grow into an even uglier duck, and she was all too painfully aware of how people saw her, all too conscious of the disdain and amusement she inspired. When the other girls—two of them in particular, interchangeably blonde, pretty in an obvious way—called Mary names she bristled in her chair as if an electric current had shot through the seat. She tucked a few thick strands of black hair behind her ear in a futile attempt to make herself look presentable and then let her hands fall to the folds of her grey skirt like a couple of buckshot doves.

"If you'd just like to give us a smile for the camera, Mary…"

She looked up and frowned at me. There was a mark on her cheek, close to the edge of her right eye. At first I thought it was a birthmark, but then birthmarks didn't look as raw and painful as that, and they rarely pushed an eye half-closed.

"Okay then, how about a smile for me?"

The frown deepened. I kept smiling. I wasn't going to let this one win.

"Trust me," I said. "I'm not going to make you look bad."

She blinked, obviously wondering if I was taking the piss.

I wasn't.

A slow smile spread across her mouth, the clouds lifted, and just as she relaxed, I clicked the mouse.

There.

The bruise didn't show, hiding in the shadow of her hair. Her smile seemed brighter, more honest, on the screen than it ever had in real life. It was almost a perfect photo, even if I did say so myself, and it would give her a nice reminder of how she wasn't a freak at all, no matter what she heard. The same couldn't be said for the two girls who giggled at Mary as she made her way back to her seat—I'd already made sure to snap those two with all their chins and bug eyes. Their cards would be their pictures in the attic.

As I was leaving the school, I saw her again, her head down and her book bag protecting her front. As she passed, I said, "It's Mary, isn't it?"

She stopped, regarded me through her curtain of hair, and then looked at her feet. "Yeah."

A crowd of kids passed, but I didn't really notice them, couldn't say if they noticed me. "That isn't a birthmark on your cheek, is it?"

She didn't say anything.

"It's okay." I dug out my card, held it out to her. "Take it."

"Why?"

"In case you need someone to talk to."

She shook her head.

"Hey, just in case."

"I don't need counselling."

"I'm not a counsellor, Mary. But I've been there, I think. So, like I said, if you feel like talking to someone…"

I saw an eye through the hair. She swallowed, then took the card with long, pale fingers.

I smiled at her, thought I saw the ghost of a smile back. "It's my mobile, so just whenever you want, give me a ring. It's always on, okay?"

"Okay."

"Okay, then. Take care."

When I drove away, she still had the card in her hand.

It took a couple of weeks, but she called one night at seven o'clock, just after dinner. It was her mother's boyfriend who'd pushed her to it. She was phoning from the bedroom, whispering into her mobile, her voice hoarse from crying and her speech punctuated with the kind of small shuddering breaks that happen when someone's cried too hard and too long. It took me a while to get her talking beyond monosyllables, but once the cracks appeared in that wall she'd built around herself, it wasn't long before the whole thing came tumbling down.

The boyfriend was called Andy. He was a barrel of shit with anger management problems and an old-fashioned idea of gender relations. He moved in about two years prior after her mam brought him home from the pub one night and fucked noisily on the green leather sofa in the front room. Andy'd had a rough time of it, according to Mary's mam. He done bird, a two stretch, come out to find his missus shacked up with some other bloke, and so that was him chucked out of his own flat and at the end of his rope. He needed a table to put his feet under while he worked out what he was going to do. So Mary's mam told her to make Andy feel at home, which Andy did within the month. He liked a clean house, regular home-cooked meals and the feel of young skin under his fingers. When Mary opened her mouth to scream, he slapped it shut, and told her in no uncertain terms that if she so much as whispered to her mam or anyone else Andy would beat her so fucking bad they'd have to wire her jaw shut.

And what about her mam?

Well, she was like anyone else who'd lost the last shred of their self-esteem, put on drinking weight and after a long period of hating men started to miss them desperately. And when she found someone drunk enough to fuck her and desperate enough to stay the night, she held onto him with both fists. In that light, Mary was nothing but another pain-in-the-arse teenager who missed a false memory of her errant dad. She just needed to grow up a bit, didn't she? Mam had needs too. One of those needs was Andy, and it didn't matter if one of Andy's needs was Mary, because Mary couldn't trust her mam enough to say anything.

And so she wished she was invisible. Beaten and raped at home, bullied at school, there was nowhere for her to go. And when she told me that, sat across from me in a café in another city two stops up the East Coast line, she couldn't stop herself from breaking down completely. People must have stared at us, but I didn't care. Instead, I held both her hands in mine and I told her my own story. I told her about how my parents were drunks like her mam, and how my sister went to live with my mother while I got stuck with my dad and his rages. I told her about how my sister went missing. There was a pain in my throat when I told her how they found her three weeks later, beaten and naked at the bottom of a quarry. I told her about how I never got over that. "I mean, a person doesn't, does he? He *shouldn't*." And by that time, she'd stopped crying and our hands had switched position.

"Listen," I said. "You can stay with me if you want."

She brightened for an instant before the inevitable clouds appeared. "They'd know."

"No, they wouldn't."

"I need to go to school."

"No, you don't. You don't have to do anything you don't want to."

When she looked at me again, and realised I was deadly serious, her black eyes filled with tears and I knew she loved me more than anyone else in the world.

It was our big fuck-you. When the papers reported Mary Yanoulis missing a week after she moved in, she smiled wider than I'd ever seen anyone smile before. When she saw her mam and Andy on the news, talking about her in bored tones, feigning concern, she sneered. Andy was stoic, frowning and saying very little. Mary's mam had the pink eyes of someone who'd spent more time rubbing them than crying. When her mam stumbled over her prepared speech and said "Shit," Mary rose from my lap and squealed with laughter.

She stayed with me for five months, all told. In that whole time, she didn't go to school and she didn't leave the house. She didn't need to, and didn't appear to want to. I brought her everything she asked for without question. We trusted each other. She did the cooking and cleaning, but she did it happily and I always remembered to thank her. When she wasn't playing the housewife, she was self-educating from my bookshelves, and I dare say she learned more in five months with me than she did in five years of school, mostly because she wasn't under constant threat of ridicule or physical attack. And so she changed, she became vibrant and assured. I'm not ashamed to say that I was in love, and so was she, and when I wasn't at work it was always just us, together against the world. And as we continued to live together, we watched the news on a nightly basis, charting the slow, irrevocable decay of her old life just as the new one blossomed. The police, having exhausted what few leads they had, gave up the search. Mary's mam and Andy didn't show up on the television again. Mary was free of her abuse, once and for all. She was happy.

At least, I thought that was the case. After a while, I noticed the change. I saw the books left half-read on the floor. I noticed that she spent most of her time asleep. Whenever I talked to her, she was sullen, negative and withdrawn. It didn't take a genius to work out what was happening, but I asked her anyway. "What's the matter?"

"Nothing."

"Tell me."

She opened her mouth, rolled her tongue. "I don't know."

"You bored?"

She shrugged.

I leaned against the doorway. She was lying on the couch, staring at the television. Some godawful brightly-coloured morning show. The adult in me wanted to turn it off, but I knew that would only make matters worse. "So what is it?"

She huffed, then shook her head. "You'll get angry."

"No, I won't."

She glanced at me. "Yes, you will."

"I really won't. Listen, I think I know what it is, anyway."

The glance turned into a stare. "What?"

"You want to go home."

She opened her mouth and then closed it again.

"You think they've forgotten about you. You think they've moved on with their lives, and you want to go round there and rub their noses in it."

"Is that bad?"

"No. No, I understand it completely. But then what happens, Mary? When you've done that, and you've made them feel terrible and guilty—if they even *do* feel guilty—and then your life goes on. Are you just going to go back to the old life?"

She blinked. The smile had gone. "I don't know."

"You don't miss them, do you?"

"No."

"And you didn't have any friends. None that I saw."

Her forehead crinkled.

"It's true, isn't it?"

"Can I not even leave the house?"

"We've been through this—"

"At *all*?"

"If someone sees you, Mary, that's it, we're both in trouble."

"But it's okay now. They've not said anything. Nobody knows who I am, I can dye my hair—"

"I can't take that risk."

"There must be *something* we can do."

"Maybe." I checked my watch then. "Look, I can't talk about this now, I'm going to be late for work. We'll discuss it tonight, alright?"

"You said maybe."

I gave her my best smile. "I know I did. We'll see."

She brightened immediately and followed me to the door. She kissed me on the cheek before I left.

I wasn't late for work. I hadn't been late for work since I started at the large multinational corporation. If anything, I had time to spare, and I used it up sitting in my car and thinking the whole situation through.

Mary didn't want to leave the house, she wanted to leave me. In the end, they always tried to leave. My sister did. She loved me for a while before she grew to hate me and went off to live with my mother, abandoning me to a childhood of barely-healed bruises. We loved each other, and then we hated each other, and then she went missing.

Nothing lasts forever, and everything decays in the same way.

So I allowed her to leave me. She even got packed. And a week later they found her in the weeds by the railway line at Easington. It took one more week to identify her and yet another to forget the whole thing. The ugly ones never stayed in the public's memory for very long.

It was a tragedy, right enough. I didn't know what I'd done wrong, so I wasn't sure how I was supposed to learn from my mistakes. In the end, I just blamed myself for falling in love with the wrong girl. It happened to everyone. In the end, you just had to pick up and move on. I threw myself into my work to forget the heartache, which the large multinational corporation loved. There were even offers of promotion, which I politely declined. They still gave me a raise.

And then here I was, a year on from meeting Mary, letting the memory of her wander through my mind as I photographed the Year Nines, thinking maybe it was the age that was the problem, that perhaps the younger girl would be more malleable. As I worked, I made sure to smile and joke with Miss Morgan every now and then, just to be on the safe side and to distract me from the task at hand.

"That's two down, only another three to go, God help us."

"Hang in there, Champ."

I did. I tried not to think about Mary, but it was difficult until Becki Fisher sat in front of me. She was fat and dimpled, her hair dirty and blonde. Her clothes looked aggrieved to be so close to her body, and her eyes were dark little dots whirring around in their sockets. Her details told me she was new this year. A couple of clicks of the mouse and I saw just the one name on the account. Single-parent family. Mother, by the name, probably just as fat as her daughter. Both of them new in town, no real friends, nobody to confide in. When I looked at Becki, she was squirming, uncomfortable. I could feel the disgust from her classmates like a warm gust of fetid air.

I smiled at her, and thoughts of Mary Yanoulis went from my mind.

"If you'd just like to smile for the camera there, Becki."

She stared at me. She looked frightened.

Baby's In Blue
Nigel Bird

There's red blood in my veins, no doubt about it. Once it's been through the heart at any rate. After that it turns blue, just like everyone else's.

And there's not many who wouldn't have done what I did. None with the red blood in them and not with spring in the air like it was.

Libby and I, we'd been trying for a nipper. Turned out she had dodgy tubes, so we were saving up to have things sorted. Get it done the right way. The way God intended only with a bit of a helping hand.

One Friday we were in the pub with Rox and Sox. We all knew each other at school and never lost touch. Best mates you could say. So what if they were lesbians?

We should have gone way before it all kicked off on account of us trying to fill up the piggy-bank, but my control's never been so good after a few beers.

Anyway, Sox was crying into her gin and tonic and Libby was holding her hand while me and Rox got down to some arm-wrestling at the other end of the table.

We were at it a while. She's got a grip like a giant bloody crab, she has. Nips just like one, too, with those sharp nails of hers. I was scratched to buggery by the time I got her down onto the table. Spilled half the beer from our pint glasses in the process, but it was worth it.

I felt a bit dizzy after the exercise. Needed a dram to get my pulse back to resting.

Rox was off before I even had to ask.

"Les will do it, won't you Les?" I heard Libby say, all soft and purry.

"What's it this time, love?" I didn't mean to sound fed up, but you couldn't blame me for that, neither. "Washing machine on the blink again?" That's the thing about two women. Useless when it comes down to it. I know Rox did all the butch stuff, but shaving your head round the sides and lifting weights don't make you a bloke.

"Provide the necessary."

"Give over talking in riddles," I told her.

"You know."

"I don't bloody know."

She leant in and her voice went quiet. "The sperm, darling. Spunk."

"Now wait a minute…" I wasn't sure what we were waiting for. Didn't have an argument to get me out of it, just didn't like the idea.

Sox burst into tears again. Stood up and ran over to the ladies'. Silly moo. Nice arse, mind.

Off Libby went, following the drama like usual, and Rox came back. She must have known what'd been going on by the looks of her. Couldn't look me in the eye. Just talked football and let me have a good gawp at her cleavage till the others came back.

Libby went at me like a woodpecker on my skull. It wouldn't be a problem and we'd have our own soon enough was what she was saying.

I wasn't having any of it. Not until the word threesome came up.

There was that red blood, simmering away and fit to boil over. I remembered Sox's arse all tight in those jeans and the way Rox's boobs had been teasing me and the word popped out of my mouth. "Yes," I said. A thousand times, yes.

• • •

I know what you're thinking. Course I do. 'Lucky bastard.' I thought so an' all.

I pictured the three of us, oiled and sweaty and rolling about in a huge bed, licking and laughing and gasping and me getting to shag myself silly. Candle-light, I thought, and music and all the trimmings. They were lesbians, after all.

Them were the pictures I had rolling through my mind when I rang the bell—if I'd unzipped my fly, I probably could have reached it with the Sergeant Major, the way he was standing to attention.

Imagine my disappointment when Sox opened the door in a big woolly jumper and pair of jogging trousers. Not even a hint of make-up.

And the wine I'd taken? They were having none of that. Bad for the sperm. Only thing I got to drink was a mug of coffee. "To wake up the little fellers," she said.

In the end it was Sox who went up first. Said we should give her five minutes.

Rox came over and straddled me. Felt like the couch was about to break, but I didn't mind.

"See the match?" she asked as she undid the zip of my jumper.

"Aye. Cracking goals, eh?"

She leaned forward. Put her mouth on mine, stuck her tongue in and span it like I needed tumble drying. Took me a while to work out the breathing, but I got there. Even enjoyed it until I opened my eyes. Soon as I saw her, the shaved head and everything, it was like I was snogging a bloke.

Christ.

So I went straight in for the jugs.

"Easy tiger," she said, giving me a break from the cement mixer. "Save yourself."

She got back to action and so did I.

There was something about her boobs. They felt perfect. Silky smooth and warm and bigger than my hands so I had plenty to work with. But they weren't fat and they weren't firm. Best tits I've come across, which is saying something.

Not only that, but all I had to do to get her purring was to tweak those nipples and she was off. And so, very nearly, was I.

"All ready," came the call from upstairs.

I thought about the football to try and cool my ardour. Didn't work at all. Even thinking about the guys jumping on top of each other when they'd scored got my nerve ends twanging.

Rox got off the couch. Gave me a hand onto me feet.

When we went up I made sure she went first. Got to watch those hips of hers rolling all the way up.

There was a heavy smoke drifting from the bedroom. Smelled of Thai curry, all sweet and sickly. I knew it was going to play hell with my allergies and I was right. Soon as I went in my scalp started itching.

Sox was lying under the bed, the duvet pulled up to her chin. The fairy-lights were shining down and making her look beautiful, like one of those statues in Greece.

She pulled the duvet back, far enough for me to get a look at her tits.
Fantastic.

"Right then, let's get cracking," I said, blowing on my hands to get them warm and making out like I was about to dive into a swimming pool.

I got straight in there, neck, nipples the lot.

Couldn't bear to wait, either.

"Wait," she said when I lined myself up for entry. "We need this to get the angles right." First time I'd ever heard of geometry in the sack, but I wasn't going to say anything to spoil the mood.

I pushed in and she were perfect. All hot and wet, just as I like 'em.

The plan, if there was one, was to take it slow. Make it last. Get to remember every last bit and save it for my old age.

She felt so good that the plan went out the window. I was at her like a road drill and when I saw that Rox was taking off her panties it was more than I could bear. I shot me load and that were that. Everything stopped.

Sox made me lie there so that gravity could get to work and Rox had her panties on before I could get my breath.

"Hang on," I said. "What about the threesome and all that?"

Sox pulled on my arse cheeks and made to get comfortable. "Steady Tiger. If it's foreplay you want, you'll need to be hanging on to that libido of yours. Besides, nobody gets pregnant first time, do they Rox?"

"Never," Rox said. "Cup of tea, love?"

"Aye lass," I told her. "Two sugars. And bring the wine up with you. I'll need something a bit bloody stronger than tea the way I'm feeling."

• • •

Them moving away like they did was probably for the best.

We kind of lost touch after that.

Not that I minded.

Things had been awkward between the lot of us.

It was like I didn't fit any more.

Libby said everything was normal, but it wasn't. Only time we got to shag was when she was ovulating—even then she were there more in body than in soul. Closest I got to making her gasp were when I pushed a bit too hard. So I pushed as hard as I could.

When we all got together, they didn't talk to me much. Just took the piss.

'Speedy', they called me after that night. 'Speedy Gonazales.' And when they said it, they burst into fits of laughter. It was like they punctured my ego every time.

Sox could hardly bear to look at me when they got the news.

Pregnant first attempt. What were the chances of that?

You'd have thought Libby might have been bitter with them, but it was me who ended up as the lemon.

Started going out without me, they did, and when Rox and Sox moved away Libby were on the phone to them every night.

I just kind of retreated into myself. Watched a lot of porn and started going down the strip-clubs just to get some kicks.

Libby said nothing about it. Just got cold on me. Like she lived in the fridge.

• • •

He was almost a Christmas baby. Rupert Arnold—Jesus Christ. Weighed 6 pounds and a couple of ounces.

Earliest we could get there to see him was the 30th. Plan was we'd stay over for New Year and have a quiet one. A quiet one? What the hell had things got to?

Worse, it meant going over the border into the land of the sheep and the 4-by-4.

The journey had been hell, motorway down to one lane on each side and the snow belting down.

If we could've, I'd have turned around.

Anyway, it put me in a filthy mood.

And it might have all melted away if they'd known how to look after my boy.

Rupert Arnold, his tiny fingers curled round mine like he knew who his dad were. I was lump-in-the-throat proud.

It's a miracle, let's face it, the way they pop out. From a tiny egg and sperm to this perfectly formed human being. I wondered for a while about God and that kind of thing, that maybe he's up there after all. That there's a better place with a help-yourself buffet and sex on a plate whenever you want it.

That's how I was feeling until Libby picked him up from under his blankets.

Pink. My boy in this pink baby vest that matched his skin.

Just seeing it had me biting my lip.

"He's gorgeous," Libby started. She sounded like she was having trouble breathing the way she said it. "Such a little star."

Rox stood proudly by as Libby and the wee man sat down, as if she'd had anything to do with it. "Isn't he just."

"He looks just like you, Sox."

A weak smile passed over Sox's lips. She was slumped into the back of her chair, pale as the weather we'd been driving through, with little sick-marks on the shoulder of the slinky black number she was wearing.

"And you'd never know he was premature, eh?"

"Takes after his dad in that department," Rox said and Libby sniggered along with her like I wasn't there.

"I'll get myself a drink then," I said and took the carrier bag into the kitchen at the back. The women just stood around the baby. Didn't lift a finger to help. I unscrewed the top from the whisky bottle and took a healthy swig to wet the baby's head. Then I had another to make a toast. "To you, Arnie. You poor sod."

I opened a beer for myself and took orders from the manger. Two coffees and a herbal tea.

While I was waiting on the kettle to boil, I watched them. Arnie was so delicate and helpless and there he was, surrounded by his lesbian parents and my wife, and him all dressed in a girl's baby-grow and this pair of yellow-flower booties. And I knew it then that his life was screwed and I knew that I was going to have to do something about it.

Half an hour I spent watching Libby and Rox holding the lad and talking all that baby language at him like he was stupid.

And Sox spent most of the time just lying back in the cushions of her chair and staring at this picture on the wall. It was one of those modern art paint-ings, all slash and splash like the artist had eaten a plate of beans on toast and thrown up on the canvas. Way she looked at it, it was like she could see some-thing in there, the bloody lunatic. And she was the one supposed to be looking after Arnie.

"Mind if I take him round the block?" I got up all cheerful. Picked him up for the first time. He weighed nothing to speak of and smelled all sweet—milk and talc and washing powder—like an angel or something. "In his buggy?"

Sox lifted her head and looked over. Like she was thinking. "If you like. But make sure you wrap him well and get him back in ten minutes for his feed."

"Will do," I said. "Come on fella."

I let Rox get him ready in his big snow-suit, putting his tiny arms and legs into the thing and zipping him up right to the top.

He had a hat and a hood and a couple of big blankets over him by the time we were ready to leave.

"Ten minutes," Sox shouted from the back as I wheeled him out the front door.

"Aye, right," I shouted back, and when the door was closed I said what I was thinking. "You can shove your ten minutes, you bloody lezzer."

• • •

I don't know what to put it down to. I reckon I was just having a really great time, me and my son just bonding out there, me telling him stories about when I was a kid and how to watch out for the women who came along. Taught him all about the four Fs. "Find 'em, finger 'em, fuck 'em and forget 'em, son." He kind of rolled his head to the side when I said that, so I think he understood.

Whatever it was, I lost track—track of where I was and track of the time.

Didn't have my phone and hadn't a clue how to get back to the house. Couldn't even remember the address.

Best I could think of was to head towards the bright lights and ask around. Maybe find a cab office and see if they might set me straight.

Before I got far, I saw this real good looking pub. The kind the Yorkshire folk do well, all big and homely.

I would have walked by if I hadn't taken a peek in at the window.

Looked like there was some kind of party going on the way they had the lights down and the way everyone was dressed up in their finest. Made me thirsty just looking in.

"You wouldn't mind, would you son?" I could tell he wouldn't. "If yer dad just popped in to wet his whistle?"

And he didn't say a thing.

I pushed the buggy through the slush and into the car park round the back and found him a nice place out of the way where the wind wouldn't get to him.

"Now lad. You wait here and don't tell anyone where I am. That's something else you need to know," I told him while I pushed the brake down with my foot, "that the lads always need to stick together."

I gave him a kiss on his cheek, pulled the blankets up to his chin and wandered over to the pub.

When I opened the door the music blared out. Pop stuff, the kind of thing Libby likes.

There was a real fire and a load of sandwiches on the bar and there were some great looking lasses dancing over on a small stage where the lights were flashing and a DJ was supping a pint.

First thing I did was wander over to them.

Had to shout on account of the tunes. "Fancy a drink, girls?"

They all giggled and pretended they weren't interested, but I could tell they were after a good time. "Three pints of Stella," the one in the middle said. She looked straight back at me when she said it then let her gaze drop down, a bit below the belt, like.

They were dynamite, the three of them. Tight dresses, firm flesh and long legs. I was finally convinced about there being a God.

I got the drinks, bought some more and gave them some of my best dance moves. Things flowed from one thing to another—a few drinks, a bit of flirting and a one-night-stand with a beautiful blonde.

Soon as I woke up I remembered the nipper. Dressed like there was a fire in the building and got the blonde to drive me back to the pub.

Ran every step of the way into the car park till I got to him.

Poor mite.

Knew when I saw him that he wasn't right. As if he was telling me. Telling me I was right about not wearing pink. That there's only one colour you should put on a boy. Turned himself blue to make sure I got the message. Telling me that whatever they'd put him through, he would have done me proud.

The Black Rose
Michael A. Black

Brax watched as the muscular men danced around the picturesque court-yard, chopping at one another with those three-foot bamboo swords, their arms, chests, and backs covered with colorful tattoos, their bodies glistening with sweat.

"They do that with real blades too?" he asked. The wood of the raised porch-like balcony that overlooked the courtyard below was hard and his legs were beginning to ache from sitting there.

"Of course." Kiroshi cast an amused looking smile his way. His English was good, but heavily accented. "Those are called *shinai*. Used for practice. But there are times when a *yakuza* must use a real *katana*."

"A what?"

Kiroshi smiled again and stood up. "A *katana*." He touched the handle of the long sword sticking out from his belt. "For us, it is part of our culture. A sacred part." With a quick movement, Kiroshi pulled the long sword from its holder and held it out in front of Brax. The shiny metal gleamed in the fading sun-light like sterling silver. "They were used to guard the Emperor and his lords. A true warrior used his *katana* as an instrument of honor. They were fashioned by . . . artists with metal. It would take them many months. They would fashion the blade over and over, never allowing any weakness or impurity." He turned it, catching the light. "During this time, they would not eat meat, bathed only in cold water, and would not have sexual relations. Not until their task was complete. Not until the blade was perfect." He swiftly raised his arm and with a quick motion sheathed the sword.

Brax shook his head. This whole country was nothing but fanatics. In the distance, symmetrical rows of trees and circular patterns of crops gave way to a once scenic mountain, now obscured by a cloud of brown fog. Like everything else here, crowded, polluted, and inscrutable. The sooner he could get himself and crazy Stevie out of this damn country, the better.

"We're used to guns in the States," he said.

"Guns are illegal in Japan," Kiroshi said, grinning as he pulled back his jacket to display the grip of the pistol, "but they are not unobtainable."

Kiroshi murdered the pronunciation of the last word, but Brax figured he'd better not say anything. After all, these were the guys who were protecting them. He looked around again at the remote house where they'd been hiding out, waiting on that flight back to the States in twelve more hours. It seemed pretty secure. They were a good distance from the city, in a maze of gardens or farms or something. The long house was set back from the yard, and the whole place was surrounded by a five foot brick wall. Embedded fragments of broken glass adorned the topping cement. Plus there must have been at least fifteen *yakuzas* here. It should be safe enough. He glanced at his watch again, wondering what time it was in LA right now, and thought about the reason he was sitting here, sweating it out.

"You're sure that Tanaka dude ain't gonna find us?" he asked.

Several of the men in the courtyard yelled in unison, brandishing their bamboo swords and charging their opponents.

"Tanaka Mishima knows where we are," Kiroshi said. "But he will not come."

Brax thought about that and decided if two foreigners had whacked his daughter, he'd be sure to try and ice them before they took off for parts unknown. He hurled another silent curse at Stevie for getting him into this mess. Taking the boss's son along on a business trip like this had been a mistake from the get-go. He'd known it, and Stevie's excesses, when it came to hookers, was what did them in. Instead of completing the simple transaction agreement like he wanted, and getting the hell back to the States, idiot Stevie had to get laid.

And how was I supposed to know he liked things rough, Brax thought. Real rough. And then the dead hooker turned out to be this ex-hitman's daughter...

"So just how good is this Tanaka guy?" Brax asked.

Kiroshi's eyes narrowed and he held up his thumb. "I trained him to be the best-best."

One of the female servants, dressed in a flowing *kimona*, stepped on to the porch and bowed, saying something in Japanese. Kiroshi grunted a response and motioned for her to set the tray down.

"He was a cast-off of your army's occupation," he said picking up one of the small cups and sipping from it. "His father was a GI, his mother Japanese. When I found him, he was an *einoko* running the streets. I took him in, raised him as my *shatei*, taught him the way of the *katana*." Kiroshi paused and Brax thought he saw something akin to pride in the older Oriental's expression. "In the years that followed, after the occupation, he became legend among the *yakuza*, able to master every technique, every weapon, and completely without fear. And yet he also had honor. He would leave a black rose with each of his...assassinations." He murdered the pronunciation again, but Brax got the idea. It sent a cold shiver up his spine. "It would be," Kiroshi continued, "the last thing seen before his *katana* struck."

One by one, the combatants in the courtyard were being eliminated in their swordfighting contest. Only two of the tattooed men remained now. Brax watched as they circled each other warily. The larger of the two made a deft movement, sweeping the other man's *shinai* out of his hands. The big guy followed up with a quick slashing motion, smacking the other man's gut and leaving a bright red welt below a feathery tattoo pattern.

Kiroshi called out in Japanese. Brax could tell that it was an order because the men quickly turned and bowed toward him. Then they picked up their gear and dispersed.

"That big guy looks pretty good with that thing," Brax said.

"Kiro was taught by Tanaka," Kiroshi said. "He is very skilled with *tanto, katana,* and guns." He turned and pointed to the tray. "Have some tea, Brax-san."

"So the guy who's stalking me is the guy who taught your crew all they know?" Brax said, ignoring the cups. "How do I know this guy ain't crazy enough to follow me once we get outta here?"

Kiroshi chuckled. "He could never find you in your country. He does not speak the language. And if he tries here, tonight, he knows it means defying me, which will necessitate his death. I am his *saiko-koman.*" His expression turned stern again. "Believe me, Brax-san, once we get you and your friend on that plane in the morning, you will be safe." He leaned forward. "Just do not let your superiors forget about our agreement. And the special reward you promised me."

One of the flunkies from the courtyard approached them and bowed, then went into a crouch, holding out his open palm like he wanted to shake hands. Brax noticed that the little finger was missing on the guy's left hand. Kiroshi regarded him for several seconds, and then said something in Japanese. The man responded, bowed again, and backed cautiously away.

"He told me your friend has refused food," Kiroshi said. "He is very strange."

You got that right, Brax thought. The dumb son-of-a-bitch.

"He's also the big man's son," he said. "My boss, Sal Payne."

Kiroshi nodded and brought the small cup to his lips, sipped, then barked out an order and two men, each with small machine guns, began walking around the courtyard.

"Looks like they're ready for action," Brax said, feeling slightly better that they were packing heat and not some kind of samurai sword bullshit. "You said that guy Tanaka is no longer with the organization?"

Kiroshi set the small cup down and nodded. Almost noiselessly, the servant girl appeared and took the tray away.

"So what did he do?" Brax asked. "Screw the boss's daughter?"

If Kiroshi got the joke, he didn't show it. He simply shook his head.

"I told you Tanaka was an *einoko* . . . Mixed blood. As it stands, it is our custom that he never marry a full blood Japanese. But he did.

"He came to me almost twenty years ago, and asked to be released from the..." he paused, as if searching for the right word, "organization. He offered me *yubitsume*." Kiroshi held up his own left hand, which was missing the tip of the little finger.

The corners of Brax's mouth turned downward. "That other guy was missing one, too. Some kind of sword-play accident?"

Kiroshi shook his head. "*Yubitsume*...An atonement. If a yakuza has offended his *oyabun*, he may offer his finger as an apology."

"You cut off your own finger?"

"*Hai*. I was his *kumicho*, but I forbade him to do it."

The image of some dude fanatical enough to go chopping off the tip of his finger flashed through Brax's mind. "Why was that?"

"Tanaka was the greatest kendo master I had ever seen. A throwback to the days of the samurai. And I owed him a debt of honor. I once saw him kill ten men at one time."

"Sweet Jesus," Brax said. "You mean with one of them swords?"

Kiroshi nodded. "Yes, with a *katana*." He stared off into space. "Tanaka saved my life that day, so I went to the *oyabun* and offered myself in his place. My *yubitsume* was accepted. I went back to Tanaka and told him our debt was paid. He left on the condition that I never see him again."

"Or what?"

"Or," Kiroshi looked toward Brax with an obvious expression of disdain. "I would kill him."

Brax wrinkled his nose. "You guys got some funny rules over here, I'll say that. But I gotta tell you, I don't get a lot of what you're telling me."

The older man smiled. His teeth were gold outlines reinforcing crumbling enamel. "I did not imagine you would. You are a westerner...An American." His word had a measured, contempt-filled tone. "I speak of *bushido*...The warrior's code. It is very important here in Japan, even today."

"I'm sure it is," Brax said, rising. "I gotta use the bathroom."

He went inside the structure and saw the shadows of a group of men moving behind the long paper wall of the main room. They were obviously playing one of their damn Jap card games. Christ, it seemed like that's all they did. He went to the third room, slid open the door, and checked to see if Stevie was still sleeping it off. The fat slob was lying on his back clad in his dirty underwear, snoring and stinking of booze.

Brax would have liked nothing better than to boogie on out of there, take a taxi back to the city, and wait by himself in the airport for the next flight out. But bringing the boss's kid home safe was part of the deal. Sal Payne's boys were almost, but not quite as serious as these yakuza fuckers. He didn't have to worry about cutting off any fingers. They'd probably cut something else off, though, before they put a bullet in his brain.

Two of the gangster dudes ran down the narrow hallway talking Japanese into a portable radio. They looked agitated and alarmed. He could see it in their eyes. He slid the door closed and followed them, noticing for the first time that it had suddenly gotten very dark. Lighted Japanese lanterns ringed the hallway and the perimeter of the courtyard.

Kiroshi stood by the doorway, his hands on his hips, surveying the yard as the other guys rushed out.

"What's up?" Brax asked.

Kiroshi frowned. "Just checking on the guards. They did not answer their radios."

Oh shit, Brax thought. That don't sound too good. "What does that mean?"

Kiroshi glared at him momentarily, then his radio squawked with some kind of jibberish, and he smiled and held the radio up. "See, it is as I told you. All is good."

Brax looked dubious.

"Do not worry, Brax-san. As I told you, Tanaka is a man of honor. He can not defy me, without it meaning his own death." Kiroshi turned and gestured down the hallway. "Do you want me to teach you how to play our game of cards?"

Brax glanced at the gesticulating images against the opaque wall again. "You guys do that a lot, don't you?"

"It is our tradition. We take our name from it. The word *yakuza* means twenty-three."

"Is that lucky or something?"

Kiroshi shook his head and smiled. "No. It means to lose."

Great, Brax thought. Just what I wanted to hear.

"Another time," he said. "I'm pretty beat."

"Go to your room, then. Rest for your long journey home."

"Ah, I'd feel better if I had a piece," Brax said. "At least until we leave in the morning."

Kiroshi shook his head. "A gun would do no good against Tanaka, and you might accidentally shoot me."

Brax swallowed hard and eyed the butt of the automatic in the other man's belt. He didn't dare to reach out and try to grab it.

"All right," he said. "But keep me posted on what's going on, okay?"

Kiroshi bowed his head slightly.

Brax went back to his room and pulled out the small mattress they'd given him.

Christ, it isn't bad enough that I have to spend my last night in Japan cooped up in some little shithole, but I have to sleep on the goddamn floor, too. He stretched out and tried to sleep, but it proved fleetingly elusive. Stevie's sonorous breathing carried through the thin wall with the precision of a buzzsaw. Brax lay on his back listening to it, strangely reassured that if he could hear it, he knew the other man was still alive.

Still alive, he thought. Something he wouldn't be if he failed to bring the idiot back unharmed to his old man.

The buzzsaw stopped and Brax wondered if he should get up and check. Then the snoring resumed and Brax felt relief wash over him as he fell into a light slumber.

• • •

He awoke from a bad dream, and lay there in the dark trying to figure out if the loud noise was what he thought it was. It had sounded like a gunshot. Or had he imagined it? Blinking, he couldn't be sure. Could he have dreamed it? Then he heard it again. A gunshot. Another one, followed by a scream. No, this sure as hell ain't no dream, Brax thought.

A shadow flickered across the translucent door panel. Someone was outside. Before Brax could even get to his feet, the door slid open. Kiroshi poked his head in, his face drawn and tight in the moonlight that filtered in after him.

"Tanaka is here," he said. "You no move." He slid the door closed.

Brax was on his feet, thinking the hell with that. I ain't gonna be no sitting duck. It took him several seconds to slip on his pants and shirt.

Better go check on Stevie, he thought.

He heard footsteps on the other side of the far wall and saw a shadowy figure running toward the front.

Must be a hallway on both sides, Brax thought. Great. Those paper walls would offer about as much protection as a silk nightgown.

He eased open the sliding door and peered out. Several *yakuza* ran down the hallway. Glancing both ways, Brax looked for Kiroshi, but saw only a lone guy standing at the end of the hallway where it opened up into the courtyard. A pistol dangled from the man's hand.

Being as stealthy as he could, Brax moved into the hall, and crept down the ten feet to the room Stevie was in. He pushed on the sliding door and slipped inside, closing it after him.

The big slob lay on his side, still snoring, his swollen gut looking like a distended bladder. Brax grabbed the other man's shoulder and shook him.

Cursing and muttering, Stevie shoved Brax's hand away.

"Whatcha doing?" he asked, his tone loud and full of anger. "I was sleeping, for Christ's sake."

Brax couldn't afford to waste time. He slapped the fat cheeks twice and put his face closer.

"Listen to me," he said, keeping his voice low. "We're in the middle of a real bad situation here, see? Now I'm going to go outside and get us a gun, then I'm coming back for you and I'll get you outta here." He stared into the pale brown eyes, hoping to see a glimmer of understanding. "But I can't waste time looking for you, so I need you to stay right here, got it?"

Stevie's hot, fetid breath stung Brax's nostrils.

"Got it?" he repeated, slapping the other man again.

"Yeah," Stevie said.

Brax knew for sure, as he got up and moved to the door that he was going to have to answer to Sal for roughing the punk up, but hell, what other choice did he have? He thought momentarily about cutting and running, but then if Stevie did survive, how would Brax's exit be explained? It'd be answered with a bullet, that was for sure.

The hallway was deserted as Brax moved toward the guard at the end.

Easy does it, he thought. All I need is for this dude to turn around and think I'm Tanaka. Staccato sounds ripped through the night again, and Brax figured the sound would cover any noise he made.

There were three more rooms separating Brax from the other man and all were standing open. That meant three more recesses. Once he got up next to the guy, he'd call out, and get him to give up a gun or something. If worst came to worst, he could try knocking the dude out and taking what he needed. From there he'd collect Stevie and make a run for the front gates while all the confusion was still going on. Who could blame him? It sounded like a war zone out there punctuated by gunshots and screams.

Brax moved down to the second open door. A running silhouette shot past on the opposite wall. It startled him, but he kept moving. Just as he reached the final door, Kiroshi appeared and began shouting orders at the guy who'd been standing guard.

The guy said, "*Hai*," bowed quickly, and moved off to the left. Kiroshi's head bobbled as he looked down the hallway and obviously saw Brax.

"I told you, stay in room," he said, his English slipping into less comprehensible pronunciations. "Now, go!"

Kiroshi raised his arms and Brax saw the man was holding a gun. A chrome, snubnosed revolver. Kiroshi opened his mouth, as if to shout another order for Brax to leave, when his lips twisted downward in a lugubrious scowl. Slowly, Kiroshi's head lowered, as if he was testing to see if he could put his chin on his chest. But out of the front of his shirt something long and pointed protruded. An arrow. Kiroshi reached up and touched it with his left fingers as a crimson stain blossomed around the point. He looked slowly up at Brax, took two steps toward him, and twisted down in a tangled heap. After a quick glance around, Brax knelt beside him and peeled the fingers off the butt of the gun. A large blood-tinctured bubble spread from over Kiroshi's lips, and stayed there without bursting.

Brax pressed the cylinder release button and checked the ammo. Six shots, all good primers. This was his ticket out. He moved to the door and looked around. At least seven guys lay in the middle of the courtyard, some with long arrows sticking out of them, others with their bellies sliced open. He estimated about thirty yards to the gate.

To his left Brax saw the *yakuza* who'd been guarding the hallway moments ago. The man stood glancing around, his eyes so large and scared-looking that Brax was afraid the guy would shoot the first thing that moved.

"Hey," Brax called, pointing down the hallway. "Kiroshi wants you."

"Kiroshisan?" the guard said, and took a step forward just as a shadow moved behind him. The guy lurched forward, crying in pain, then as he whirled around, trying to raise his pistol, Brax saw a flash of light as a blade whistled up and back. The *yakuza* twisted, stumbling down the walk-way, his expression stupidly benign. He gripped his abdomen, which had an immense slash across it, the dark intestines rhythmically winding out from between his fingers with each step. The gun he'd been holding clattered to the floor and fell over the edge into the darkness. When the guard fell after it, Brax saw a figure in a black pajama-looking outfit standing there holding a long, bloody sword.

Tanaka!

Raising the gun, Brax started to squeeze the trigger, but the figure dashed to his right, into the adjacent hallway.

Brax ran back into his hallway and threw open the first paper door. Nothing. He ran to the second room where the door was already open. The shadow in the pajamas was silhouetted against the white rice paper wall. Brax brought his gun up and fired once, twice, three times. The shadow on the other side fell out of sight.

Never take a sword to a gunfight, Brax thought, and moved down to Stevie's room. It was still time to get the hell out of there, and he had three shots left as a buffer.

He threw open the door and yelled.

But Stevie stood there dumbly looking back at him, his fat cheeks covered with sweat. He was standing at the far wall, in the corner.

"Let's go, dammit," Brax said.

"Is it..." Stevie finally muttered, "is it safe?"

"As safe as it's gonna be," Brax said. But before he could add anything else, Stevie stiffened and rose up on his toes, the point of a *katana* protruding from his chest. The blade rotated, and Stevie did a little dance step before crumbling to the floor. Brax fired at the shadow behind the wall, aiming for the open slit as the blade withdrew.

He couldn't tell if he'd hit the guy, or not.

His mind raced: But, Christ, I thought I hit him before.

An eerie silence crept over everything, punctuated only by the racking coughs of Stevie's death throes. Nothing to do but get out myself, Brax thought, looking at what was now the corpulent corpse of his boss's son.

Turning, Brax moved down the hallway, the gun extended in front of him, ready to fire at whatever moved. Nothing's gonna stop me from getting to that gate, he thought.

He came to the edge of the hallway exit. Moving to one side, he surveyed the flat platform that led to the stairway down to the courtyard. Once he got down there, he could cover the distance in a few seconds. Zigzagging to make himself a harder target for the arrows. Unless Tanaka had picked up a gun along the way... That would be a problem. But Kiroshi had said the guy didn't operate that way. Old school, he'd called him. Traditional. A samurai.

Putting all that bushido crap out of his mind, Brax moved to the other wall and checked that direction also. It was clear, as far as he could see. Stepping onto the wooden platform, he did another fast survey and went to the steps. It was perhaps eighteen feet down to the court yard. How many rounds did he have left? He'd used three at the first shadow, one at the slit. That meant two left. Plenty of cushion. Something creaked under the porch as Brax stepped forward, but a quick look indicated nothing. He could feel the sweat starting to wind down his face, collecting on his neck and running onto his back.

"Like I said," Brax muttered, "Never take a sword to a gunfight."

The best thing would be to just make a run for the front gate. Go out and try to find some way back to Tokyo. Maybe a cab or something. Hell, he'd even pay one of these farmers for a ride.

Brax turned and worked his way cautiously down the stairs, wheeling quickly from side-to-side.

He thought about calling out to Tanaka, telling him he had no quarrel with him. That he only wanted to leave. Maybe it would buy him passage, or trick the Jap into showing himself so he could get a clear shot. But yelling would only give away his position.

No, he thought. Got to keep moving. If the guy showed himself, he'd shoot first and say he was sorry later.

Two more steps and he'd be at the bottom. He surveyed the yard again. Nothing, except for a whole lot of bodies. Brax felt his feet on solid ground and was moving forward, toward the gate when a noise over to his left made him whirl. Nothing. He started to turn back, his gun arm still outstretched, when a shadow moved from under the wooden porch's support pillars, and something flashed in front of him.

He turned, trying to pull the trigger but his hand wouldn't work. Instead, he felt a strange numbness, and looked downward. The gun lay there, in front of his feet, his fingers still curled around it, the bloody cut that severed it from his wrist looking smooth and even. Like a chopped-off piece of meat. Something flittered in front of him and landed next to the gun on the ground. He squinted to see what it was in the poor light, and then, suddenly, he understood.

It was a black rose.

Last Orders

Tony Black

A GUS DURY STORY

There was something about this prick, got me thinking.

I took a deck at his shoes, brogues. His type have a name for the colour, ox-blood. Oh, yeah. I wear Docs, same colour, I call them cherry. Go figure.

He strolled over, "Mr Dury, I have something to say and I will not..."

He stopped flat.

I put the bead on him. My hand went up, slowly.

"*Yes...*" It was a question, really, the pause told me. Like I needed the nod too, that I clocked as—*affectation*.

"Call me Gus, I hear the mister in there, I think you're after money, or worse, mistaking me for my old man." The bold Cannis Dury, not a man you'd like to be confused with. Trust me on that. I know.

He looked to the ceiling. Huffed. Was that a tut? I let it slide.

I stood.

He said: "A-hem, are you?"

"Leaving? Oh yes."

"But we have business."

"You think?"

That was when I noticed the tweed cap in his hands. He twisted it. Like he was wringing the neck of a pheasant on his country estate. It boiled my piss. I'm working class, c'mon, it's in the contract.

I reached the street in a heartbeat, as they say Stateside, tugging the zipper on my denim jacket. I know, I know, sacrilege: buttons are the thing for denim—go tell Mr Wrangler. These days, fashion, the whole world...don't get me started. No, really, don't.

The hand on my shoulder told me I'd been followed out. That, I did not like. Too close to keeping tabs. Or worse, control.

"I have a daughter and she is no longer contactable through the proper channels," he said, a pause, then, "Gus."

*The proper channels...*he spoke of his daughter like he was some ponytailed ad-man at a PowerPoint presentation.

I eyeballed him, "And this is my problem, why?"

I sensed his distaste at the way I talked, not my accent, though that was bad enough—heavy on the Leith—what got him was what riled teachers in school, made them say, "The temerity!"

He looked skyward. Wanted to bolt, turn on his heels, throw up his hands. Days of Empire, I'd be flogged where I stood. But this was 2008. Say you want a revolution—bring it right on.

He checked himself, two yellow tombstones bit down on his lower lip. His pallor was grey as concrete. He spoke, slowly, "I believe you are a man of some...reputation."

I allowed myself a blink. But, no more.

He went on, "You have, I understand, some background."

"*Background?*"

"I took the liberty of, oh what's the demotic? Checking you out."

The hand again. I blocked his words. Funny how, you're in a situation, you act out old habits.

"And how did you manage that?" I said.

There was a spit of rain in the air, threatened more of the same. Edinburgh, could be coming down in stair rods inside a minute. He sussed this too. "Mr Dury, can we return indoors?"

His face changed shape. I'd seen the look before, what the Scots call, *thrawn*. I thought, fuck the ox-blood brogues, if he's buying, then...

Truth told, was close to last orders anyway.

• • •

There were one or two old soaks propping up the bar, bluenoses with tractor tracks cut in their brows. Rough's the word. Knew I'd be there soon enough myself, but was there a point in hastening it? You bet. Ordered up a Guinness, pint of, and a double whisky chaser.

"A malt?" said ox-bloods.

"Is there another kind?" Like I was settling for a blend on his time and dime.

We collected our drinks, headed for the snug. I felt like sparking up, had a pack of Rothmans raring to go, but the smoking ban had me beat to the punch.

The pint of dark settled a craving, tasted like old memories. I was heading for the wee goldie when himself removed his scarf, revealed a dog collar.

"You're Church?"

"I am, yes, Church of Scotland...that makes a difference?"

The short answer was, "Yes", the easy one was, "Should it?"

"That would be an ecumenical matter."

I picked up my pint again, supped, said, "I believe you're right...can we skip it, get down to business?"

"Indeed."

His name was Urquhart. A Church of Scotland minister from the North; the trip to Edinburgh had left him, he said, "Unsettled".

"How come?"

"I have what you might call, no good reason to be here."

Hadn't we all, played him with, "Should I get my coat?"

"No. No. Please, if you'll indulge me, Mr Dury."

"Gus."

"Of course…Gus."

He played with the lid on his mineral water, Highland Spring, still. Sparkling just too exciting an option, "My daughter…"

"Yeah, you mentioned her."

"I'm afraid, she has, erm, well…it's rather embarrassing, gone missing."

Embarrassing? Somehow, that didn't seem the right word. A daughter gone from home was a cause for sleepless nights, not a cause for losing face. I eyed him cautiously over my pint, gave him some more rope.

"She got herself mixed up with the wrong crowd some time ago, my parish is a very poor community, we once had mines but they are long gone and I'm afraid in their wake came some rather extreme views."

I knew pit communities had it tough after Thatcher, they lost their livelihood so the old bitch could prove a point. Some got paid off, a few grand to piss up the wall, called them six-month millionaires.

"Extreme?"

"Well, yes…anarchists, Mr Dury."

"Go, on…"

He poured out his mineral water, drank deep, he had quite a thirst on him, I knew the territory. "My daughter, Caroline, she was a very willful child and…"

"Whoa, back up…was? What makes you think we're talking past-tense here, Minister?"

He bridled, removed a handkerchief and wiped his palms, "A figure of speech, I have no reason to believe…I mean, I have nothing to go on, Gus, that is why I have come to you."

I'd say one thing for him, he had my attention. These days, my situation, wedded to a bottle of scoosh and forty, scrub that, sixty, smokes a day, that was no mean feat. I pressed him for some details, jotted them down.

"I'll need five-hundred in advance and another five when I conclude."

"Conclude?"

"That's right…I don't have a crystal ball, Minister. I go digging, what I find is what I find. What I get, is a grand for my trouble. We understand each other?"

He nodded, took out a cheque book.

"Cash."

"I'll have to go to a bank."

"Then, let's."

I drained my pint.

On the way out the door, Urquhart placed a hand on my elbow, spoke softly, "One more thing, I neglected to mention..."

"Yeah?"

"My daughter, I believe, is...with child."

· · ·

Papers had been full of scare stories coming out the hospitals. We had a power of superbugs rampaging through them. Resistant to treatment, the red-tops said; was the new plague. I'd watched a documentary about the issue, doctors were in the clear, so were nurses, the blame was being planted firmly at the feet of...immigrant workers. I'd been a hack, knew a beat-up story when I heard one. Everyone needs a scapegoat, welcome to Scotland, scapegoats a speciality, we've a history littered with them.

I traipsed through the main doors of the Royal Infirmary and looked for the maternity ward. Figured a young girl—Urquhart had said she was barely eighteen—wouldn't be too hard to find. Women were having kids later and later, right? Wrong. They had a ward full of them. Gym-slip mums they called them in my day. Christ knows what they called them now...Britney had kids, last I looked, was probably the fashion. Me and fashion, we don't get along.

I grabbed a nurse as she passed me in the corridor, "Hello, there..."

Eyed with suspicion, got, "Yes."

"I was wondering if you might be able to help me."

Now I got the full head-to-toe eyeball, "Visiting hours are four till six."

"No, sorry, I'm not visiting. I'm just looking for someone."

"Looking for someone?"

"Yes, a girl...name of Urquhart, about eighteen." I knew the chances of her using her own name were slim to none, but chanced it.

"Are you a relative?"

Fuck it, the boat was out, I pushed it further, "Yes. I'm her brother."

I knew at once she wasn't buying it. I was only in my thirties, but the sauce had added a few years to the dial of late.

"Do you have any identification?"

I stalled, "Can I show you a picture?" Urquhart had supplied a photo, a few years old I'd say. Caroline was still in school uniform, one of those dreadful posed, say-cheese numbers that everyone has tucked away in a sideboard at their parents' home. Not me, though. What I have tucked away at my parents' home is…skeletons.

The nurse took the photograph from me, looked at it, said, "This girl has red hair."

"Yeah?"

"And blue eyes."

"You caught that."

"If you and her are related…I'm a monkey's uncle."

I snatched back the picture, "Are you in charge here."

"I'm the ward sister."

"Well look, *sister*, this young lass is missing, her father is very concerned and if I don't find her soon who's to say what might happen to her."

Hands on hips, I got hands on hips from her. "I'm calling the police."

"Y'what?"

"If you're not off this ward, and out of this hospital, in the next thirty seconds, I'm calling the police."

I pocketed the photograph. Turned, fired out, "Nice bedside manner you have there."

A finger pointed to the door.

"Out!"

"Don't worry, I'm gone."

Felt a torrent of abuse at my back, caught the words, "come in here stinking of drink" and knew I'd reached the end of one line of inquiry.

• • •

Before I got my jotters from the paper, I had a helper. Not quite an assistant, more a Girl Friday. Amy was work experience, had a thing for old movies with journalists cracking big stories. Had a thing for old journalists too, but that's another story. I caught up with her in Deacon Broadie's pub on The Mile.

On any given day of the week, Amy, you can bet your hat, is dressed to impress. She sauntered in, white mules, white jeans (skin-tight) and a pillar-box red crop top that showed a stomach so flat you could eat your dinner off it. The diamanté stud in her navel, you could argue was over the top…but who'd listen.

"Gus boy, how do?"

"Mair to fiddling." That's a Scots spoonerism for you, does it have a meaning? Does anything?

Amy settled herself at the bar, ran her fingers through long black hair. She was a show stopper, men's eyes lit up like Chinese lanterns about the place.

"I need your help?"

She ordered a rum and coke, fastest service I'd ever seen, "Yeah, help with what?"

"A case."

A smile. Wide, a from the heart job, "Great!"

"Calm down, I wouldn't get too excited about this one."

"Work's work...beats staying home watching Antiques Roadshow."

"Maybe not this one...I warn you, I don't see much scope for excitement."

"I'm an excitable girl! Try me."

I gave her the details. My main concern was just what was behind Urquhart's tale.

"You think he's hiding something?" said Amy.

"Dunno."

"He's a minister, though."

"There's no sin but ignorance."

"Is that a quote?"

"Sure is."

• • •

I stood in the carpark of the Royal Infirmary. Couldn't believe I was about to do this. Had to call and double check.

"Fitzsimmons, please?"

"Inspector Fitzsimmons, connecting you now."

Fitz the Crime and I went way back. In my time on the paper, I'd kept a couple of his indiscretions out of the headlines. Plod tends to turn a blind eye to its own lot's peccadilloes, but seeing them in print is a whole other matter.

"Hello."

"Fitz, I wanted to check..."

"Dury, by the feckin' cringe, what in the name of Christ are ye doing calling me here?"

"Calm down, man, all I want is a little confirmation."

"By the holy, it's my bollocks in a jar yeer after! I'm certain of it."

I let him settle, grab a hold of himself, said, "It's definitely the blue Micra, L89 KLP?"

"Jeez, didn't I tell ye it was?" The Jamieson we'd tanned over lunch was rising in him, brought out some more Irish, "It is her and that's that...why are ye doubting me?"

I could see the nurse by the car, she was chatting with a young lad of about twenty, the blue shirt a giveaway that he was also a member of staff.

"It's just I have her in my sights, and well, we've already spoken and she was none to keen on filling me in."

"Dury, I have no such qualms, I will gladly come down there and fill ye the feck in if I hear one more word out of ye. I cannot believe you would call…"

I hung up.

If this was our one, there was no choice. I let her wave off her co-worker and headed for her car.

The Micra had central locking, I opened the passenger door and got inside. "Hello again."

She looked, there's a phrase, shook. "What are you doing here?"

"Don't worry, I'm no mentaller. I want to talk to you about Caroline Urquhart and don't play coy, I know you treated her when she came to the Royal."

"Get out of my car."

"Look, lady, I don't care what you think of me but that girl and her baby need help, now either you're going to be the one to help her or we're relying on someone else out there being a very good Samaritan."

She fiddled with the keys in her hand. She looked at me, in the eye, then averted her gaze back out towards the hospital carpark. A sigh, "I haven't seen her in weeks."

"How many?"

"Two, three…maybe a bit longer. She's due you realise."

"What, now?"

"Very soon. I have to admit, I've been a bit worried, she gave us an address for a place down in Leith and I went there, twice now, but it's boarded up. I don't think anyone is living there."

"Did she have any associates?"

The nurse's top lip twitched uneasily, she looked out the window again, "There was a boy, erm, he was a bit…rough."

"How do you mean?"

"Rough, rough. He was tattooed from head to toe and I think he had beaten her."

"Beaten?"

"There was a black eye once and a few cuts on her face."

"The baby?"

"Healthy. I think the child was fine, it was just male dominance issues."

"Backhanders."

She nodded.

"This guy, you know anything about him?"

"No. I don't think he had a job. I think he was wary of Caroline coming to the hospital. I know he had told her that he thought we suspected he beat her and…look, I really can't tell you any more."

I took out my notebook, "Just let me have the address and I'll be on my way."

• • •

I grew up in Leith. Parts of the place, now, I hardly recognised. There was chrome and glass eyesores springing up every week it seemed. When my brother and I were young enough to go bikes we played boneshaker over the cobbles. I couldn't see any kids nowadays doing that, unless you can get it on the Nintendo Wii.

I found the address quickly. This part of town, the developers had left well alone. Give them a few more months, there'll be bulldozers in. Then the chrome and glass.

The stairwell was covered in graffiti. Tagging mainly. You get your school of thought that this kinda thing ruins an area; me, I say, how much worse can they make it? Scrubbing it off's only turd polishing.

The landing smelled of piss. Even with all the windows panned in, the piss was still rank enough to make me want to chuck. I stuck my face behind my jacket and waded through the detritus of aerosols, needles and White Light-ning bottles. The address was the last in the line I wondered, end of the road?

I could see why the nurse would think nobody lived here. Like she would? Uh-uh. I pressed on the door's windowpane, there was no movement, it wasn't opening up. Looked in the letter box, a blast of damp, but also, I'm sure some movement.

I banged on the door.

Nothing.

Tried again.

A clang of, was it, a door?

I hollered in the letterbox, "Caroline, is that you? My name's Gus, Gus Dury, your father asked me to find you?"

I put my ear to the slot.

No movement anymore.

I knew there was someone in there. Toyed with the idea of putting my foot to the door when, suddenly, a whoosh of stale air as the glass pane came through. I caught a set of wooden step ladders in the mush.

I fell back. My back smacked off the concrete landing just as I saw a blur of shaved head loom over me and cosh me across the face with a heavy pot.

Next thing I saw was the dancing canaries.

• • •

"Hello, can you hear me? Hello…hello."

My head felt like Chewbacca had taken a dump in there. I was still on my back as I opened my eyes to find a young girl looming over me with dark panda eyes.

"Can you hear me?"

"Yeah. Just, maybe lower the volume."

"I'm sorry. Are you okay? Can you move?"

I tried to steady myself, "I think so."

"Would you like to come inside?"

I got on my feet, knees caved. The girl, heavily pregnant, put an arm around me. "Can you manage, this?" I said.

She smiled, a sweet smile, real heart-melter. Wondered why anyone with a smile like that needed to live in a place like this.

She sat me on an old crate, an orange velour cushion the only concession to comfort.

"You would be Caroline?"

She brought me a wet cloth, said, "We've no ice."

"You've not much of anything."

She gripped her palms, looked at the floor.

"Caroline, your father..."

She turned away, "Don't. Don't say his name to me."

I tried to regain control of my balance, stop the room swaying, "Look, he's worried about you."

"No he's not."

"Sorry?"

The sweet demeanour vanished in a second, she turned, rushed towards me but seemed suddenly cut down in her tracks. She bent like a hinge, gasped.

"Are you okay?"

Breathless, "I think the baby's coming."

"Oh, fuck."

A shriek.

Pain.

"You'll have to help me."

"What? I mean, how?"

Another shriek.

She fell to the floor, started to scrunch up her eyes.

"Help me, please!"

• • •

At the hospital we went our separate ways.

"Will she be okay?" I asked as they wheeled Caroline away.

No answer.

Some bright spark put a wheelchair down for me, motioned 'in'.

"No chance. I walk fine."

Got two steps and the knees went again. Had been running on my last reserves of adrenaline.

"Like I thought, that gash tells a different story," said the paramedic.

I touched my head, felt blood on my fingertips. It had soaked all the way down into my shirt collar and into my waistband.

"Looks like you took quite a clatter."

Wanted to say, "No shit, Sherlock." Went with, "Yes, quite a clatter."

They spent an hour or so patching me up. Had stitches and a nice head bandage to complete the look.

Amy brought in the news: "She had a little girl."

I tried to smile, but my head hurt too much, even on the codeine, "Great, she's okay?"

"Chirping away like a budgie."

I sat up, "Do tell."

Amy had on her shit-stopping seriousness look, "It's not pretty."

I motioned to my head, "I look like someone who needs sugar-coating?"

Amy stood up again, looked agitated. She took off her coat and placed it over the chair by the bed. "Well, I checked out our Minister..."

"And?"

"Well, let's just say you were right to have your suspicions. He's in line to be the Moderator of the Church of Scotland."

"That's a big gig."

"The biggest, comes with the Right Reverend title...you could see why he has Oscar night nerves."

"He does?"

Amy put her arms round her slim waist, hugged herself, "Gus, I feel strange talking about this, but, Caroline said some stuff when she, well after the birth, I think she was still under the drugs, but..."

I sat up in the bed, motioned her closer, "Look, if there's something I need to know, you better just spit it out."

Amy started to cry. She was a tough lass, I'd never seen this before.

"Hey, what's the matter?"

She put her hand to her mouth, "Caroline says...he's the father."

I slumped, "*What?*"

The dam had burst, "She says he raped her. She hates him, got into trouble at home and got into this neo-Nazi crowd because she thought it was about as far away from what he stood for as she could get...Gus, it's too sad for words."

I couldn't listen any more.

"Give me my phone over."

"You can't use a phone in hospital."

"Fuck it. Give me it."

She passed me the mobi, it smelled of fags, Benson's.

I dialed Urquhart, he answered on the second ring, "Hello, Minister, this is Gus Dury."

"Oh, hello ... have you uncovered anything?"

"You better believe it."

"Well, that's wonderful news."

"Is it?"

"Well, yes, I-I..."

"Not so fast. I have found your daughter, but let's just say I've ran into a few extra expenses along the way."

"I don't understand."

"Understand this, the price is now two-thousand in cash by this afternoon."

"*What?*"

"You heard, Minister...you ever want to hear that Right Reverend bit upfront then you better be where I first met you on time."

I cut the line.

• • •

I took Amy, not as back-up, or decoration, but because she set the tone I wanted. She had—edge.

Urquhart was sitting in the snug with a bottle of Highland Spring. Still.

On our approach he stood up, eyes lit on my bandaged head, then shifted, "Who is this?"

Amy looked him up and down, she blew out her Hubba Bubba, popped the bubble fast. Sat right up front. Urquhart had a view of her cleavage most men would have paid money for, but it set his nerves jangling.

"You don't ask any questions, Minister," I said.

I nodded to the barman, "Rum and coke, twice."

There was silence around the table. Amy eyed Urquhart with derision. Once in a while she'd blow out another bubble, just to put the knife in him.

"Could you stop that, please?" said Urquhart.

"Why?" said Amy.

He clammed, mumbled, "It's vexatious."

Amy fluttered her eyelashes, leaned forward, close enough for the minister to scent the Hubba Bubba on her breath, "If someone says stop, do you always stop, Minister?"

"I beg your pardon?"

A smile, wide white teeth, "No never."

Our drinks came.

The barman left.

I spoke, "Now, let's get down to brass tacks. The cash."

He ruffled, "I think I shall have my side of the agreement fully realised before I part with any..."

I raised a hand, "Hold it right there."

Amy slurped rum and coke through a straw.

The minister shuffled on his seat, "I have had quite enough of this performance, Mr Dury! Now I engaged your services to locate my daughter and I demand to know what progress you have made towards that end."

"The money."

Silence.

Amy leaned forward, yelled, "The money!" She slapped her hand on the table, yelled again, "Now!"

Did the trick.

He produced a long manila envelope from the inside pocket of his Barbour jacket.

I opened the package, peered inside.

"There's no need to count it, it's all there."

It looked about right. I peeled out two fifties, gave them to Amy, said, "Here, you've earned that."

She took them greedily, sat them under her glass; returned eyes to the minister.

I resealed the envelope, handed it back to Amy, said, "Take this to Caroline...that girl deserves all the help she can get for making a fresh start."

Urquhart's face reddened, "Now look here, I paid you to find my daughter."

"I did."

"Then, where is she?"

"I never said I would tell you that."

He made an O of his mouth, fumbled for words, we have a phrase in Scotland, "Are you catching flies, Minister?"

"I-I can't believe this...you have swindled me!" He rose, went to do up his jacket. "I'm not standing for this," he said.

I motioned, "Sit," patted on his chair, "unless you'd like me to fuck up your chances of becoming Moderator once and for all."

His eyes widened. He lowered himself, slowly.

Amy sighed, blew another bubble, got up to leave.

"I've seen all I can stomach," she said.

Urquhart lowered his head, looked into his palms, "What has she told you?"

I tipped up my glass, drained it, "Everything."

"She lies you know."

"Will the DNA?"

He turned to me, quickly.

"Didn't think so."

I stood up to leave, moved towards him and lowered my mouth to his ear, "If I ever hear you have been within a country mile of that girl, I will personally preside over your crucifixion. Do you understand me?"

He said nothing.

"Is your hearing off, I said do you understand me?"

Nods. Rapid. "Yes, yes, I understand." He took out his handkerchief, pressed it between his hands, then carefully began to fold it away again.

I moved off, left him staring at the tabletop. As I walked, I expected him to ask about his daughter, either one. He stayed silent.

At the door, my heart pounded. I turned, thought I might see a broken man, in tears perhaps. He was pouring out the mineral water. Face, stone.

Repossession

R. Thomas Brown

Daryl dimmed the lights on the tow truck as they turned down the alley. Looming lamps from the nearby streets provided enough light to see turns, but the screech that tore through the silence illuminated that not everything was visible.

"Shit, Daryl, did you just kill a cat?" Bill stuck his head outside the window and looked down. He jerked it back in with the sting of a branch slapping his face after being bent by the oversized side mirror.

Daryl tossed back a handful of sunflower seeds while laughing. "Watch yourself, newbie. You'll get plenty of scars in this business." He pointed at fresh wounds on his face. "No need to add a few from just being stupid. 'Sides, you'll do worse things in this job than kill a few cats."

Bill rubbed his cheek with his palm and his tongue. "What are we doing down this stupid alley anyway. I thought the guy lived three streets over."

Daryl shook his head. "Yeah, but he knows someone's coming for the car. He'll park somewhere away from the house, but close enough to walk to it." He spit the chewed seeds out the window and downed another handful. "They all think they're so fucking smart, but we always find it."

"Sure, but I hate being out here in the dark. Can't see if anyone's out there."

"Nut up, newbie. Ain't no one gonna be out here if the car is. Who'd just wait by a car while we roll up. They'd drive off, see. And, even if they was, I got this." Daryl reached between them and tapped the shotgun that rested on the seat.

Bill looked off. He'd only been doing repo for couple weeks, and was happy to get to work vehicle skip tracing. He felt like a PI hunting down clues and interviewing people of interest on the phone. Daryl was a legend at the shop, and Bill wanted to learn everything he could. At first.

They'd found a car parked behind a strip mall the previous week. Owner's sister worked there. Bill was happy with himself for finding that out, and Daryl had a big grin on the way there. Kept talking about how the newbie was learning. How he'd have a truck of his own in no time.

After they matched the plates, they were hitching up the car when a woman came tearing out of one of the back doors. Screaming at them to stop. Dragging her daughter behind. She kept screeching that it wasn't right. They had the wrong car. She'd sue. She'd call the police. Bill was working the hitch. She jumped Daryl. Clawed at his face.

Daryl tossed her off. Kicked her when she tried to jump in for more. Knocked her into the kid who fell. Started bawling. He told them both to sit, and Bill kept hitching the car. Everything calmed down, until someone else came out. Woman screamed for help. The dude ran over. Daryl pulled the shotgun out of the truck. The hero took the woman inside. Daryl belly laughed while Bill finished up.

"Bill, what kind of car is that up on the right?"

Bill shook the thoughts out and grabbed the flashlight from the dash and aimed it out the side of the truck, careful to keep his head safe inside. He moved it around the vehicle. "It's a Magnum. No plates."

"They always take off the plates, idiots, we'll just check the VIN."

Daryl pulled the truck past the vehicle and backed up. Bill hopped out and read the numbers back. A match. Daryl slipped out of the truck. "Let's get this done." He began working the gear.

• • •

At the other end of the alley, a man exited his car. He'd been waiting for the two bellowing buffoons to exit. Waiting for them to find their next target. He needed them on foot.

He'd followed the pair for a week, waiting for the right situation. Too many parking lots. Busy streets. Driveways in daylight. They were at their worst without prying eyes. He'd match it this time. The woman had needed help. He needed to make sure her and her daughter were okay. It wasn't the right time, then.

The big one beat that woman. Beyond need. And laughed. Hurt the kid without giving a shit. No need to report. She'd gone at him first, the man knew that, but it was all sideways. The big one reveled in it. The power was in his eyes and the man knew that black heart was drunk on it.

The little one stood back. Didn't join in, but didn't help. He was just craven. Cared for his own. Just doing his job. Let the coward inside put job over people. Let it make money precious and people replaceable.

Lessons needed to be taught. Values put in perspective. But those lessons needed private instruction. He needed the right classroom. The alley looked good.

When the driver exited the truck, the man began walking. Slow, steady steps. Keeping to the shadows. The street lamps cast long fingers, and under the canopy of trees, he was hidden. He needed to get close. Close enough to take the cannon out of the equation.

Once he was close enough, he didn't care if he was seen. He was a nobody. Everybody. The most average person that could be found. Once he'd been irritated when everyone thought they had met him before, now he knew the gift he'd been given.

He crept closer, moving as the wind blew, his steps mixing with rustling leaves. Closer. Closer still. They worked the hitch and had the car ready. They were looking away. Time for class.

"Hey. What's going on?"

· · ·

Bill looked up at the man coming toward them. He was sure they were alone. His heart jumped but he took a deep breath and kept working. He figured Daryl would do the talking.

"Just workin'." Daryl stepped toward the cab of the truck. "You know the owner of this car?"

The man shook his head. "No. I was just out for a walk. Don't normally see anything going on in the alley this late. Figured I'd see if you needed any help." He stepped toward Daryl. "Name's James Smith." He reached out his hand.

"No, we got it." Daryl ignored the gesture. "Thanks anyway." Daryl turned and reached in the window of the cab.

Mr. Smith lunged and drove his shoulder into Daryl, knocking him against the truck and onto the ground. "Now, I was being nice. Why'd you go for the weapon, Daryl?" He kicked the large man in the side and took the shotgun out of the truck.

"How'd you know my name?" Daryl scurried back until he hit the truck.

"It didn't take much work." He pointed at the shirt. "Name's on the tag, dumb ass."

Bill stopped work and stepped toward them, but the pointed barrel stopped him. "Hey, I'm just doing my job, man. I don't want any trouble."

Mr. Smith waved him over to Daryl and motioned for him to sit. "Just doing your job, huh? You people are always just doing your job while someone else is being railroaded. People just did their job while they pinned those repos on me. People did their job while I got escorted out of the building. People did their job when my house got taken away. And you did your fucking job, while this asshole beat a woman and hurt a kid. And laughed about it."

Bill squinted. "You were the guy in the alley, weren't you?"

"Yeah. I saw it all. Saw fatso kick that woman. Saw the kid get hurt. Saw you not do a damn thing. Well, now there's no one around. Now, there's no shotgun to save you." He pointed the barrel at Bill. "You, get that car down."

Bill stood up and took a step.

"Don't do it, Bill."

Bill stopped. Remembered what Daryl said. People act brave, but they don't really want to shoot. Daryl always said it was what let him be fearless. He knew how far he would go. Most didn't.

Daryl stood. "Listen, James, we're taking that car. I don't care if it's yours, a buddy's, or you really are just some stupid wannabe hero. We're taking it."

Mr. Smith stood.

"Bill, the car secure?" Daryl kept his eyes on Mr. Smith.

"Yeah. It's good." Bill swallowed and watched the two men.

Daryl smiled and stepped to the truck. "Get in, Bill. Time to go. Pleasure to meet you, James."

Bill walked around the car, to the opposite side. He heard the truck door open. He exhaled. He was glad Daryl was right. Still, he didn't like this part of the job. He was thinking about quitting when he heard a sickening crack. He looked across the cab and saw blood splattered on the inside of the windshield.

He ran around the front and saw Daryl on the ground, holding his jaw.

"Your friend didn't want to listen. I suggest you sit your ass down."

Bill scurried over to Daryl and sat. His jaw was loose and blood poured out of this mouth with a few teeth in the river of red.

"Now." Mr. Smith exhaled. "Bill, right?"

He nodded.

"Bill. Slowly, go take that car down. I don't think Daryl will be arguing this time." Mr. Smith paused while Bill walked over to the hitch. "See, Bill, it's simple. We need different priorities in our lives. Need to keep things in their proper place."

Bill lowered the car and removed the gear. "Sure. Okay. Whatever you say."

Mr. Smith tapped Bill's head with the barrel. "Don't patronize me. You don't understand a damned thing I'm talking about." He walked back. "Now. Get him in the truck."

Bill nodded and struggled to get Daryl up and into the cab. He set the larger man in the passenger side. Backing away, he was sickened by the blood on his clothes. "Now what?"

"Now. Get out. Leave. Take him to a hospital."

"What?"

"He has a fucking broken jaw, Bill. Take him to an emergency room. You're such a self-centered prick, Bill. Doing your job. Worrying about yourself." Mr. Smith leaned toward him. "You need to start thinking about other people, Bill. Keep being that egocentric, and it'll all catch up to you."

Bill swallowed and hurried to start the truck. The diesel engine sputtered and roared and he drove off. Behind, he could see Mr. Smith standing there. Staring. Bill checked in front of the truck and then back to the mirror. He was gone.

He drove straight to Century Hospital and helped Daryl in. While he was waiting, he called work and quit. After a while, an officer showed up. Bill described Mr. Smith as best he could.

The officer flipped his pad closed. "Well, we'll do our best to the find a medium height, medium build, brown eyed, brown haired man by the name of," he made a show of looking at his pad again, "James Smith. But don't hold your breath."

• • •

James Smith sat in his Camry outside the hospital as the cruiser drove away. He took a sip of his soda and watched the ER entrance. Waited. About an hour. Bill came out.

A minivan pulled up and Bill hopped in the passenger side. James pulled out of his space and followed. He watched from behind as Bill leaned over for a kiss from the driver. A knot formed in James's stomach thinking of the woman in his own life who couldn't endure the job loss and anger.

James followed them out of the parking lot, on and off the highway, and into their neighborhood. He drove past them as they pulled into the garage of a modest home. He noted the address and was on his way. He had hope for Bill. Maybe he could turn it around.

Maybe.

With a few more lessons.

Spectre In The Galway Wind

Ken Bruen

He was a ejit
A bollix.
A daily, no worse, morning, drinker
But
Most of all
He was my partner.
Barret.
Of the Galway tribes.
Least in name.
We'd been young Guards in Templemore. Graduated on
Poiteen.
That's Irish moonshine with malice.
Cured the ferocious hangover with the carbo nightmare
Like this
3 fat sausages
3 rashers.
Runny egg
Black pudding.
Mushrooms.
Beans.
And, lashing of scalding tea.
We'd a lot in common, well
We had hurling.
You play it with hockey in mind, murder as out rider.
Barret was good and I was dirty.
Worked.
My first assignment was the border town, bandit country, Drogheda. I learned
a new set of dirt.

Barret got home, Galway.

He'd always been lucky and when he made detective, in the shuffle of the
Northern counties disgrace, he got me re-assigned to Galway.

Busted back to street shite but home anyway.

My sister, Kaitlin, a head case of epic size and the fook, the love of my mates
life.

That's when he stopped being lucky and became prone.

Prone to

Life

In the worst form, the form that gets you caught.

• • •

Drogheda, the border outpost, precarious the pose, twixt the Republic and the North. If the peace process was seen as a wonder globally, the news had yet to filter through to the inhabitants of the town. In two years I learned most you'd ever need on the human condition. Drugs and weapons. Sex too but that was like an Irish afterthought. Drogheda was vital in my career as it was then I first met Brian Deacon. I'd been called to a domestic. The worst kind of call. You learned early, watch your back and never take sides. The wife you offered sympathy to, a moment later was putting the bread knife in your neck. So, you stood well back and on occasion, handed out a slap to one of the parties. It was a flat above a pub. I was partnered with an old sergeant, Flanagan, who gave cynicism a whole new flight.

We stood in the apartment, as a man in his early forties, wearing just a shirt and briefs, seemed stunned we were there. A woman, who looked closely underage, screamed

'Yah bollix, you said you loved me.'

Am...

Flanagan, seemed amused, not a trait he much showed and might explain his turning his back on the girl.

Who lunged with a knife.

More accident than reflex, I pushed Flanagan aside, and as she drew down the knife, it caught me below my right eye. The pain took a moment, the blood as afterthought. I shot out my right fist, knocked her on her arse. My blood covered the front of the man's shirt, he muttered

'Holy fook.'

He was Deacon, then a junior minister in the Labour Party. A party then in the wilderness. As I tried to stem the blood, he moved to me, said

'I owe you lad.'

Flanagan said

'Put your pants on for Christ sakes.'

We got the woman in the car, Deacon asking Flanagan

'Any chance you could ... you know, keep this out of the news?'

Flanagan, not big on politicians, snapped

'Any chance you can keep it in your pants?'

As I led the girl to the patrol car, I looked back, to see Flanagan accept a wad of notes from Deacon. He waited while they stitched my face in the hospital, the doctor saying

'Going to be quite a scar there.'

Flanagan snorted, said

'Give him a bit of a rep.' leaving, the doctor gave me a shitload of pain killers, cautioning

'Avoid alcohol.'

Flanagan asked

'A drink then?'

Absolutely.

Went to a seedy dive off the main street, frequented by The Boyos. What that meant was, it was unlikely to be bombed unless the UVF took a day trip. On the other side of large Jay's, black pints, I asked

'So, no formal report I'm thinking?'

A foam moustache added an almost softness to his granite face. He drained the pint, said

'You saw that huh?'

The Guards were still regarded in a good light and the scandals of Donegal had yet to come blue down the pike. I nodded, not feeling a whole lot of anything, the shock of the knife still hadn't kicked in, it would but the Jay was fighting a rear line. He added

'No harm to have an ally in them circles.'

I looked at him, his battered face, asked

'Those circles being the ones where they beat the shite out of women?'

A flash of anger, then

'Ary, you're young, but hang in there, like me, you have a dirty soul.'

He reached in his ash strewn tunic, began to peel off some notes, I said

'No thanks.'

He shrugged, said

'I want half though.'

The fook?

I asked

'Half of what, my scar?'

He yawned, said

'Those pain killers, Those babies have the oul jolt.'

'You're in pain?'

He laughed

'I'm a fecking Guard, pain is me business.'

• • •

A

   DIRTY

      SOUL.

Spectre;

An apparition.

A ghost,

A person, event or thought, causing

Alarm or threat.

Being Jewish in a green land.

Worse, a deeply catholic one.

Deeply Catholic being the Spanish version, ie, religious when it suited their bigotry.

Spectrematz.

My great grandfathers name, changed to Spectre by the Ellis island hard arses. I was born in the US, Irish mother, and living in Ireland since I was two years old.

A mongrel they said.

Neither here nor there.

Christ killer the kids at school taunted, and encouraged by the priests, gave me some good fooking grief on Good Friday. My father met and married my mother in New York, she was a chamber maid, like, she said

'Nora Barnacle.'

A beat

'But your Da, he was no James Joyce.'

Indeed.

He was a hustler.

Of varying levels of success.

Truly, t'was, all or nothing.

Precarious the pose. We had to flee NY due to some guys who Dad owed a small country to, and my mothers home of Galway was certainly far enough away. To stay until the heat ebbed.

Right.

I got my height from my father, all six foot and my mouth, attitude from my mother. My accent would always be a hybrid, of NY and Claddagh and that is not an asset, just a surprise. Our house, rented, was in The Claddagh and from our front door, you could literally feed the swans. I think, cross me heart most ways, my earliest memory is of a King Charles puppy, asking my Dad

'What shall we name him?'

One of his perennial cigarettes fired up, he said

'Best not name something we might have to eat.'

Was he kidding? All I know is the nameless one gave him a wide berth from then on.

• • •

There was a time when we had a shit load of money, brief but beautiful. My father got in on some Pyramid scheme, when it crashed, he narrowly avoided jail and incredibly kept most of the cash. My sister was sent to a posh boarding school, I was sent to hell. Because he started to drink and could afford it, we couldn't. Not the ones who took the brunt of the hangovers.

Those times, he'd wax Hebrew lyrical. My mother sneering

'Oh yeah, Hasidic my arse, how come you married a Mick?'

Wreathed in smoke, he'd mutter his almost mantra

true heroism, contrary to military heroism, is always bound up with insults and contempt.

(Theodor Fontane)

As always, when this rigmarole began, I'd stare out the window, could see the swans drifting by, as if they'd had massive shots of Valium, or religion. I envied them. As I heard a black guy mutter on Law and Order.

'That is some fucked up shit, yo.'

When you were envious of a dumb bird, floating on a basin that was rank with poisonous chemicals, rain pelting down and not a sign of a landlubber bearing bread.

Maybe and I know this is pure fancy but in, around that time, Fleming got started,

Started on his odyssey, I fooking flat out refuse to call it a crusade, though those arguments are being put forward.

But having Irish blood, I'm allowed a little stretch of the narrative and who knows, on his first outing, did he glance in our window?

That outing, where he lured the most beautiful swan of the flock, snared him in a make do garrotte, then poured petrol on the creature, lit a long kitchen match and pushed the flaming spectacle out on to the bay.

The burning swan, silhouetted against the Galway night, the coast of America, almost, palpable, in the misted distance.

While Fleming refined and honed his killing instinct, I'd finished school, and ended up with my mate, Barret at Templemore. Fleming, already on a collision course with my life, learned to fly under the radar and on the streets of Drogheda, I learned to walk the wet, cold miserable streets. Because of my refusal to, am share in the spoils of my sergeants spoils, I got night duty every fooking weekend.

The drunks

The insane

The predators

The scum

Who saw an unarmed Guard as a turkey shoot. Too, I was dealing with the fallout of the so termed peace treaty. Being within spitting distance of the Border, we got the dregs of both paramilitaries seeking new trade and these apprentice thugs were lethal. Eighteen months in, I began to change, realising a lousy baton was just bait to the violence, I acquired, in no particular

A cut off hurley.

Mace

Knuckle dusters

Steel toes boots

And used on both sexes as required.

In short, I got mean, and got promoted. My arrest record was batting out of the park and it seemed I couldn't be bought. I could be bought but no one had yet offered me what I wanted.

Juice.

Oh yeah, that bit of power that makes you ape shit. My crazy sister had taken to visiting me every weekend. My flat was vacant weekend nights as I trod the weary streets of loathsome destiny. She was banging every minor villain she met. To support her growing coke jones. God, she was pretty, I can say that because she was. Red hair that, I kid thee not, get this, *cascading* down her slender frame, a face that was pixie in its appeal and a mouth that rattled off such madness it sounded like cook rap.

But fook, enough is not even Irish enough. I was ready to throw her bodily on to the street, a Saturday, when I'd come home to find three punks urinating on my bed. One of them, all of seventeen, eyes dusted, dead, sneered

'The keystone cop is back.'

Broke his nose.

Broke some bones on his mates for blending and then grabbed Kaitlin, shouting

'crazy bitch, it's over.'

And she gasped

'Spec, wait.'

Even my own sister used the name I went by. I had her by her hair, my temper in riot gear, stopped, asked

'What? You want money, one more weekend, well fookit.'

And she turned that elfin face, said

'I got you a transfer.'

'What?'

'To Galway, cross me heart, I swear on Daddy's grave.'

Not the most convincing oath, as dead he was but you never knew with him, some sort of con yet again. I let her hair go, sat down, pulled off my vomit covered tunic, twisted the cap of a cold one, said

'Right.'

She moved to me, grabbing a brew her own self, said

'I've been seeing this politician, a guy on the way up, with clout and when I mentioned you, he said, get this Spec?'

I waited

'He said he owed you.'

I drained half the bottle, Jesus it was good, looked at her

She rushed

'Deacon, in the Labour party, he's on the telly all the time and he said you helped him once so he's got you transferred to Galway.'

I said what I deeply felt

'Bollocks.'

• • •

A PIXIE.

A FAIRYLIKE OR ELFIN CREATURE.

ESPECIALLY ONE THAT IS MISCHIEVOUS; A PLAYFUL SPRITE.

Kaitlin was dreading hitting twenty five, felt her best years were already gone in a wisp of dust, angel or otherwise. Her current interest was Zen, not that she studied it in detail, some guy gave her a calendar with Zen sayings and she thought they were kind of, like cool. The young irish were all cursed with a kind of American speak that was mostly irritating but she was half American so some leeway was given.

Not that she gave a flying fuck.

Her only abiding love was The Pixies. The four iconic albums were nigh worn to thread until she downloaded them to her iPod. Times, she could go with

The Suicides

Florence and The Machine

The Pogues

But they were just vegan, when she needed meat, it was The Pixies.

She lived in a former squat along the University canal, not a mugging from the college. The house had been bought by Mencap and she'd persuaded a doctor she was in need of sheltered housing, thus she was there legit. The doctor, after twenty minutes of her *mental preoccupations* had thought of actually having her committed but fear over rode that. She was he knew, the type who'd burn your home in the middle of the night. Like a lot of current doctors, he was heading Stateside, screw the sinking ship and all the lunatics he met daily.

She was listening to the new song from the Saw Doctors, with get this shit

Petula Clark.

Down fucking town.

Hardcore.

She was getting the spare room ready for Spec, her brother, returning to duty in Galway with The Guards, thanks to her wiles. This task didn't take long, she simply closed the door. Checked her watch a slim fake Rolex, an hour till her brother arrived.

So, time for a wee pick me up. Did two fast lines, let her head back, the long red hair literally floating down her spine, the icy trickle hitting the back of her throat, she croaked

'Fucking awe SOME.'

A sip of Bailey's as a girl needed a touch of sweet to her life.

Right?

A large poster behind her showed

'Death to The Pixies'

And underneath, singed by

Get this

Dave Lovering, Kim Deal, Charles Thompson and her hottie, Joey Santiago. A surfer dude had offered her an ounce and two hundred bucks for that, She'd said

'get fucking real'

It was never, never for sale. Everything else was.

Sure.

Her land line shrilled, and coke alert, she grabbed it, nigh sang

'Yeah-oh.'

A tight arsed lady reminding her of her doctor's appointment the next Monday. She went

'Yeah, like whatever.'

Hung up.

Truth to tell, she liked the doctor, he made her, giddy. Said aloud

'You're alright Dr Fleming.'

• • •

SCIENTOLOGY

FOR

PSYCHOS.

PART ONE.

'Just a little flutter of metaphysics.

Fleming muttered.

The emigration papers had been approved and he shouted

'And pray tell, why fucking not, am I not, Le professor, El docteur, the cat's bollix, n'est pas?'

Among the varied psychoses bidding for prominence in his frenzied mind, at any given time, were the smattering of languages he prided himself on. He liked to slum in about five different tongues.

'None of them civil.

Said his mother.

His late, not lamented Mama.

He whispered

'The cold mad bitch.'

Black cat, black kitten?

'Café au lait mon ami?'

He asked.

Reasonably politely. That there was no one in his living room, was neither here nor there. His own frenzied mind provided enough personalities to run a small corrupt country, or even Ireland, if there's a difference. He was medium height, thick blond hair, bad nose, bad mouth and eyes that seemed to hold a black tint, so he wore blue tinted lenses. Fuckers hurt at the end of a killing day. He was lean, not from the gym but simple frenzy.

He had what he termed his *Snap* ABILITY, a deadly focus on one thing until it was complete. He'd used that to blend, pass, for the years of medical school. Learned early, medical qualification needed just

Arse licking

Learning by rote

An ability to parrot

Volunteering.

Yup, no matter the crap assignment, up snapped your hand, you got on the credit ledger. The fact all the other students hated you, what?

You gave a flying fuck?

Money.

Money sure paved the way and so ok, your final diploma came from the University of Panama, few saw beyond the doctor tag. His practice was on The Crescent, the Harley St of Galway. If that isn't the final word in absurdity. The new shingles there, gave witness to the medical schools of

Cairo

Nepal

Rawalpindi.

And with the Government fucked, The health Service in tatters, did a new breed of almost doctor make a whole lot of difference?

People were lying on trollies in hospital corridors for days. A bed was as elusive as the sun. Fleming had figured four years in Galway, fine tune his project, then the promised land. New York.

His project.

Red-19.

Kill nineteen girls with red hair in the shortest time possible. That he could split the task between Ireland and US seemed fair.

Only seventeen to go.

A Tall House

Bill Cameron

"David, take your lunch. You're late."

David sat at the kitchen dinette, English muffin and juice untouched in front of him. He gazed up at Elsa's back as she stood at the counter closing the bread and peanut butter, wiping up crumbs. Her round shoulders and the tight grey hair encasing her head made her look like a football player. She put the bread and peanut butter in the cupboard, then turned to him, his sack lunch in her hand.

"You haven't eaten a thing." He followed her eyes to the clock above the sink. Eight twenty-six. "You'll know better tomorrow. Now take your lunch. You're late."

David's eyes remained fixed on the clock—a cheap plastic thing like you'd get at Fred Meyer's. There used to be another clock, David remembered. An old clock, made from dark, carved wood with chain weights and a ticking pendulum, a chime every hour. He remembered long, long ago his mother let him pull the chains every Saturday morning. He'd liked the sound of the chime.

"David. Take your lunch. You're late."

He looked at her. "I'm not going," he muttered.

Elsa's eyes narrowed. "What did you say?"

David felt his stomach flip-flop. For a moment, fear of Elsa battled his defiance. It wasn't the first such battle waged inside himself, especially in the months since he'd turned ten. But it was the first in which defiance won. He glared up at Elsa. "I'm not going," he said, his voice rising. "I am not going!"

The strength of his words seemed to surprise Elsa almost as much as himself. Her jaw took on a firm set that made her cheeks bulge. *Elsa Jaw.* How often had David seen that? Elsa Jaw meant she was getting serious. It meant she didn't intend to take any lip. It meant ear pinching and restrictions if David didn't comply.

"Don't be ridiculous," she said. "Take your lunch. You're late."

She set the lunch sack on the table in front of him, put her hands on her hips in stern supplement to Elsa Jaw. But he only shook his head. "I'm not going. No matter what you say, I'm not!"

"David, if you don't take your lunch this instant, I'm calling your mother."

"Fine! Call her. I don't care. I'm not going."

Elsa Jaw wavered. It wasn't the first time she'd invoked the threat of a call to his mother, but he'd always backed down before. "David, you'll upset your mother. You don't want to do that. You must take your lunch. You must go to school." Elsa Jaw clenched and unclenched. "You're late."

"You can't make me." He looked back up at the cheap clock. Eight twenty-nine.

• • •

Elsa's breath whistled through her nose. "You're going to have to tell that to your mother," she said tightly.

David felt himself perk up. "Can I go see her?"

"You know better than that."

He sagged. "I'm tired of only talking to her on the phone. I want to go see her."

"That's impossible, and you know it. She's terribly ill. She doesn't want you to get sick."

"That's stupid!" David pushed his chair back and stood up. "You get to see her. You go up and down those stairs fifty times a day. You *never* get sick."

Elsa pursed her lips and reached toward him. The pinching fingers. He ducked under her hand and retreated, pressed himself against the basement door. "How come you get to go see her and I don't? She's *my* mom. You're just the stupid housekeeper!"

Elsa gasped, raised fingers to her lips. Sudden tears glistened in her eyes.

He'd gone too far. He realized it in a skipped heartbeat. "I just want to go see her," he said. "That's all." But it was too late for defense. Elsa's face betrayed only dismay. Without any clear idea of what might happen next, he fumbled frantically behind himself, grasped the door knob. Elsa reached toward him as he turned and pulled the door open. "David! Don't be ridiculous!" He didn't stop to flip the light switch at the top of the stairs, just charged down into darkness. He stumbled at the bottom. Backed up against the wall out of the light that fell through the open doorway.

"David—!" Elsa called out. "Stop this! Stop." Elsa didn't follow. He knew she wouldn't. She hated the basement. Bugs and dirt, cobwebs in the corners—Elsa was very tidy. "David, come out of there. You're upsetting your mother." David stood in shadow, breathing heavily. "She's very ill. Take your lunch, please. You're late." When David didn't answer, she closed the door and left him alone in the dark.

David liked the basement. He liked its quiet, and he liked the smell of earth in the crawl space under the porch, of the mold that grew on the shelves that held Elsa's preserves. He liked that she never came down here. It was his job to haul her canned vegetables and jam down and up the stairs.

But always with the light on.

His legs trembled with fear—fear of the dark, but also fear of his rebellion against Elsa. He listened to the sound of her footsteps as she paced the kitchen. He could hear her muttering to herself up there—a strange, bewildering sound. He wondered why Elsa didn't just call upstairs to his mother. There was an intercom phone in the kitchen.

He'd never done anything like this before. In all the years she'd cared for him since his mother got sick and his father went away, David had fought Elsa only in small ways. Wouldn't do his homework, wouldn't eat his squash. If a restriction didn't solve the problem, a call to his mother would. But this morning David had crossed a line. Elsa seemed to know it too. Maybe she was building up her nerve to come downstairs after all, grab his ear and haul him the heck out of there. At least she'd turn the light on. But then, abruptly, her footsteps trailed out of the kitchen and into the hallway from the dining room. He heard a distant door close, followed by the fading tap of Elsa's feet climbing to the second floor.

Relief flooded through him. He pressed forward, his arms stretched out in the dark, breath in his throat. He found the stairs with his bare shin. Pain stabbed up through his leg and he crumpled onto the steps, strangling a cry in his throat.

He grasped his shin and felt wetness. Blood. A whimper escaped his lips. He was bleeding in the dark basement and the only person who could help him was Elsa. Tears dribbled down his cheeks and he wished he could run up to his mama, have her bandage the hurt. But after a moment the pain in his leg dulled to an aching throb. All he could think to do was avoid Elsa as long as possible. As he started up the stairs, he imagined leaving a trail of blood that Elsa would follow wherever he went.

He moved carefully but quickly. At the top step, he paused only long enough to listen for sounds of Elsa's return. All was quiet. He pushed the door open and breathed as he stepped back into the light.

His lunch sack sat on the table, beside the remains of his breakfast. He glanced up at clock—eight thirty-five. He'd been downstairs hardly any time at all, though it felt like ages. He glanced at his leg, surprised to see only a small cut and tiny trickle of blood that hadn't even reached his sock.

He wasn't sure what to do. Take his lunch and go to school, maybe. But he was sure to be punished anyway, whether he went or not. He slipped out of the kitchen, through the empty dining room and into the living room. Maybe there was somewhere he could hide. In the living room, he stopped in front of the shabby couch under the huge front window. For a moment, he gazed sightlessly out the window as he considered possible hiding places.

It was a big, old house, on the dead end of a short block, surrounded by old trees. Elsa had told him what they were. Sycamore. Birch. Hawthorn. The hawthorn was a ratty mess, though David recalled a time when a man came and trimmed it. Elsa said they couldn't afford that anymore, what with his mother's sickness. His favorite tree was out back, a great white oak growing up through a split in an ancient boiler that had been abandoned in the backyard before it had been a backyard. The boiler was rusted and mostly hidden by mats of creeping phlox and wildflowers, but it was sturdy enough as a first step whenever David wanted to climb the oak. Elsa tried to keep him out of the tree, but he often climbed it when she wasn't looking. It was the best climbing tree in the yard.

As he stood there thinking of the tree, the intercom phone on the end table buzzed. A part of his brain told him not to answer it. But he knew he wanted to talk to his mama, tell her that he just wanted to come see her—that's all. Then he'd go to school. She'd understand. He picked up the phone.

"Hello?"

"Davey, what's going on? Why won't you go to school, honey?"

He didn't know how to put it into words. He struggled for a way to describe the feelings he'd been having lately—about being the weird one at school with no father and a sick mother; feelings about living with Elsa alone, his mother so close and yet so far away. All he could think to say was, "I want to come see you, Mama."

"You know that's not possible, honey. I'm ill."

"But what about Elsa? She never gets sick. If she doesn't maybe I won't either."

He could hear her breathing. It comforted him to know she was breathing even when she wasn't talking. He realized, suddenly, that he couldn't recall her face, that he knew her only by the soft sound of her voice over the phone. The idea made him feel strange. "Davey, it—it affects children differently. I can't take that chance. You do understand, don't you?"

He didn't. It sounded stupid, but he didn't want to say that to his mama. Now it was his turn to breathe into the phone. She was so close, just up a flight of stairs, and yet all this time had passed. And nothing.

"Davey, sweetie? Are you there?"

He wasn't sure why, but he said, "What happened to the old clock?"

"What's that, honey?"

"There used to be an old clock in the kitchen. It's gone. So's the dining room furniture. We used to have lots of stuff, but it's all gone. We don't even have a TV anymore."

More breathing, faster now. He'd made her nervous. After a moment, she said, "That's not your worry, okay? You understand that? Your worry is to go to school."

"I don't want to go to school. I want to come see you."

She started crying. Tears welled up in his own eyes. He couldn't remember ever making his mama cry before. He felt like he should run to the kitchen, grab his lunch, run to school—just to make his mama stop crying. But it wouldn't be that simple anymore. Something had changed this morning when he refused Elsa's commands.

"Mama?" he said. "Please?"

"I'm sorry, Davey. You know I love you."

He heard the phone click. She was gone. He gazed through the doorway into the hall. He could just make out the door leading upstairs. So close, yet so far away. He hung up the phone. Go to school, he told himself.

Then he heard a sound, footsteps on stairs. Elsa was coming. His impulse was to flee, but he could already hear Elsa's hand on the doorknob at the foot of the stairs.

He scanned the room. There was only a low table against the wall opposite the couch. The living room had once been packed with furniture—a pair of ceiling-high bookcases; a hutch filled with china figurines; a piano. Now, all that was gone. Even the couch was different, small and tattered. But it offered him his only refuge. As the stairway door opened, he scrambled over the back and dropped down beneath the window.

Elsa's footsteps clicked into the room. Just keep going, he willed. But Elsa was too elemental a force to succumb to the psychic energies of a ten year old boy. She paused, then crossed the room. He saw her hands grasp the back of the couch, then her face as she leaned forward and peered out the window. His heartbeat pounded in his ears.

"Oh, David," she muttered. "What's happened?" She raised one hand, trembling and uncertain, to her cheek.

David felt his stomach drop. Normally she was as strong as the old oak in the backyard, a stern word from her the only word. But now her voice faltered. It was beyond the scope of his experience. He shivered with confusion and dread.

She stared out, whispering, "David, you're upsetting your mother. Take your lunch. You're late." She sighed, pushed herself up off the couch. "What have you seen?" she muttered as she left the living room. "You've upset your mother so..."

Silence descended, punctuated by the distant sound of the back door slamming. Tremulous, he slid out from behind the couch. The faint floral scent of

Elsa hung in the air. He shuddered, but then he realized that nothing could stop him from going upstairs. Elsa had gone outside. He looked at the phone. His instinct was to call, ask his mother if he could come. She'd say no. She might not even answer. She couldn't always handle the phone without Elsa's help.

A shadow passed the window. David looked and saw Elsa on the front lawn. He quickly ducked into the hallway, then peered around the door jamb out the window.

She didn't see him. She gazed up the street, her lips mumbling. Her eyes seemed unfocused, her cap of hair in disarray. She was looking for him, but before she could find him, he'd already be upstairs. He took a deep breath and turned into the hall.

Half fearful, half-excited, he crept toward the stairway door. His mama was so close. Just steps away. But the air in the hallway oppressed him, constricted his chest. The stairway door stood open a couple of inches. He couldn't remember ever seeing it like that. His mother's door was always shut. He reached out to grasp the knob, but his hand recoiled. In the dim light, he saw steps climb into darkness.

There had been a time, dimly remembered, when he had been allowed to climb those stairs. But the facts of his mother's illness and Elsa's rule had dominated him for too many years. He tried to open the door, but he couldn't. He backed away, pressed himself against the door opposite his mama's.

"I want to see you, Mama," he said. If she heard, she didn't answer. In sudden anxiety, he backed away, grasped the doorknob behind him, pushed the door open without thinking. And stopped. In a heartbeat regained his senses.

It was Elsa's room. Quiet and clean, filled with muted colors and the smell of mothballs. A place as forbidden as upstairs.

David still remembered when Elsa first showed up, years before. There had been a fight. His mom and dad yelling at each other upstairs. Mama put him to bed early, because the fight started right after supper, and she always put him to bed when fights started. David didn't know what the fight was about. He hardly remembered even having a father, let alone what he and his mama had fought about. But that particular fight stuck in his mind. It went on long through the night, the yelling from atop the stairs, muted by the walls but loud enough to keep David awake. He recalled the sickly feeling of listening to their voices, as though the sound would smother him. He tried hiding under his pillow, tried to imagine a time and place when they never fought again. They just kept screaming at each other, so close, so far away.

Then there was a final, lone shout, and silence. A long deep quiet that descended so suddenly that the ticking of the radiator seemed loud. After a while, his mother came in and kissed him, told him everything was fine. She promised it would all be okay. Just go to sleep and everything will be fine. She wiped away his tears, but a tear of her own dripped onto his face. She kissed him again, and left the room.

The next morning, when he awoke, Elsa was there—grey-haired and stern. *Your mother is ill,* she said. Something like that. *You can't see her, she's catching.* David didn't remember exactly, but Elsa had repeated herself so many times that he was sure that was what she'd said. "She's catching." His father was gone, run off into the night. "A man who gives himself to alcohol has no business being around a family anyway," Elsa told him. He never came back.

Elsa had moved into this room. Once the guest room, now it was Elsa's, completely and utterly off-limits. If she caught him here, he couldn't imagine the consequences. The bed was perfect, its white spread smooth as glass. It was hard to believe she slept in it. A glass lamp stood on the bedside table, centered on a lace doily. Another doily draped across the dresser, and on it sat a bible, its black leather cover crisp and shiny. David touched it but didn't open it. A ceramic dish held a collection of hairpins, beside it an ivory hairbrush. David ran his finger under the clasp of a small wooden jewelry box, feeling the thrill of illicit intrusion. His own room was heaped with treasures by comparison— books, drawings, toys. He didn't expect Elsa's room to look like his, but this sterility baffled him. For a moment, the place radiated the apprehension he'd felt when he saw Elsa's uncertainty from behind the couch.

The back door slammed and dread rumbled through him. He went to the door, heard footsteps in the dining room. He didn't know what she'd do if she caught him in her room. He stepped out into the hall just as she turned the corner from the living room.

"David! My goodne—" Then, she noticed that her door was open. Her fingers twitched at her side and her jaw clenched and unclenched rhythmically. David wished he could disappear, run away—anything. But the force of Elsa's voice kept him rooted in place. "David?—what have you been doing?"

"Nothing." Automatic response.

She shook her head. "What's going on? Your mother's worried to death." She advanced toward him, and he backed up until he pressed against his mother's door.

"Nothing's going on," he muttered. He felt stupid saying it. He wanted to ask her why her room was so cold and empty, why he wasn't allowed to go upstairs. But her hard face silenced him.

Elsa pulled her bedroom door shut. "I don't know why you're doing this." David stared at her. "I just want to see my mama."

"You know better than that. She's catch—"

"You always say that!" he blurted. A rush of heat and chill swept over him, as though his frustration and fear were battling for control. Elsa gasped at his outburst. "I'm tired of always hearing the same thing. You never tell me anything that's real!"

She flinched, a gesture both strange and unsettling. "She—she has a disease."

David felt himself start to quiver violently. "You always say that. You never tell me what disease. It's always, 'she's catching she's catching' but everything's just all weird." He didn't want to shout, but the words poured out of him. "All the furniture is gone and your bed is perfect! Do you even sleep anywhere or what?!"

"David. Please—"

"I just want to go see her!" He felt tears on his cheeks and fire on his neck. "I just want to see her and I'm going to go see her and you can't stop me!" With a cry, he spun around and grabbed the doorknob. Elsa clutched at his shoulder, but he twisted and thrust the door against her. She grunted and stumbled away from him. He slammed the door around against the wall, then dashed up the steps into darkness, stopping only as he neared the closed door at the top. He looked back over his shoulder, but Elsa didn't follow. He could see her in the open doorway at the foot of the stairs, gazing up at him, her body framed by light. Her face was dark, but the light glinted off her eyes.

"David, David," he heard her say in a broken voice. "What have you seen?" Then she turned and was gone.

For a long moment he just stood breathing. Then the realization settled onto him. She couldn't stop him. He grasped the doorknob, listened in the darkness. It was quiet on the other side. Perhaps his mama was sleeping. It didn't matter. He was going to see her at last. He felt himself tremble as he pushed open the door.

It was a small room with three walls of windows. The white curtains were drawn, but let in a pale, diffuse light. He smelled a faint odor of mildew. Along the walls were stacks of magazines and old newspapers. Beneath the far window stood a battered dresser, its top a mess of lotion bottles, heaps of paperback books. The bed was old and sagged in the middle, its sheets dingy and its spread thrust carelessly aside. The bedside table was stacked with papers. A pale green robe hung from the bedpost.

"Mama?" he said quietly. There was a closed door off to the side, a bathroom, he recalled from the dim past. She must be in the bathroom. He went to the bed, sat gingerly on the edge to wait. His mama's bed.

As he waited, he glimpsed his mother's name on the papers on the bedside table. Idly, he picked up the top sheet and started to read, "...120 days past due. Please remit immediately..." The words confused him, and he looked at several more pages. Different kinds of bills, he figured, and all saying the same thing, *past due, remit immediately*. Whatever that meant. He set them down and stood up, suddenly uncomfortable. It was a money thing. That must be where all the furniture went. Something to do with money. But why would a money thing make his mother sick?

He didn't want to wait for her to come out. She was being too quiet. Slowly, tentatively, he went to the bathroom door. "Mama?" No sound from within. He knocked, gently at first, then with more strength. "Mama?" Nothing. He drew a couple of deep breaths, and opened the door.

The light was on, but no one was there. He saw a bar of soap on the sink, a well-chewed toothbrush. There was a shelf over the toilet with a couple of bottles of shampoo and a piece of round Styrofoam like a head. He'd seen one before, through the window of that hair place on Hawthorne. A wig form.

He backed away from the bathroom door, and gazed around the empty room, and suddenly everything looked strange and terrible to him. "Mama?" he said into the silence. But no one answered.

He heard a sharp sound from outside. He went to the rear window and pushed the curtain aside. Down in the yard Elsa knelt before the white oak that grew up through a crack in the old boiler. She had something in her hand, a rock or a brick, and she was hammering at the hatch on the boiler.

"Mama?" He looked back through the open bathroom door at the wig form for a long moment, then he fled the room. He stumbled down the stairs and up the hall into the living room. He passed through the dining room to the kitchen. He could hear Elsa's sounds more clearly now, the sharp rap of stone on metal. He went to the door and looked out. Her back was to him, but he could see that she was unkempt, her hair in disarray on her head.

David slid quietly out the back door and down the steps. As he drew near her, he could hear her breathe and mutter as she hammered. "What have you seen? You weren't supposed to see anything. I told you to stay out of this goddamned tree." She slammed the rock against the boiler again and something gave. The hatch popped open and cloud of dust pillowed around her. She bent down to gaze through the hatch, but her body blocked his own view.

"Mama?"

Her round shoulders jerked and she spun around. "Davey!" She stared at him, eyes wild. "Davey. David. Take your lunch. You're late."

He struggled to hold onto his tears. She looked back down into the hatch. Then she started to cry. "I didn't want you to know. All these years—it was just an accident, but I thought you would stop loving me if you knew. I thought

Elsa would make sure you'd keep loving me. You were never supposed to go into her room."

David stared at her, her eyes sunken and dark, the wig askew on her head. "Davey, please, take your lunch. You're late," she said. Over her shoulder, through the open hatch of the old boiler, he saw a man's leather shoe, half-rotten, and a collapsed trouser leg partly covered with dirt.

"Okay, Mama." He turned away, headed around the house and up the street toward school. He forgot his lunch, but that didn't matter. He didn't feel very hungry anyway.

Seven Ways To Get Rid Of Harry

Jen Conley

Harry twists his head around and shouts, "We ain't going through the god-damn Safari!"

Danny sulks immediately and stares through the open car window, muttering how it isn't fair. His sister, Lisa, the older one, kicks him to shut up.

He doesn't.

"Nobody ever takes me through the Safari," the boy says under his breath.

Harry has bionic ears. "Stop talking about it!"

"I did."

"No, you didn't!"

Harry shouts some more, this time facing the front windshield, spit landing on glass. "We ain't going through the Safari because it will cost me extra and it's nothing but a bunch of bug-infested jungle animals from Africa and me and your mother got no interest in jungle animals from Africa! Got that?"

Danny says nothing, just looks out the window. Harry has problems with Africa, with black people in general. He calls them the N-word, says the country went to shit the day Lincoln freed the slaves, stuff like that. Danny once told him—back when Harry first started coming around—that they aren't supposed to be prejudiced because they live in the North. Harry told Danny to shut the hell up.

"Well?" Harry says now, peering into the rearview mirror. "Got it?"

Danny doesn't respond. Just listens to the bugs in the trees while the car idles in the Parking line.

"Didn't hear you!"

"I got it," the boy finally says.

Harry glares at Danny's mom, Judy, who is in the front seat, fanning herself with her hand.

"I know," she says. "He won't give up."

It is hot, July, and they're waiting in a long line of cars for Great Adventure. Judy lights a cigarette, hands it to her boyfriend. Harry just takes it, doesn't say *thank you* or anything. He has no manners, Danny thinks. Judy lights one for herself. She's got her hair pinned up and a gold necklace sticks to her sweaty skin.

She turns around and says, "This is supposed to be a day of fun. Please, Danny, just try to be happy with what you're getting."

Danny shifts in his seat, sulks even more.

After a while, the car inches around a bend in the road and the amusement park comes into view. Lisa leans over and points to Rolling Thunder, the wooden rollercoaster. "We're going on that."

Danny scrunches up his face. *No, I'm not.* It's the scariest coaster in the park. That and Lightnin' Loops. Rolling Thunder is tall and the biggest hill rises way above the pine trees. Danny has been to Great Adventure several times because they live nearby in Manchester, but he has never been on Rolling Thunder. A few weeks earlier, the school took the sixth graders to Great Adventure for their class trip—a bargain for the Board of Education because half the kids have season passes—but Danny refused to ride Rolling Thunder, along with Lightnin' Loops. And Freefall, which is not really a rollercoaster. That thing shoots you 150 feet into the sky and then drops you like a broken elevator.

The school didn't take the kids through the Safari, either. The last time Danny went through the Safari was with his dad. His dad understands him, knows his kid likes animals. Danny's dad is sick with MS. Danny and Lisa haven't seen him since March.

Lisa nods to Rolling Thunder and then nudges her brother to look at her hand, which is resting on the car seat. She shows him three fingers. Danny squints at her because he doesn't quite get the full meaning and she shakes her head. *I'll tell you later.* Still, he knows it has to do with her new list: "Ways to Get Rid of Harry."

Number One: Rat poison in one of his beers. Danny told her it probably wouldn't kill him, but Lisa said that was okay. The object was to get rid of Harry, dead or alive. If the poison made their mother's boyfriend sick and it scared him off, then so be it. Number Two was busting into the bathroom when he took one of his long baths and knocking the radio into the water. Lisa suggested that when Harry was listening to his stupid doo-wop music from the '50s, she or Danny could burst in, claim they had an emergency, trip, knock into the little stand with the radio, and send it sailing into the bath. Danny said that was too dangerous. "One of us could get electrocuted, too."

Number Three has something to do with Rolling Thunder. Danny guesses Lisa plans to push him out of the rollercoaster, probably from the top of the first hill.

"Goddamn lines," Harry mutters, sucking on his cigarette. Harry doesn't live with them, thank God, but Danny and Lisa are very afraid he'll be moving in soon. He is there enough. Some of his clothes hang in their mom's bedroom closet. Shaving cream and a razor are in the bathroom. For Danny, they are demented replacements of his father's things. Even Harry's footfalls across the house, the empty coffee cup in the sink in the mornings, it all reminds him that his father once lived there and now another man sometimes does.

"We're almost there, babe," Judy says, tossing her cigarette out the window.

"I know," Harry says softly, placing his hand on her cheek.

Lisa shifts in the back seat. She looks at her brother and curls her lip in disgust.

Harry lives in a crummy, small, white house in Bricktown near the water. Danny and Lisa have been there few times, when Judy drives there on rainy days to pick him up. Harry doesn't have a car because he owns a motorcycle. He has an old dog that he kicks when it gets in the way. Harry never kicks the dog hard enough to kill it, but enough to make the poor beast whimper. Danny feels such sorrow for the dog and he has dreams of rescuing the animal. He even pressed his friend, Joe, to ask his dad to drive them to Harry's house. The two boys have concocted a plan—Joe will be the lookout, Danny will smash open the window with a bat. "We'd have to bring a towel to put over the window pane so I could get in," Danny says. "There'd be some left-over glass." Joe likes dogs and he's all for it. But no matter how many times he asks, he can't get his dad to drive them to Bricktown.

"Want no part of that," the man always says.

After Harry pays for parking, he drives Judy's car to a spot. Judy makes the kids roll up the windows but leave a crack. The summer sun shines relentlessly as they walk with dozens of other people towards the amusement park gates. Music blasts out of the speakers, playing "Mr. Roboto." Lisa and Danny sing the lyrics, falling behind their mother and Harry who are now holding hands.

"Gross," Danny says. Then he asks his sister what Number Three is—her Rolling Thunder idea to get rid of Harry.

"Right before we get to the top of the hill, I'm gonna scream that there's a spider or a snake. He'll jump up, fall out. It's perfect."

Danny is immediately disappointed. This is the worst suggestion of them all. Only one person has ever died on Rolling Thunder and that was because the guy was standing up, goofing off. Danny knows there is a safety bar holding people in their seats. In fact, after the guy died, Great Adventure made sure the Rolling Thunder safety bar was even stronger than before. Joe told him this when they were on the sixth grade trip. "You can't fall out."

Danny relays the information to his sister and she frowns. "Shit. Didn't know that."

But Number Four comes quickly to her, as soon as they get into the park. A group of black people dart out of nowhere, laughing loudly. They are soaking wet, probably from the Log Flume or maybe Roaring Rapids. Danny and Lisa are right behind their mother and Harry. Both kids flinch when Harry snarls his favorite slur.

Immediately, Lisa jumps on it. She tugs Danny back and whispers, "I could scream, 'He just called you the N-word!' They'll beat him up. Number Four."

"Maybe." Danny rocks his head back and forth. He likes it. It's realistic. "Do it."

Lisa doesn't do anything, though. Just watches them walk away. "Nah."

• • •

The four of them go on the small rides, like the Sidewinder and the Buccaneer, things that twirl around or rock back and forth. They eat lunch at a hotdog stand. About two in the afternoon, Harry and Judy hit the Beer Garden, while Danny and Lisa go through the Haunted Castle. For all of his fears about rollercoasters, Danny doesn't spook easily at the traditional horror stuff. When he was nine, he watched *The Exorcist* by himself and didn't have a single nightmare.

"This is dumb," he keeps saying as he and his sister wander through the dark catacombs, strobe lights flashing, witch's screams in the background. But the air conditioner is blowing through the vents and it's a nice relief from the heat.

"Number Five," Lisa says when she sees a skeleton with a hatchet sticking out of its skull.

"Huh?"

"I read this story in school called 'The Black Cat.' This man kills his wife with an ax to the head and then walls up her body in the basement."

It is so dark, they could hardly see each other's faces. "Cool," Danny says.

"Yeah. So we can kill Harry with an ax and then wall him up in the basement. If we do it right, nobody will find him for years."

Danny rolls his eyes at the absurdity. "It's stupid. We don't even have a basement."

They say nothing to each other until they are outside, back in the heat. "Well," Lisa says. "Why don't you come up with a better idea?"

"I will," Danny snaps.

They walk over to the Beer Garden and find their mom and Harry. Judy's cheeks are pink and her eyelids hang heavily.

"Beer goes right to my head," she trills, leaning into her boyfriend, who puts his arm around her.

Lisa slips behind Harry and motions hitting him with an imaginary ax.

Eventually, they make their way to Lightnin' Loops and stand for a few minutes, watching the two monster coasters loop through one another. It is a short ride—down the hill, around the loop, up to the end. Then the coaster moves backwards—down the hill, through the loop, halting where it began. Danny doesn't want to go on.

"Come on, Danny," his mom says, the words slurring just a bit. "It'll be fun. Don't be scared."

"It's nothing," Lisa says. "But I have to go to the bathroom."

"Me too," says Judy. In seconds, they are gone.

Harry stands, smoking his cigarette, scowling at the boy.

"What?" Danny snaps.

Harry's eyes widen and cigarette smoke comes through his nostrils like a dragon. He leans close to Danny. "Don't be scared, *Danielle*."

"Don't call me Danielle."

Harry smirks and with the quickness of a snake attack, shoves his hand into the armhole of Danny's shirt and pinches the skin near his armpit.

Danny twists away, screaming. A few people look but no one intervenes.

Harry smiles, licks his lips, sucks on his cigarette. He's done this to Danny once before, when they were in the garage.

Tears spring to the boy's eyes. He holds his hand underneath his arm. "Jerk," he mutters.

"*Jerk*," Harry mimics.

When Danny's mom and his sister appear, Danny is standing away from Harry, fighting back tears. He concentrates on Lightnin' Loops. The noise is loud, like a mini-train with loose cargo. Down goes the coaster, through the loop, people screaming, up again, stop. Then it repeats, backwards.

"Let's go, honey," Judy says, approaching her son. Her face is still flushed but she sounds more sober. Harry and Lisa are several feet away, standing way apart from one another.

"Ready?" she asks.

Danny shrugs.

"What's wrong now?" Judy says, exasperated.

Danny eyeballs his mother. "Harry pinched me."

Her face twists into disbelief. "What do you mean?"

"He pinched me here." Danny lifts up his arm and goes to push up his sleeve but his mother turns and walks away.

Just then, the rollercoaster catapults its riders down the hill and through the loop. "Come on!" Judy shouts excitedly, twirling around, gesturing towards Lightnin' Loops. "Let's go!"

"I'm staying here," Danny calls, crossing his arms.

"Fine," Judy calls back, grabbing Harry's hand. Lisa trails after them.

Danny finds a bench underneath a large oak tree and sits, watching people walk by. He doesn't understand his mom. Lisa says that their parents got divorced because their dad was running around. "He cheated," Lisa insists.

Danny doesn't believe her. "Dad wouldn't do that. Bet Mom was cheating with Harry."

But this isn't true, and he knows it. His father moved out of the house two years ago, when Danny was eight, going on nine. Harry wasn't around back then and Danny's father wasn't sick either. He used to come get his kids on the weekends and take them to their grandmother's house where he still lives. Now Danny's grandmother won't let the kids near their dad. "He's too sick," she says when Danny phones her. "The doctors say he'll get stronger in a few months."

No, he won't, Lisa says. She's an advocate of preparing for the worst.

Harry began showing up around January. He just popped out of nowhere and suddenly his mom started referring to him as her boyfriend. His mom is young, neighbors said. Thirty-two. She's still pretty, still has her figure, still deserves a boyfriend, especially a cool one with a motorcycle. Joe's mother says that. Joe says, even though his mom is married to his dad, she has a crush on Harry. But she doesn't know that when Harry gets annoyed with Judy, when she says something dippy or wrong, Harry reaches across the table and smacks her. Not really hard, just a quick slap. Danny has seen it happen three times.

"He's old fashioned," his mother explains when Danny reminds her that men aren't allowed to hit women anymore. They used to be able to, but not anymore.

"And Dad never smacked you."

"Your dad got mad at me once and threw me into a wall."

"That's not true!"

"Believe what you want."

Danny knows his father used to be tough when he was a teenager—was in the bad crowd. Still, he doesn't believe his mother's story. Lisa says she doesn't know what to believe.

• • •

Harry, Judy, and Lisa come off of Lightnin' Loops an hour later. It's a popular ride, so the wait was super long. The three of them are grinning.

Judy looks at her watch. It's four-thirty already. "You kids go off by yourselves and meet us by the fountain at seven. We'll get dinner then."

"Are we old enough to go by ourselves?" Danny asks. His mother was never the type to let her kids loose in a mall, never mind an amusement park. Danny understands that this new freedom isn't really freedom—Judy and Harry just want to go back to the Beer Garden.

Harry appears to catch on to the boy's train of thought and the man doesn't like it: he narrows his eyes and says meanly, "Yeah, Danny, you're old enough."

Danny looks at the ground.

Judy gives both kids five dollars and then in a minute, his mom and Harry are walking away, arms around each other like teenagers.

Lisa flips them the bird.

"They can't see you," Danny grumbles.

"I know," she snips.

Brother and sister stroll by ride after ride, but the long lines deter them. It seems to be hotter than before. Drops of sweat roll down Danny's freckled face. Perspiration beads on Lisa's nose. They stand in front of the big yellow Ferris Wheel with only ten people waiting.

"That'll do," Lisa says.

It's a very high Ferris Wheel but Danny doesn't have a problem with heights or Ferris Wheels. He just doesn't like rollercoasters. The combination of height and speed frighten him.

The two jump into a red square car, enjoying the breeze as they slowly rotate towards the top—the ride halts every minute to unload and load passengers below. Eventually, they are way above the treetops and Danny stares across the amusement park with its confectionary colored rides and buildings, searching for a glimpse of the Safari. He can't find it. Too many trees in the way.

But they can see way beyond the park—a panoramic view with water towers popping up in the landscape like gophers in a field. Very far away, they can see a huge gray hangar that is the Lakehurst Naval Base.

Lisa points to it. "That's where the Hindenburg crashed."

"I know," Danny says. They live right near Lakehurst. "I'm not stupid."

The Ferris Wheel spins again, gently rotating towards the bottom, then towards the top. The breeze is cool and Danny closes his eyes, wishing his dad were with him.

"Where to next?" Lisa asks when they get off.

"Skyride?"

So back in the air they head, boarding a small car attached to a cable. This time they slide above and across the park, passing other cars moving in the opposite direction. Kids call to them, mimicking the Grey Poupon commercial. "Pardon me. Do you have some Grey Poupon?" Danny plays along, saying, "But of course," and leans over the side to hand over an imaginary jar of mustard. A few cars later, a group of girls sing, "Beat It."

Danny shouts, "Michael Jackson sucks!"

"No, he doesn't!" screams a girl's voice.

"Yes, he does!" Lisa yells back. Danny laughs and gives his sister a high-five and then asks himself why he even said that. He owns *Thriller* and doesn't think Michael Jackson sucks. Three cars later, when they are at the highest point of the Skyride, they pass two guys and a big white butt. They are being mooned.

"Oh my God!" Lisa squeals, hiding her face in her hands

Danny explodes with a great cackle and full body shake. It's the funniest thing he's ever seen.

The ride ends in the Wild West section of the park. They hop on the Runaway Train, a wimpy rollercoaster Danny's not afraid of, and then wander into the Big Teepee, picking up and putting back souvenirs—drinking glasses or wallets that say *Great Adventure*.

When they get bored, they leave the Teepee and go to the Log Flume but Lisa doesn't want to get wet. They have their money so they walk to the game area, trying their luck at shooting ducks, but neither kid wins. "It's fixed," Lisa gripes. The air is still humid, sticky and smelling of sweat, fried food, and cotton candy. They enter the arcade. The air conditioner is blasting, as is the music. They play each other in Pac-Man. Lisa wins the first round, Danny the second. They drift apart. Danny drops quarters into more video games. Eventually Lisa finds him again and reports it is six-thirty. "Better head to the fountain," she announces grimly.

• • •

Harry and Judy are not at the fountain. Danny and Lisa wait, sitting on a bench near a candy shop, watching people step into the fountain, splash each other.

"Should one of us go to the Beer Garden?" Lisa says.

"I'm not going," Danny says.

"Fine, I will."

She's gone for over an hour.

The sweet smell of candy stirs Danny's hunger, but he has no money left. He doesn't even have enough money for a phone call, although who would he call? His dad? Danny's grandmother would probably make up some excuse, like she always does. *Your dad is too sick today. We're letting him sleep.* Danny's not sure his dad is even sick. Maybe it's a lie. Maybe his dad is working in a foreign country, which is why he can't come to the phone. Maybe it's a secret job, something he can't tell anyone about, and after he makes enough money, he'll return home, punch Harry in the face, and take his kids away to live with him.

Danny likes this story and he sits back, replaying the part where his father punches Harry over and over again.

When the sun is setting, casting a beautiful peach-orange blaze throughout the park, Lisa comes walking up with Harry and Judy in tow. Judy is smashed. She leans against Harry who glows with drunkenness himself. Judy laughs and laughs and then mumbles how hungry she is. Danny is embarrassed and hopes nobody notices them. Lisa leads them to a pizza stand near the Rotor.

The Rotor is the cruelest ride in the park. People step inside a cylinder and are advised to stand against the wall. The cylinder rotates, faster and faster and faster, until you're stuck to the wall by the pressure. Then the floor drops. People barely can move, their mouths and cheeks rippling from the wind, their bodies plastered to the curved wall like dead bugs. Eventually the torture ends. The floor comes up, the spinning slows, stops. People stagger out of the cylinder and down the gangplank like drunks, hooting and laughing at each other.

Judy decides everyone is going on the Rotor.

"I don't think that's a good idea," Lisa says, collecting the paper plates littered with pizza crusts.

The guy running the Rotor says Judy shouldn't go on. She's still visibly drunk and he says if she throws up while they're spinning, it will splash back in her face and choke her to death.

Judy grimaces and advises Harry to forgo the Rotor with her. "That might happen to you, too."

"No, it won't," Harry says, snickering. "'Cause I ain't half-gone, like your drunk ass."

Judy frowns, then tilts her head. "Babe," she says gently. "I'm just trying to help."

"Go lay down."

Even through her intoxication, Judy is clearly insulted, hurt. She doesn't respond, though. Just shuffles away, heads towards a bench.

Danny is so embarrassed, so humiliated that she actually listens to him, he hates her.

"Let's go," Harry says.

So Lisa, Danny, and Harry, along with a few other people, walk into the cylinder. "Stand by the wall," the guy running the Rotor announces through a loudspeaker. He's speaking to Harry who is near the center. Harry nods and backs up. The rotation begins. Round and round and round, faster, faster, faster. People begin to stick to the walls. The floor drops. And Danny catches site of Harry, his long face rippling in the spinning, his eyes wide and sick. Danny looks across the cylinder at his sister, who has also seen Harry. With her hands up against the wall like she's in a hold up, she shows six fingers. Number Six, Danny comprehends. Harry will vomit and choke to death. It's brilliant.

But he doesn't choke to death. The floor rises up, the spinning stops.

Outside, as they stumble down the gangplank, Danny and Lisa laugh at each other while Harry is quiet. Judy is lying on a bench. Suddenly, Harry lunges towards a garbage can and begins to throw up. People walk by and chuckle. Lisa shakes her head and smiles. And Danny cannot resist. He approaches Harry—the man is still bent over the garbage can, still hurling up pizza and beer—and Danny sneers, "Are you okay, *Harriet?*"

• • •

He expects to be smacked, punched, beaten, so Danny backs up, prepares to run, but there is no retaliation. Harry finishes vomiting, wipes his mouth, doesn't even look Danny's way. He staggers over to the bench, pushes Judy up into the sitting position and slides next to her. He orders the kids to go away for a half hour.

The sky has gone completely dark but the park is lit up with fabulous colored lights that flash and glitter. Danny and Lisa wander around the fountain, run into someone they know from school. The kid is with his parents and little sister, so he's not very talkative.

When the half hour is over, they return to Harry and their mom. Judy is sitting up now, more alert. "One more ride," she says. Rolling Thunder.

Lisa pushes her brother to take a chance, ride the rollercoaster. She talks on and on, promising it's better to ride Rolling Thunder at night because then he won't see how high he is.

"I don't have a problem with heights," Danny explains. "Just speed and heights."

Still, Danny can't do it. When they get to the coaster's entrance, he plops down on a bench and prepares to hang out by himself.

Then Harry announces he's not going on either.

Danny's stomach tightens and he feels the pizza rise in his throat. Harry lights a cigarette. Lisa and Judy walk away, Lisa taking a last solemn glimpse of her brother before she and her mother disappear into the dark wooden tunnel that will lead them to the ride. Anxiety rips through Danny's bones. He and Harry are in a corner, alone, and nobody can see them. Danny knows he has to get out of there, get to the gift shop where there are people.

Again, Harry seems to know Danny's thoughts. Within seconds, Harry leans over and grabs Danny by the back of the neck with a grip so fierce, so dangerous, so meant for a man and not a kid, Danny knows he's as good as dead.

"You're a little fucking wise ass, aren't you?" Harry growls. His voice is low, sizzling like burning meat, and the words come out clipped because the cigarette is in his mouth. With his hand still on Danny's neck, Harry pushes the boy up from the bench, squeezing, Danny bent over, trying to get away.

"Huh, you little shit?"

Danny cannot speak. He lets out little cries of pain.

"Stop fucking moving," Harry orders and the boy does. There is some let up in the grip and Danny is thankful, hopeful he may survive after all. But a moment later, Danny sees the orange glow of a cigarette near his left eye.

"I'll do it, you shit," Harry says, his words clear and punctuated. "I will."

The cigarette is so close, the heat and smoke burn already and Danny clamps his eyes shut.

Suddenly, Danny hears another man's voice. "What's your problem?"

Harry's grip and the cigarette are immediately gone. Danny stumbles forward, falls on the concrete. When he rolls over, he sees a man push Harry against the wall.

There is second man and also a woman.

"Only a bastard would pick on a kid!" she screams.

The second man stands behind the first guy.

It's pretty dark and their faces are not really visible. But Danny can see the men are strong. They tell Harry off, call him names, threaten to fucking kill him. Harry threatens back, has his arms tightened, his chest puffed out, but it's two against one and the men are as big as him.

The woman finds Danny, places her hands on his face, asks if he's okay. He can see her a little more clearly because she moves him into some light, away from the men. The whites of her eyes are glassy with tears and she has a lot of teeth.

In the end, there is no fighting. Just words. The one guy is piss angry and rants about when he was a kid. "I had a father like you and he knocked me around and shit and you know what? You know what?"

Harry says nothing.

The man steps towards him, points and says, "I got bigger. Your boy, he's gonna get bigger."

"He ain't my boy," Harry barks.

But the man doesn't care about that information. He turns and walks towards Danny. Then he looks at him and says, "You're gonna get bigger. Just remember that."

• • •

The two men and woman wait with Danny until his mom and sister show up. Harry stands off to the side smoking. When Judy arrives, the woman tells her the story and Judy finally gets angry. She yells at Harry and he promises it won't happen again. She accepts this and the men and the woman reluctantly walk away.

The drive home is quiet. Judy passes out in the front seat, Lisa conks out in the back. Danny wants to tell his sister about Number Seven, had wanted to do it when she and Judy got off Rolling Thunder, but didn't get the chance. Still, the revelation is perfect without anyone knowing yet: he's gonna get bigger. The whole time Harry's been around, Danny has never thought of it.

Now he scowls in the back of the car, shooting death thoughts at his mother's boyfriend, hoping they get delivered. *I'm gonna get bigger. That's right, asshole, I'm gonna get bigger.*

He rests his chin on the open window and lets the wind blow into his face.

Dark Eyes, Faith, and Devotion

Charles de Lint

I've just finished cleaning the vomit my last fare left in the back seat—his idea of a tip, I guess, since he actually short-changed me a couple of bucks—and I'm back cruising when the woman flags me down on Gracie Street, outside one of those girl-on-girl clubs. I'll tell you, I'm as open-minded as the next guy, but it breaks my heart when I see a looker like this playing for the other team. She's enough to give me sweet dreams for the rest of the week, and this is only Monday night.

She's about five-seven or five-eight and dark-skinned—Hispanic, maybe, or Indian. I can't tell. I just know she's gorgeous. Jet black hair hanging straight down her back and she's all decked out in net stockings, spike heels, and a short black dress that looks like it's been sprayed on and glistens like satin. Somehow she manages to pull it off without looking like a hooker. It's got to be her babydoll face—made up to a T, but so innocent all you want to do is keep her safe and take care of her. After you've slept with her, mind.

I watch her in the rearview mirror as she gets into the backseat—showing plenty of leg with that short dress of hers and not shy about my seeing it. We both know that's all I'm getting and I'm lucky to get that much. She wrinkles her nose and I can't tell if it's some linger of l'eau de puke or the Lysol I sprayed on the seat after I cleaned up the mess my last fare left behind.

Hell, maybe it's me.

"What can I do for you, ma'am?" I ask.

She's got these big dark eyes and they fix on mine in the rearview mirror, just holding on to my gaze like we're the only two people in the world.

"How far are you willing to go?" she asks.

Dressed like she is, you'd be forgiven for thinking it was a come-on. Hell, that was my first thought anyway, doesn't matter she's playing on that other team. But there's that cherub innocence thing she's got going for her and, well, take a look at a pug like me and you know the one thing that isn't going to happen is some pretty girl's going to make a play for me from the back seat of my cab.

"I can take you any place you need to go," I tell her, playing it safe.

"And if I need something else?" she asks.

I shake my head. "I don't deal with anything that might put me inside."

I almost said "back inside," but that's not something she needs to know. Though maybe she already does. Maybe when I pulled over she saw the prison tattoos on my arms—you know, you put them on with a pin and the ink from a ballpoint so they always come out looking kind of scratchy and blue.

"Someone has stolen my cat," she says. "I was hoping you might help me get her back."

I turn right around in my seat to look at her straight on. I decide she's Hispanic from her accent. I like the Spanish warmth it puts on her words.

"Your cat," I say. "You mean like a pet?"

"Something like that. I really do need someone to help me steal her back."

I laugh. I can't help it.

"So what, you flag down the first cab you see and figure whoever's driving it'll take a short break from cruising for fares to help you creep some joint?"

"Creep?" she asks.

"Break in. But quietly, you know, because you're hoping you won't get caught."

She shakes her head.

"No," she says. "I just thought *you* might."

"And that would be because...?"

"You've got kind eyes."

People have said a lot of things about me over the years, but that's something I've never heard before. It's like telling a wolf he's got a nice smile. I've been told I've got dead eyes, or a hard stare, but no one's ever had anything nice to say about them before. I don't know if it's because of that, or if it's because of that innocence she carries that just makes you want to take care of her, but I find myself nodding.

"Sure," I tell her. "Why not? It's a slow night. Where can we find this cat of yours?"

"First I need to go home and get changed," she says. "I can't go—what was the word you used?" She smiles. "Creep a house wearing this."

Well, she could, I think, and it would sure make it interesting for me if I was hoisting her up to a window, but I just nod again.

"No problem," I tell her. "Where do you live?"

• • •

This whole situation would drive Hank crazy.

We did time together a while back—we'd each pulled a stretch and they ran in tandem for a few years. It's all gangs inside now and since we weren't either of us black or Indian or Hispanic, and we sure as hell weren't going to run with the Aryans, we ended up passing a lot of the time with each other. He told me to look him up when I got out and he'd fix me up. A lot of guys say that, but they don't mean it. You're trying to do good and you want some hardcase showing up at your home or place of employment? I don't think so.

So I wouldn't have bothered, but Hank never said something unless he meant it, and since I really did want to take a shot at walking the straight and narrow this time out, I took him up on it.

He hooked me up with this guy named Moth who runs a Gypsy cab company out of a junkyard—you know, the wheels aren't licensed but so long as no one looks too hard at the piece of bureaucratic paper stuck on the back of the driver's seat, it's the kind of thing you can get away with. You just make a point of cruising for fares in the parts of town that the legit cabbies prefer to stay out of.

So Hank gave me the break to make good, and Moth laid one piece of advice on me—"Don't get involved with your fares"—and I've been doing okay, keeping my nose clean, making enough to pay for a room in a boarding house, even stashing a little extra cash away on the side.

Funny thing is I like this gig. I'm not scared to take the rough fares and I'm big enough that the freaks don't mess with me. Occasionally I even get someone like the woman I picked up on Gracie Street.

None of which explains why I'm parked outside a house across town on Marett Street, getting ready to bust in and rescue a cat.

My partner-in-crime is sitting in the front with me now. Her name's Luisa Jaramillo. She's changed into a tight black T-shirt with a pair of baggy faded jean overalls, black hightops on her feet. Most of her make-up's gone and her hair's hidden under a baseball cap turned backwards. She still looks gorgeous. Maybe more than she did before.

"What's your cat's name?" I ask.

"Patience."

I shrug. "That's okay. You don't have to tell me."

"No, that's her name," Luisa says. "Patience."

"And this guy that stole her is...?"

"My ex-boyfriend. My very recent ex-boyfriend."

That's what I get for jumping to conclusions, I think. Hell, *I* was cruising Gracie Street. That doesn't automatically put me on the other team either. Only don't get me wrong. I'm not getting my hopes up or anything. I know I'm just a pug and all she's doing is using me for this gig because I'm handy and I said I'd do it. There's not going to be any fairy tale reward once we get kitty back from her ex. I'll be lucky to get a handshake.

So why am I doing it?

I'll lay it out straight: I'm bored. I've got a head that never stops working. I'm always considering the percentages, making plans. When I said I'd come to enjoy driving a cab, I was telling the truth. I do. But you're talking to a guy who's spent the better part of his life working out deals, and when the deals didn't pan out, he just went in and took what he needed. That's what put me inside.

They don't put a whole lot of innocent people in jail. I'm not saying they aren't biased towards what most people think of as the dregs of society—the homeboys and Indians and white trash I was raised to be—but most of us doing our time, we did the crime.

Creeping some stranger's house gives me a buzz like a junkie getting a fix. I don't get the shakes when I go cold turkey like I've been doing these past couple of months, but the jones is still there. Tonight I'm just cozying it up with a sugar coating of doing the shiny white knight bit, that's all.

I never even stopped to ask her why we were stealing a cat. I just thought, let's do it. But when you think about it, who steals cats? You lose your cat, you just go get another one. We never had pets when I was a kid, so maybe that's why I don't get it. In our house the kids were the pets, only we weren't so well-treated as I guess Luisa's cat is. Somebody ever took one of us, the only thing Ma'd regret is the cut in her cheque from social services.

You want another reason? I don't often get a chance to hang out with a pretty girl like this.

"So what's the plan?" I ask.

"The man who lives in that house is very powerful," Luisa says.

"Your ex."

She nods.

"So he's what? A politician? A lawyer? A drug dealer?"

"No, no. Much more powerful than that. He's a brujo—a witch man. That is not a wrong thing in itself, but his medicine is very bad. He is an evil man."

I give her the same blank look I'm guessing anybody would.

"I can see you don't believe me," she says.

"It's more like I don't understand," I tell her.

"It doesn't matter. I tell you this only so that you won't look into his eyes. No matter what, do not meet his gaze with your own."

"Or what? He'll turn me into a pumpkin?"

"Something worse," she says in all seriousness.

She gets out of the car before I can press her on it, but I'm not about to let it go. I get out my side and join her on the sidewalk. She takes my hand and leads me quickly into the shadows cast by a tall hedge that runs the length of the property, separating her ex's house from its neighbours. I like the feel of her skin against mine. She lets go all too soon.

"What's really going on here?" I ask her. "I mean, I pick you up outside a girl bar on Gracie Street where you're dressed like a hooker, and now we're about to creep some magic guy's house to get your cat back. None of this is making a whole lot of sense."

"And yet you are here."

I give her a slow nod. "Maybe I should never have looked in your eyes," I say.

I'm joking, but she's still all seriousness when she answers.

"I would never do such a thing to another human being," she tells me. "Yes, I went out looking the way I did in hopes of attracting a man such as you, but there was no magic involved."

I focus on the "a man such as you," not sure I like what it says about what she thinks of me. I may not look like much, which translates into a lot of nights spent on my own, but I've never paid for it.

"You looked like a prostitute, trying to pick up a john or some freak."

She actually smiles, her teeth flashing in the shadows, white against her dark skin.

"No, I was searching for a man who would desire me enough to want to be close to me, but who had the heart to listen to my story and the compassion to want to help once he knew the trouble I was in."

"I think you've got the wrong guy," I tell her. "Neither of those are things I'm particularly known for."

"And yet you are here," she says again. "And you shouldn't sell yourself short. Sometimes we don't fulfill our potential only because there is no one in our life to believe in us."

I've got an idea where she's going with that—Hank and Moth have talked about that kind of thing some nights when we're sitting around a campfire in the junkyard, not to mention every damn social worker who's actually trying to do their job—but I don't want to go there with her anymore than I do with them. It's a nice theory, but I've never bought it. Your life doesn't go a certain way just because other people think that's the way it will.

"You were taking a big chance," I say instead. "You could've picked up some freak with a knife who wasn't going to stop to listen."

She shakes her head. "No one would have troubled me."

"But you need my help with your ex."

"That is different. I have looked in his eyes. He has sewn black threads in my soul and without a champion at my side, I'm afraid he would pull me back under his influence."

This I understand. I've helped a couple of women get out of a bad relationship by pounding a little sense into their ex-boyfriend's head. It's amazing how the threat of more of the same is so much more effective than a restraining order.

"So you're looking for some muscle to pound on your ex."

"I'm hoping that won't be necessary. You wouldn't want him for an enemy."

"Some people say you're judged by your enemies."

"Then you would be considered a powerful man, too," she says.

"So the get-up you had on was like a costume."

She nods, but even in the shadows I can see the bitter look that comes into her eyes.

"I have many 'costumes' such as that," she says. "My boyfriend insists I wear them in order to appear attractive. He likes it that men would desire me, but could not have me."

"Boy, what planet is he from?" I say. "You could wear a burlap sack and you'd still be drop dead gorgeous."

"You did not like the dress?"

I shrug. "What can I say? I'm a guy. Of course I liked it. I'm just saying you don't need it."

"You are very sweet."

Again with the making nice. Funny thing is, I don't want to argue it with her anymore. I find I like the idea that someone'd say these kinds of things to me. But I don't pretend there's a hope in hell that it'll ever go past this. Instead I focus on the holes in her story. There are things she isn't telling me and I say as much, but while she can't help but look a little guilty, she doesn't share them either.

"Look," I tell her. "It doesn't matter what they are. I just need to know, are they going to get in the way of our getting the job done?"

"I don't think so."

I wait a moment but she's still playing those cards pretty much as close to her vest as she can. I wonder how many of them are wild.

"Okay," I say. "So we'll just do it. But we need to make a slight detour first. Do you think your cat can hold out for another hour or so?"

She nods.

• • •

She doesn't ask any questions when I pull up behind a plant nursery over on East Kelly Street. I jimmy the lock on the back door like it's not even there—hey, it's what I do; or at least used to do—and slip inside. It takes me a moment to track down what I'm looking for, using the beam of a cheap key ring flashlight to read labels. Finally, I find the shelf I need.

I cut a hole in a small bag of diatomaceous earth and carefully pour a bit of it into each of my jacket's pockets. When I replace the bag, I leave a five-spot on the shelf beside it as payment. See, I'm learning. Guys back in prison would be laughing their asses off if they ever heard about this, but I don't care. I may still bust into some guy's house to help his ex-girlfriend steal back her cat, but I'm done with taking what I haven't earned.

• • •

"You figure he's home?" I ask when we pull back up outside the house on Marett.

She nods. "He would not leave her alone—not so soon after stealing her from me."

"You know where his bedroom is?"

"At the back of the house, on the second floor. He is a light sleeper."

Of course he would be.

"And your cat," I say. "Would she have the run of the house, or would he keep her in a cage?"

"He would have...other methods of keeping her docile."

"The magic eyes business."

"His power is not a joking matter," she says.

"I'm taking it seriously," I tell her.

Though I'm drawing the line at magic. Thing is, I know guys who can do things with their eyes. You see it in prison all the time—whole conversations taking place without a word being exchanged. It's all in the eyes. Some guys are like a snake, mesmerizing its prey. The eyes lock onto you and before you know what's going on, he's stuck a shiv in your gut and you're down on the floor, trying to keep your life from leaking out of you, your own blood pouring over your hands.

But I'm pretty good with the thousand yard stare myself.

I get out of the car and we head for the side door in the carport. I'd have had Luisa stay behind in the cab, except I figure her cat's going to be a lot more docile if she's there to carry it back out again.

I give the door a visual check for an alarm. There's nothing obvious, but that doesn't mean anything, so I ask Luisa about it.

"A man such as he does not need a security system," she tells me.

"The magic thing again."

When she nods, I shrug and take a couple of pairs of surgical gloves out of my back pocket. I hand her one pair and put the other on, then get out my picks.

This door takes a little longer than the one behind the nursery did. For a guy who's got all these magic chops, he's still sprung for a decent lock. That makes me feel a little better. I'm not saying that Luisa's gullible or anything, but with guys like this—doesn't matter what scam they're running, magic mumbo-jumbo's not a whole lot different from the threat of a beating—it's the fear factor that keeps people in line. All you need is for your victim to believe that you can do what you say you'll do if they don't toe the line. You don't actually need magic.

The lock gives up with a soft click. I put my picks away and take out a small can of WD-40, spraying each of the hinges before I let the door swing open. Then I lean close to Luisa, my mouth almost touching her ear.

"Where should we start looking?" I say.

My voice is so soft you wouldn't hear me a few steps away. She replies as quietly, her breath warm against my ear. This close to her I realize that a woman like her smells just as good as she looks. That's something I just never had the opportunity to learn before.

"The basement," Luisa says. "If she is not hiding from him there, then he will have her in his bedroom with him. There is a door leading downstairs, just past that cupboard."

I nod and start for the door she pointed to, my sneakers silent on the tiled floor. Luisa whispers along behind me. I do the hinges on this door, too, and I'm cautious on the steps going down, putting my feet close to the sides of the risers where they're less liable to wake a creak.

There was a light switch at the top of the stairs. Once I get to the bottom, I stand silent, listening. There's nothing. I feel along the wall and come across the other switch I was expecting to find.

"Close your eyes," I tell Luisa.

I do the same thing and flick the switch. There's a blast of light behind my closed lids. I crack them slightly and take a quick look around. The basement is furnished, casually, like an upscale rec room. There's an entertainment center against one wall, a wet bar against another. Nice couch set up in front of the TV. I count three doors, all of them slightly ajar. I'm not sure what they lead to. Furnace room, laundry room, workshop. Who knows?

By the time I'm finished looking around my eyes have adjusted to the light. The one thing I don't see is a cat.

"You want to try calling her?" I ask.

Luisa shakes her head. "I can feel her. She is hiding in there." She points to one of the mystery doors. "In the storage room."

I let her go ahead of me, following after. Better the cat see her first than my ugly mug.

We're halfway across the room when someone speaks from behind us.

(I knew you would return,) a man's voice says, speaking Spanish. (And look what you have brought me. A peace offering.)

I turn slowly, not letting on that I know what he's said. I picked up a lot of Spanish on the street, more in jail. So I just look surprised, which isn't a stretch. I can't believe I didn't feel him approach. When I'm creeping a joint I carry a sixth sense inside me that stretches out throughout the place, letting me know when there's a change in the air.

Hell, I should at least have heard him on the stairs.

"I have brought you nothing," Luisa says, speaking English for my benefit, I guess.

(And yet I will have you and your champion. I will make you watch as I strip away his flesh and sharpen my claws on his bones.)

"Please. I ask only for our freedom."

(You can never be free from me.)

I have to admit he's a handsome devil. Same dark hair and complexion as Luisa, but there's no warmth in his eyes.

Oh, I know what Luisa said. Don't look in his eyes. But the thing is, I don't play that game. You learn pretty quickly when you're inside that the one thing you don't do is back down. Show even a hint of weakness and your fellow inmates will be on you like piranha.

So I just put a hand in the pocket of my jacket and look him straight in the eye, give him my best convict stare.

He smiles. "You are a big one, aren't you?" he says. "But your size means nothing in this game we will play."

You ever get into a staring contest? I can see that starting up here, except dark eyes figures he's going to mesmerize me in seconds, he's so confident. The funny thing is, I can feel a pull in that gaze of his. His pupils seem to completely fill my sight. I hear a strange whispering in the back of my head and can feel that thousand yard stare of mine already starting to fray at the edges.

So maybe he's got some kind of magical power. I don't know and I don't care. I take my hand out of my pocket and I'm holding a handful of that diatomaceous earth I picked up earlier in the nursery.

Truth is, I never thought I'd use it. I picked it up as a back-up, nothing more. Like insurance just in case, crazy as it sounded, Luisa really knew what she was talking about. I mean, you hear stories about every damn thing you can think of. I never believed most of what I heard, but a computer's like magic to someone who's never seen one before—you know what I'm saying? The world's big enough and strange enough that pretty much anything can be out there in it, somewhere.

So I've got that diatomaceous earth in my hand and I throw it right in his face, because I'm panicking a little at the way those eyes of his are getting right into my head and starting to shut me down inside.

You know anything about that stuff? It's made of ground up shells and bones that are sharp as glass. Gardeners use it to make barriers for various kinds of insects. The bug crawls over it and gets cut to pieces. It's incredibly fine—so much so that it doesn't come through the latex of my gloves—but eyes don't have that kind of protection.

Imagine what it would do if it got in them.

Tall, dark and broody over there doesn't have to use his imagination. He lifts his hand as the cloud comes at him, but he's too late. Too late to wave it away. Too late to close his eyes like I've done as I back away from any contact with the stuff.

His eyelids instinctively do what they're supposed to do in a situation like this—they blink rapidly and the pressure cuts his eyes all to hell and back again.

It doesn't help when he reaches up with his hands to try to wipe the crap away.

He starts to make this horrible mewling sound and falls to his knees.

I'm over by the wall now, well out of range of the rapidly settling cloud. Looking at him I start to feel a little queasy, thinking I did an overkill on this. I don't know what went on between him and Luisa—how bad it got, what kind of punishment he deserves—but I think maybe I crossed a line here that I really shouldn't have.

He lifts his bloodied face, sightless eyes pointed in our direction, and manages to say something else. This time he's talking in some language I never heard before, ending with some Spanish that I do understand.

(Be so forever,) he cries.

I'm turning to Luisa just then, so I see what happens.

Well, I see it, but it doesn't register as real. One moment there's this beautiful dark-haired woman standing there, then she vanishes and there's only the heap of her clothes left lying on the carpet. I'm still staring slack-jawed when the clothing moves and a sleek black cat wriggles out from under the overalls and darts into the room where Luisa said *her* cat was.

As I take a step after her, the man starts in with something else in that unrecognizable language. I don't know if it's still aimed at Luisa, or if he's planning to turn me into something, too—hell, I'm a dyed-in-the-wool believer at this point—but I don't take any chances. I take a few quick steps in his direction and give him a kick in the side of the head. When that doesn't completely stop him, I give him a couple more.

He finally goes down and stays down.

I turn back to go after Luisa, but before I can, that black cat comes soft-stepping out of the room once more, this time carrying a kitten in its mouth.

"Luisa?" I find myself saying.

I swear, even with that kitten in its mouth, the cat nods. But I don't even need to see that. I only have to look into her eyes. The cat has Luisa's eyes, there's no question in my mind about that.

"Is this...permanent?" I ask.

The cat's response is to trot by me, giving her unconscious ex's body a wide berth as she heads for the stairs.

I stand there, looking at the damage I've done to her ex for a long, unhappy moment, then I follow her up the stairs. She's sitting by the door with the kitten, but I can't leave it like this. I look around the kitchen, not ready to leave yet.

The cat makes a querulous sound, but I ask her to wait and go prowling through the house. I don't know what I'm looking for, something to justify what I did downstairs, I guess. I don't find anything, not really. There are spooky masks and icons and other weird magical looking artifacts scattered throughout the house, but he's not going to be the first guy that likes to collect that kind of thing. Nothing explains why he needed to have this hold over Luisa and her—I'm not thinking of the kitten as a cat anymore. After what I saw downstairs, I'm sure it's her kid.

I go upstairs and poke through his office, his bedroom. Still nothing. But then it's often like that. Too often the guy you'd never suspect of having a bad thought turns out to be beating on his family, or goes postal where he works, or some damn crazy thing.

It really makes you wonder—especially with a guy like Luisa's ex. You find yourself with power like he's got, why wouldn't you use it to put something good into the world?

I know, I know. Look who's talking. But I'm telling you straight, I might have robbed a lot of people, but I never hurt them. Not intentionally. And never a woman or a kid.

I go back downstairs and find the cat still waiting by the kitchen door for me. She's got a paw on the kitten, holding it in place.

"Let's go," I say.

I haven't even started to think about how a woman can be changed into a cat, or when and if and how she'll change back again. I can only deal with one thing at a time.

My first impulse is to burn the place to the ground with him in it, but playing the cowboy like that's just going to put me back inside and it won't prove anything. I figure I've done enough damage and it's not like he's going to call the cops. But the first thing I'm going to do when I get home is change the plates on the cab and dig out the spare set of registration papers that Moth provides for all his vehicles.

For now I follow the cats down the driveway. I open the passenger door to the cab. The mama cat grabs her kitten by the skin at the nape of her neck and jumps in. I close the door and walk around to the driver's side.

I take a last look at the house, remembering the feel of the guy's eyes inside my head, the relief I felt when the diatomaceous earth got in his eyes and cut them all to hell. There was a lot of blood, but I don't know how permanent the damage'll be. Maybe he'll come after us, but I doubt it. Nine out of ten times, a guy like that just folds his hand when someone stands up to him.

Besides, the city's so big, he's never going to find us, even if he does come looking. It's not like we run in the same circles or anything.

So I get in the cab, say something that I hope sounds calming to the cats, and we drive away.

· · ·

I've got a different place now, a one-bedroom, ground-floor apartment which gives me access to a backyard. It's not much, just a jungle of weeds and flowers gone wild, but the cats seem to like it.

I sit on the back steps sometimes and watch them romp around like...well, like the cats they are, I guess. I know I hurt the man who had them under his power, hurt him bad. And I know I walked into his house with a woman and came out with a cat. But it still feels like a dream.

It's true the cat seems to understand everything I say, and acts smarter than I think a cat would normally act, but what do I know? I never had a pet before. And anybody I talk to seems to think the same thing about their own cat or dog.

I haven't told anybody about any of this, though I did come at it from a different angle, sitting around the fire in the junkyard with Hank one night. There were a half-dozen of us. Moth, Hank's girlfriend Lily, and some of the others from their extended family of choice. The junkyard's in the middle of the city, but it backs onto the Tombs and it gets dark out there. As we sit in deck chairs, nursing beers and coffees, we watch the sparks flicker above the flames in the cut-down steel barrel Moth uses for his fires.

"Did you ever hear any stories about people that can turn into animals?" I ask during a lull in the conversation.

We have those kinds of talks. We can go from carbs and engine torques to what's wrong with social services or the best kind of herbal tea for nausea. That'd be ginger tea.

"You mean like a werewolf?" Moth says.

Sitting beside him, Paris grins. She's as dark-haired as Luisa was and her skin's pretty much covered with tattoos that seem to move on their own in the flickering light.

"Nah," she says. "Billy Joe's just looking for a way to turn himself into a raccoon or a monkey so he can get into houses again but without getting caught."

"I gave that up," I tell her.

She smiles at me, eyes still teasing. "I know that. But I still like the picture it puts in my head."

"There are all kinds of stories," Hank says, "and we know one or two. The way they go, the animal people were here first and some of them are still living among us, not looking any different from you or me."

They tell a few then—Hank and Lily and Katy, this pretty red-haired girl who lives on her own in a schoolbus not far from the junkyard. They all tell the stories like they've actually met the people they're talking about, but Katy's are the best. She's got the real storyteller's gift, makes you hang onto every word until she's done.

"But what about if someone's put a spell on someone?" I say after a few of their stories, because they're mostly about people who were born that way, part-animal, part-human, changing their skins as they please. "You know any stories like that? How it works? How they get changed back?"

I've got a lot of people looking at me after I come out with that.

Nobody has an answer.

Moth gives me a look—but it's curious, not demanding. "Why are you asking?" he says.

I just shrug. I don't know that it's my story to tell. But as the weeks go by I bring it up again and this time I tell them what happened, or at least what I think happened. Funny thing is, they just take me at my word. They start looking in on it for me, but nobody comes up with an answer.

Maybe there isn't one.

So I just drive my cab and spend time with these new families of mine—both the one in the junkyard and the cats I've got back home. I find it gets easier to walk the straight-and-narrow, the longer you do it. Gets so that doing the right thing, the honest thing, comes like second nature to me.

But I never stop wondering about what happened that night. I don't even know if they're really cats who were pretending to be human, or humans that got turned into cats. I guess I'm always going to be waiting to see if they'll change back.

But I don't think about it twenty-four/seven. Mostly I just figure it's my job to make a home for them and keep them safe. And you know what? Turns out I'm pretty good at doing that.

Adeline

Wayne D. Dundee

AUTHOR'S NOTE: *This story is based on historical fact. The Orphan Train program operated in the United States for nearly eight decades, starting in the early 1850s and ending in 1929. Abandoned, vagrant children were taken from the cold, dirty, danger-ous streets of eastern cities like New York and Boston and transported to foster homes in rural Western states. In all, over a quarter-million children were relocated in this manner. Like so often happens, the original intent was good, but the execution came with flaws and unintended consequences. Regulation improved in later years, but during the 1870s and 1880s, the turbulent times following the Civil War, the operation ran under its loosest control. Many children went to farming/ranching families where they were treated as little more than slaves or indentured servants; others, like the title character of this story, were destined for even worse fates*—WD

"It's what you do, ain't it? Bring back people for money?"

"Bring back people who got wanted papers on 'em, yeah … But not just any old 'people'."

"This ain't any old person. This is the sweetest little girl you ever saw. Tiny as a tick, with big, innocent, trusting eyes, and—"

"Is she a criminal? A wanted fugitive?" Rawson interrupted.

"Of course not. I told you, she's just a little girl. It's what's about to happen to her that's criminal … As far as that goes, so is what's *already* happened to her."

"You said she came through on the Orphan Train, right?"

"Uh-huh."

"I thought that was supposed to be a good thing—Getting those abandoned kids out of the overcrowded orphanages and filth of the big cities back east and delivering 'em out here to folks in smaller towns or on farms and ranches ready to welcome 'em into their own families."

"It might *sound* like a good thing," Miss Maybelle responded, frowning. "It was probably meant to be, and I'm sure it seemed all fine and uplifting to who-ever thought it up and the politicians they got to sponsor it. Hell, when I first heard about I thought it sounded kinda good and noble, too. But once you see how it actually gets conducted, the way those kids are treated … No, there's a lot about it that ain't good and noble. Not by a damn sight. It's downright degrading and humiliating, is what it is. And that's not even the worst part, for sure not in the case of this little girl I'm talking about."

Clete Rawson leaned back in his cushiony chair and drew thoughtfully on the fine cigar Miss Maybelle had provided once he'd been ushered into her private quarters. The latter were quite handsomely appointed, especially for a no place little town like Hesterville on the far edge of western Nebraska. Miss Maybelle herself was quite handsomely appointed, too, with her piled high hair, glittering jewelry, and a form-fitting dress that showed an intriguing flash of leg and a daring amount of cleavage.

She remained among the most requested in her house of "soiled doves", despite her maturity in years and the fact she herself had long since stopped entertaining clients. This didn't prevent her from being on hand each evening to greet and mingle with the guests, however, and to do so while always dressed enticingly—either as an example for her girls to emulate, an added stimulant for the men, or simply to satisfy her own vanity. Perhaps all three. The only thing Rawson knew for sure was that whenever he stopped by Miss Maybelle's place during the times he passed through Hesterville, he looked forward to drinking in the sight of her as part of his visit, even though he knew it would be one of the other girls he'd be going upstairs with. So tonight, when summoned to join the renowned madam in private, he'd been equal parts surprised, puzzled, and excited by the invitation.

"I went down to the station when the Orphan Train stopped here two days ago," Miss Maybelle continued. "Curiosity, I guess—like most of the others who showed up. Except for those actually looking to adopt one of the children, that is. Seeing how they went about making their selections was where the whole thing started to go sour for me."

"What do you mean?"

"It was like they were examining livestock they might be interested in buying, that's what I mean." Miss Maybelle's nostrils flared indignantly. "For starters, they had the children parade out onto this platform that had been set up. The kids all did their best to manage smiles, some of them pirouetted in little circles—like they obviously were trained and encouraged to do. A couple of them even did dance steps and sang some song refrains ... Then, if that wasn't humiliating enough, the people who'd signed up as being interested in adoption took turns getting up on the platform for a closer look. They poked and prodded. Made the kids open their mouths so they could check their teeth. Felt their muscles ... Made me half sick, just watching."

"I saw some slave tradin' once, down South before the war," Rawson recalled. "Don't sound too much different from that."

"Exactly. Eight children were adopted that day. I'd like to think at least a couple of them went to homes where they'll be welcomed into a family and loved like a kid oughta be. But it was clear that some of the others, for sure the older ones who were selected for their size and strength, are going to end up little more than an extra pair of hard working hands on the ranches they went to … And then there was Adeline, the little girl I mentioned. And Hiram Fortner, the man who adopted her."

"How old is this girl?"

"Can't be more than eight or nine."

"You said before she was small. Tiny. Don't sound like a child who was picked for hard labor."

Miss Maybelle shook her head. "No, that would almost be a kindness. What Hiram Fortner picked Adeline for is a whole lot worse than hard labor."

"Sounds like there's more to tell on this Fortner fella."

Miss Maybelle's face clouded. "Hiram Fortner is the lowest form of vermin you can ever imagine."

"In the bounty huntin' business," Rawson replied, "I've encountered just about every kind of vermin there is. Ain't much left I need to use my imagination on."

"The thing about Hiram Fortner," Miss Maybelle argued, "is that he likes little girls. And I don't mean he likes them in a good way … I mean in a way that ain't normal or healthy. A way that's sick."

She paused, letting her words sink in. Watched the grim expression settle over Rawson's face.

"I don't make a habit of talking about the peculiarities of the men who come to visit my gals. If I wanted to, believe me there's plenty to tell. But obviously that wouldn't be smart for business. Only, in the case of Hiram Fortner, I'm willing to make an exception."

"Think I'm already beginnin' to get the picture," Rawson said.

"He comes round every couple months or so," Miss Maybelle went on. "Always asks for my youngest gal. Always picks the slimmest, most girlish one out of the lineup. When he gets her up to the room he has her put her hair in pigtails, dress in the closest thing she has to little-girl clothes. Insists she call him 'Daddy' the whole time, even when they're—"

"I said I got the picture."

"I wanted to make sure."

"So when he heard about this Orphan Train, Fortner saw it as a way to hand-pick his very own little girl—a real one, instead of pretend—to satisfy his sick desires. That what you're tellin' me?"

"If you saw the way he looked at Adeline up there on that platform. The way he stroked her hair, her shoulder." Miss Maybelle shuddered. "To anyone else looking on—anyone who didn't know about his peculiar tastes in the sex department—it might look like any loving parent affectionately touching their child. But I knew better. I saw it for what it truly was."

"Don't this sick bastard have a woman of his own?"

Miss Maybelle nodded. "That's the excuse for adopting a little girl. Fortner's wife never healed right after a bad fall on the ice last winter. She has a lot of trouble getting around, even for simple house-hold chores. They never had children of their own, so a daughter in the home would be able to help Mrs. Fortner and sort of look after her while Hiram works the ranch."

"Is the wife in on what *else* their new daughter will be expected to do?"

"No way of knowing for sure. But not likely, would be my guess. At least not at this point. Elsie Fortner is one of those browbeat, worn-down-looking women who never lifts her face in public and always walks a step behind her husband. Hiram bosses her like a work mule and seldom has an un-harsh word for her. Leastways that's how it was *before* her accident. She don't make it into town with him much any more these days … No reason to expect it's any different, though."

Rawson's grim expression grew grimmer. "In other words, anything Fortner does in his own home—even if comes to makin' visits to little Adeline's bed-room at night—ain't gonna get spoken out against by his wife."

"I'm afraid not. That's why the only chance for the little girl is to get her out of there as soon as possible. That's why I'm offering to pay you—a bounty, if you will, just like you're used to collecting—to ride out there and bring her back."

"What about the sheriff? Or a federal marshal? Ain't what we're talkin' about *illegal*, for Chrissakes? Shouldn't they be the ones to handle something like this?"

"Based on what? What proof do I have? Only the events I claim took place in a bawdyhouse, and what I feel and know in my gut. Hiram Fortner might not be the biggest rancher around, but he's got a decent-sized spread and he's never caused anybody any trouble. It'd be his word against a bunch of whores, and that's if the law would go far enough to even question him."

"If I was to ride out there and snatch the girl—kidnap her, in other words—*that* for damn sure would be illegal. Be no question about it."

"It might be illegal. But it would be the right thing. No question about that, either."

Rawson scowled. "If I was to bring Adeline back, what would you do with her? You surely ain't plannin' on keepin' her and raisin' her here, are you?"

Miss Maybelle smiled faintly, pleased that the bounty hunter was clearly considering her proposal. "Of course not. Don't be ridiculous," she said. "But it so happens I've stayed in contact with one of my gals who left the business a couple years back. She ran off with a ranch hand who'd fallen in love with her and they moved across the border into Wyoming and got married. The kind of thing that's supposed to happen only in storybooks, except sometimes it actually does in real life, too. Anyway, they've got their own spread now and, slowly but surely, they're making a go of it. The only thing is, they've found they can't have kids of their own. They'd welcome little Adeline like a gift from Heaven and I know Marilyn—that's the name of the gal who used to work for me—would be a wonderful mother."

"Sounds like you've got it all figured out," said Rawson, rubbing his jaw.

Miss Maybelle regarded him. "Why do you think I care so much about this little girl I barely laid eyes on, Rawson?"

"Been wonderin' that."

"Yeah, I've wondered on it some myself." One corner of her mouth lifted wryly. "The thing is, there's nothing much in this old life that's more pure and innocent than childhood. At least, that's the way it *should* be. I'm not making excuses, mind you, but in my years working this trade I've met way too many gals who started down this path because their childhood was robbed from them. Either by abandonment or physical abuse … or, maybe worst of all, the kind of treatment that's in store for little Adeline. I'm not saying she's guaranteed to end up a whore. And I'm not even saying that's the worst thing she could be. But however she turns out, her innocence will have been robbed from her and it will have been done in the worst way possible—by somebody pretending to be a parent, a person she ought to've been able to trust above all others. Any way you slice it, that's a hell of a cruel blow for a little kid to try and make it past."

Rawson didn't say anything right away. When he did: "What's to prevent Fortner from comin' after the girl? And, even if we manage to get her away and keep her away, what's to stop him from waitin' for the next train and 'adopting' another little girl?"

"If you work it right, Fortner will have no idea who took her," Miss Maybelle answered. "Maybe he'll think she just ran away. Wouldn't be the first time one of these Orphan Train children did that. As far as him getting his hands on another girl … well, we can only fight one battle at a time. We can't do any-thing about the future, Rawson, but we can damn sure do something about the here and now—if, that is, you're willing to sign on for what I'm proposing."

• • •

Rawson rode out to Fortner's place the following day. The ranch lay more than a dozen miles from town, over rugged country, so it was late in the afternoon when he arrived.

He approached cautiously, wanting neither his presence nor his interest to be known. In a hilltop stand of cottonwoods, he found a well-concealed position with a clear view of the house and outbuildings. Using his spyglass, he was able to closely and leisurely monitor the activities around the house as he mentally put the final touches on how he was going to go about getting the girl out of there.

As evening was settling in, he got his first look at Adeline when she appeared on the front porch and tossed a pan of table scraps out onto the ground. A flock of scrawny chickens and two pot-bellied shoats came scurrying to make short work of whatever had been in the pan. Adeline paused to watch them for a moment, her mouth curving into a wide smile before she turned and went back inside.

She was indeed a lovely child. Big, luminous eyes, rosy cheeks, golden hair dangling in loose ringlets. Watching her, Rawson's gut knotted like a clenched fist at the thought of what lay in store for this frail innocent if Hiram Fortner had his way.

The bounty hunter swore under his breath. He was damned if he was going to let that happen.

He'd gotten plenty of looks at Fortner, too, as the man busied himself with chores around the property before calling it a day and going inside for supper. Stocky build, average height, with bristly mutton chop sideburns and a weary yet purposeful stride. Outwardly just another hard-working rancher, a common enough type to these parts … except this one harbored a dark evil on the inside.

The way he'd work it, Rawson had decided, would be to wait until well after full dark, close to midnight. Then, when everyone was sleeping their soundest, he would steal into the house and simply take the girl. He'd long ago learned the art of stealth from an old Indian fighter and it had served him well more than once in the bounty hunting business. In his saddlebags, he even carried a pair of whisper-quiet moccasins he could slip on when the need arose.

The biggest risk would be that of alarming Adeline and having her cry out. He'd have to deal with that if it became necessary, but for the girl's sake it was something he hoped to avoid. In addition to startling the child, any outburst resulting in a confrontation with Fortner was almost certain to turn violent and, as a result, could have an even more traumatizing affect. The whole idea was to spare Adeline exposure to things that would strip away more layers of her childhood innocence. Still, worst case, even if an alarm somehow *was* raised, Rawson's main objective remained to rescue her from this place and he would do whatever it took to succeed in that. He'd solved problems in the past with bullets and, if given no choice and that's what it came down to tonight, he would again. On a strictly personal level, he couldn't deny he'd get a measure of satisfaction from pumping a couple slugs into the likes of Fortner.

In the meantime, now that he'd seen the layout of the place and had a plan fixed in his mind, all he could do was wait. The old Indian fighter had taught him patience, too. But that didn't mean while he was waiting he couldn't make himself reasonably comfortable. The early spring day had warmed nicely but now, with the sun gone and no cloud cover to retain any of the afternoon's heat, the night was quickly growing chill.

Rawson withdrew a quarter mile and found a shallow gully where he could build a small, unseen fire to warm himself and cook some coffee. It was there he waited. A thin slice of moon rose and the cloudless, now-darkened sky became sprinkled with glittering stars. That was good, it would provide illumination for making his approach on the house. In case of pursuit, however, it could work against him—but Rawson didn't plan on allowing any pursuit.

He drank coffee. Smoked another of the fine cigars Miss Maybelle had given him. Waited.

The problem with holding off like this was the nagging question that kept creeping through Rawson's mind—the question of what Adeline might be going through in the meantime. He had no idea how someone like Fortner would proceed with his vile plans. Would he immediately brutalize and abuse the girl? Or would he work up to it more slowly, like some sort of sick seduction?

Adeline had been at the ranch for two nights now. If Fortner meant to force his way with her, then it might already be too late. If otherwise—which, needless to say, was Rawson's fervent hope—then another few hours shouldn't be crucial. He reminded himself that when he'd seen Adeline on the porch earlier she hadn't shown any signs of being misused or troubled in a way you might expect if the actual molestation had begun. He recalled her big smile when she paused to watch the pigs and chickens go after the scraps she'd thrown to them.

He told himself that was a good sign ... and hoped to hell he was right.

When it was finally time, Rawson kicked out his fire then mounted up and rode back toward the Fortner ranch.

• • •

From the same stand of cottonwood trees as before, Rawson again paused to gaze down on the layout below. The starlight cast everything in a bluish silver glow that revealed details almost as clearly as in the daytime.

Everything was quiet. No lights were burning. No signs of movement or activity anywhere in or around the house. He heaved a sigh of relief that his earlier reconnaissance had determined the premises was free of any damned dog for him to worry about.

Dismounting, Rawson sat down on the grass and exchanged his boots for the moccasins he'd pulled from his saddlebags. Then, after stuffing his dusty boots into the same leather pouch the moccs had come out of, he took his horse's reins in hand and led the way slowly down the slope.

About fifty feet from the main house, he tied the animal to a rough-bark corral rail. The horse's nostrils flared at the scent of the other horses in the corral and some of them stirred and snorted in response. "Easy, boy," Rawson soothed. He wanted the big gelding close by when he made his exit from the house but couldn't afford for it to cause a disturbance.

Once the animals seemed settled down, he turned and started toward the house. As he walked, he reached down to slip the hammer thong from the Colt riding on his hip and lifted the gun a couple inches to make sure it rested loose in its holster.

A moment later, the first gunshot blasted apart the silence of the night!

Rawson immediately threw himself to the ground and scrambled for the cover of a piled-stone well housing. A second shot rang out and, from the corner of his eye, Rawson caught the flash of gunfire through the darkened windows of the house.

He squirmed in tight behind the piled stones, Colt now clenched tightly in his fist. Everything had gone quiet again, except for the chugging of his breath and the hammering of his heart. After several tense seconds, Rawson came to the realization that neither of those shots had been aimed in his direction. He removed his hat and slowly peered around the edge of the well housing. The front door was still shut and the glass in the front windows was intact, unshattered. Everything inside remained dark ... but no, peering closer he could now see a faint glow way back toward the rear. Where the bedrooms most likely were located.

Adeline!

Rawson gathered his feet under him and rose to a crouch. He continued to watch the house intently. The glow—a softly burning lantern, he'd decided— remained steady but motionless. Sucking in a deep breath and holding it, Rawson shoved away from the well and, staying in a half-crouch, covered the remaining distance to the house at a hard run. Leapt onto the porch, plastered himself against the outside wall just to the right of the door.

More tense seconds, but no more gunshots. Silence again, interrupted only by his heavy breathing. Cautiously leaning to peek around the edge of the nearest window, Rawson got a closer look at the lantern glow but there appeared to be no change in either its location or brightness. Leaning back the other way, he thumbed the door latch and gave a hard push.

The door swung inward, creaking faintly on its hinges, and a wedge of silver-blue starlight bathed the interior. Rawson could see a tidy kitchen area off to the right, a simple but comfortable-looking parlor area off to the left. Straight back, where the shadows converged again beyond the spill of starlight, there was a short hallway with the faintly pulsing lantern glow emanating from a corner at its far end.

Rawson stepped quickly through the doorway and cut immediately into the dense shadows on the kitchen side, mindful not to silhouette himself against the window. He stood frozen there for several beats, Colt held at the ready, willing himself to keep his breathing under control.

Nothing but stillness and silence all around him.

Sticking to the shadows, Rawson began moving toward the hallway and the lantern glow. His moccasin-covered feet glided ghostlike across the wood plank floor.

He'd taken his first step into the hallway before he was able to make out the bulky shape lying on the floor at the opposite end. After another step he was able to determine that the bulky shape was the head and shoulders of a man, the rest of his body extending through an open doorway into the room where the lantern was burning. It wasn't hard to guess that the man must be Hiram Fortner, and the milkweed-like tufts of mutton chop sideburns caught in the lantern glow was enough to confirm it.

Rawson covered the rest of the hallway quickly and then, stepping over Fortner's prone body, went through the doorway with his Colt raised and ready.

He found himself in a bedroom. A disheveled, frail-looking woman sat on the edge of the bed, staring blankly down at the man on the floor. A pistol lay on the blanket beside her. The softly flickering coal oil lantern rested on a nearby nightstand.

Rawson leaned over and lifted the pistol from the bed.

"Go ahead and take it," the woman said dully, her eyes never leaving the weapon's apparent victim. "I'm done using it for what needed doing."

"Are you Elsie Fortner?" Rawson asked, seeking to confirm what seemed obvious.

"I am."

"What happened here?"

"I just shot my husband. Killed him, I expect … I had to do it. No other choice. He was fixing to bother our little girl." Now her eyes lifted, twin pools of anguish that bored deep into Rawson. "Bother her in a real bad way … You understand?"

"Yes, I'm afraid I do."

"Who are you?" the woman wanted to know.

"I was ridin' by—I heard the gunshots."

It was a poorly constructed lie but she seemed to accept it.

"I had a feeling right from the start ... but I fought against admitting it," Elsie Fortner went on. "I chose to believe he only wanted to take in one of those Orphan Train girls to help me around the house, like he said, since my accident left me limited and all ... Deep down, though, I knew there was more to it ... I always knew he had a—a *problem* when it came to his feelings for young girls. He said he could control it ... I let him convince me. What woman wants to believe otherwise about the man she married?"

"Where's the girl now?"

Elsie Fortner lifted her arm feebly, pointing. "Across the hall, in her bedroom ... The shooting must have frightened the poor dear terribly. Please, somebody should go check on her."

Rawson started to do as she suggested, but paused. Turning back, he said, "Why tonight? What happened tonight to cause you to use the gun?"

The woman's eyes took on the blank look once more. "He was heading back to her room again," she said in a voice as far away as her gaze. "I caught him in there last night ... I woke up and he wasn't in bed next to me. I looked in across the way ... He was sitting in a chair beside Adeline's bed, just watching her sleep. But his nightshirt was pulled up and he was—was touching himself ... I knew that, sooner or later, it would turn into more. I told him what I'd seen, told him he could never go to her room like that again. Said what I'd do if he did. Warned him ... Tonight, when I felt him getting out of bed, I turned up the lamp and tried to warn him one last time. He just laughed at me. Told me it was all my fault, that if I wasn't a dried up old cripple he wouldn't have to seek his pleasure in other ways ... He was still laughing when I brought the gun out from under the pillow and pulled the trigger."

• • •

"I sure had her pegged wrong." Miss Maybelle's tone carried a kind of wistful sadness. "I never figured Elsie Fortner for having enough sand to stand up to her husband at all, let alone have what it took to shoot the bastard."

"She had sand alright," Rawson allowed. "She might've been a little slow finding it in herself but, when it counted, she had plenty."

They were seated at a varnished wood table on the broad, open back porch of Miss Maybelle's house. Miss Maybelle was sipping from a cup of tea; another of the fine cigars she'd provided Rawson was burning in a cut glass ashtray pulled over in front of him. Out on the grassy back lawn, in a wash of bright and warm early afternoon sunshine, two of Miss Maybelle's doves were stick-rolling a large wooden hoop back and forth between them. A laughing, energetic Adeline was running alongside the hoop, trying to jump through it without disturbing its roll.

Two days had passed since Rawson's return to Hesterville, arriving in the pre-dawn hours with a blanket-bundled Adeline clutched in the saddle before him. He'd taken her directly to Miss Maybelle's, making sure no one saw them.

Back at the Fortner ranch, Rawson had found the little girl hiding in her bedroom closet—frightened by the gunshots, just as Elsie Fortner predicted. Once he managed to convince her he posed no harm, Rawson wrapped her in a thick blanket and carried her out to his waiting horse.

The cover story Rawson and Elsie had quickly concocted to tell Adeline went like this: Rawson was a family friend who'd stopped by for a visit after Adeline was in bed. Undefined "robbers" allegedly showed up, looking to break in and loot the house. Hiram Fortner bravely fought them off and then gave chase, requesting Rawson get Adeline to safety by taking her to town. Mrs. Fortner, it was explained, had been injured by a stray bullet but would be okay once Rawson sent a doctor back to tend her.

The child seemed to accept these unlikely events in a sleepy, dumbfounded sort of way. Since that night, she'd been dutifully entertained and kept distracted by Miss Maybelle and her doves while being further told only that Hiram hadn't yet returned from chasing the robbers and Elsie was recovering but still too ill for visitors.

For his part, Rawson had left the Fortner ranch without knowing exactly how he was going to play it as far as following through on getting the girl successfully spirited away yet at the same time not leave Elsie Fortner completely in the lurch. Once again, it was Elsie herself who supplied the solution. "Send the sheriff back if you want … I won't be going nowhere," she'd told him after eliciting from him a promise that he would look after Adeline.

A short time later, when Rawson had ridden barely out of sight from the ranch, he heard the sound of a distant gunshot once more slicing through the still night. He turned in his saddle, careful not to disturb Adeline who now rode bundled in front of him, and looked back in the direction of the Fortner spread. The pulsing, steadily increasing glow of light coming from the other side of the rolling hills told him everything he needed to know. With crystal clarity he realized exactly what Elsie had done. As soon as he was gone, she'd set the house ablaze and then put a gun to her own head. Not the same one she'd used on Hiram—Rawson had taken that one with him. But a ranch house was bound to have other guns, at the very least a hunting rifle.

"Send the sheriff back if you want … I won't be going nowhere."

Albeit inadvertently, Elsie had cleared the way for Rawson and Miss Maybelle to complete their covert rescue of Adeline with no questions ever being raised. When neighboring ranchers saw the lingering smoke next morning and subsequently found no sign of any survivors in the burnt remains of the Fortner house, the only conclusion the sheriff could logically reach when called in was that the entire family had tragically perished.

"We need to finish this," Miss Maybelle was saying now, as they continued to watch Adeline and the two doves playing on the lawn. "We need to get her out of here and on over to Wyoming, before somebody spots her and maybe recognizes her."

"And before you get so attached to her you ain't gonna want to let her go," Rawson pointed out.

"I'm already dreading the thought of that," Miss Maybelle admitted. She looked at Rawson sharply above the rim of her teacup. "But what if I am? I still know what has to be done ... And it ain't like I'm the only one Adeline has turned into a sentimental old fool—is it?"

She was referring to the fact that the rough-hewn bounty hunter had refused any payment for his part in rescuing the little girl, instead insisting the money be placed for her benefit in the hands of the new parents she would soon be acquiring.

Rawson flushed slightly at the reminder, but did not acknowledge it. "All I know," he said, "is that I got a team and wagon lined up for the trip, as soon as you give the word. Something else we need to take care ahead of that, though, is findin' a way to ... well, you know, explain to her how she won't be seeing the Fortners no more."

"I got a hunch she'll be able to handle that easier than you might think. After all, it ain't like she had a lot of time to get attached to them, or barely even know them. On top of that, she's a tough kid who's already made it through plenty."

"Thanks to you, she didn't have to make it through even worse."

"Don't you mean 'thanks to *us*'?"

"Okay. Us, then ... including Elsie Fortner."

Miss Maybelle sighed. "Yeah, there'll always be that. My hope for Adeline is that she never has to have any more bad memories in her life. But at the same time I can't help thinking how sad it is that one of the things she probably *won't* remember is the woman—the mother, no matter for how brief a time—who stood up so bravely for her. Yet no one must ever tell her the whole truth."

"Sometimes," Rawson said, "the truth ain't everything it's cracked up to be. Seems to me that if we're able to give Adeline a fresh start and leave her simply knowin' there were people in her life—never mind exactly who or why—who cared about her at a time when she needed it the most ... well, then I'd say we haven't done too bad a job."

Go Away

Chad Eagleton

Mercer didn't speak during the drive. He rubbed the orange locker key in his jacket pocket and stared out the passenger window, watching his former hometown through the nicotine-stained glass and feeling nothing at all. Coming back there, he had expected more than a faint sense of familiarity in the stretch of houses and trailers along the highway. He had figured maybe nostalgia and probably hatred. At the very least, he had hoped for the sort of satisfaction one feels when meeting an old lover and realizing even lust was gone.

Instead, there was nothing.

When they reached the border of the student ghetto and Section 8 housing, they pulled off the highway and drove toward Whitcomb Park. Three blocks away, Mercer could see the streetlights through the trees. The first tinge of memory misted through the dim glow and he could hear the rusted squeak of the swings. Before the things they carried on their lonesome echo drew too near, the car was even with the row of shotgun houses. Raab turned down a narrow gravel alley, and Mercer was again alone and empty, rolling slowly through the darkness.

Midway through the alley, Raab eased over into the grass. He killed the engine and pointed to the long, thin house beside them. "This is it."

Mercer followed his partner to the backdoor. Raab knocked once and waited. The man named Tully answered the door with a nod and led them both down the hallway into the front room where Mercer finally spoke, "We here alone?"

"Yeah."

A noise too indistinct to name came from somewhere behind them.

Mercer looked back down the hallway. "We here alone?"

"Yea—oh, that? S'nothin'." Tully turned his head and yelled, "Shut up!"

The noise again, louder.

"It's just my kid." Tully leaned over the couch and hammered the wall with a thick calloused fist until plaster shook from cracks in the ceiling seams and the single panes rattled in their rotting casements. The noise rose a final time before quieting.

Mercer looked at Raab. The younger man lit a cigarette and pretended not to notice.

"She's like 14," Tully said, sitting on the couch and wiping dust from his shoulders. "Pain in the fucking ass and only getting worse. Boys over here all the goddamned time sniffing around."

Raab shrugged and exhaled. Mercer sat and Tully leaned forward. "Hey, you got kids?"

"No."

"Me either." He laughed at himself, jerked a thumb toward the wall and continued, "I didn't squirt her out. Old lady came with baggage, but watchu gonna do?"

"She gonna stay put?"

"Ain't gotta worry about her. She won't come out till I say and her mom don't get home till late."

Mercer nodded, then listened to the fat man repeat everything Raab had already told him. He works as janitor at The University of the Midwest, in Roosevelt Hall where they house the Bursar's Office, and he wants to rob it. "On Family Weekend this town will swell with mommies and daddies throwing a lot of money around paying a lot of bills. Easy peasey."

"With cash?"

"Oh yeah. Just downstairs, they have a window. Like a teller window. Quite a bit there."

Mercer ground his teeth. "I don't want to rob some $8 an hour employee for the change drawer."

"Who does, right? It's not just the change drawer. We're talking tuition payments, health center bills, and fines. Plus, all the other bullshit they gouge you on."

"We *are* talking cash?" Raab repeated. "They pay in cash?"

Mercer shook his head. "I googled the cost. No way even in-state parents are dropping cash for that."

"Some do," Tully said. "Honest. And we're not just talking tuition."

"How do you know?" Mercer asked. "You're the janitor."

"Cops told me."

Raab gagged smoke.

Tully made a face, shrugged. "Yeah. See, two of 'em show up at least twice a day to pick up the deposits. Here's the kicker—ain't real cops." He grinned, running his tongue across a brown incisor. "University PD. And a lot a times? Student cadets."

"They just told you this?"

"I jaw-jack with 'em. They pull round back where I smoke, by the loading docks."

"And they just told you all this? You didn't pump them for info and then call Raab?"

"There's nothing to pump. Don't hide it—pull right around, park, walk inside, come back with deposit bags. Everybody sees. Everybody knows. Surprised they don't get robbed every day."

Mercer started to answer, but caught movement in the hallway. "Company."

"Huh?" Tully rose, peering out the front window.

"Other way," Raab said.

Tully turned and saw his stepdaughter. He jerked her to her tiptoes. "What the fuck did I tell you?" She fled from the front of her eyes just before the smack. A loud overhand blow, it stung her pale cheek a deep red and echoed through the quiet house.

Mercer felt something dislodge.

"You never fucking listen—never." The girl's eyes remained empty. "Like talking to the fucking wall."

Mercer lit a cigarette. The crackle wasn't loud enough to smother the sound of Tully dragging the girl down the hallway. He watched it burn until Raab said, "So, what do you think?"

"Don't know yet." Mercer got up and walked back to the car. He waited there in the gloom with the cigarette as his only light. It burned out before Raab followed and found his friend standing there in the darkness, the first ghost in the long night to come.

• • •

On the silent drive back to the motel, Mercer remembered his father and the time he locked his bedroom door. That night, his old man had been too drunk to pop the twist-lock with a bobby pin or simply shoulder it open. Other than several hours of door-banging and slurred curses, it was the quietest night he ever knew.

And the beginning of new torment. The next day, sobered and still angry, his father took the door off its hinges. It was a lesson in determined aggression Mercer carried with him into adulthood and prison.

He was still remembering it at 3 AM. Restless and knowing sleep would not come, he quit fighting the insomnia and left his room ahead of the rain. He walked across the highway intersection and bought a 20 oz. cup of coffee. One the way back, he tossed the lid in the ditch, letting the damp wind cool the contents.

By the time he returned to the parking lot and sat on the low stone wall circling the office, the temperature had plummeted and lightning flashed in the distant sky just beyond the city nightglow. The coffee was barely warm and tasted awful, but Mercer didn't mind. He liked his coffee desperate. The familiar anguish comforted him. He and his sister had always made coffee last by squeezing two pots out of a single basket of grounds.

Mercer took a sip, then lit a cigarette and looked across the shared parking lot at the other motel. The only thing keeping it in business was the lounge in the back. There was nothing else appealing in the long, low building. It was badly in need of repair, and painted one of those odd pastel shades that disappeared in the sixties. The same shade his father had kept the kitchen.

Mercer gritted his teeth and watched the people sitting near the window, trying to not to think about anything. Everything else was pointless. Got you nowhere but sad. He had accepted a long time ago that life was mapped out from cradle to prison. Only the grave broke the suffering.

He watched until it started raining. The downpour came quickly, gathering intensity before the first drops plunked on the concrete. Looking but not seeing, he stood and cupped his cigarette in his palm, smoking quickly and thoughtlessly until the last drag nearly burned his hand. He let it fall, listened for an extinguishing hiss, heard none over the hard splatter of rain, and walked back to his room.

He unlocked the door, pushed it open and waited. The downpour dimmed the harsh light from the parking lot to a marsh light glow. In the gloom, he thought he saw a young woman, lying there, shadowed and sheet-wrapped.

Mercer breathed ragged—*fuck*. Inside, he closed the door softly against the growing volume of the rain and the imminent threat of thunder. The ghost faded as he moved through emptiness. Once near the window, he took his wet jacket off, draped it on the back of his chair, and scratched the ink sleeving his upper arm.

He sat and tried not to think about his sister, but the thunder came and she followed. Behind him, he heard her stir. Rhythmic breaths from a long-quiet chest punctuated the rain beat. The bed groaned. Nails clacked against the nightstand. A lighter wheel rolled, clicked, and sparked. Heavy inhale, a red glow and a hazy smolder filled his darkened eyes.

How many times had he woken up to that? Her smoking in the darkness and rubbing the key to the orange bus locker where she kept her secret things?

Aloud he said, "Next she'd say," because she always did, but he let the words hang in the air before finishing, so he could hear it in her voice, in his head: *Go away.*

He had never understood what she meant by that. What or who was supposed to go away? He had been so desperately afraid that she meant him, he had never asked her.

Mercer closed his eyes, breathed and opened them again as lightning flashed in the parking lot. Close and bright. Phantom images silhouetted against cheap curtains. He thought of Saturday morning cartoons and electric shock X-ray scenes.

Mercer felt sick to his stomach and desperately wanted to leave, desperately wanted what had been dredged up earlier in that little house across town to sink back down to the bottom, to rot and be forgotten. He wanted to leave but didn't know where to go. *I should have never come back here. Never thought I could plan something like this. I'm nothing. Nothing.*

He choked his disgust down, stood and, pulling the curtain, looked out at the heavy rain filling the ruts in the parking lot. He watched until the memory of his father's voice, the slurred and slow cadence, filled the pauses between the thunder—*You'll never amount to shit, boy.* He let the curtain fall and pressed his head against the glass, imagining he could feel the rain and the thunder through the thick pane, hoping the fury would pull everything down, down, back down and far away. Very quietly, he said, "Go away."

• • •

Mercer had lived in this town until he was fourteen, but he had never gone anywhere near campus. It always seemed like a whole other world. One that wasn't his. Two days after the meet, when he and Raab cruised around the university, gauging traffic flow and scouting escape routes, it felt that way again. Most of the students looked too young. The rest looked too old. Several were too pretty, like a film with attractive 30-somethings playing the teenagers.

"Before I called you, I went to the library," he said. "Googled Bursar robberies."

"Yeah?"

"Didn't get a lot of hits."

"That a good thing or that a bad thing?"

"Little of both."

Raab chuckled. Mercer tried not to flinch. The younger man had a wide gap in his front teeth that made his laughter whistle and sound a little wet, like when his father removed his ill-fitting partial. "You're the man who'd know."

Mercer had met Raab during his last stint inside. His pod mate at the time had been a bank robber named Harrison Odets. Raab was convinced their six months together had been a thief's apprenticeship, that Odets had bequeathed Mercer some secret knowledge before he died.

He hadn't.

The geriatric gunman had told him stories, but none of them were useful. Just con talk—bullshit about women, crimes, and cops. The only advice he ever gave was, "Don't get caught." Odets thought it was funny, but Mercer never laughed. Ever.

He changed the subject. "Wanted to ask you about Tully," Mercer said.

Raab slowed as they approached the busy intersection near the Student Union. "You mean the kid? The girl? Uh, what the hell's her name? It's something normal. Ashley, I think, but spelled weird."

"I wanted—"

"Look, man, I don't know what's up with that. She's not my kid. She's not even his. I don't think he should be smacking her around neither, but it's not my business. And besides, it's not like he's fucking her or something. Who didn't get whipped when they were a kid? Shit, I wish my old man had whipped me more—"

Two girls stepped off the sidewalk in front of them.

Raab slammed on the brakes. Horns blared as he locked the wheels into a rubber-burning skid and careened onto the curb. "Use the fucking crosswalk, you little bitches!"

The girls kept walking, not picking up any speed until they hit the sidewalk. On-the-right was still a girl. Puppy bellied and awkward in her femininity, trying hard to fit in, she was wearing the same clothes as everyone else, only they didn't look good on her. On-the-left looked like his sister. Walked like her, too. Tall and thin, slightly boyish, but obviously girl. It coated her sexuality with a safety some men found attractive.

Watching her, Mercer remembered the kid down the street with the big Fred Flintstone nose. One day, throwing rocks at the neighbor's cat, he said it was freaky sexy when his sister walked. "A little butch, kinda like a boy, but it gives me a huge boner, dude."

Mercer had splattered his nose before he finished the last syllable. It was the only time he had done something that he didn't remember getting beat for. He had been happy with himself, until his father beat his sister for walking like a whore.

Raab gave the car behind them the finger, yelling for them to back up as he tired to right the car back into the flow of traffic. "Goddamn wonder I didn't hit both of them."

Mercer cracked the window and lit a cigarette. "Fucking teenagers," he said. "Haven't learned fear yet. Most of them, anyway."

Raab cornered onto the main drag and thumbed to their left. "Police station is awful close."

Mercer shrugged. "University PD."

"Cell phones and 911 reach the real cops."

"Nothing we can do about that."

"So what do you think though?" Raab moved his hands on the wheel like he could give it an Indian burn. "I don't know, but I kinda like it. It seems low risk, you know?"

Mercer didn't hear him. He spotted the girls in the side mirror. Watching on-the-left standing there, he remembered the last time he saw his sister. Looking at her in the doorway was the first time he realized she was pretty. The weight of everything she had given up came crashing down on him and he said, "Pretty dies quick."

"Huh?"

Mercer chewed the end of his cigarette. "Nothing."

Raab shrugged. "Well? What do you think?"

Mercer checked the side mirror again and saw only strangers. "Tully's an idiot. And there's a reason why he's a janitor. I don't see a whole hell of a lot of cash. I think we're going to end up with checks and credit card receipts and shit."

"No one pays in cash anymore."

"Plus, we're robbing a state school. That'll get noticed."

"Hadn't thought of it like that."

"But…" He shrugged. His time with Odets *had* left him with something. A hunger for respect. Even if it came from cast-offs and criminals. "Let's do it."

"Yeah?"

"Couple things—I want a campus map and a schedule for Family Weekend. Events and shit. Where the parents gotta go and when."

"What made you change your mind?"

You'll never amount to shit, boy. "No else seems to have it done before."

• • •

The door opened a crack. Through the sliver, a big curl of bleached hair and clumps of dark mascara blacking a single blue eye. "You're Tully's friend," Ashleigh said. "He's not here."

Mercer nodded. "Can I wait?"

He watched her weigh outcomes.

"Sure."

He walked past her and sat on the couch. Ashleigh shut the door, turned and leaned against it, standing there awkwardly in her skinny jeans and shiny black boots, rubbing her thin fingers together so the cheap kiosk rings clinked like badly played drums. "Well," she said eventually, before lowering her head and walking down the hall.

Mercer gave her five minutes before he trailed after her. He found her in her room, typing on an old computer whose internal fan sounded like a dying jet engine. He watched her, straining to hear the music until her head moved and she shifted in the rickety office chair. "Tully be home soon?"

Ashleigh didn't look from the screen. "Hard to say. Sometimes, he'd be home by now and, sometimes..." She shrugged.

"Where's he go?"

"Don't know."

"Why don't you get us some food?" Mercer took a roll of money from his front pocket, thumbed a twenty free, and offered it to her. "You can keep the change."

"I'm not supposed to leave." She swiveled, staring at the bill. "On a school night."

"I'll take the flack. Two blocks down and three over, there's a Burger King."

She chewed her lip until she found an answer. "What do you want?"

"Just a sandwich."

"Not a meal?"

"Just a sandwich. Hamburger. No cheese."

"Don't steal anything," she said, plucking the twenty from his fingers.

Mercer laughed. He patted her shoulder as she walked by. She tried not to flinch and he tried not to notice.

When she was gone, he searched the house. Mercer had told himself he was there to protect his ass. He told himself he didn't know Tully. Part of planning a real job, a big money job, was covering all bases. He was the one putting all this together. He was the brains with the few thousand in cash to back this play at the big time. That's all. Nothing to do with the girl. He was good at lying to himself. His father taught him that.

He moved quickly, starting with the living room. The walls were empty. The furniture cheap. The television looked tax-check expensive. *Thousand bucks a kid*, he thought. There were only two pictures on the small end table. Grandparents on a porch swing. The other was the girl—still didn't know her name—when she was young. About six, maybe, and looking up at the camera the way you did before you were afraid it would capture something you didn't want anyone to know.

The kitchen was the same. Not a single anything from the girl. No homework assignments. No notes. No little photos held with cutesy magnets. Not even a school calendar or a lunch schedule. Mercer stared at the crushed cans in the red recycling container walking down the hall.

In the bathroom, he looked under the sink and rifled through the medicine cabinet. The only thing of interest he found was a mostly full 90-count bottle of Xanax. He dry swallowed one and pocketed a handful before hurrying back down the hall.

He wanted to search the girl's room, but couldn't. He stood on her shag rug, looking at everything—the couple of posters, the two photos taped to the cheap mirror, the ragged stuffed animal perched on the lumpy pillow, the single shiny knickknack on the wobbly nightstand, and the scattered collection of makeup still tagged with burnt orange 99 cent stickers—and it was all too familiar. The desperate and disparate attempts at comfort and meaning conjured from daydreams and imaginings.

He tried to remember what his sister's room had looked like then. But he couldn't. His thoughts were lost in a collection of moments that weren't his, but might have been. Not knowing what else to do, he sat at the foot of Ashleigh's bed and stared at the poster of a young man he didn't know.

Mercer didn't move until he saw the computer screen flash and blacken. He walked to the desk and resuscitated it with the mouse. She had left her e-mail up.

Mercer sat and read until he heard the front door open. He met Ashleigh in the kitchen. Together they sat at the island. Neither speaking, both eating slowly. Each throat raw from swallowing too many secrets.

• • •

The day before the robbery, Mercer switched motel rooms. Raab thought it was slick. Planning and scheming. Covering tracks. Mercer being the Mercer he thought he knew. The guy Mercer wanted to be.

It wasn't.

The other room reminded him too much of his sister. Lying on the bed made his head hurt. When he tossed and turned, rolling desperately after sleep, the springs on the mattress squeaked and each squeak came with a stab that sent his brain going again, either chasing after the ghost of his sister or trying to kill the image of Tully's face when he told him the job was a go.

He had tried eating Xanax to kill his thoughts. The pills did nothing but lock him into a panic-filled catatonia, giving the visions of his sister's face dominion over the width and breadth of his mind until there was no Mercer, only her. Her face. Always her face. Sad. Bloody. Sad and bloody. Bloody and sad. Reflecting everything back at him through the red sheen shining across her cold and slack expanse while Tully looked on, pleased with himself.

Mercer couldn't take it.

The new room wasn't much better. The carpet was shag and it made him think of Ashleigh until he could do nothing, again, but sit and stare out the window.

Through the night, he felt a nameless and blinding rage growing inside him. He wanted to break something, feel it shatter and splinter. He wanted to find someone, anyone—just someone somewhere—and he wanted to hurt them, to punish them with an explosion of savage and graceless violence.

The feeling remained until morning when the horizon brightened, and shades of orange and yellow sparked across the city like a thousand little fires. He watched them grow, flaring into a single brilliant haze spreading over everything like he was watching it all burn. Only then did his thoughts clear enough for him to plan.

. . .

When the MUPD squad car turned down the narrow road winding behind Roosevelt Hall, Mercer pulled from the curb, easing up to the stop sign. The squad car drove over a little bridge then disappeared behind a line of trees shading the shallow creek and the rear of the brick building. Oak Avenue traffic broke for barely a car length and Mercer punched it. He roared across the street, nearly barreling over a bicyclist before cautiously slowing to a mile over a crawl.

Raab should already be waiting in the basement's dimly-lit hallway. Looking ahead, Mercer could see a crew-cut cadet heading downstairs while his dark haired partner waited behind the wheel, chewing his nails.

Everything was on schedule.

. . .

The day of the robbery, just after 3:30, Ashleigh got off the bus at the top of the block. She waited till it rolled to the next intersection before taking the crumpled Blue Devil soft pack from her messenger bag. She lit a bent cigarette and watched the bus disappear down the road.

Ashleigh liked to imagine it was a real bus that had dropped her off somewhere far away like the ending scene to a movie when the plucky heroine finally escapes the small town and delivers some voice-over everybody thinks is clever. She forked smoke from her nostrils and wished she had a voice-over like that. A clever one. Maybe written by Diablo Cody.

But she didn't. All she had was a cigarette. Ashleigh smoked and walked, kicking a shard of broken concrete all the way down the uneven sidewalk to her front stoop.

. . .

Rounding the building, Mercer moved the gun down to his thigh. The officer glanced at him once but didn't spot the piece. Mercer nodded back. As soon as the cadet looked away, he crossed quickly to the car, reached through the window and gun-butted the officer in the face. His nose popped, head rocking back and hands clawing air.

"Out!" Mercer pulled the door open, snatched his collar and jerked the cadet to the pavement.

• • •

Ashleigh slammed the door closed with her heel, tossed her bag onto the couch, and walked into the kitchen, hoping this time would be different, but knowing it would be the same as always. The fridge full of condiments and beer. Nothing in the cabinets but those gross Vienna sausages Tully liked to take for his lunch, a few cans of tuna fish—in oil—that her mother used for her a once-a-month attempt at dinner, and a single jar of store-brand peanut butter.

It was the same. "Some fucking food would be nice," she said and kicked the loose corner tile by the stove. After months of blows, her methodical and clandestine act of defiance broke the tile in two. It split with a heavy clink that sent her fleeing down the hall.

• • •

Mercer secured the zip tie. He pulled the blindfold tight as the mailroom door opened and Raab led Crew-Cut in by gunpoint. Seeing his partner trussed on the floor and another man with a gun, the cop began panicking. His fingers twitched and his eye raced, strained to see as far over his shoulder as possible while still keeping Mercer in his peripheral.

"Knees," Raab ordered.

The officer wetted his lips.

Mercer grunted and moved gun-first, raising his pistol to forehead height. "Down. Fucking down!"

Crew-Cut retreated. Raab stepped on the back of the cadet's knee at the first movement, sending him toppling forward into the swinging blow of Mercer's Browning. The gun cracked against his skull, splitting a jagged crescent of skin across his temple.

"Shoulda listened," Raab said, pulling his zip tie from his back pocket.

• • •

Ashleigh stopped in the doorway.

Everything was exactly how she had left it. It looked like nothing was open and nothing had been moved, but she knew from experience—someone had been in her room.

"Tully!" She rushed to her computer.

. . .

Mercer opened the mailroom door for Tully. He handed the fat man the green North Face backpack. "Help Raab with the deposits."

Tully licked his chapped lips. "Where are you going?"

"Pulling the car around." He slapped the fat man on the gut. "Hurry. Lock the door behind you. Don't open it till I come back."

When Tully went inside and he heard the lock click into place, Mercer took the prepaid cell phone from his front pocket. He dialed on his way up the stairs.

. . .

The 37 dollars and 63 cents she had saved over the last year were still in the zipper storage bag taped to the inside of the computer's case cover. She didn't know if was the best hiding place for her stash, but so far it seemed to be the only place that Tully couldn't find.

Ashleigh added the $11.26 left over from her trip to Burger King and replaced the cover. Without anywhere else to go and not knowing what to, she pushed the power button. The computer groaned to life with a low warble that rattled into a loud and labored whirl of air. The screen flashed twice before blinking to life.

She'd email her Facebook friend. Though she couldn't help directly, the purple-haired Filipino girl almost always made her feel better and, if nothing else, Ashleigh liked looking at her pictures. It was the only time she didn't think about being stuck here, in this town, forever.

. . .

Mercer didn't know they were there until the first squad car raced over the bridge, bounced down the narrow road, and skidded through the gravel to come to a front-facing halt by the loading dock. Two officers banged the doors open, dropping to kneeling positions with weapons pointed through their open windows.

The silence broke under the sudden onslaught of sirens up Oak Avenue. Mercer stood, watching the two cars that followed. They rocketed nearly bumper to bumper and fought for traction as they slide into awkward defensive positions that blocked any attempt at getaway and granted cover against the threat of weapon fire.

Mercer thumbed the safety and dropped the Browning. He laced his fingers, and turned his back to the officers while slowly dropping to his knees.

• • •

Ashleigh pulled the chair from under the desk and saw what had been left for her. An orange locker key atop a thick wad of bills held tight by an intricate web of blue rubber bands.

Slowly, she picked the key up. It was old and worn. The numbers along the side faded to little more than bumps and depressions that looked something like Braille. She didn't understand it and sat it aside to stare at the money. Through the latticework of rubber bands, she could see a hundred dollar bill.

Ashleigh reached for the roll and noticed the small scrap of white paper beneath the money.

She pulled it free and read it aloud. "Go away," she said. "Go away."

You Don't Know Me

Les Edgerton

I shot her.

Twice.

The first time so she'd feel it.

I wanted to talk to her a bit before I finished.

I told you, you didn't know me, I said.

You kept giving me that stupid grin and saying—I lived with you for twenty-five years. I know you.

But you don't, I said. See?

Then, I shot her the second time. The first time it was a gutshot and the second I put a hole in her forehead.

I imagine she believed me now, I thought. For a few seconds anyway. Between the first bullet and the second.

She never said anything, either time. But then, she didn't need to. Her face said it all. She realized I was telling the truth after all.

After the second shot, the one that quieted her for good, I sat there awhile, waiting for the emotion to come, but it never did. Not even a general feeling. Nothing. Nada. That was what I was trying to tell her—had always been trying to tell her.

I sat there, in the chair across from her. From what wasn't her any more. Now it was just a body. I thought about what memories I'd carry with me of her after twenty-five years of marriage.

All I could come up with was our nightly routine. At nine sharp, each evening, we'd turn off everything downstairs and come up to bed. I'd go in the bathroom first, and sit on the stool, lid down, and read something, usually a novel. I'd have my last cigarette of the day. Take my pills. Open the window so the smoke would go out. If it was summer, I'd close it before I left to keep the air conditioning in. Same thing in the winter, for the furnace. Those times when neither was on, I'd just leave it up.

I'd leave a cigarette for her on the sink counter. We kept a lighter there, all the time.

I'd go to bed, turn down my side and climb in. She'd usually have the TV on, the remote tossed on my side of the bed. That was because she'd go to sleep before me. I was a night owl. From my days in the joint. I couldn't go to sleep without TV or some kind of noise going on. Since our neighborhood was quiet, it was the TV's job to get me to sleep.

She'd go in the bathroom and smoke the cigarette I'd left for her.

You may wonder why she didn't have her own. Years ago, she'd quit. Only she hadn't. She just quit buying cigarettes. She just smoked mine.

Depending on the day of the week, she'd have whatever she liked that day on. On Thursdays, it was always The Office, either a rerun or a new episode. If the office wasn't on, it would be Court TV for a long time and then the Identification Channel (ID). Both featured murder cases.

After she finished her cigarette, she'd come in, turn down her side, throw the covers off and lay there. For what seemed all of our married life, she had heat attacks as soon as she came to bed. Menopause, she said, but it was sure a long menopause. It lasted for at least the last fifteen years of our marriage.

Until I shot her. Twice. Then the menopause thing was over and done with.

We watched Court TV and then ID TV for the same reasons. At least, I think so. To watch for the mistakes others made when they killed their spouses. So we didn't repeat the same mistakes those folks made, you see. That's why I watched it and I'd bet the house that's why she watched the shows. I could feel her thinking beside me and that's what she was thinking. I'm pretty sure of that. She'd shush me during the show if I said anything. Didn't want to miss any crucial information.

I already knew how to kill her and get away with it. Several ways, in fact.

A cop told me years ago that all those shows were bullshit.

All you have to do, he said, is just break their necks in a car, stick 'em behind the wheel, and then have the car roll down an embankment and into a tree. Cops never investigate deaths like that, he said. Just make sure the neck is broken in the right direction and you'll be fine.

I had an even better plan. I just didn't use it or my cop friend's idea.

I just got tired of all the planning.

Security

Andrew Fader

A booming sun blazes down on me as,
from a distance, I hear my name called
softly. I grow smaller and more alert.

I pretend the voice summons someone
other than me: a stranger, a sibling,
a relative visiting for the day.
My name announces the silence
that knells between all sound.

Later, I hear my name again
but now I am tucked in safely
under the dining room table,
its cloth hanging to the floor.

A full moon shines through the window
when I peek from beneath the cloth.

It is night already;
except for the calling of my name,
all sound has washed away.
I laugh warmly like a blanket
wrapped tightly around a loving voice.

Planning For The Future

Matthew Funk

Charlotte's stomach turned to ice and began boiling the moment she heard the last bell ring. She dragged her feet down the marble steps of Sacred Heart. Her After School Program made her nervous.

It usually did. The familiar aches were all there: The clench in her belly. The blank space in her head. The chills. Today was much worse.

"Hit me up later, Charlotte, and we'll have a G+ hangout," Lacey said, and Charlotte could barely raise her hand to wave.

Today, Charlotte was almost certain the After School Program meant she and Mama were going to Hell.

Her Mama, Sandy, was waiting with the Lexus's door open under the oak-cooled curb on St. Charles.

"Hey, angel," Sandy bent in for a kiss of Charlotte's brow. "8th grade alright today?"

Charlotte nodded. Words wouldn't make it past the clot in her throat.

"I'm making Alfredo tonight." Sandy pulled away from the curb, smiles all around. "Your mostest favorite."

Charlotte tried to lift a smile of her own. Her eyes caught on the bulge in her Mama's purse. The outline of the gun pulled them in and wouldn't let go.

Sandy's grin splintered when she noticed Charlotte staring.

"Something wrong, baby?"

Charlotte couldn't shake her head.

"You don't want to tell me?"

Charlotte nodded.

"Give a try anyway." Sandy pet Charlotte's platinum ponytail.

"I'm worried about the After School Program."

"Stage fright again? You've been at it two years, Charlotte." Sandy put on another smile, flat as the rouge on her cheeks. "Find your confidence there."

"I saw a video on it today."

"Really?"

"Yeah. Isn't it a sin?"

"Honey." Sandy took her hand off Charlotte and gripped her purse. "It's not about sin. It's about your future."

"I don't want to go to Hell, Mama."

"You won't go to Hell." Sandy's eyes swept everywhere along the gilt buildings and grand oaks of St. Charles Avenue. Her mouth carved into a frown.

"You're going to college. That's what this is about. Getting you the best opportunities."

"Will the others go to Hell?"

"I know it's hard," Sandy talked over her, "but remember Susan B. Anthony?"

"Yes."

"Remember Rosa Parks?"

"Yes."

"Women have it hard. We have to work ten times as hard as men to get where we want to be."

Charlotte hung her head and fused her eyes shut. It only made the cold tumble in her stomach worse. Black space burned in her skull.

"Charlotte, look."

Charlotte wished she could grind her teeth. She wished she could forget the gun. She wanted out of here, anywhere but here.

"Charlotte, open your eyes and look."

Charlotte did. Sandy pointed at the houses as they went by—stately as wedding cakes, fluttering lanterns on their drowsy porches, plantation pale under the oaks.

"That's where you're going."

Charlotte saw. She nodded. She swallowed and could breathe again.

"And this is how we get there." Sandy pat her purse. "We're planning for your future."

"Will anyone get hurt?"

Sandy drove the rest of the way to their crumbling Upper Garden District apartment in silence.

• • •

Charlotte got ready as Mama made dinner in the next room.

She could hear everything through the thin studio apartment wall. She focused on getting presentable—on the task at hand.

Mama had taught her that early: Focus on what you're doing. Not on the past. Not on the future. On being the best you can, now.

Charlotte rubbed rouge on her cheeks and ignored the drunken shouting from Mr. Carlyle next door.

She brushed on mascara and didn't hear the police sirens. Spraying and primping her hair shut out the rap music throbbing on the street. Puckering for lipstick closed her ears to the scratching of mice in the walls.

Charlotte rose and inhaled deep. It almost melted the ice in her. Her hands stopped shaking long enough to smooth her golden dress.

They calmed for good as Charlotte looked at her posters.

Harriet Tubman in sepia tone. Harriet had to be brave. She risked her life for freedom—hers and others.

So could Charlotte.

And next to Harriet, Marie Curie in black and white, who gave her life for science that now saved lives. And Emmeline Pankhurst, whose jail cell was smaller than Charlotte's studio. And Florence Nightingale, who cared for others in a Hell far worse than New Orleans' slums.

"Charlotte angel?" Sandy called. "You ready Freddy?"

Charlotte nodded, staring long enough at the great women so that when she shut her eyes, she would see them. She would see them and it would be like looking in a mirror.

"I'm ready."

One day, Charlotte told herself as she left her room, she would leave this city. She would leave all this pain behind. She would be on her way to a poster on a young girl's wall.

• • •

The ride to the After School Program was so dark, and the sepia portraits Charlotte saved behind her eyelids began to fade.

She felt chill again, lost, shaky. She wanted to cry. But crying would ruin her mascara. And that would ruin everything.

She couldn't stop herself from talking.

"Mama, what's the gun for?"

Sandy drove faster.

"Is it if something goes wrong?"

"It's to make sure nothing does."

"Is the After School Program wrong?"

"Charlotte, Jesus." Sandy's hands were trembling too. She popped her brown bottle and shook out the last pill.

Charlotte pursed her lips. Best not to say more. Mama got testy on her pills.

"Your father leaving us with his debts was wrong." Sandy crunched her pill. "Paul kicking me down the stairs, into traction for half a year, was wrong. What you're doing is to escape that kind of life and those kind of men."

Charlotte nodded, anxious to be done. She wanted out. Away from shaking hands and pain and unpaid bills.

"You're going to be a great woman." Sandy pulled over in front of a yellow house. "For now, just be a beautiful girl. That's what fills your college fund."

"Yes, Mama." Charlotte opened the door.

They traded kisses. Charlotte slid out and made her way up the steps.

She was ice all the way through as the door opened: Blank. Cold. Frozen in the moment.

Charlotte saw the man who led her in already had his fly open. The hand he put on her head already stank. She knew from much experience that meant her time with him might be over quick.

• • •

Sandy waited in the Lexus until she was sure Charlotte would be too busy to notice she was not waiting outside like she promised.

She hated to think what would happen if something did go wrong when she was there.

She looked at herself in the Lexus's vanity mirror, searching her eyes to see something in them that would make her certain she could pull the trigger. The men certainly deserved it. But that had never moved her to action against men before.

Her thoughts slid toward Paul, toward Charlotte's father, toward her own father.

Sandy shook her head to clear it. She gripped the Lexus's wheel. She had to focus on the moment, on what she had to do, on what was important.

Sandy drove to the Magnolia Projects, thinking on how much Oxycontin she could buy.

Things I Know About Fairy Tales

Roxane Gay

When I was very young, my mother told me that she didn't believe in fairy tales. They were, she liked to say, lessons dressed in fancy clothes. She preferred to excise the princesses and villains and instead concerned herself with the moral of the story.

• • •

Once upon a time, not long ago, I was kidnapped and held captive for thirteen days. Shortly after I was freed, my mother told me there was nothing to be learned from what had happened to me. She told me to forget the entire *incident* because there was no moral to the story.

Little Red Riding Hood didn't see the danger she was facing until it was too late. She thought she was safe. She trusted. And then, she wasn't safe at all.

• • •

My husband Michael and I, while visiting my parents in Port-au-Prince, decided to take our son to the beach for the afternoon. As we backed out of their long, narrow driveway, three black Land Cruisers surrounded us. In the end, the details of the *incident* were largely irrelevant. What was done could not be undone.

On that day, Michael and I looked at each other. We knew what was happening. Kidnapping is all anyone with any kind of money talks about in Haiti, everyone in a fragile frenzied state wondering when it will be their time. It was a relief, in a sense, to know that my time was up—to know that this day was the day I would be taken.

Two men with dark, angry faces broke the car windows with the butts of their rifles. The man on my side reached through the broken glass, unlocked my door and pulled me out of our car. He sneered at me, called me *diaspora* with the resentment that those Haitians who cannot leave hold for those of us who did. His skin was slick with sweat. There was no place for traction. When I tried to grab onto the car door, he slammed the butt of his gun against my fingers. The man on Michael's side hit him in the face and he slumped forward, his forehead pressed against the horn. They put a burlap sack over my head and shoved me into the backseat of one of the waiting cars. They told me, in broken English, to do as they said and I would be back with my family soon. I sat very still. The air was stifling. All I heard was their cruel laughter, my son crying and the fading wail of the car horn.

My father is fond of saying that a woman's greatest asset is her beauty. Snow White had her beauty, and her beauty was her curse until it became her greatest asset.

Before the *incident* my mother and I often had very frank conversations about being kidnapped. She was always very concerned with the logistics of the thing because she's a woman of manners and grace. It's the kind of quotidian conversation you have in a place where nothing makes sense and there is no respect for life. She told me that she wouldn't be able to survive the indignity. I told her she would have to do whatever was necessary to get through it because we needed her. As I sat between two angry men, being jostled as we sped over the broken streets of Port-au-Prince, I remembered that conversation. I realized my arrogance.

· · ·

Sleeping Beauty was cursed by her birthright, by her very name. In one telling, her fate was sealed by Maleficent before she ever had a chance. Even hidden away, she could not escape the curse placed upon her. There was nowhere for her to run.

· · ·

I couldn't take it personally, being kidnapped. That is what I told myself. It was a business transaction, one that would require intense negotiation and eventually, compromise. One of the accountants who worked for my father, Gilbèrt, was kidnapped the previous year. His kidnappers originally asked for $125,000, but everyone knew it was simply a starting number, an initial conversation. Eventually, with professional assistance and proof of life, his family paid $53,850 for Gilbèrt. My negotiations would be somewhat more complex and far more costly. A good family name comes at a high price.

After the first stifling days of my abduction, when negotiations began in earnest, I understood that the money my family would pay for my safe return was not for me. It was for the daughter, wife, mother they had last seen. I had become a different person entirely. It seemed, somehow, unfair for them to not get what they were paying for.

After the *incident*, when Michael and I returned to the States, a gaggle of reporters greeted us, waiting just past the crowded, suffocating customs area in the Miami airport. Reporters lined the street where we lived. They followed us for weeks until a white woman went missing and then my story no longer mattered.

• • •

The thing about Rapunzel was that she had the means to her own salvation all along. If she had only known that, she would have never been cast out by the enchantress and been forced to wait to enjoy her ever after with her prince.

• • •

My family hired an American firm that specializes in negotiating for U.S. citizens who have been abducted abroad. They were efficient. Within 24 hours, they had demanded proof of life. I was able to call my husband from a disposable cell phone. I said hello. At first, it was a relief to hear his voice, to remember his smile, the softness of his lower lip, the way he always wanted to hold my hand. But then, he started blathering about how I was going to be okay and that he was going to do everything in his power to get me back. I hung up because he was lying and he didn't know it.

Although my kidnapping was a business transaction, my captors enjoyed mixing in pleasure at my expense. I fought, but I also begged them to use condoms. I did what I had to do. Worse things could have happened. I was not broken. That's what I tell myself now, when I close my eyes and see their gleaming white teeth leering at me. It's what I tell myself when I smell their stink and their sweat or remember the weight of their thin, sinewy bodies on top of mine, taking things that weren't theirs to take. It's what I tell my husband when he thinks he wants to know what *really* happened. It is mostly true.

My parents' friend, Corinne LeBlanche, was kidnapped not long before I was taken. She and her husband and four children lived in Haiti year round. She always swore, to anyone who would listen, that if she were ever kidnapped, her husband Simon best meet her at the airport with her passport and children once she was returned because she would never spend another night in the country. Simon was a fat, happy, prominent businessman who owned a chain of restaurants and gas stations that did quite well. He laughed when Corinne made such declarations. He didn't yet understand that these things went differently for women. She and the children now live in Miami. She called me when Michael and I returned to the States. Even though we said very little, we spoke for a long time.

My kidnappers took me to a small, two-story house without air-conditioning in a cramped neighborhood on the outskirts of Cite de Soleil. They kept me in a back room furnished with a small cot and a green paint bucket filled with brackish water. Throughout the day, I could hear children playing on the street below, music from a house near by, a car now and again, the occasional gunshot. I didn't scream or try to escape. There would be no point. Anyone I might run to would just as soon take me for themselves rather than rescue me because compassion wasn't as valuable as *une diaspora*.

Two years ago, the matriarch of the Gilles family was kidnapped. She was 81. The kidnappers knew the family had more money than God. They failed to realize that she was frail and diabetic. She died soon after she was abducted. Everyone who knew her was thankful that her suffering was abbreviated, until the kidnappers, having learned the lesson that the elderly are bad for business, kidnapped her grandson, who at 37 promised to be a far more lucrative investment.

• • •

At least Cinderella had her work to keep her busy—the familiarity of sweeping floors and washing windows and cooking the daily bread. If nothing else, because she had truly suffered she could truly appreciate her ever after.

• • •

What you cannot possibly know about kidnapping until it happens to you is the sheer boredom of being kept mostly alone, in a small, stifling room. You start to welcome the occasional interruption that comes with a meal or a bottle of water or a drunken captor climbing atop you to transact some pleasure against your will. You hate yourself for it, but you crave the stranger's unwanted touch because the fight left in you is a reminder that you haven't been broken. You haven't been broken.

• • •

Beauty learned to love the Beast. She forced herself to see past the horror of his appearance, past his behavior, past the circumstance of how they came to know one another.

On the tenth night, Ti Pierre lies next to me, staring at the ceiling. He tells me his name, after he's had his pleasure and I've had my fight. His skin is caked beneath my fingernails and my body is stiff. A bruise is forming along my jaw. I cling to the edge of the bed, trying to create as much distance as possible between our bodies until I regain the energy to fight, to remind myself that I am not broken. Ti Pierre talks to me about his life, his young son, how he wants to be a nightclub deejay because he loves American hip hop music. "We could be friends, maybe," he says, "We are close in age." I roll onto my side and bite my knuckles. He rests a tender hand on my back and I cringe, repulsed. It is the closest I will come to crying. These are the things I will never tell anyone.

At a dinner party once, with some of my colleagues and some of Michael's and lots of wine and music and excellent food and pretentious but engaging conversation, talk turned to Haiti. Everyone leaned forward in their seats, earnest in their desire to be genuine in their understanding of the world. One of my colleagues mentioned a magazine article he read about how Haiti had surpassed Colombia as the kidnapping capital of the world. Another colleague told us about a recent feature in a national magazine. Soon everyone was offering up their own desperate piece of information, conjuring a place that does not exist.

On the fourth day of my captivity, I thought about that silly evening, and the new bits and pieces my friends were adding to their portrait. Three years later, I would overhear one of these colleagues, trying to be charming at a cocktail party, telling a precocious graduate student that he knew someone who had been kidnapped in one of *those* Third World countries. When I walked by, he wouldn't have a strong enough sense of shame to look away. Instead, he would tip his wine glass in my direction before taking a long sip and continuing to regale his audience with the few lurid details he knew.

My kidnappers and my family's negotiators finally came to an agreement on the thirteenth day. My kidnappers shared the news gleefully. I could hear them in the next room, talking about all the things they were going to do with their money. Their plans were modest, really, which made it all so much worse. They wielded cartel-like precision, and for a long while the only sound I could hear was the bills sliding against each other as they were counted into $1,000 stacks. This is what my worth sounds like, I thought. How lucky I am.

• • •

A Cuban friend once told me of a popular lullaby from her country, about a mother with thirteen children. The mother kills one child to feed twelve, so on and forth, until she is left with one child, whom she also slaughters. Finally, she returns to the middle of a cornfield where she slaughtered the other children, and slits her own throat because she cannot bear the burden of having done what needed to be done. After telling me this story, my Cuban friend said, "A West Indian woman always faces such choices."

• • •

When my kidnappers were satisfied that I had been properly bought and paid for I was cleaned up, shoved into the back of the Land Cruiser, and dropped off in the center of an open market in Pètionville. I stood there in what remained of my shirt and my filthy jeans, my feet bare, my hair a mess. My hands were in my pockets, my fingers clenched into tight fists. I stood there and waited. I tried to breathe. I was not broken. I remember these details more than any others. Around me, men and women haggled over chicken and vegetables and water and Cornflakes and radios. I was invisible, until I wasn't—until I heard my husband shout my name and run toward me with a group of men I didn't recognize. As Michael moved to embrace me, I stepped back. His expression, in that moment, I also remember. "You're safe now," he told me as if he understood the meaning of the word.

• • •

Alice had choices in Wonderland. Eat me, drink me, enjoy tea with a Mad Hatter, entertain the Queen of Hearts, down, down the rabbit hole.

• • •

I didn't speak for hours, not when I saw my parents or my child, who patted my cheeks with his chubby, wide-open hands. I took a long shower. I washed my hair and tried to scrub away the stink and sweat that comes with being trapped in a dark, hot place with strange angry men. Michael came into the bathroom to check on me, and when he saw the bruises, the weight I had lost, the bowed frame of my body, he gasped. I wrapped my arms around my body. "Get out," I hissed. "I'm not broken."

Afterward, I took my soiled clothes to the fire pit behind my parent's house and smoked cigarette after cigarette while I watched the clothes burn. For years, I had hidden my smoking from my parents, told them I'd quit, but that lie no longer seemed necessary. We ate dinner together that night, as a family, acid burning my throat with each bite. Everyone watched me intently. I smiled politely, tried to give them what they needed.

In bed that night, Michael lay on his side, watching me as I sat on the edge of the bed. "When you're ready to talk, I'm ready to listen," he said. His tone was so kind it made me nauseous. I wanted to tell him that I wasn't the woman he married, that I knew things now. Instead, I nodded and kissed his shoulder. After he fell asleep, I slipped next door into the room where Christophe slept. I picked him up, inhaled the scent of soft skin, and sat on the floor, watching as his lower lip quivered and his tiny chest rose and fell with his rapid baby breaths.

My husband found me the next morning, asleep on the floor holding our son. "You don't have to be so strong. You can cry if you want to," he said over breakfast, as if I were waiting for his permission. I didn't know how to tell him that I felt nothing at all. I held myself together until three days later, after we said goodbye to my parents under the watchful eye of their new security detail and boarded our flight to Miami. The plane took off. My chest tightened because I knew I would never really get away from that place. "Are you okay?" Michael asked, brushing his fingers across my cheek. I shook my head, got up, and locked myself in the first class bathroom. After I threw up, I stared at the stranger in the mirror. I imagined going down, down the rabbit hole of my own happily ever after.

The Lawyer

Edward A. Grainger

A trail of blood flowed gently downstream, pulled by the lazy current of the Louisiana bayou. Slowly it dissolved into the muddy water, telling every creature with olfactory organs that a human was helpless and bleeding somewhere upstream; they could taste the fear. A raccoon dipped its meal of shellfish into the bayou, then sniffed at the smell of raw human blood. It licked at the clam. Washed it again. Sniffed. Dropped the morsel and retreated into the woods. A water moccasin cut across the dissolving blood, wiggling its way toward the far bank. A snout pushed upstream, breathing in the bloody scent, followed by a sinuous body and long serpentine tail. Not much blood can be shed in a Louisiana bayou without a gator coming to investigate.

A thick-muscled body lay on the bayou embankment, bound hand and foot, the source of the blood that drew the alligator. The reptile slowed, wary of the upright human standing over the blood source.

The man they called The Lawyer knelt by the bleeding giant. While his stature didn't measure up to that of the unconscious blacksmith, the Lawyer had the fire of revenge on his side. He worked his fingers into the matted mass of the blacksmith's brown, shoulder-length hair. He jerked the unconscious man's head back, exposing the throat with its prominent larynx. The gator fastened its eyes on the prize and wiggled a little closer.

The Lawyer rolled the big man over. His head lolled, blood still making a pathway down his face from a horribly broken nose. The Lawyer slapped him. It wouldn't do for the blacksmith to die. That would be too easy for him. Another slap. And another.

The eyes fluttered. The Lawyer leaned down to shout in the blacksmith's ear. "Wake. Up. You turtle shit. Wake. Up!"

The blacksmith gurgled. He opened one eye, just a sliver. He saw the Lawyer. He cringed. "No. No. Not again. No. Don't. Mister, don't kill me." He pleaded. He groveled. "Not ready to die." The gator hung in the water just out of the Lawyer's reach. It watched every movement of the two pieces of meat on the shore. It waited.

The Lawyer leaned down close to the blacksmith's ear. "I'm not going to kill you, asshole." He jerked the blacksmith's head around so he faced the gator. "*That* is."

"Oh, God!" The big man struggled against his bonds. "Oh, God. Mister. Don't. I never killed none of your family. Not one. You can't do this."

"You were there. You watched. You liked watching. As far as I'm concerned, that's the same as cutting or stabbing or shooting."

The gator edged closer, its eyes on the meat standing up and its nose full of fresh blood from the meat lying down. The lawyer grabbed hold of the blacksmith's belt and heaved him closer to the edge. The gator hovered. One more heave and the blacksmith's head touched the water. The gator lunged, jaws lined with three-inch teeth clamped over the blacksmith's shoulder. The gator heaved backward, pulling the screaming blacksmith further into the water. It changed its position, biting deeper into the man's arm. Then it started its death roll. In seconds, the blacksmith's arm was a bloody stump. The gator had ripped it from his body and pulled it from the ropes around the wrists. Blood spurted from torn arteries. The blacksmith's screams said he was no longer human, just prey. The gator struck again, fastening its jaws over the blacksmith's face and neck. The roll started again. This time the gator pulled the meat off the embankment and into the water. Mud bubbled to the top as the gator continued its roll of death down, down, down to the bottom of the bayou.

The Lawyer stood with his hands clasped behind his back, watching the roiling water. Neither blacksmith nor gator came up. Only blood, and mud. The surface of the bayou eventually quieted. The moccasin wiggled back across the water. One more burble of blood rose to the surface. The Lawyer smiled. He adjusted his wide-brimmed Stetson down over his eyes, then strode to his horse. He coiled the lariat he'd used to drag the blacksmith to the gator's dining table, mounted the blood bay mare, and fastened the lariat to the saddle horn. He patted the Morgan mare on the neck. "That's it, Redemption, Baker was the last of them." He neck-reined the bay around, and took the levee road to the riverboat landing.

• • •

The Hale and Hawkins stage made its usual entrance in a cloud of dust. And as usual, Scarecrow Jim sawed at the reins like the veteran driver he was. But instead of pulling the Concord to a stop in front of the H&H Stage Station, he drove the big coach right on by to Pritchard's Boarding House, a two-story yellow-and-white building at the far end of Main Street.

Two well-dressed men climbed out of the coach. "Driver," shouted the first, a rotund man in his fifties with a leonine shock of white hair. "Driver. I'd be obliged if you'd toss my bags down. Here's a dollar for your trouble." He held a rumpled greenback.

"Shit, Senator Woodruff. I'd toss yer damn trunks down fer nothin', far as that goes." Scarecrow Jim plucked the bill from the fat man's hand anyway.

"And how is it that you know my name?"

"Folks ain't always who they say they is," the driver said. He pulled a newspaper out from under his offside leg and handed it down to Woodruff. The *Cheyenne Gazette's* headline touted, "Senator Woodruff's Plan for Indian Replacement." Beneath the headline, surrounded by type, was an etching of Senator Woodruff himself, the man who now held the newspaper.

The second man out of the coach put on a top hat as he exited, and he sported a fine hickory cane. He stabbed a finger at the caricature. "No mistake, Senator. That's definitely you, sir." Half a smile played on the thin lips of his thin face. "Shouldn't we get inside?" He, too, held up a dollar bill to Scarecrow Jim. "For my baggage, driver."

The driver plucked the bill from the man's hand and started undoing the ropes that held the baggage in place.

"Inside, yes. Well..." Senator Woodruff glanced up and down Main, which was quiet on that Wednesday night. "I suppose you're right, Mr. Smith."

"Your bags, Senator." Scarecrow Jim handed the two heavy leather bags down. Woodruff accepted them one at a time and wrestled them to the boardwalk.

Smith untied his Morgan mare from the rear of the coach, then came back in time to accept his own small bag. The other passengers stayed inside.

Scarecrow Jim cracked his whip above the ears of the lead team and sawed the horse reins, turning the coach around in a broad circle that barely fit the confines of Main Street. A hundred yards down the street, he whipped the teams around again to face the way they'd originally entered town. He whoaed them in front of the H&H station so the other passengers could get out.

Senator Woodruff, obviously not used to carrying his own bags, struggled down the boardwalk toward the front door of the boarding house. Smith led the bay Morgan to the hitching rail, where he looped the reins. The Morgan immediately went hip-shot as if he'd spent the best years of his life hitched up.

The door opened before Smith and Woodruff reached it. "Good day, Senator. I am Anne Pritchard." The woman stood almost as tall as the Senator, but had less than half his girth. Her face said she was in her forties, but her hands said she'd lived a hard life. She glanced at Smith, who stood behind Senator Woodruff.

"Pardon me," Woodruff said as he swept a hand toward Smith. "This is Tom Smith. He did me a favor this evening and I hoped you might provide him with a room."

Anne Pritchard pursed her mouth. "Well, all the rooms are taken, but I can fix up a couch in the den if that is acceptable. Such temporary accommodations are less than room rates, of course."

Smith tipped his tall top hat. "A couch would be more than ample, madam."

"There's a livery about three blocks back down Main...."

"Thank you Mrs. Pritchard, but I'd prefer that Redemption stay close at hand."

"He defecates in front of my boarding house and you'll clean it up, Mr. Smith." The owner of the boarding house didn't seem happy at the idea of Redemption standing in front of her establishment all night.

"Yes, ma'am," Smith said. "May I point out that Redemption is a she, if you please."

She gave Smith a curt nod. "Come along, Senator. Mr. Smith can come after he's tended to his animal friend."

Smith chuckled. He unsaddled the Morgan mare and threw the horse tack over the hitching rail. From the bulging saddlebags, he extracted a gunnysack that had been made into a nosebag. It contained a good quart of oats, and he fitted the bag over Lucinda's ears so she could eat while he looked into his accommodations.

• • •

Mrs. Pritchard left Smith in the den and showed Senator Woodruff to his room on the second floor. It proved somewhat larger than the normal hotel room, and it contained a large four-poster, an ornate commode with a china washbasin and water pitcher, two cedar dressers, and luxurious floor-length curtains that set off the carpeted floor.

"Thank you for allowing Mr. Smith the use of the den for the night, Anne," said Senator Woodruff.

Mrs. Pritchard swept across the room to open a curtain. "I do run a boarding house, Senator, and extra income in these hard times is always appreciated. Is this Mr. Smith an acquaintance, then?"

"Oh no. We first met on the stage, well, he arrived at the stage at a most fortuitous time."

"Intriguing. Intriguing indeed."

Woodruff poured himself a liberal dollop of bourbon from the complimentary bottle on the nightstand. "Highwaymen assaulted us not long after we left Casper," he said. "Mister Smith appeared and drove off three of the bandits with the most expert shooting I have ever seen. He shot two of the men in the shoulder and blew the horse out from under the third. He claims that he abhors killing and shot only to wound. Damnedest thing I ever saw."

"What happened to the outlaws?"

"Smith left them trussed up by the side of the road with a note pinned to the unwounded one proclaiming them outlaws and highwaymen. He said that stretch of road is frequently traveled by lawmen and they would likely be picked up soon. I, of course, invited him to ride in the coach as we were going the same way."

"He seemed quite gentlemanly," Mrs. Pritchard said. "Not at all one who would go in for fancy shooting."

"He shoots extraordinarily well," Woodruff said, stifling a yawn.

"Oh, you must be dead tired. Let me turn down the bedclothes." She went to the four-poster, turned down the covers, and fluffed the pillow. "There. Now, what time do you wish to arise?"

"Six thirty in the morning, if you don't mind. The stage east leaves early, and I must get back to Washington to vote on the Indian bill."

"As you wish, Senator."

"Oh, could you also package some victuals for Mr. Smith, compliments of me, please? And I will pay his room fee as well."

"Very good, Senator. Would that be all?"

"Yes, it would. Excuse me now, it's been a long day and I'd like to retire."

"Certainly," Mrs. Pritchard said. She swept from the room with her back straight as an iron rod and her skirts swirling.

Senator Woodruff realized he'd kept Scarecrow Jim's newspaper. He sat down in the overstuffed chair near the lamp to read the editorial on his Indian bill. "Lies," he muttered. "Balderdash and lies." He rolled up the paper, smacked his leg with it, and tossed it on the nightstand.

Something tapped at the window.

Woodruff pulled back the curtain to see what. The wind was blowing and the limbs of a big old oak tree brushed the side of the building, making the noise.

Finding the room a bit stuffy, Senator Woodruff decided to open the window. He gave the window frame an upward push. It refused to move. He felt around the frame and found the latch on its top. This he undid, then lifted the window and drank in the warm Cheyenne air.

The senator went back to his overstuffed chair as the breeze ruffled the curtains. He picked up his half-empty glass of bourbon and sipped. A good fragrant whiskey, he found. He picked up the bottle. Old Grand-dad. Not the most expensive, but excellent as a complimentary bottle. He tipped a bit more into his glass.

He did not even sense the garrote that slipped over his head and drew up tight on his throat. He could not shout for help. He could not breathe. He could not think straight. He struggled to put fingers beneath the cord. He couldn't. The world turned red. He struggled for breath, then struggled for life, kicking and bucking and using the last of his failing strength in trying to escape the cord of death. Thirty long seconds elapsed before Senator Josiah B. Woodruff shuffled off his mortal coil. His sphincter opened. His bladder voided. He died, his bulging eyes wide open.

• • •

U.S. Deputy Marshal Cash Laramie stepped into the room where Senator Woodruff had been killed, then moved aside as Chief Devon Penn escorted the local doctor toward the exit.

"Thanks, Doc. I'll send someone over for your report later on. And remember," Chief Penn's voice turned hard, "no talking to any newspaper men, or anyone else, for that matter. Don't want rumors getting started, hear?"

The portly doctor shot a glance at Penn's hard face. "Won't, Chief. Trust me. Don't like whispering in the dark, and you'll not find rumors starting with me."

"Good, good. Thanks again for coming over." Penn motioned with his hand for the doctor to leave. The medico glanced at Cash as he left, but obviously didn't recognize him. Penn leaned out the door after the doctor left. "Mayo, no one comes in."

"Right, Chief," came the reply.

Penn turned to Cash. "A mess, Laramie, a goldam mess."

Cash stepped around the spraddle-legged corpse in the overstuffed chair. "Smells like a goldam mess, Chief. Someone did the country a favor. Senator Josiah Woodruff ain't gonna be doing no more voting," he said.

Woodruff's face was bloated. His tongue protruded, stiff and bloody. The bulging eyes stared vacantly into space. Woodruff had not died a pleasant death.

"Hear the senator from Virginia was campaigning to relocate some of our native citizens to lands other than their own," Cash said. He fingered the Arapaho arrowhead he wore on a leather thong around his neck. "Reckon that measure will never pass now."

"But you're not Arapaho." Penn said.

"Naw. All white, whatever that means. Raised by Arapahos, though. Damn good people."

A woman sat in a chair by the window, staring at the floor and wiping tears from her face as they dripped from her eyes. Penn indicated her with a wave of his hand. "This is Mrs. Anne Pritchard, Cash. She found the body. You can get her statement while I take care of the newspaper people. Damn horseflies. Always buzzing around."

"Will do'er, Chief," Cash said.

"Mrs. Pritchard," Penn said.

The woman made no move. She stared at the floor as if she, too, had been garroted to death.

Penn raised his voice. "Mrs. Pritchard!"

She jumped. Her eyelids fluttered. She turned her face toward the Chief. "Y-y-es," she managed to say.

"This is Marshal Laramie. He will ask you a few questions, and I'd appreciate it if you gave him full and truthful answers."

The woman blinked, then her back stiffened. "Yes," she said. "Of course."

Penn left the room as Cash grabbed one of the chairs, turned it around and straddled it, arms on the back. "Your statement, ma'am," he said.

The woman said nothing. She just sat there, staring past Cash at the horrible dead body of Josiah Woodruff.

Cash stood, took a blanket from the bed, and covered the corpse. He pulled a tally book and pencil stub from his vest pocket, and sat back down, straddling the chair and balancing the little book on its back. "Statement, Mrs. Pritchard?" he said.

"Thank you, Marshal," the woman said.

"Call me Cash, Mrs. Pritchard," he said.

"I'm Anne."

"Tell me what happened. Start when you first saw the Senator, please."

Anne Pritchard recounted how the Senator and Mr. Smith had arrived, and what had happened when she came to wake the Senator early in the morning.

"So you were full up, then, with guests I mean?"

"This is a small guest house, Marshal, er, Cash. Besides the Senator and Mr. Smith, there're only two others. Their names are Gramlich and Randall."

Cash nodded. He knew the two gamblers, and figured neither one was a murderer of the kind that would sneak up behind a man and choke him to death with a garrote. That said, Woodruff was a politician, and that meant enemies. In fact, John Wilkes Booth, who shot President Lincoln, was considered an upright citizen before he gunned down the President.

"What about this Mr. Smith?" Cash asked.

Pritchard perked up a little. "Mr. Smith seemed a fine sort," she said. "And he saved the Senator during a highwayman holdup of the stage." She repeated the story the Senator had told her.

"Do you know where this Smith was headed?"

"He said he was going back to Louisiana."

"Did he say Louisiana was his home?"

"We didn't actually have much of a conversation. He went right to bed, as did I."

"Did he have breakfast?"

"He was gone by the time I went to call the Senator at six thirty, so I must assume he didn't eat. And he left his horse tied up outside all night."

"Hmmm. Okay, Anne. That's all. If I think of anything else, I'll look you up."

"Thank you, Cash. I've got cleaning to do, and should be here at the boarding house all day."

"Good. Stick close. The killer may come after you, too. Who knows?"

Anne Pritchard's hand went to her mouth. "Surely..."

"Don't worry. We're around, and Matthew Mayo's a good guard."

Cash watched Anne Pritchard leave the room, appreciating her upright bearing and the graceful sway of her hips. He turned to the window, rereading the notes he'd taken as she talked.

A rap came at the door. "Undertakers," one of the two men standing at the door said. "Come to get a body."

Cash waved at the blanket-covered body, and turned again to the window to read his notes.

"Draw!"

Cash spun to the right as he drew his Colt, earing the hammer back with the web between his fingers and thumb. The undertaker men dropped the body back into the overstuffed chair and took cover behind it. Cash leveled his Colt, but didn't pull the trigger. A slight blond man with battered Stetson and a modified rifle in a holster against his leg stood crouched with his hand held out, his forefinger pointing like the barrel of a gun.

"Josh Randall!" Cash said, smiling. "Pulling that kind of a trick's gonna get you killed one of these days."

Cash reholstered his six-gun, tossed the notebook on the table, and stood up to meet Randall's firm handshake. "How the hell are you, bounty hunter?"

"Well as can be expected, Cash. Doing fine." He looked at Cash and his eyes turned the color of hard blue agates. "You know, Cash. I seen something last night that you just might be interested in. Let me tell you about it."

• • •

"Cash, this telegram don't mean nothing."

"Lemme see." Cash reached over the counter and snatched the yellow paper from the telegraph operator's hand. "It's just Miles' jibberish," he said. He put a dime on the counter. "Get yourself a sarsaparilla, Henri. I can read his message."

Cash Laramie and Gideon Miles, U.S. Deputy Marshals both, often exchanged telegrams in code. This was one of the simpler ones. The codes were not meant to stand up to close scrutiny, but they served to keep casual readers from understanding the contents. Helped stave off gossip. Cash picked out his friend's message from the clutter of redundant words and words spelled backwards.

THE LAWYER IS WORKING IN CHEYENNE STOP

• • •

Penn read the message twice, the real words written by Cash below the jibberish code. "So you think the man in the stovepipe hat, that Mr. Smith, you think he killed the Senator?"

"Not ready to bet my whole hand on it, but I'd like to find him and ask him a question or two. Up close and personal." Cash smoothed the rim of his Stetson and put it back on his head. "You know, I kinda thought all that talk about The Lawyer was a story, but like some other stories you hear, there's a lot of fact mixed in with the fantasy. Killer all right. But not just one. No one man could do all the slaying he has been accused of. My reckoning anyway."

"Could be. Those dime novels don't help either. But we've cleaned up before, we can do it again." Penn leaned back. His chair creaked under his weight. "You've got an idea where the stovepipe man is, then?"

Cash handed over another telegram. "I've got a gambler friend who says he played with Smith at the Gray Fox in Linden. I'd like to go over and play a hand, see what I can dig up."

"He the same one that saw him at Pritchard's boarding house?"

"No, that was Josh Randall. Charlie Gramlich—he's a gambler and sometimes hired gun—he's in Wounded Dove. From where I stand, his word's as good or better than that of any lawman in the territory."

Penn leaned forward, and the chair complained again. He ignored the screech. "My secretary will give you some traveling money. You'll have to sign for it and you'll have to bring back what you don't use."

"How many times do you think I've done this, Boss?" Cash's smile took the sting from his words.

"Man forgets," Penn said. "Wire me when you know something. Newspapers are bloodhounding, and Washington wants results."

Cash set his black Stetson low on his forehead. He put a finger to its brim. "Yes, sir. Anything you say, sir."

Penn laughed. "Ignorant ass," he said. "Get outta here."

• • •

Wounded Dove, Wyoming, had the world by the tail with a downhill pull. Men knew they could go to its saloons for friendly card games, a little bucking the tiger, and for warm friendly conversation and other things from the doves who worked the floors. Its general store held the supplies people needed. Wyoming ranches were thriving. The winter had been mild, and Wounded Dove the town was reaping the rewards. New people came every day, and a gaggle of pumpkin rollers had taken out claims on land watered by Rock Creek to the south. Growth. That was the name of the game. Growth.

Cash Laramie recognized the town though he'd never been there before. It was the same as other new towns in the territory—lusty, energetic, loose in some ways, hard and tough in others. It was the kind of town that made a country grow. A little wild, maybe, but full of vitality. He pulled Paint to a stop in front of the Black Mask saloon, dismounted and looped the reins over the hitching rail. He slapped the dust from his clothing, then unpinned his badge and slipped it in a vest pocket. Putting a hand on each side of the batwing doors, he pushed them open.

The room, like the town, was familiar. Bar down the left-hand side of the room. Tables down the right. Desultory card game going on at the far table. None of the players was Charlie Gramlich and none matched the description of Mr. Smith. Cash moved to the bar, and the barman behind it moved to meet him.

The barkeep swiped at the bar top with a damp towel. "What'll ya have, sor?"

Cash looked closer. "Ronald O'Hara? Is that you, man?"

"Aye, but it is, sor. Are ye still toting a badge, sor?"

Cash lowered his voice. "Not so's you'd notice, Ronald. Not so's you'd notice." He winked. "Tell me. Charlie Gramlich been around?"

O'Hara swiped the bar with the towel again and leaned closer to Cash. "Charlie's been here all right, Cash. Been and gone. Dunno why he left in such a hurry, but he did. Done and gone, he is."

"What're the poker stakes like?"

"Right now, penny ante. Ain't nobody over there who rolls on the high end."

"Ya got Maryland Rye?"

"Have we got Maryland Rye? Is Hell hot? Do angels have wings? Bet your bottom cookie we've got Maryland Rye. Why?"

"I'll have a bottle."

"Sor, that's a sissy drink, it is. Have something with body, like Jameson's."

Cash shook his head and smiled. "Know where you're coming from, O'Hara, but I've got to keep my head on my shoulders. Can't afford to get tipsy."

"If you say so, sor." O'Hara went to get the drink.

Cash took the opportunity to watch the card game. The players looked like ranchers, except for the house gambler, a man in a white shirt with garters on the sleeves.

"Yer rye, sor," O'Hara said.

"Thanks. How much?"

"Two bits, Cash, sor."

Cash laughed. "Always preferred that," he said. "That's how I got my name." He paid, took the bottle by the neck, and wandered over to watch the card game.

When one of the ranchers pulled out, Cash said, "Gentlemen. Mind if I sit in?"

The card players swept him with hard glances, measuring him as an opponent. All they saw was a trail-worn rider with dust on his hat, black shirt, vest, and trousers, and black boots that had seen better days. Cash's Arapaho arrowhead and its leather thong hid beneath his shirt.

"Help yourself," the oldest rancher said.

Cash sat down and put his bottle on the table. "Five card stud?" he said.

"You got it," the old rancher said. "Nickel ante."

"Fine with me." Cash would be paying with expense money from Penn's secretary, but he didn't worry about it. He won more often than he lost at poker tables.

Over a slow half hour, Cash managed to lose three times out of four. *Not my money.* The men were not good poker players and kept their stakes low. No wonder Gramlich had moved on. He did find out that a man called J.D. Smith usually came in to gamble in late afternoon, often staying until dawn, if there was any action.

"Seems a nice chap," a rancher said. "Plays for the fun of the game. Never seen him upset over a hand, his or another's."

"Reckon he'll be in today, then?" Cash asked, looking at his cards with a serious expression. "Might he play for a little more than nickel ante?"

The game went on. The mousy looking girl who served drinks lit the coal-oil lamps. "Hey, Mona," a man at the far table hollered. "Gimme another whiskey, would ya?"

"Hold your damn horses, Cowboy. Can't you see I'm lighting the goldam lamps?" She laughed, as a floor woman should. Never pays to rile a customer. Cash watched her.

"Hey, mister. We got a card game going here. Wanna watch the butts and tits, go back to the bar." The rancher who spoke was a steady loser, but didn't seem to worry about it. He seemed to enjoy the bluff and counter bluff.

About the time Mona finished lighting the lamps, J.D. Smith walked in. He took a moment to note the position of everyone in the saloon. His eyes stopped at the card table. Two of the ranchers who'd been playing poker had already left, so Cash, the gambler whose name was Henry, and a rancher named Franks were the only ones at the card table.

Smith ordered a whiskey from Mona, removed his stovepipe, and came over to the poker table. "Mind?" he asked.

Cash shrugged. Franks nodded. Henry indicated an empty chair. "Five card stud," he said. "Nickel stakes."

"Thank you." Smith sat. "Gentlemen," he said. "Shall we begin?"

Henry held up the deck, and O'Hara came with a new one.

Cash sized Smith up, without seeming to watch him. Height: five eight. Weight: a hundred fifty pounds or so. Late thirties. Seemed a bit of a dandy, but also had an electric aura of danger that showed from deep within his black eyes.

Smith sipped his whiskey, a slight smile on his face. He kept his eyes straight ahead, looking at a place somewhere between Cash and the bar. Cash knew Smith was watching with peripheral vision. This was a man to steer clear of.

After the third hand, Smith beckoned Mona over. "Could you get me a plate of that good roast beef from the Garvey Hotel restaurant? Baked potato, too. Lots of gravy. Hmm?"

"Yes, sir, Mr. Smith. Right away." Mona hustled out the batwings and around to the restaurant, which was next door to the saloon.

Cash won the next hand. He left his winnings on the table in front of his chair and stood. "Henry, I'm gonna stretch my legs and have a cigar. When I get back, I'd like to play another round. Okay?"

"You got it," the gambler said.

Cash seemingly paid no attention to Smith, but he felt the man's deadly eyes following him as he left the saloon. He reached into an inner pocket of his vest and withdrew a cheroot. He paused a moment, hunching his shoulders to shield the cheroot as he lit it with a lucifer scratched against the saloon wall. He ambled past the window behind the card table and continued down to the telegraph office on Commerce Street. There was no reply to the wire he'd sent earlier. He returned to the game.

Smith was still eating his meal, but when he finished, he came back to play with Cash, Henry the gambler, and a wealthy rancher named Harlow Wilson. Franks had left as soon as the stakes went up. Before long, raises were a minimum of five dollars, then ten. News of the big money game flew around Cheyenne and people gathered to watch the card players. Wilson dropped out, for all his claims of wealth from a ranch in Arizona, another in Texas, and a beginning in Wyoming. Henry dealt. Smith and Cash played.

"What's that I see around your neck, sir?" Smith asked. "An arrowhead. Unusual to say the least."

"Won it in a poker game," Cash said. "Dodge City."

"Is that right? Earp still the tin star there?"

Cash sipped at his Maryland. "Last I heard, Dodge was under the thumb of a man named Dillon. Matt Dillon. Big tall sucker."

"Dillon? Never heard of him."

Henry dealt the cards. Smith picked up his and fanned them out for a look. He rubbed the bridge of his nose, his eyes calculating.

Cash got an ace and some garbage. He decided to talk. "If you don't mind my asking, where you from?"

"Don't mind at all," Smith said. He tossed a card and Henry gave him a new one. "Rayne, Louisiana," he said.

"You're a long way from home, Mister...." Cash fished for a name.

"Smith. J.D. Smith. I travel around on business."

Came time to put up or shut up and Cash folded, losing more of Penn's money.

"What about you? Don't believe I got your name."

"Some call me West. James West," Cash said. "I do some of this and some of that. Up here because I heard there's mining interests coming in, and that interests me."

"Mining interest, shit," said an onlooker. "Only ones making money from mining interests is them with money. Them's the ones bringing in Chinks 'cause they work cheaper than micks or spades. Mining interests, my ass."

The argument spread and the noise level in the saloon went up three levels. Good thing a man doesn't think with his ears. Cash signaled for a card to replace the one he discarded. Henry dealt it with a deadpan face. Smith acted as if they were playing cards on some distant shore with no more than the lap-swish of waves to disrupt the silence.

"Mining, Mr. West," Smith said. "That could be quite risky. Would you be accustomed to taking big risks?"

"Done it a time or two," Cash said. "Raise you ten." He shoved a chip into the middle of the table.

"You really shouldn't do that, West. This will make the fourth hand you've lost in the last hour, and your pile of chips looks rather thin." Smith showed a whisper of a smile, but didn't look at Cash as he spoke.

"I'll damn well play cards the way I want to play them," Cash said, his voice a little louder than necessary. Talk of mining lapsed and the onlookers turned their attention to the game once more.

Smith's little smile remained. His black eyes were flat, expressionless, deadly. On the table before him lay one card face down, a jack of spades, a jack of diamonds, and a deuce of clubs. On the surface, Cash had the advantage with two queens and a ten of spades.

"Check," Smith said. Henry dealt two more cards, an eight of hearts to Smith, a four of clubs to Cash.

Smith's bet.

"Well, West. It comes down to the hole card, does it not?" Smith rubbed the bridge of his nose with a forefinger. "Ten," he said, shoving a chip to the center of the table.

Cash pasted a matching little smile on his own face. "Match ten, raise ten." His blue eyes bored into Smith's.

Smith nodded. "Call."

Cash flipped over his hidden card. A queen of diamonds. "That gives me three of a kind," he said. "No way you can top that."

Smith nodded again. "Almighty lucky all of a sudden," he said.

"Gotta win once in a while. You've been mowing 'em down all evening. How'd you work it so's I'd win, sharpy?"

Smith eyed Cash with quiet disdain. "Are you saying I cheated, West?"

Cash fastened Smith with smoky eyes. He reached across to the empty chair where Smith had deposited his stovepipe hat. Calmly he placed his palm on the top and squashed it flat. "If the hat fits, Smith, wear it."

Smith stood smoothly, his eyes never leaving Cash's face. He stepped back from the chairs surrounding the table to a clear space, then took a ready stance. His hand hovered over the walnut handles of a Remington Army .45. Spectators cleared out from behind him.

"How do you want to call this one, West? You can only insult a Southern gentleman so far, you know."

Cash kept the thin smile on his face. His blue eyes harkened back to the sundance trial of his youth. His face could have been hacked from granite. He opened his mouth, but the double-click of shotgun hammers being eared back cut him short.

"Alright," the bartender said. "No shooting my place up. Understood?"

Cash let his body relax. He retrieved his Stetson and placed it low over his brow. He smiled the thin smile at Smith. "Never you mind, Ronald. Mr. Smith and I will settle our differences elsewhere. Is that not correct, Smith?"

"We will do that, West. We surely will."

"Cash me in, Henry."

"Will do." The gambler counted out bills for Cash's chips. Not as much of Penn's money as he'd laid down, but a decent repay.

"Later then, Smith." Cash touched a finger to the brim of his hat in salute.

"Yes, West. Later." Smith sat back down.

Cash left the saloon, not worrying about a back-shot from Smith or anyone else. And they would have been surprised to see the broad smile on his face.

• • •

On his way out of town, Cash stopped by the telegraph office so the sun was long down by the time he got to Snooker Ridge. Cash tied Paint off the trail and out of sight, then took cover in a jumble of boulders. He heard the clip-clop of Smith's walking horse minutes before it came abreast of his hiding place. He could tell The Lawyer was in no hurry.

Just before he passed Cash, Smith spoke. "That you, Laramie?"

"It is. Just keep your hands on the saddle horn and we'll be just fine."

"An execution? Not like a U.S. Marshal, I'd say." Smith's voice carried a hint of irony, but there was no tremble of fear in it.

"Thought we could palaver a bit," Cash said.

"We could've talked at the card table."

"How'd you figure out who I am?"

"Arrowhead. Heard of a U.S. Marshal named Cash Laramie who always wore one. Besides, James West hasn't been around these parts for years. The Secret Service only scouts the way when the President heads in that direction."

"James West's a pretty common name."

"But you're not a common-appearing man. So. What do you want?"

"Why the stovepipe. That went out with Lincoln."

"Haberdasher friend made it for me. What of it?"

"Josh Randall saw you making a quick exit from Anne Pritchard's boarding house. And I've got a copy of the telegram you sent to Washington. It says 'JOB FINISHED STOP MAKE FINAL PAYMENT'. Reckon the money's why you're still in these parts."

Smith said nothing for a long moment. Then, "Is that all, Laramie. Nothing you've got'll stand up in a court of law, you know."

"The Lawyer, eh? Why would a defender like you start killing?"

"None of your concern, Laramie. None at all. I'm going to start my horse down the trail. If you shoot, you'll shoot me in the back."

"Whoa. Who said anything about back-shooting? Besides, sometimes killing is more than justified. A rich kid shot my friend in cold blood, just because he was Arapaho. I killed him. It was a gunfight, but I killed him."

Smith heaved a sigh. "So what."

"So a bunch of rowdies fired up on bad whiskey and worse opium raped your Cheyenne wife, then killed her and your children, hacking them up in a frenzy, leaving their bodies scattered all over your house. Right?"

The Lawyer's shoulders hunched as if he were enduring incredible pain. Words hissed from his clenched jaw. "None. Of. Your. Fucking. Business, tin star."

Cash released the hammer of his Colt and returned it to its holster. He stepped out of the jumble of rocks and walked up alongside The Lawyer. "Smith, I'm not trying to egg you. I know exactly where you're coming from. Those hard cases that did your family in, they died. I know they died. I have no proof, but if I'd been you, they'd die. And I reckon that's what put you on the side of justice."

"Justice. What the hell is justice, Laramie." The depth of The Lawyer's pain was mirrored in his words.

"I know you kill for hire, Smith. I also hear that you never kill just for the money. I hear there's got to be a miscarriage of justice involved."

"How do you figure that? You as much as accused me of killing Senator Woodruff, whose life I saved from a bunch of stagecoach robbers."

"But you didn't kill those owlhoots. You left them wounded for me or another lawman to find."

"Well. Yeah. They weren't nothing to me. Who knows? They might go straight after some time in jail."

"See? Justice. So there's got to be some justice involved in the Woodruff killing."

"The people he's moving off their land are relatives of my wife."

"And the Senator's vote was the deciding one," Cash said. "But I'd sure be interested in knowing who paid you to do it, but I don't reckon there's any kind of a trail I could follow to the source of that money." Cash sighed, and holstered his Colt. He paid no more attention to Smith while he walked back to Paint, untied him, and mounted. When he reached the trail, Smith was waiting, his Remington in his hand.

"Sometime you may trust the wrong man, Laramie." The Lawyer said. He leveled the six-gun at Cash.

Cash grinned and adjusted the black Stetson on his head. He turned his back and kneed Paint on down the trail. But the horse had only taken two steps when The Lawyer's Remington crashed. A pine bough, snipped from an overhanging limb, dropped on Cash's shoulder. He reined Paint to a stop.

"Sometime you may trust the wrong man, Laramie," The Lawyer repeated. "But this time, trusting my honor served you well." Smith holstered his Remington.

Cash pulled a cheroot from his vest and bit off its end. He rolled it into the corner of his mouth without lighting it. "Pay you to stay out of my neck of the woods, lawyer man," he said.

The Lawyer removed his stovepipe and smoothed it into its proper shape. "Done," he said. "Good day, Marshal."

A Blind Eye

Glenn G. Gray

"Have you been using the drops I prescribed last visit?" I scan her chart. It says Mrs. Jankin brought her infant daughter here to the clinic about two weeks ago. I vaguely remember her but I definitely remember her cute baby, Molly.

"Of course," Mrs. Jankin says.

Molly had what I thought was bacterial conjunctivitis of both eyes. I noted subtle corneal abrasions as well, possibly from scratching or rubbing. I prescribed antibiotic drops last visit. She was supposed to follow-up a few days later but didn't show. The note in the chart indicated that the clinic staff had tried calling but the listed number was apparently disconnected.

"Well." I look down at Molly on the exam table; puffy eyes, red and indurated. I tuck the blanket back up around her chin. "It seems she's gotten a little worse. Have you noticed any other problems? Like fever, diarrhea, cough?"

"Nope."

"She eating okay?"

"Seems."

"Sleeping well?"

"Yup. Seems real tired. Sleeps all the time."

"Well, her exam is okay except for the eyes. And her vital signs and temp are normal. So, I'm going to prescribe something a little stronger. But you really need to come back in a couple days. We need to check. Keep on top of this."

"Okay, Doctor."

I wink at Molly, touch her smooth cheek. She kicks, chubby legs pedaling. Her arms flail in jerky circles. I fill out a script, rip it from the pad and hand it over. Mom and baby are on their way.

I take a moment to write my note, and decide to review the chart in its entirety. I had a feeling that maybe something was a tad off. A gut thing. Missing appointments was always a red flag but people have busy lives, right?

I look at the address. A nearby lower middle class neighborhood. Not that that means much. Mom is thirty-two years old. No other children. Unemployed. Divorced. The ex-husband's details are not listed. I feel like I'm being stupid, maybe even a bit paranoid. But I've been down this road and so have several of my colleagues. I've called Child Protection Services before, only to come up empty handed. And then that family is unfairly flagged.

A case that still haunts me occurred when I was an intern. I saw a baby during a routine well-visit and the mom expressed concern over two small bumps on the baby's chest. The bumps seemed bony and I was not that worried, but I consulted the covering attending physician and we ordered X-rays. There were two healing rib fractures. The chief doctor called Child Protection Services, thinking they were the result of abuse. More X-rays were ordered and several other old fractures were noted.

The parents were questioned and it seemed the answers were not good enough, even though the baby was clean, well-dressed, well-fed, and happy. She even had painted toenails. I remembered the mom telling me that bone problems ran in her family and I relayed that information to the senior doctors, but no one listened. The baby was admitted to the hospital for observation. The next day a social worker informed the parents that due to the injuries and the interviews the baby was going to be put in foster care. They were told making a scene would certainly make things worse.

The parents reluctantly handed over their baby and wept. The parents wrote out her schedule and helped buckle their baby in the car seat. The car pulled away. The mother bolted after the car in the parking lot screaming, "They stole my baby!" The father ran too. They both fell to the ground in the rain sobbing, the mother curled into a ball in a puddle.

A series of emergency hearings were held. A judge ruled that there was abuse and the baby was to remain in foster care. The husband was arrested. The parents fought back. They fought with everything they had, which wasn't much, and eventually lost everything. First their jobs, insurance, then all of their savings. But they didn't lose hope.

After a year and a half, I heard, the baby was found to have osteogenesis imperfecta, a genetic disease that affects collagen production and weakens bones, resulting in multiple fractures at the slightest trauma. Funny thing is, this disease was suggested to the social workers and others by the mother after doing her own research but was dismissed as an excuse; a cover-up for the husband.

After finally getting the attention of a lawyer, and much legal battle, the baby was eventually returned to the family but of course not without significant psychological, financial and emotional trauma to the family.

The case is now back in court, the family suing the hospital and social-service agency, and rightly so. A classic case of misunderstanding and error heaped upon error. And a system all too quick to judge.

I've been overly cautious since. And as far as Mrs. Jankin and little Molly go, I had a baby with an eye infection. As of now, all Mrs. Jankin was guilty of was a missed follow-up appointment. Hardly a crime. And she did come to the clinic today, no?

Mrs. Jankin placed Molly in her crib. Molly had wailed all the way home from the clinic. And it was such a long walk. Mrs. Jankin's feet hurt. Mrs. Jankin didn't stop at the pharmacy for the new prescription. Passed it right by. Heck, she had no insurance. No money. How was she supposed to pay for that stuff?

She had lied to the doctor at the clinic. She did have eye drops left. Just not the ones from the pharmacy. She never filled that first prescription either. She made her own "special" eye drops. Like a home remedy. What did those doctors know anyway? She had plenty of drops left. See? Much cheaper too.

She wrapped Molly tightly in a soft blanket, like a cocoon, to keep her arms and legs from moving around, messing things up. She filled the dropper with a gentle squeeze, then applied firm pressure to Molly's forehead with the palm of her hand, to keep her head still. With thumb and forefinger of the same hand, she separated the lids of Molly's right eye. She positioned the dropper overhead, steady, watched the liquid form into a drop, then elongate and plop, right onto the eyeball.

Molly shrieked as usual, a blood curdling high-pitched sound like babies do, till her face reddened. This annoyed Mrs. Jankin. *What the heck was she screaming at? I'm just trying to help.* Mrs. Jankin made her scrunched-up face. The one that made her feel all put together. She took a breath and let it out through pursed lips.

Molly had a hard time getting her breath for a moment. When she cooled off a little, settling down like a good baby, Mrs. Jankin moved her hand so that her fingers could spread the left eyelids.

From the next room, Mrs. Jankin's new boyfriend Max, who had been trying to take a nap, yelled, "Shut that kid up will ya!"

Under her breath, Mrs. Jankin said, "*Chillax, Max.*"

"Whassat?"

"I said okay, Max!" Mrs. Jankin smirked. Shook her head. She steadied the dropper over Molly's left eye, watched the drop form and ever so slowly, stretch and elongate.

Then fall.

• • •

"What happened?" Molly was on the examining table in front of me, somewhat lethargic, both eyes massively swollen, discolored. There was a new bruise over the left side of her head.

"She fell off the changing table."

I didn't like the look of this. I motioned the nurse over. She came at once, recognizing the panicked expression on my face. "Yes?"

"Call CT. Now." I held Molly's tiny hand. "We need to scan this baby's head."

The nurse darted off and I turned back to Mrs. Jankin, who seemed oddly calm.

"Have you been giving Molly the drops?"

"Yes."

"You filled the prescription I gave you?"

"Well."

"Well what?"

"I have my own drops."

"Your own?" My head hurt. This wasn't making sense. "You have them with you?"

Mrs. Jankin stared blankly into space.

"I need to see them. Please. Molly is critically ill."

She slowly turned, unzipped the tattered purse on her shoulder, dug around. "Here."

I grabbed the dropper bottle, examined it. Clear, no label.

"What are these?" I started to unscrew the cap. "Where'd you get them?"

"I made them."

With that, I passed the open bottle under my nose and immediately whipped my head back, swung my hand to face. My nostrils burned, eyes watered. I involuntarily let out a muffled gasp.

"What *is* this!?"

Mrs. Jankin stared at me, shrugged.

Transport appeared, angling a stretcher alongside the table for Molly.

I stepped back while they transferred Molly to the stretcher.

"Non-contrast Head CT," I told them, capping the bottle. I turned to Mrs. Jankin, my fury starting to take shape, build. "What the hell is this, lady!?" I blurted, losing control, holding myself back, wanting to shake some sense into this woman.

Mrs. Jankin looked dazed. All she said was, "Drops."

I called security.

· · ·

Two hours later I was in the pediatric ICU. Molly was sedated and intubated. The head CT had revealed a small subdural hematoma. The bruise on her scalp was felt to be made from an open hand.

She was going to be okay. At least as far as the bleed goes.

Earlier, I sent the homemade drops to the hospital lab for stat analysis. The head tech called me frantically a short time later; given the slip we sent for request stated: "Evaluate contents of eye drops."

"You wrote that these are eye drops?" The tech said over the phone.

"Yeah." I couldn't see his face but I could pretty much guess the expression by the sound of his voice. "What's in it?"

"Oh boy," he said, probably shaking his head. "You ready?"

"Yeah."

"Bleach."

"Bleach?"

"Yup," he said. "Pure… household… bleach."

Silence.

"You okay, Doc?"

"I guess."

After I hung up, I could hardly talk. I took a few minutes, then called the security office. Broke the news. Social Services was already there. Mrs. Jankin was subsequently taken into police custody.

I rushed up to the ICU.

I looked at Molly there in the bed, intubated, swollen slit-like eyes, bruised head. My heart sunk.

Pure bleach?

I'm not sure how much vision little Molly lost at this point, but there's a good chance she'll be totally blind.

I fought back tears.

Could I have done more?

I shook my head, ran a finger along Molly's cheek. Never again was I going to question my gut. The monitors buzzed and hummed. Molly's limbs lacked the usual excited baby kicks, swings and jabs. Her arms slumped at her sides, due to sedation, the small endotracheal tube jutting from her lips, taped to her cheek. Her bulbous eyes crusted, glistening from ointment. I cursed under my breath, my fists balled.

I decided right there in the ICU, that from now on, I had a new mission. I wasn't going to let gut feelings go unchecked. I wouldn't let someone I had a strange feeling about just walk away without at least discussing it with a colleague or some other third party. Without probing just a bit deeper. From this moment on, I would err on the side of ultra-protector.

For Molly.

Lettie In The Ozarks

Jane Hammons

After the government mowed their houses under along with shriveled stalks of corn, everybody went to California to pick things she'd never heard of.

Artichokes and avocados.

Or tasted.

Limes and grapefruits.

So she followed the old ones to their house in the mountains because it was in the opposite direction of California, a place too far from home.

But the old people's house in the Ozarks is just something made of skins hung over planks nailed together at the front of a cave. For food, they cook leaves and berries in steamy pots of nothing, strip pieces and parts from carcasses piled like cordwood at the back of the cave. Everything smells like blood dried up and underground. A wisp of smoke threads the air. The old ones wrap Lettie in animal hides. Where the paws have been cut off, the skin flaps like useless little wings. Every morning the old man nudges her and puts a sticky bowl of something by her pallet. The old woman peers into Lettie's green eyes and growls like a big cat.

There is not a book to read or one pretty thing to look at except for the piece of teacup she took out of Mama's hand. It broke when Pa shot her. He said it was better for them to die together than to starve to death one by one. Lettie wanted to stay with them, but when he pointed his rifle at her, she couldn't help but run away.

In her pocket she keeps the broken cup decorated with Texas Bluebells like the ones Mama planted in front of their house even though they lived in Oklahoma. At night she holds the rim between her pointer and thumb, sticks out her pinkie like a lady, and wishes she'd let Pa kill her the way he wanted to.

Once her grandma told her that when you are dead and buried your hair keeps growing and fills up the coffin. Mama got mad and said *Don't scare her*. Back then Lettie wasn't afraid of anything. Now when she sleeps, Mama's sweet face unfolds like a valentine in her dreams. She sees her mother's pretty red hair curling around tree trunks and covering rocks like moss. Underneath the ground it grabs on to roots and ties up the whole world.

When Lettie decides to leave, she walks to the door and lifts the skin flap. The old people watch her go. She finds a riverbed and follows it because rivers used to have water and lead somewhere.

Back when there was school, her teacher, Miss Jenkins, had a conch shell on her shelf of special things, and she said if you held it to your ear, you could hear the ocean. The only thing Lettie heard was the wind that howled and blew all the crops away. In music class they sang counting songs like This Old Man, reels and rhymes to dance to, Jimmy Crack Corn and Skip to My Lou.

Lettie picks wild grapes from the vines that twist between thorny bushes. If she's really hungry she eats dirt and all the things that live in it. There are other raggedy girls in the woods, but she never talks to them because they are all her and only crazy people talk to themselves. To keep herself happy she sings *Jimmy crack corn and I don't care Jimmy crack corn and I don't care Jimmy crack corn* and with every step she drops words like breadcrumbs along a trail to an old story she's forgetting but it doesn't matter because it can't take her home and nobody is looking for her anyway.

1983
Amber Keller

"Reggie!"

Troy sat on his bike in Reggie's driveway, the sun beating high in the sky, baking Troy's skin to a deeper golden brown. Football practice had started a few weeks ago, signaling the inevitable end to summer vacation.

This summer, the boys had found an abandoned rock quarry where they spent most of their time. As a bonus, the rain had gathered in the bottom of the large pit and provided the perfect place to swim on hot days.

"Hang on, hang on!" Reggie's squeaky voice came from the depths of his house. Soon a small figure appeared from the darkness of the open garage. "And I told you to call me Grandmaster G."

Troy choked back a laugh. He knew that Reggie was desperate to be seen as a cool kid, always had been, but the irony was that somehow, defying the laws of the universe, he was a geek yet the coolest geek at school. And he was way more comfortable being him than the cool kids ever were.

Troy was a jock and big for his age. At 14 he was already 5'11" and he weighed 185 pounds. He was pure muscle. The girls loved him, but he was incredibly, painfully shy. At 130 pounds and barely five foot tall, Reggie was a stick next to Troy, his polar opposite. Troy had always felt protective over Reggie since they'd met years before, but Reggie never really needed him. He did pretty good on his own. Reggie had a smooth way of talking that inevitably worked magic on the girls. Reggie liked to give him hell about his shyness.

Reggie pushed his bike out of the garage and into the sun with a backpack slung over one shoulder.

Reggie's mom appeared in an upstairs window, waving at Troy. "Hi Troy! Sorry he kept you. Reggie had to finish his chocolate chip cookies. Do you want some? They're fresh out of the oven."

"No thanks, Mrs. Taylor." Reggie's mom was almost perfect. She looked like June Cleaver and was always baking things in the kitchen. Most of the time their house smelled of warm apples and cinnamon, and it seemed like there was always a roast on the table waiting as soon as Reggie's dad got home from work. Troy had wished she had been his mom since he had met Reggie in kindergarten.

She waved her goodbyes to the boys and shut the curtain, disappearing into the darkness of the room.

"What's in there?" asked Troy nodding at the backpack.

"This is a surprise." Reggie grinned his best opossum eating shit out of a barrel grin and patted his backpack. Troy shook his head. Reggie never failed to have something up his sleeve. Reggie pushed his glasses up his nose and hopped on his bike.

The ride to the quarry was nice. On these late summer days the air felt like an oven, and the breeze folded around their faces. They hopped over the curbs and swerved around trashcans, cutting to the alleyway. Taking the shortcut behind old lady Stendman's house allowed them to get a great view of the pool in the Taylor's back yard, and that meant they might have the chance to see Trisha in a bikini. Troy would sneak the quickest of peeks, and then look down at his handlebars, but Reggie being Reggie would wink and nod, sometimes adding a cool, "Hey babe," for prosperity's sake. Troy had heard her giggles and knew that she liked their little visits. This route hadn't let them down too much this summer, and today was no different, except today there was someone with her. It was Ashleigh.

Ashleigh was beautiful. She had long brown hair the color of a chestnut that ended in deep, curling waves down her back. Her deep brown eyes were almond shaped and fringed with thick, dark eyelashes, and her skin was the color of peaches and cream. Troy had liked her for the last year, but didn't have the courage to tell her. They sat next to each other every day last year in English, and Troy could smell the perfume she wore. He always made it a point to take a deep breath before he got up to leave the class each day. She never knew.

When Ashleigh saw Troy, her eyebrows raised in surprise then just as quickly came down and her mouth formed the largest of smiles. Trisha glanced back at Ashleigh and a moment passed between them that spoke in silent volumes.

Troy could hear his heart beat in his ear, rushing like rapids on a river. Spots formed in his eyes, and he thought he might faint. He recovered before Reggie had even turned his head back to the road.

When they were out of earshot Reggie said, "Damn, Trisha's so fine. You just let her get a few years on her and..." His voice trailed off and Troy saw that Reggie's eyes were glazed over.

Troy was still fighting to regain his breath, but was able to choke out, "What do you know about a few years?"

"Girls only get better, you know. We've gotta be patient, savor them like a good cheese."

This time Troy let his laugh go. His tension released with the laugh, and it went on a little longer than it should have. When he caught his breath, he could see from Reggie's cool expression that he had been serious. "Don't you mean a fine wine or something?"

Reggie's eyes narrowed. "You're never going to get anywhere if you don't take this serious," he said with a solemn look. Troy felt like he was being lectured by his coach.

"Yeah, yeah, I got it. Cheese." Again Troy let loose with a burst of laughter.

Reggie joined in soon after and they rode the rest of the way laughing.

At the quarry there was plenty of abandoned equipment sitting around. The two of them hung out today on the side of the big rock crushing machine.

Reggie opened his backpack and pulled out one of his dad's Playboy magazines and an opened pack of cigarettes.

"Where'd you get the cigarettes?" asked Troy.

"My uncle left them at the house months ago. For some reason my mom put them in a drawer in the kitchen. I guess she thought she would give them to him when he came back, but he hasn't been over since." He slid one out and flicked a lighter, holding it to the end.

Reggie took a deep draw on the cigarette and his face turned bright red. He let out a succession of short, barking coughs and spit went flying. When he caught his breath again, Reggie handed the cigarette over to Troy.

"You don't need this stuff," said Troy, chucking it out into the deepest end of the quarry.

Reggie smiled slyly and said, "Yeah. I think you're right." He followed with another round of coughs.

Reggie settled down on the crusher with the Playboy and Troy hung over the edge, scooping up rocks and seeing how far he could throw them.

They had been there a long time when a familiar voice broke the silence.

"Hey pansies."

It was Troy's older brother Sam and his loser friend, Larry.

Troy knew this was no good. Sam never came to the quarry.

"I've been looking for you," said Sam. He was clumsily walking over the rocks and kept twitching and pulling at the bottom of his shirt.

Troy sat up straight and looked back at Reggie who was stuffing the magazine and cigarettes into the backpack. He finished and scooted back against the metal.

Sam made his way to the machine and stood with his hip pointed out, his fists balled. Larry was jumping and running erratically behind him, whooping cries of nonsense. They were messed up and Troy didn't like it one bit.

Sam inched forward into the shadow of the crusher and Troy could see white powder lined around his nostrils and on his upper lip.

Reggie sang a Grandmaster Flash verse in a low voice, "White lines, blowing through my mind."

"What'd you say, you little punk?" Sam moved forward lifting his fist.

Reggie said nothing.

Troy felt his cheeks burn. Sam had been rough on him for many years. He held a power over him. Troy saw how his mom had struggled since their dad left and if he complained about how Sam treated him it only made it harder on her. He had told her once and the beating that Sam gave him after was unforgettable. Sam also knew how to hit him so that there were no marks their mother would see. His ribs were still sore from one of Sam's outbursts a few days ago.

"Why were you looking for me?" asked Troy, trying to take Sam's attention away from Reggie. If Sam got hold of Reggie, he was afraid he might kill him. Sam wasn't half as big as Troy, but Reggie was small, and Sam, when he was hopped up on something, could be amazingly strong.

"Hey Larry," Sam said, turning to look at his friend who was playing a particularly vicious air guitar. "Why don't you come over here and teach his little friend some manners?"

Larry slowly made his way to the crusher, now fake drumming in the air and wailing some unnamable tune in a whisper-like voice.

Reggie moved his feet, scooting as far back as he could. Troy knew he was scared, and inside a voice screamed at him to do something, to buck up and take care of Sam once and for all. At the same time, a picture of his mother's red and cracked knuckles, the dark bags under her eyes, and her bent back flashed through his head. He fought his silent war as Larry hopped up onto the platform and grabbed Reggie by the shoulder, lifting him half way up into the air.

Troy jumped to his feet before he realized it.

"Let him go!" Troy yelled at Larry, but Larry ignored him and hit Reggie hard in the nose. Reggie squeaked and his glasses flew off his head. Reggie's hands went to his face, streaking the blood that had spurted onto his cheeks.

Troy ran toward Larry and was caught off guard when Sam reached through the handrails and pulled on his feet. Troy went sprawling to the ground, banging his shoulder on the metal floor, knocking the breath out of him when he landed.

Sam turned around and threw his hands high into the air, raising his arms in victory, and let out a whoop.

"Touchdown!"

Troy watched Sam dance on the rocks, kicking his feet up and laughing with joy at the cleverness of tripping Troy.

When Troy looked back and saw Reggie, his head bent down, with blood trickling between his fingers, something snapped in him.

In one quick move, Troy rolled and slid off the side of the crusher. When his feet hit the ground, he ran straight at Sam's back.

Troy ducked and tucked his head, hugging his arms around Sam's thighs. They both tumbled forward and slammed into the rocks, with Troy landing on top.

"I'm going to kill you!" Sam screamed in a high-pitched voice.

Troy didn't hear him; he only rode the anger and rage that coursed through him. He flipped Sam over with one strong arm and saw that his face was cut in several places from the rocks. Sam gave a feeble swing at Troy, but Troy grabbed his fist in his and squeezed.

As Sam cried out in pain, blood dripped into his mouth and over his teeth, leaving a dark red trail.

Troy used his free hand to punch Sam in the face two times, his arm moving in a blur. All of the anger and resentment he had harbored over the years welled up inside of him, spilling over and into his arms. And he didn't even care. Sam went quiet after the third punch. Troy heard nothing and saw nothing as he swung repeatedly.

"Hey man, get off him." Larry's voice sounded like it was under water. The sound snapped Troy back into the world, his eyes slowly coming back into focus, and he saw Sam's red, swollen face. The white powder under his nose was now stained pink.

Sam moaned and shook his head.

Larry walked the long way around Troy to avoid him and got behind Sam to lift him up.

Sam had trouble staying on his feet, so Larry propped him up.

Troy stood up and faced them both.

"Never try to hit me again," he said, staring straight at Sam.

Sam's eyes were wide in terror and he spit out what looked like a bloody tooth.

Troy didn't move.

Larry dragged Sam out of the quarry and Troy didn't move until they were out of sight.

Reggie's hand on his shoulder caused Troy to jump.

"You did good, man. He had it coming." Reggie smiled up at Troy with blood smeared cheeks. Reggie's nose had a small nick across the bridge and was starting to swell. When he spoke, his d's were coming out as th's. "You had to do it."

Troy knew he was right. Sam would have continued to hit him as long as he allowed it, but he wouldn't allow it anymore. He felt strong, like his chest had been inflated and his muscles were bulging. He felt alive. Suddenly remembering that Larry had hit Reggie, Troy asked, "Are you ok?"

"Yeah. Guys with broken noses are always more sexy to the girls." He put his fingers lightly on his nose. Leave it up to Reggie to make a broken nose about girls, Troy thought with a smile.

"Come on, let's go." Reggie put his glasses back on and turned back to the crusher, slinging his backpack over his shoulder.

Troy said, "Let's go back by Trisha's. I want to see if Ashleigh wants to go see a movie this weekend."

Reggie's head snapped toward Troy. Lifting one eyebrow he said, "Are *you* feeling ok?"

Troy smiled and squinted into the setting sun.

"Sure, Grandmaster G. I feel great."

Reggie grinned and started singing. "It's like a jungle sometimes it makes me wonder."

They jumped on their bikes and rode out of the quarry, heading toward Trisha's house.

The Boy Who Became Invisible

Joe R. Lansdale

The place where I grew up was a little town called Marvel Creek. Not much happened there that is well remembered by anyone outside of the town. But things went on, and what I'm aware of now is how much things really don't change. We just know more than we used to because there are more of us, and we have easier ways to communicate excitement and misery than in the old days.

Marvel Creek was nestled along the edge of the Sabine River, which is not a wide river, and as rivers go, not that deep, except in rare spots, but it is a long river, and it winds all through East Texas. Back then there were more trees than now, and where wild animals ran, concrete and houses shine bright in the sunlight.

Our little school wasn't much, and I hated going. I liked staying home and reading books I wanted to read, and running the then considerable woods and fishing the creeks for crawdads. Summers and afternoons and weekends I did that with my friend Jesse. I knew Jesse's parents lived differently than we did, and though we didn't have money, and would probably have been called poor by the standards of the early sixties, Jesse's family still lived out on a farm where they used an outhouse and plowed with mules, raised most of the food they ate, drew water from a well, but curiously, had electricity and a big tall TV antennae that sprouted beside their house and could be adjusted for better reception by reaching through the living room window and turning it with a twist of the hands. Jesse's dad was quick to use the razor strop on Jesse's butt and back for things my parents would have thought unimportant, or at worse, an offense that required words, not blows.

Jesse and I liked to play Tarzan, and we took turns at it until we finally both decided to be Tarzan, and ended up being Tarzan twins. It was a great mythology we created and we ran the woods and climbed trees, and on Saturday we watched Jungle Theater at my house, which showed, if we were lucky, Tarzan or Jungle Jim movies, and if not so lucky, Bomba movies.

About fifth grade there was a shift in dynamics. Jesse's poverty began to be an issue for some of the kids at school. He brought his lunch in a sack, since he couldn't afford the cafeteria, and all his clothes came from the Salvation Army. He arrived at history class one morning wearing socks with big S's on them, which stood for nothing related to him, and they immediately became the target of James Willeford and Ronnie Kenn. They made a remark about how the S stood for Sardines, which would account for how Jesse smelled, and sadly, I remember thinking at that age that was a pretty funny crack until I looked at Jesse's slack, white face and saw him tremble beneath that patched Salvation Army shirt.

Our teacher came in then, Mr. Waters, and he caught part of the conversation. He said, "Those are nice socks, you got there, Jesse. Not many people can have monogrammed socks. It's a sign of sophistication, something a few around here lack."

It was a nice try, but I think it only made Jesse feel all the more miserable, and he put his head down on his desk and didn't lift it the entire class, and Mr. Waters didn't say a word to him. When class was over, Jesse was up and out, and as I was leaving, Mr. Waters caught me by the arm. "I saw you laughing when I came in. You been that boy's friend since the two of you were knee high to a legless grasshopper."

"I didn't mean to," I said. "I didn't think."

"Yeah, well, you ought to."

That hit me pretty hard, but I'm ashamed to say not hard enough.

• • •

I don't know when it happened, but it got so when Jesse came over I found things to do. Homework, or some chore around the house, which was silly, because unlike Jesse, I didn't really have any chores. In time he quit stopping by, and I would see him in the halls at school, and we'd nod at each other, but seldom speak.

The relentless picking and nagging from James and Ronnie continued, and as they became interested in girls, it increased. And Marilyn Townsend didn't help either. She was a lovely young thing and as cruel as they were.

One day, Jesse surprised us by coming to the cafeteria with his sack lunch. He usually ate outside on one of the stoops, but he came in this day and sat at a table by himself, and when Marilyn went by he watched her, and when she came back with her tray, he stood up and smiled, politely asked if she would like to sit with him.

She laughed. I remember that laugh to this day. It was as cold as a knife blade in the back and easily as sharp. I saw Jesse's face drain until it was white, and she went on by laughing, not even saying a word, just laughing, and pretty soon everyone in the place was laughing, and Marilyn came by me, and she looked at me, and heaven help me, I saw those eyes of hers and those lips, and whatever made all the other boys jump did the same to me…and I laughed.

Jesse gathered up his sack and went out.

• • •

It was at this point that James and Ronnie came up with a new approach. They decided to treat Jesse as if he were a ghost, as if he were invisible. We were expected to do the same. So as not to be mean to Jesse, but being careful not to burn my bridges with the in-crowd, I avoided him altogether. But there were times, here and there, when I would see him walking down the hall, and on the rare occasions when he spoke, students pretended not to hear him, or James would respond with some remark like, "Do you hear a duck quacking?"

When Jesse spoke to me, if no one was looking, I would nod.

This went on into the ninth grade, and it became such a habit, it was as if Jesse didn't exist, as if he really were invisible. I almost forgot about him, though I did note in math class one day there were stripes of blood across his back, seeping through his old worn shirt. His father and the razor strop. Jesse had nowhere to turn.

One afternoon I was in the cafeteria, just about to get in line, when Jesse came in carrying his sack. It was the first time he'd been there since the incident with Marilyn some years before. I saw him come in, his head slightly down, walking as if on a mission. As he came near me, for the first time in a long time, for no reason I can explain, I said, "Hi, Jesse."

He looked up at me surprised, and nodded, the way I did to him in the hall, and kept walking.

There was a table in the center of the cafeteria, and that was the table James and Ronnie and Marilyn had claimed, and as Jesse came closer, for the first time in a long time, they really saw him. Maybe it was because they were surprised to see him and his paper sack in a place he hadn't been in ages. Or maybe they sensed something. Jesse pulled a small revolver from his sack and before anyone knew what was happening, he fired three times, knocking all three of them to the floor. The place went nuts, people running in all directions. Me, I froze.

Then, like a soldier, he wheeled and marched back my way. As he passed me, he turned his head, smiled, said, "Hey, Hap," then he was out the door. I wasn't thinking clearly, because I turned and went out in the hall behind him, and the history teacher, Mr. Waters, saw him with the gun, said something, and the gun snapped again, and Waters went down. Jesse walked all the way to the double front door, which was flung wide open at that time of day, stepped out

into the light and lifted the revolver. I heard it pop and saw his head jump and
he went down. My knees went out from under me and I sat down right there
in the hall, unable to move.

• • •

When they went out to tell his parents what had happened to him, that Marilyn was disfigured, Ronnie wounded, and James and Mr. Waters were dead,
they discovered them in bed where Jesse had shot them in their sleep.

The razor strop lay across them like a dead snake.

Take It Like A Man

Frank Larnerd

Squeak tried to make himself invisible.

He was small, even for a seventh grader with soft brown eyes and large ears that he hadn't grown into. He sat quietly with his hands in the pockets of his grey hoodie, head down, concentrating. There were more insults from the back of the bus, but Squeak ignored them. He imagined fading away, leaving only his Ben-10 book bag behind on the seat. If they couldn't see him, they couldn't hurt him.

"Don't you hear me, gaywad?" The stocky red-headed ninth grader said. "I asked you if your mom gives good blowjobs."

Squeak wasn't sure what the kid's real name was, all the kids at the trailer park just called him "Stomper." He was two heads taller than Squeak and a hundred pounds heavier with thick shoulders and solid arms.

Squeak kept his head down, focusing his eyes on the tips of his Nike rip-offs, focusing on turning them invisible.

The ginger kid came toward him, as the bus hobbled past the bowling alley and the Pristine Tanning Salon. Grinning, Stomper picked Squeak's bag off the seat and slid it down the aisle to the back of the bus.

Stomper dropped into the seat, smiling. Squeak cringed, but didn't look up.

"With those big fucking ears, you'd think you could hear better." Stomper gave Squeak's ear a flick.

"Just leave me alone," Squeak said, ashamed of how weak his own voice sounded.

Smiling, Stomper patted Squeak on the head. "I'll leave you alone, after you sing The Mouse Song."

"Please."

Stomper slammed a freckled hand into Squeak's face, driving his head into the bus window. He held Squeak there, pressing him against the glass.

From the back of the bus, a Korean kid with a giant mole shouted, "Make that pussy sing!"

"Mouse song! Mouse song! Mouse Song!" chanted a kid next to him with jagged yellow teeth.

Stomper leaned his weight against Squeak. "Sing it, bitch."

The pressure strained on his skull and Squeak screamed. Stomper pushed with varying force, making him cry out in different panicked pitches.

It seemed like everyone laughed.

Stomper let him loose, and a tear rolled down Squeak's face.

"Take it like a man," Stomper said, and backhanded Squeak in the nose.

. . .

When Squeak got home, his mother was cooking noodles in the sunlight of the kitchen's tiny window. Nana sat on the plaid couch in the living room, clutching a cold cup of coffee and watching Wheel of Fortune with a vacant stare.

"I'm home," Squeak said, and slunk down the hallway.

Neither one looked up.

The narrow trailer hallway was lined with family photos, birthdays, and vacations, all of them featuring a dad who wasn't around. Squeak ignored them, and went into Nana's room and shut the door.

He knew right where to look. His father had shown him the box two months ago, back when his father could still walk and had all his hair. Back when Squeak still had some hope left.

Squeak got down on his belly and squirmed under the bed, pushing his way past pink hatboxes and cardboard crates. The box was still there, dark green and rectangle shaped, wedged against the wall under the head of Nana's bed.

Setting the box on the bed, Squeak undid the metal clasp. Inside was all that was left of his father: a stack of faded photos, a belt buckle, some odd coins, two sets of cufflinks, and the gun.

It was shiny and black with a brown handle. The gun's weight felt solid and comforting in his hand.

Squeak pointed the pistol at Nana's mirror. "I've tried being nice to you. I've tried to ignore you, but you just couldn't leave me alone. Now, this is what you get. Look at me. You're gonna leave me alone. Understand, Stomper? From now on, you don't talk to me; you don't even look at me. If you do, you're dead."

Maybe it would work; all he had to do was scare him.

Squeak pushed the box back under the bed, wondering whose bed the photos in the hallway would end up under.

. . .

Crouching low, Squeak moved through the weeds and bushes, pretending to be invisible.

The woods surrounded the back half of the trailer parks and stretched from Creeker Hill to Morningside Cemetery. Squeak moved through the brambles and thorns, careful not to make a sound.

Through the leaves stood Stomper's trailer, close enough to read the numbers on the door. It was lime green and white, with rusty lines streaking down from its squat roof. In the driveway was a faded blue Chevy Cavalier, its rear bumper dented and held on with duct tape.

Squeak gripped the gun in his pocket. The squirming feeling in his stomach had settled and he felt oddly calm and numb.

"Clint, please don't!" A woman's shout echoed from the trailer, followed by a slamming door.

A man roared, "Get in here!"

Squeak lowered himself on his stomach and inched closer.

"Did you make this fucking mess?" The man shouted.

"I was gonna clean it," Stomper answered, his voice high and shrill.

Something slammed into the wall of the trailer, rattling the wind chimes on the porch. From inside, Stomper started to scream, the sound reedy and fearful.

Squeak's face cracked into smile.

From inside the trailer came more slams, bangs, and screams. Slapping sounds cracked in rapid succession. Squeak giggled and cupped a hand over his mouth.

The woman yelled, "Stop it, Clint. You're hurting him!"

Stomper's screams turned into billowing howls of pain.

"Take it like a man!"

The smile dropped from Squeak's face.

The door to the trailer blasted open and Stomper ran down the porch steps, his face red and streaked with tears.

A skinny man with a dark goatee slung the door open and called after him. "You'll fucking listen next time, won't you?"

Stomper ran toward the woods as trailer door slammed shut.

Stumbling and crying, Stomper tore into the woods, tripping over the undergrowth. He collapsed under a maple tree, clutching his arm and weeping, ten feet from Squeak.

Squeak pushed himself up, and pulled back his hood.

"You OK?"

Stomper turned toward his voice, pulling an arm across his runny nose. "Go away, faggot."

Squeak's fingers tightened on the gun. "Are you hurt?"

"It feels like he broke my arm," Stomper wept, his voice hiccupping.

Squeak pulled his hands out of his pocket and knelt beside him. "Can you move your fingers?"

Stomper gave his fingers a halfhearted wiggle.

"My dad used to tell me that if you can move your fingers, it's not broken."
Through gritted teeth, Stomper said. "It hurts."

"Come on," Squeak said. "I'll help you up."

• • •

By the time they reached Morningside Cemetery, Stomper had stopped crying.

The boys sat together in the graveyard on a granite visitor's bench. The sun hung low, casting streamers of pink and orange across the sky.

"My dad is buried here." Squeak said.

"How did he die?"

"Cancer."

Stomper rubbed his eyes. "Clint is just my mom's boyfriend. My real dad is in Pensacola."

"She needs to dump him."

Stomper stood up and stretched his arms. "She's tried. After he went to jail, she said she was done with him. Two weeks on parole and he's back putting out cigarettes out on my arm."

"You should tell someone."

"Like that would work," Stomper said. "My mom would probably get in trouble and then they'd ship me to some fucking orphanage."

"There's got to be something."

Stomper's voice grew cold. "I'm just waiting. One of these nights, I'll go in while he's sleeping and stab him."

The gun felt heavy in Squeak's pocket. He opened his mouth to speak when a voice made him jump.

"Hole-E shit! Stomper caught a mouse."

Mole and Fangs, the kids from the bus, approached on the graveyard's stone walkway. Squeak's eyes turned to his shoes.

Stomper cleared his throat. "What's up, bros?"

"Chilling," Fangs said as he slapped Stomper's hand.

Mole kicked over a vase of wilted orchids. "What are you doing with this faggot?"

"Oh my God, encore Mouse Song!" Fangs shouted as he leapt on a tombstone.

Squeak slipped his hand into his pocket.

"Just chill. Squeak's cool," Stomper said.

Mole stood in front of Squeak, leering over him. "Fuck that. He's a little fag."

He gave Squeak a shove.

"Mouse song! Mouse song!" Fangs shouted as he danced and gyrated.

Mole pushed him again, rocking him backward. "What are you going to do, pussy?"

Squeak's hand tightened around the gun.

"You're gonna take it like a man." Mole smiled and reached toward him.

Stomper roared and threw himself at Mole, tackling him into the grass. Straddling him, he hammered Mole's face.

"Get off! Get off!" Mole shrieked.

Squeak put his hands on Stomper's shoulder, pulling him back. "That's enough."

Mole sat up, blood streaming from his nose. His eyes shimmered with tears as his lower lip twitched.

"Hole-E shit!" Fangs said and hopped down from the marker.

Mole touched his nose and looked at his bloody fingers. "What the fuck, man?"

Squeak helped Stomper to his feet.

"From now on, nobody messes with Squeak," Stomper growled.

He grabbed Squeak by the arm, pulling him back toward the woods. "Come on. Forget these monkey dicks."

• • •

It was dark by the time Squeak and Stomper returned to the trailer park. The scattered lampposts hummed, casting down pale light and collecting bugs. In the distance a train blew its whistle.

"Katy Perry has the best boobs ever," Stomper said. "I'm gonna marry her and make her my queen."

Squeak shoved him. "You're on crack! Megan Fox is the queen of boob city."

"She's got jacked up thumbs."

"I wasn't looking at her thumbs."

They stopped in front of the green and white trailer. Clint sat in a plastic chair, smoking under the porch light. He flicked his greasy hair out of his eyes and stared at them.

"I gotta go," Stomper said and slunk toward the trailer.

Clint stood as Stomper came up the porch steps. "Where the fuck you been?"

"Nowhere," Stomper said, opening the trailer door.

Clint kicked him as he passed. "Get inside, dumbass."

Turning, Clint's eyes meet Squeak's.

"What the fuck are you looking at?" Clint snarled and tossed his cigarette at the kid's feet.

Squeak didn't look away; he wanted Clint to see him.

"Fucking kids," Clint grumbled as he went inside and slammed the door.

Squeak wandered to the driveway as the screams and slams rattled the trailer. He opened the passenger door of the blue Cavalier and slid inside. The car smelled like old cigarettes and moldy food. The floor littered with McDonald's bags, soda cans, and empty packs of Winston's. Even inside the car, Squeak could hear Stomper screaming.

Shaking, he opened the glove box and slipped the gun inside.

After leaving the car, Squeak walked out of the trailer park. He followed Chester Avenue south for six blocks, past the old folks's home and rows of pawn shops, until he reached the Speedway.

Squeak looked around. A grey-haired man with a bulging belly was filling up his truck. A woman in a dirty orange Tweety Bird shirt stood in front of the gas station, counting her change. No one seemed to notice him.

The payphone stood off by itself under a tiny light. It was sticky and marred with graffiti, but it worked.

After his call, Squeak pulled up his hoodie and pretended to be invisible. He walked past them and once he was out of sight, he ran.

He was out of breath and walking by the time he reached home. From the rear of the trailer park, blue and red lights pulsed like fireworks. A few of the residents stood in the street or craned their necks from their windows for a better look.

Squeak walked closer. Four police cars had surrounded Stomper's green and white trailer. Clint was in the driveway, shouting at the officers, while Stomper and his mother watched from the porch.

A bald cop emerged from the blue Cavalier, holding the pistol in a plastic bag.

"That's not mine, man!" Clint shouted, his voice horse and cracking.

The officer next to him put a hand on Clint's wrist. "Settle down."

Clint pushed him aside and sprinted out of the driveway. He made it two feet into the street before a stocky lady cop Tasered him in the ass. Clint dropped to the ground, howling and jerking as the officers surrounded him. The bald cop put his foot on Clint's neck as the other officers yanked back his arms.

"Oh, Jesus, you're hurting me!" Clint cried out.

Squeak moved closer and pulled back his hood. "Take it like a man."

Stoop-It

Gary Lovisi

Jack smacked me upside the head so hard I swore I could feel my eyeballs rattle inside their sockets.

Jack liked to smack. He was very good at it.

"Wha?" I stammered confused. I was just happy to be out of my cage and working again with Jack.

"Stoop-it!"

Jack said it like that, using separate words: "stoop" and "it".

"Look, Jack, I know I'm stupid for losing the cash and all..."

He glared at me. That was not a good sign. I can be slow sometimes.

"Not stupid," he barked, pronouncing it correctly for once like they do on TV, "but block-head, thick as a brick, shit-for-brains stoop-it! Stoop-it! Stoop-it!"

I nodded. I was used to this from Jack. We were partners. By now you probably figured out that I was the stoop-it one.

We'd been doing jobs all along the East Coast, but it had gotten too hot so we decided—well, actually Jack decided—we'd take a trip out West and check out the lay of the land as he put it. Plenty of young gash and green cash he said out in La-La-Land. I didn't really know what he was talking about, but I went along like I always did. I had no choice, really. So we took the plane ride—wow!—got a place, then Jack made calls to people he knew. The bad kind. Then he began to line up jobs for us.

"Now listen to me, moron! Don't be getting stoop-it like you were back in New York. This here ain't New York City and don't let the freaking palm trees fool you, the skells out here may have blonde hair and perfect tans but they'll cut out your heart, eat it raw, and then crap it back out at ya before you ever know what hit you. You got it?"

"I understand, Jack," I said, trying not to be scared. Sometimes I think Jack told me stuff just to make me scared and then he'd laugh at me, but he wasn't laughing now. I knew that he was dead serious, he didn't want me going soft in the head like I do sometimes. He told me I had to focus, pay attention to business and above all remember the rules. The rules were very important.

I broke the rules when I lost all that cash the first time. Or was it the second time? I forget which. Then I got punished. I don't want to remember that. Jack could be mean. Jack gave me cash to take some place and someone would always try to take it from me, but Jack was always right there to surprise them.

Then he took back the cash, they were made dead, and I was safe. That was our main rule. I always did what Jack told me to do, just the way he wanted me to do it, and he always made me safe after. Jack was happy because he got his cash back from the bad man he had to pay. That was good. Jack liked money and it made him happy.

Jack told me we was partners in crime and partners in blood. He told me we were identical twins, meaning we looked so much alike no one could tell us apart—'cepting that I was the stoop-it one.

Jack always told me I was a shit-for-brains, numb-nuts, brain-dead cretin. I used to laugh at them words because they sounded so funny when he said them. I didn't even know what cretin was. But I wasn't all that stoop-it, and even if I was, I was glad to have Jack to look after me. I called him my saving grace, like mama used to say before Jack made her go away. I think Jack made mama dead, but he still did a good job raising me even if he would lose his patience at times. I mean, I was stoop-it, so I guess I deserved a smack now and then.

Thankfully I had Jack to look out for me. He was real smart, so I knew I had it made.

Out here in LA no one knew us, and Jack said that was a good thing. I shrugged, I always agreed with Jack. After all, Jack was always right and he was real smart. A lot of times when he would work what he called a set-up, he'd have me come out and show myself, then the bad men would all come after me. See, I was Jack as far as they were concerned and then Jack would 'slam the mark with a heavy hit', as he told me. I don't know what that meant either but the guy would go down, made deader than dead, never knowing what hit him. It worked good.

Jack always kept me out of sight until he needed me. I had a cage in the basement and he gave me a bed, and I even got a TV. I watch it all the time. Mostly cartoons. I love cartoons.

I always knew we had a new job coming up when Jack came into the basement and unlocked my cage. Then he'd shout at me, "Hey, Stoop-it moron! Wake the hell up! We got work to do!"

Then Jack would shave me, put me in the shower, fix my hair, and give me new clothes to wear. Clean clothes that I hadn't made any business in yet. When I was all cleaned up and dressed I looked exactly like Jack!

You could not tell us apart.

I liked that. I liked it when I looked like Jack. I felt important. Special. But I don't think Jack liked me looking like him at all. He said he only tolerated it because we had a job to do and we got money for it. Jack got all the money, I never saw any but I didn't care none. I didn't need no money and Jack said he needed money real bad. He always seemed to need more and more money.

My part was always simple. Jack told me two, maybe four times already—made me speak it all back to him so I'd be sure I got it all right.

"The job," I told Jack, thinking hard to remember it all correctly so I wouldn't get smacked, "is we make some bad people think that I am you. I pretend to be you and go where you tell me to go, then I walk around like some dumb-ass without a care in the world."

Jack nodded, holding his temper, waiting.

I swallowed hard, said, "I act…o-bliv-vi-ous?"

"Know what that means, stoop-it?"

"Ahhh…?" I stammered, it was a big word. Big words confuse me. "Ahhh, Jack…?"

He smacked me upside the head. "Now pay attention, moron! It means, like you don't know shit. Which you sure as hell don't! Understand? I don't know why I have to explain this to you every time we have a job. We always do the same plan. It's always the same. They're gonna follow you, thinking you are me, so they can get the drop on you. When they do, I surprise them. Got it?"

I smiled, said, "Yeah, Jack, sure, you surprise them."

I didn't let on to Jack that I had no idea why we were doing these things, nor why we were out here in LA doing them. It didn't seem right at all but I knew Jack was my saving grace and that he'd be there to save me if there was any trouble, just like he always did.

• • •

I walked to where Jack told me to, at a corner by an alley. I never saw anyone following me, but Jack said they'd be there. I didn't care, I was acting o-bliv-vi-ous, just like Jack had told me to do. So I walked down Sunset and then cut into an alleyway. It was dark and quiet, real scary, and then I heard the footsteps behind me.

There were two of them. Big guys and they looked mean. They had guns out but Jack had told me to expect this and not to worry. So I did not worry. They walked closer and I tried to walk back away from them, pretending not to notice them as Jack had told me to do. I walked farther back but I was running out of alleyway. I was in a dead end.

One of the men said, "This is great, almost too easy. Jack Rawlins, trapped like a rat, and now he's going to die like a rat."

"Pretty damn stupid, Jack," the other guy said, pointing his gun at me. "We figured you for better than allowing yourself to get caught in a fix like this, but me and the boys appreciate you making it so easy for us."

I got nervous. It looked like they were going to shoot me and that would make me dead. I wondered where Jack could be. He should be here by now. I knew they thought I was Jack, but I wasn't!—but of course I couldn't tell them that. Jack said that was against the rules.

Finally I saw Jack by a window, looking down at me in the alley below. He was smiling, watching, but not doing anything. I saw him and knew that he saw me, but instead of him giving me the signal that he'd be coming down to help me—he turned his face away and closed the curtains.

"Jack?" I whispered. "You're my saving grace. I don't know what to do without you."

The two men with the guns just laughed and came closer. I knew now they were going to make me dead and that Jack was not going to come to save me like he always did. Something was wrong. Jack knew what was going to happen and he had turned his back on me. I could hardly believe it, and it hurt so much. I couldn't figure why Jack had broken the rules and left me to be made dead. I did not want to be made dead. I was in a panic when the truth suddenly came to me. I finally figured it out so I guess I wasn't that stupid. Instead of Jack setting up these men for the fall as he had told me so many times, Jack had set *me* up for the fall.

"*Why*, Jack? That's not right, you broke the rules!"

I figured they were after Jack in New York. Now these men thought I was Jack. If they made me dead here now then they could go back home and tell their boss that *Jack* was dead. Only Jack wouldn't be dead, he'd be alive and safe from them being after him ever again.

I'd be the one who would be made dead.

I stood frozen as I realized what had happened while the men drew closer to me. I didn't like this. I had to do something. Jack had broken the rules. Now I knew I had no choice but to break the rules too.

"You have the wrong guy!" I blurted to the two men.

They laughed, then aimed their guns at me.

I had to think fast. I said, "You've gotta listen to me, Jack and me are twins, I'm his brother. I'm...slow. Jack uses me to..."

They were on me now, shoving me to the ground, holding me down with a gun pressed to my head. I was scared to death but not so scared that I couldn't talk.

I shouted, "We're twins and Jack is up there watching us right now! Jack thinks if you make me dead he'll get away scot-free. Look up there, up at that window there, you'll see him watching us. Look up!"

One of the men did look up. I saw a strange expression come to his face, then he turned to his partner, "Joe, that rumor might just be true after all. I think I saw him, or someone who looked just like him, and just like this guy here. I'm going on up there and find out what the hell's going on. I don't wanna off some freakin' retard and let Jack get away again."

The man named Joe got up and left, the other man stayed with me, keeping his gun to my head, telling me, "Now don't be stupid, shut-up and lay still."

I said, "But I am stoop-it. Jack always told me that I was brain-dead stoop-it, you know, like having no sense and when I talk too much I…"

He smacked me in the head, "Shut up!"

I said, "You smack just like Jack."

The man just looked at me then, said, "Damn, I guess it is true, twins, and a freakin' retard at that."

I said, "I'm the stoop-it one, I'm…slow."

"Slow ain't the word, buddy, now shut up." Then he lowered his gun, "If what you say is true you won't get hurt."

I said, "Thank you, I don't want to get hurt or be made dead."

The man just shook his head.

• • •

I heard the shots from inside the building behind us soon afterwards. Then I heard a crash of glass and saw something fall down at us. It was Jack. He was screaming but when he hit the ground he was very quiet and still. He was bleeding.

"Jack?"

He coughed blood, tried to talk, said, "Damn-it, I screwed up."

The other man ran away now and I went over to Jack. We were alone. I tried to help Jack. I held him in my arms and tried to wipe away the blood but it just kept flowing and he couldn't move or talk much.

Jack just kept mumbling, "I had it all planned so well but I never figured on a stoop-it brain-dead moron screwing it all up for me."

I said, "I'm sorry, Jack. It's all my fault you're going to be made dead now but what you did wasn't very nice. You broke the rules. You were supposed to save me. Those men were going to make me dead and you were going to let them do it!"

Jack just laughed, more blood gushed out of his mouth. I wiped it away. He said, "It should be you laying here instead of me, stoop-it. I'm the smart one, I'm the one that had a life and a future, not a shit-for-brains nothing retard like you."

That hurt. Jack could say some hurtful things sometimes. I just said, "Well, Jack, I may be the stoop-it one, but I ain't the one that's going to be made dead. Goodbye Jack, I don't think I want to partner with you anymore."

Jack's last words were, "Stoop-it! Stoop-it! Stoop-it!"

But for the first time in my life they didn't bother me because I knew Jack was talking about himself and not me.

Monsters

Mike Miner

I am going to hurt you. Very badly.

We watch until it is over. It takes a long time. We shiver. We know how she feels, his victim. We remember, there are many reminders. Remember his touch, his stink, his salacious eyes. The pain. Unforgettable pain. We watch and feel the echo of our own wounds.

We wish we couldn't see what happens after we die. The alarming rites performed then are perhaps the most disturbing, when his voice becomes gentle, tender. The child becomes a puppet in his hands as he croons to himself.

The room is almost always the same, cheap, rented by the hour, shabby, generic. Sometimes a public restroom. An abandoned warehouse. Always the cracked ceiling, the last thing most of us see through our real eyes.

He hunts, this predator. We march, single file, behind him, pulled like magnets, falling like dominoes. He prowls the combat zone streets of Los Angeles. The parks of Beverly Hills. Schools, beaches, playgrounds, church fairs. We follow, a tail of victims. Like a lion, he searches for herds, waits for the young to get separated, fall behind, then he strikes.

We were his prey.

Now we exist in a twilight limbo, a murky between-land of long shadows. We can't see things as we used to, but there is another way of seeing.

We see our killer as a bright, loud flame, burning those he touches.

If only we'd had these eyes in life.

Time doesn't behave like it used to in this new realm, it folds and twists and resembles a complex origami design, an Escher maze. But we are too close to know what the shape means, if anything.

There are so many children among us. Covens of young girls. Sad, we keep each other company. At night, we cry for our mothers. We fall asleep to the sounds of our longing.

Then there are the dreams. His? Ours? Difficult to know. In these dreams time is further fractured and compounded and we relive the moments of our deaths, our murders, the scabs open, the blood, our blood, oozes. Through his eyes, we see ourselves, beg, scream and die.

We learn to hate. We discover that we can still feel pain, still hurt each other.

The riddle that was our lives is made only more mysterious by our deaths. What is the reason for our existence? What purpose, this endless marching? We think therefore we are. What are we?

We have become aware of another. A policeman. A detective. Another hunter, another killer. He has caught our scent. We reenact our deaths for him as well. In slow motion he lingers over every detail. He doesn't enjoy it, we can tell. But his anger burns, white hot. It won't let him sleep, it blazes brighter when he closes his eyes.

We begin to wonder. What will happen if our demon should die?

He has wings, this pursuer, visible in our side world. Once white, now bloodstained and bent. We have become his obsession. He has abandoned his life, his wife, his job, only the hunt now, for him, for us. He follows our cold trail, revenge-thirsty. The wickedness must stop here, and he must stop it. He will stop it, he tells himself, and plunges into the bottom of a bottle of whiskey, moves to skid row. He doesn't recognize the face in the mirror. With each new victim, a piece of his sanity is chipped away.

Our paths cross in the bad parts, the sad parts of town. East on Hollywood Boulevard, after the stars stop, when the walk of fame becomes the walk of shame, and the streets start speaking Spanish. In back alleys and dive bars, we see our knight in rusted armor. A mournful air surrounds him, he does not smile, he winces when something amuses him, out of reflex. But his eyes still burn, don't miss a trick.

He begins to haunt our dreams and in that nightmare landscape we see a familiar child, our monster's first victim, the Detective's daughter. We would gasp if we had mouths. This child figures heavy in both their dreams. We try to feed clues to the father, the one clue that will connect them, our tormentor and our avenger.

A necklace. An add-a-pearl necklace. Our captor keeps it with him always, a talisman, fondles it like a rosary. It holds nine pearls. One for every year she lived.

We place it in her father's dreams, make it loom, glow, hum. He wakes in tears, grasping for the thin chain, his fingers struggle with empty air.

For every birthday since she died, her father carves a slash on his arm with a clean, sharp knife. There are six such scars. After each wound, the blade lingers, at his wrists, his throat, but finally he throws it down. Opens the wrinkled, much handled case file. His eyes scour the pages, pleading for a breakthrough. He lets the wound bleed.

So when it appears, a sudden glimpse of gold and white, across a dirty bar, in a dirty fist, then vanishes, he doubts his eyes. He worries that his obsession has veered into madness, that this clue is just a mirage in the lonely wasteland of his quest.

He sees what we saw. A harmless man with a chubby, baby face. A runt, no taller than most eighth graders. His diminutive size is the only memorable thing about him. He is utterly ordinary. In his hand the pint glass he drinks from seems enormous. The other hand is in his pocket, touching his lucky charm. His voice, when he orders another round, is tiny, polite, a slight Mexican accent. His behavior is timid, nervous.

A brood of urges paralyzes him. Violence, murder, fear, the rusty taste of blood in his mouth makes him want to spit, and underneath everything, the car crash of his emotions, is a deep empty hole of despair. The hole crowds his insides, makes it hard to breathe. He waits, he watches, chokes down his feelings with warm beer and cheap whiskey. Tries to keep the voice in his head in his head. But his muttering, his occasional outbursts only complete the illusion of a crazy man, rendering him nearly invisible.

Days and nights pass and our knight becomes a shadow, always there, in the dark, out of sight, observing. We watch him, silently pleading for action, our phantom voices pierce the land we live in now, startle the bats in this Hell but do not reach his ears.

Eventually the murderer finds a new target, a defenseless prey. He stalks the child without knowing he is being stalked. A mall. A merry-go-round. *Mamacita, one more ride,* she begs. We remember our own last words to our parents. The mother will be right back. *Wait here.* We watch our captor lick his lips, grin. He waves to the girl, makes silly faces.

A delirium takes hold of our rusty knight, the sad joy of vengeance. There is no doubt now. He bides his time. He could arrest him, put him in jail, but this was never the goal. It is a private justice he is after. The odd little man performs a coin trick for the girl, lures her away. The policeman follows carefully.

We dare to hope, using muscles we have almost forgotten how to use.

The familiar moment comes. The young quarry alone in a dark room with the grinning monster. The familiar words, *I am going to hurt you.* He becomes incandescent at these times, we see unreal flames course over his body, engulf his hands, agents of pain. The beautiful child, with brown skin and chocolate eyes, must feel like her nightmares have come to life. She clutches helplessly at the ropes tying her. We all rub at our invisible wrists, remember the burn of those cords. The fear is like cold water soaking her, drowning her. She shivers. Tears choke her.

Then in a burst our dirty savior is here, his ruined wings restored and spread, his hand glowing white and shouting bullets that mash into our monster's knees; his flames ebb, he crumples. The father unties the terrified child. She flinches when he tries to comfort her. His broken heart cracks more. He tells her to wait outside, call 911, don't hang up until the police are here, don't come back in this room, ignore the noises you hear. She just shudders. He picks her up, carries her out of the room.

We watch her leave with not a little envy. He comes back, shuts the door. Approaches the bleeding heap of evil in the corner. The sharp blade is in his hand. He takes his time and in that alternate, nether world it appears that the creature is being skinned, of its scales, its teeth, until all that is left is an ordinary man's corpse.

The father kneels over the body, quaking, for a long time. He clutches the long lost treasure, the pearls feel like hardened teardrops. When he leaves, we see the terrifying monster, a dragon with its head bowed, trailing after him, last in a short line of other defeated villains.

We are alone with the body and with our other eyes we see something stir. The monster, just a man now, not even that, just the shape of a man, stands.

Some of us lick our lips. This shadow of the man squints, his new eyes adjust, when they do, he sees us, he knows us.

We are every temperature of anger, piping hot, ice cold. His eyes tremble as we occur to him, tall, winged, fierce, a gang of pure reckoning. Our tormentor appears small now, weak and pathetic. He is awash in fear, he tries to run but he is trapped, we are aware now of strength we didn't know we had, we look at each other, my how we have grown.

We lean in, anxious, but a voice stops us. The first victim, nine years old in life, infinite in suffering, has a thought, a plan. We feel something coming from her, a warmth, a pleasant breeze, of memories; not the bad ones we share, her life before. Before the villain entered it, ruined it, ended it. Before we learned what he taught us. It stirs something in us, touches parts of us we've been hiding, protecting. Remembering our families is like hearing a language we used to know. We're rusty at it. But once we get going, a torrent swirls out of us and bathes the evil creature in the room with us.

He is unfamiliar with this language, of affection of love. Gentleness is an alien concept to him. Hands are meant to hurt, to hit, to grab, not to touch, to stroke, to hold. He is basking in our old memories. His heart seems to grow, a kind smile comes to his face. He is almost human again.

The first victim nods in approval, guides us. We form a line, from last to first, and say in a haunting chant, *We are going to hurt you. Very badly.*

We are patient and careful and thorough. His screams summon a thunderstorm to smother the noises in the physical world. We go in order, waiting our turns, taking back our memories, forever, and then we begin to hurt him, slowly. He is delirious with pain and confusion. *Why are you doing this? How could you do this?* His questions echo in the small room, abandoned, unanswered. We laugh at him. Just like he laughed at us.

As we finish, savoring his last throes, we look up into a starless night sky and see others. They call us. We join them, one at a time.

Until there is only me. The first. The worst. I have learned my lessons well. I have been sharpening my teeth. There is nothing left of the child I was. Nothing but bitterness and anger. Bile and rage have shaped me into the monster before you. Your torment blooms like a well-tended poisonous flower, slowly from seed to bud, from spark to inferno. I metamorphose, sprout multiple limbs, I spin a web to trap you. Do you recognize the web's pattern from the cracked ceiling of the filthy room in which you murdered me, defiled me? No, your miser's eyes saw only your victim.

Behold me now, this spider queen. I will never look up, there is nothing for me in Heaven. I have no wings, just these legs, one for you and each of your kind.

Beware, fiends, I am waiting for you, watching with infinite, unblinking eyes.

In this special chamber of Hell, my parlor, I will keep you company.

There is no time here. No death, only pain.

Community Reintegration

Zak Mucha

<<

Subject: T. Gaylen

Date: 7/29/11

Thank you for agreeing to meet with our client. We hope you will be able to assist with Troy's reintegration into the community.

Casey Turwill, LCPC, CADC

DCFS 2610 W. Roosevelt Rd. Chicago, IL

Cturwill@DCFSill.gov

>>

Date: 9/25/11

Mr. Turwill,

Enclosed you will find interview excerpts, pertinent clinical narratives, and our team's psychosocial assessment of Troy Gaylen with concurrent documentation of interviews with collaterals. Please note the included release of information for family contact and audio recording of the assessment interviews.

• • •

PSYCHOSOCIAL HISTORY SUMMARY

Patient Troy Gaylen (TG) is a 20 year-old Caucasian male currently hospitalized at Lakeshore Hospital following his assault of a female staff member at Stony Grove. TG currently has three felony charges for separate incidents involving physical assaults against residential staff members. He has been a resident of Stony Grove since the age of 17.

Stony Grove is under court order to find placement for the patient. TG has continued to refuse to participate in treatment at the residential program while filing multiple complaints with the Office of Inspector General. All complaints were adjudicated to be unfounded. TG also refuses alternate residential placements. At his 21st birthday, he will no longer be a ward of the state and will be released for independent living in the community.

Between the ages of 8 and 17, TG has had multiple unsuccessful residential placements. Prior to the age of eight, he lived with his biological mother, and then his maternal grandmother. After the death of his grandmother, TG (age 9) went into foster placement at six residences and five residential facilities. Later reunification with his mother (age 14) resulted in the client's placement at Ridgeway Residential, Bridgeview, and Stony Grove.

Following his first suicide attempt at the age of eight, the patient has had over 20 psychiatric hospitalizations. TG has presented with a history of violent behavior and appears to present with some secondary gain in describing these past acts and his "fantasies" of violent acts.

Past mental health assessments report the patient's difficulty in "identifying and sharing background information…(TG) has vacillated between denying any physically violent or sexually reactive behavior and stating he does not remember anything about his past."

In his equivalency courses, TG is at 9th grade level only due to his refusal to participate in coursework. Past DCFS records note an IQ of 122 with verbal testing exceeding his cumulative testing scores. In 2005, the client participated in art programs with the City of Chicago's Teen Living program and was awarded a foundation grant for continued studies.

TG's left arm is scarred with self-inflicted cigarette burns and parallel razor cuts. His right forearm has a large tattoo of a crucifix. TG stated the crucifix is "upside down" (i.e. anti-Christian, but the image is inverted to benefit his own POV, not the POV of others).

• • •

CLINICAL NARRATIVE 9/14/11 INTERVIEW 2:00 PM
The interview was conducted in the patient's hospital room. Lakeshore staff offered security measures to be available during the session. The patient requested "no other people" attend the interview, stated he felt hospital staff was "biased against" him.

Patient (TG) remained in his bed during the first interview session.

When the clinician's notebook fell off the desk, TG accused the clinician of making a loud noise "on purpose." Startle response—rapid breathing, agitated movements, "searching" the room visually for potential threat— appeared incongruent with TG's physiological responses throughout the entirety of the interview. No psychomotor retardation or agitation was observed. The patient's eye contact was poor, but verbal responses appeared to consistently present no deficits. The patient appeared oriented to time, place, and situation.

TG denied any perceived need for psychiatric assistance, but stated, "I want to get my own place. They said you can help me with that."

The clinician explained interview results would determine whether the patient was accepted into the program. TG responded: "If you tell me what kind of answers you want, that would help me."

• • •

Int: How have you been doing here?

TG: They said I'm doing better here. It depends who's looking at me. And I can change how they look at me.

Int: How do you do that?

TG: By knowing the rules and picking which ones to follow. It's a game. You get gamed if you don't know the rules, or you game the people who don't know the rules.

There's rules everywhere. Sometimes the surface rules are fake and the real rules are beneath. For staff, too, not just the kids.

Int: So how do you learn the rules?

TG: You see who gets away with what. Different people have different rules. But how the rules work—that's the same all over. When you're a kid, you can't usually see past the surface rules.

The kids who do see past the surface, but don't know the difference, they go insane.

The surface rules are easy, as long as you decide to follow them or ignore them. But you can't do both.

Like, one place I was at, you get points if you make your bed and brush your teeth. If you got enough points each week, you could exchange them for "trade money" and buy candy on Friday. Or you could "give" the trade money to another kid. Administration doesn't like that, but staff will let you do that, just to keep things quiet. Those are the unwritten rules.

But if you decide you can ignore their rules, they can't do anything, not really. You never get candy, or go bowling. Big deal.

If you watch, you can see who doesn't have to follow the rules. Those kids get to do other things—like they were junior staff. Those kids said the right things and broke all the rules. They were bigger cowards than me, but they got permission.

If you break *all* the rules *all* the time, they decide you're crazy.

I can make myself sound crazy. You can make me sound crazy. The therapists always say they're on my side. It's going to be a partnership where we learn more about me. It's all bullshit. It's hard to describe, but you can see it for real when you know they can't hurt you. If you believe them, they can backstab you.

Int: Have you been anywhere where the rules were fair to everyone?

TG: It's the same everywhere—my Mom's or the Audi home, Maryville or jail. Jail isn't so bad. I know what to say to make sure I go to the psych unit in Cook County. You have to do some days in the hospital there first, but then you move downstairs.

Int: How many times have you been in?

TG: Twice, not counting Juvie. The psych unit in the jail, Division 8, used to be one big dorm room—like summer camp with thirty bunks and one big bathroom with stalls. All sortsa guys in there.

People don't bother with you until the middle of the second shift. No one bothered me though, not after one time I flipped out. That's how I ended up at the state hospital.

If you're too crazy to stay in jail, they send you to the state hospital to make sure you're sane enough to go to trial. They have therapy groups where you get trained to stand trial. "Court bingo"—you play bingo, but instead of numbers on the card, it's all the personnel and job titles for court. The counselor calls out the definition and you see if that person is on your card. When you win enough, then you're sane enough to go back to jail.

If you're too crazy for jail, but not sane enough for court, you can go back and forth for a long time.

Int: How did you do?

TG: I don't remember.

Int: You could have left Stony Grove when you were eighteen, what do you like about the place that you stayed?

TG: I hate the place.

Int: So why stay?

TG: Because I was a ward of the state, the state will pay for my college.

Int: But you're not passing your high school courses.

TG: Only because I don't want to. Do you think I'm telling the truth?

• • •

FAMILY HISTORY/ COLLATERAL INTERVIEWS SUMMARY

Phone interviews conducted by ACT clinicians on 9/18/11.

Mother (Deborah Gaylen) and sister (Melissa Perry) were both interviewed. The sister terminated the interview prior to providing or verifying any information.

The patient's mother denied any history of physical or sexual trauma in the household. TG's mother cites no difficulties regarding the child's developmental markers or learning, noting the patient was placed in "gifted" classes during grade school.

The mother stated the aberrant behavior of the patient was exacerbated by foster care and residential placement. While she has had minimal contact with her son in the last 12 years (TG lived with his mother for four months at the age of 14, and has returned to his mother's apartment during the last two elopements), she stated that TG "could" live with her when he is released from Stony Grove.

"He's my boy, I couldn't kick him out. He's a part of me," the patient's mother stated, citing the only reason TG is in residential placement is due to DCFS intervention.

The patient's mother appears to externalize responsibility for her own conduct. DCFS reports cite three arrests for forgery between 1997-2000. When queried, the patient's mother presents conflicting rationales for this behavior, first denying, then accusing collaborators (husband, boyfriend), and concurrently accepting varying degrees of culpability.

The relationship between the patient and his mother appears to be iatrogenic and stressors for both persons prompt interactions with blurred boundaries and role identification.

• • •

CLINICAL NARRATIVE 9/18/11 9:30 AM
The second interview was held after TG was placed on one-to-one monitoring on the psychiatric unit. Following a verbal altercation with his roommate, which was de-escalated by the ER crisis team, TG walked from the north to the south end of the unit and assaulted a staff member not on the crisis team. TG was subsequently transferred to the quiet room where the remaining interviews were held.

At the time of this writing, Lakeshore staff had not verified whether criminal charges would be filed.

• • •

ASSESSMENT INTERVIEW 9/18/11. 9:30AM—10:45AM
Int: What do you do when you stay out (of the residential facility)?
TG: When I'm "on-run", at night, I just watch people. By Clark and Halsted, I see the crowds of people, but I never go over and talk to them. I make sure nothing bad happens. If I leave them, then something bad happens to them. I've been blamed in the past.

Int: What do people accuse you of?

TG: Different things. One woman said I followed her into a store.

Int: But you didn't go in.

TG: I held the door for her. I was going in, anyway. I tried to talk to her and she told the counter guy I exposed myself.

I wish women were nicer to me. But I have a girlfriend. When I get out of here, we're going to move in together.

Int: Where is she at?

TG: She's in the city.

Int: How often do you get to see her?

TG: We Facebook a lot. I have other people. I know one guy on the south side, he runs a chop shop and wants me to drive cars for him. I know another woman with a house on the north side—six bedrooms—and she'll put me up for as long as I want.

Int: Out of all the people you know, who are you closest to? Who's the one person you trust?

TG: I know the answer I'm supposed to give. So, It'd be a lie to tell you that, even though it could be true. But, really, my mom.

I have one best friend who I trust, but I don't have his number any more. I met him in the hospital last year.

Int: You got into a fight the other day. What happened?

TG: I get mad when people lie to me. People don't keep their word. It's my symptoms.

Int: What was the lie the person told?

TG: It doesn't matter. People see what they want to. If you want me to be crazy, tell me so. What do I have to do to stay out of Stony Grove? I know I'll get out of here eventually. I have Medicaid. The longest they can keep me is five days. They don't want to take me to court to make me stay. So I get quiet for two days and they say I'm better.

The doctors see you for fifteen minutes, maybe, and they look at what the other doctors wrote down. That's how you get a diagnosis. There's kids in Stony who are a lot sicker than me who have the same diagnosis. There's kids who act worse than I do, but they have a better diagnosis—they're not as sick, but they know how the rules work.

Did I tell you ever I wanted to be a social worker?

Int: No.

TG: I don't, but I say that sometimes. People like hearing that. Sometimes I want to be a teacher or a therapist. I could do that.

Really, I want to be able to say what things are and have people listen to me. I want to be able to change what things are, just by saying so.

You going to say I can be in your program?

Int: Do you want to be in this program?

TG: Yeah, if it'll get me out of Stony, I do. But I'm just not used to being out in the world. I tried to stay with my grandmother and my mother, but they couldn't really teach me. Maybe I need professionals like you to help me. My social worker here told me I could go with your program. Do you subsidize rents?

Int: People working with us have to pay their own rent.

TG: I only get 698 a month. That's not a lot for the north side. I want to stay up here. Except not in the gay neighborhood. One time, I ran away and took enough money from my mom. I had a room in a hotel right by the gay neighborhood. I went to the gay parade that year—I didn't like it, it's gross, but I was able to get free food from people and this other guy gave me a ride home. He wanted to come upstairs with me and I had to pull a knife.

Int: What happened?

TG: Nothing. He left me alone. I want people to leave me alone.

Int: What do you do when you're alone?

TG: At night sometimes, when I'm "on-run", I just ride the bus all night. I'll pick someone out and follow to see where they live.

Int: How do you pick?

TG: If they look interesting.

• • •

MENTAL HEALTH REPORT HISTORY—SUMMARY (Restricted to records provided by Stony Brook)

Correlate past reports cite hospitalizations starting at the age of 8 (Jun 1999).

At Riverside residential program, TG "choked a peer in the bathroom, justified the peer attempted to assault him"...TG "attempted to stab a peer with a pencil...was found by the police to have a boxcutter and letter opener in order 'to stab people'" (Aug 2007). TG reported: "I was told if I got straight A's in class, they would have a birthday party for me, so I got straight A's. They didn't have a party, so I quit."

March 2006, "He reports, 'I was hospitalized only once. The school thought I wanted to kill myself. I never had suicidal thoughts. I never had homicidal thoughts. I just wanted to get my way.'" TG diagnoses at that time: Psychotic Disorder NOS, Oppositional Defiant Disorder, Impulse Control Disorder, and Posttraumatic Stress Disorder.

Neurological examinations in 2004 ruled out organic precipitants for petite mal seizures. Neuropsychological evaluation quotes TG: "I get seizures from anything. It used to be from video games. Now it's from stress. I take Depakote for epilepsy, not my moods. I know as much as the psychiatrist."

TG stated during his mental health assessment of 2010: "They don't like how I think…they say I manipulate people to get my way. I tore out the phones because I couldn't make calls. If I can't why should they? It's not fair. If you follow the rules, they don't bother with you, but if you throw a chair at them, they ask "What do you want?""

Psychiatric testing from Northwestern University (2009) cites the "precise" descriptions of TG's hallucinations and "ego-syntonic content" of his self-reported psychotic symptoms. The evaluation conclusion notes a potential for "ample evidence of symptoms exaggeration." TG described first suicide attempt (age 8) "by hanging" while DCFS records note overdose on mother's prescription medication. The patient's parasuicidal attempts and his suicidal acts have been performed in secure settings where emergency response would be immediate.

DuPage County court hearing of 2010 notes TG began swallowing razor blades and screws in order to "get his emotional needs met." His therapist, S. McLean, noted that "(TG's) progress appears to be minimal…he often presents with regressive or primitive behavior ('childlike', 'splitting'), by triangulating staff to 'overrule' seemingly inconsequential decisions." Therapist McLean reported, "(TG) shows little remorse and was once caught writing letters to a female peer to whom he had previously exposed himself. (TG) denied the letters were his, stating that his handwriting was perfectly copied."

Between 2002 and 2011, little consistency appears in TG's diagnoses: Bipolar Disorder NOS, Schizoaffective Disorder, Conduct Disorder, Oppositional Defiant Disorder, ADHD, PTSD, Impulse Control Disorder, Major Depressive Disorder with psychotic features, Seizure Disorder, Enueresis, Depressive Disorder NOS, Narcissistic Personality Disorder. No prevalent Axis I disorders appear consistent…Since 2007, the patient had been adjudicated by the Social Security Administration to have a psychiatric disability.

• • •

CLINICAL NARRATIVE 9/20/11
Re: T. Gaylen discharge plan
Concurrent notes—scheduled phone conf. w/ Delia R. DCFS sup and TG mother. 9/20/11. 10:00 AM—10:45 AM. DCFS conf call line 5559865

The patient's mother agreed to allow TG to return to her home, but on the condition that she is assigned as the patient's representative payee, responsible for managing the patient's Social Security entitlements. The patient declined, stating he would rather "sleep on the street." The patient and his mother respectively accused each other of attempting to "get the money" and "live for free." The patient's mother withdrew her offer.

Conference call was terminated without confirmed discharge plans.

• • •

ASSESSMENT INTERVIEW 9/21/11 5:00PM

Int: Do you agree with any of the diagnoses you've had over the years?

TG: Sometimes. When I'm Bipolar, I get really mad and go off on people. I can't help it.

Int: What makes you mad?

TG: In here, I get mad at people. I get mad at everybody, but I don't show it on everybody.

Int: Why not?

TG: On some people, getting mad doesn't feel as good. The people who don't freak out on you...sometimes they just whale on you.

Int: Which people do that?

TG: The ones I shouldn't get all Bipolar on, they whale on me.

I been Bipolar since I was a kid, they didn't know why I would just get so mad. It was because I wasn't getting what I wanted. The first counselor I saw ever, she had me seeing a psychiatrist in grade school. I had already been to the hospital by then, but my grandma sent me that first time. Then they told me I could never go back to her house. She would have let me, but the doctors wouldn't. She died when I was locked up. I never saw her again.

Int: Did you ever get mad at her?

TG: I got mad at her all the time. One time I tore down all the curtains. She would lock herself in the bathroom or in the basement. But she didn't get along with my mom, either. Grandma said how she made mom too soft and made fun of mom because mom cried all the time.

When I was fourteen, I was staying with my mom for a while. It was pretty normal. One time, she called the cops on me.

Int: What did she think you did?

TG: She thought I was going to stab her, but we were just arguing. That was when she learned I don't go to jail, no matter what. I go to the hospital when I hurt someone. They can't take me to jail because I'm disabled.

Int: What's your disability?

TG: I'm Bipolar and Schizophrenic. They also said Antisocial Personality Disorder, but you don't get Social Security for that. I don't have a low IQ. They said I'm 120. Which is smart.

Int: What does the Bipolar feel like when symptoms come up?

TG: I snap off on people. I want to hurt them real bad. Sometimes I hurt myself instead. I like watching the blood drip or the skin burn.

Int: How do you decide whether to hurt yourself or someone else?

TG: If I want them to think I'm schizophrenic, I hurt myself.

Int: That's not schizophrenia.

TG: I'm not Schizophrenic. I just say that to them so they leave me alone. The pills make me fat and that sucks. I can't get a girlfriend like that, but I won't go to jail. The one time I did, I had to swallow my watch to get out of General Population.

I ended up in the jail hospital with a guy who said he was going to kill Obama, but he said that just so he didn't have to go to General Population. He was going to try to get disability. He said he was in therapy all his life, but his mom had money and his dad was a real prick. I think he had a thing for his mom—telling me how he only wanted mom in the house, not dad. I wanted that too, except I didn't have a dad around.

That guy was a lot like me. If he's sick, I am, too. He didn't look scary or anything. No one would be scared of me if they didn't know my records and I walked up correctly and acted appropriately. I know how to do it.

Int: Do what? Act appropriately?

TG: 'Appropriate' means different thing different places. It doesn't matter. They can't make me stay in jail for long. No matter what I do.

Did you see that one governor's son—the governor who yelled at Obama? Her kid was in the hospital thirty years for kidnapping and rape. I'm not going to do that, though.

I want to have a normal life. If I stay in the system, they have to pay me for college. Even if I don't want to go to college, they can't keep me forever.

I can go back to my mom's for a while, no matter what she says, and save some money. I'll get a disability check. I can get an apartment. Maybe only a part-time job—because if you work too much, you lose the disability checks.

I want to have some free time. I'll get to do what I want somewhere. I'm tired of people telling me what to do.

Done For The Day

Dan O'Shea

10:00 a.m.

The pain woke me up. Slept on my left side, and now my shoulder didn't feel like a ball-and-socket joint. It felt like a slurry of super-heated broken glass joint. Usually, if I roll over on my left side, the pain's enough to wake me up straight away, but I'd taken a couple of the pills last night and doubled down with a few fingers of Jack, so I was paying for it now, instead.

One sure thing in life, you're gonna pay, one way or another.

Sun was up, that's good at least. Means I've got a couple hours in the bank already, burned part of another square off the calendar without having to think about it. The more of a day I can spend unconscious, the better.

TV's going, the Game Show Network. So Billy's up, too. I look at the clock. Almost 10:00, Jesus. Although it was what, going on 4:00 when I gave up and knocked back the Oxy, so it kinda figures. Kid was gonna be hungry.

• • •

Billy sat cross-legged on the floor in front of the TV, rocking back and forth, his hands flapping up by his ears. Just gave me a little peek when I walked in the room, tilting his head to the side so he could look at me out of the corner of his eye.

"Mommy is done for the day," he said

"Mommy is done for the day," I answered.

Mommy'd been done for the day coming up on two years now. Pancreatic cancer. Usually, that's a man's disease. Usually after fifty. Grace had been 42. Would have been 43 if she'd made it two more days. Billy still had a card for her around here somewhere.

He seemed OK just now. His behaviors were getting worse, had been ever since his mom died. She'd always been with him, understood him, did everything for him. Me, I'd usually been a few thousand miles away. Me and Billy, we were getting used to each other, but the behaviors were getting worse. The doc was keeping them manageable with the meds, but he'd topped out on the dosages. And Billy's hands were starting to tremor.

One of the side effects, and it would only get worse the longer he stayed on the drugs. I'd seen people my age, people who had been on this shit most of their lives, hands shaking so bad that they spray painted themselves when they tried to eat, so bad they couldn't dress themselves. We'd worked too hard with Billy building his skills, too hard to give him a little independence, too hard give it all up.

Who was I kidding? Grace had worked too hard. Everything Billy could do, Grace had taught him. I was just trying to keep him from losing ground. It's not like the autism left him a lot of dignity. I wasn't going to let it take back the little he had earned.

There was a new drug, new psychotropic. Doc wanted to try it, but that meant backing Billy off the old meds first. All the way off. I'd started cutting the dosage a couple days ago. One big meltdown last night. Kid took me down on my left shoulder, took me down hard. That's why I couldn't sleep. That's why I took the pills.

"It's just you," Billy said

"Just me," I said.

He nodded, like that confirmed an unhappy suspicion. Same conversation we had every morning.

Lingo was on, some word game show, the last bit where the winning team tried to fill in a mess of words to win twenty grand. I knew not to disturb Billy until it was over. His rocking sped up while they took their shot, his hands flapping a little faster. They came up one word short. Billy stopped rocking and stood up.

Billy was 22, had a couple inches on me, 6'1" maybe, about 220 now. Child's mind, and a broken one at that, inside a man's body. Not always the best combination.

"I want a fried egg sandwich," he said.

"Fried egg sandwich it is."

He looked back at the TV, the game show host schmoozing the contestants while the credits ran.

"They didn't win," he said.

I just nodded. Who does?

• • •

11:30 a.m.

I walked out to the end of the drive to get the mail, flipped through the envelopes. Gas bill, something from Blue Cross, a mailer from Ultra Cosmetics addressed to Grace. That used to get to me, getting mail for Grace, but I was over it. Pretty much over it. Nothing from DCFS. Had to call them again today.

Mrs. White was out watering her flowers. Her grass looked like Astroturf—a perfect, uniform green. The evergreen shrubs that lined her front porch were trimmed flat and even. Red impatiens swelled out in a lush ruffle at the base of the evergreens. Yellow house, white shutters. Lived next door to her for better than twenty years, still didn't know her first name.

"Your son was up early again today," she said. If you didn't know her, if you were hearing her voice for the first time, you'd think it was concern.

"I'm sorry," I said. "Was he being loud?"

"The TV." He did that sometimes, turned the TV all the way up. Volume 100 he called it. That's the number that showed on the digital read out if you pegged the sound.

"I'm surprised it didn't wake you," she said.

"Couldn't sleep last night, so I guess when I did, I was out pretty good. What time was this?"

"Before six. I'm a light sleeper. If you could talk to him?"

I nodded. "I will, but, you know." I gave her a little shrug. She knew about Billy.

"Yes," she said. "I'm sure it must be difficult."

"Worse some days than others."

She smiled a little. Concern, you'd think, if you didn't know her. In the window, one of her cats did a pirouette and jumped down off the sill.

She turned back to her flowers, I turned back toward the house. Lawn needed mowing. Better get to that today or I'd hear about that next.

• • •

"Yes, Paul, we did lose a resident last week." Mark Adams on the phone, the executive director at The Friends. Billy'd gone to school there for years until he aged out of the program. Best program of its kind in the state. Grace and I had been trying to get Billy into one of their adult group homes ever since. I still was.

"I'm sorry," I said. "I was just wondering if there was a memorial fund or anything. I thought I'd make a donation."

A pause. "I can e-mail you some info on that." Another pause. "Paul, it's not that we don't appreciate your generosity. With the state paying a year late when they pay at all, we need every cent we can get. But you know donations can't influence placement decisions."

"I know."

That's what I said. But money talks. Sometimes it gives orders, sometimes it just whispers in your ear. But it never shuts up. Any of the good programs, the donor lists and the resident lists, they tended to overlap eventually. So we'd been doing what we could. We'd carried a lot of life insurance on Grace, loaded up after Billy's diagnosis, figuring if she died young, I was going to need the money. Threw a good chunk of that at The Friends after Grace died, big enough chunk they'd named the art room where she used to volunteer after her. We had what insurance we could get on me, too, but in my line of work, life insurance was hard to come by.

"Have you heard from DCFS?" Adams asked.

"No. Should be any day," I said. "Of course, it should have been any day for a while now."

"They are slow. You know if you could get Billy on the emergency placement list, we'd take him in a heartbeat. He's one of our own."

The emergency list. Funding for placements in adult group homes came through the state. And the state had been cutting back for years, balancing the budget hole they'd dug through decades of corruption and nepotism on the backs of the weak and the helpless. If you had an adult child with a disability living at home, then the kid had a place to live and you weren't an emergency. Hell, I knew single parents in their seventies with fifty year old kids at home, seventy year olds rolling two hundred pound kids out of bed so they could change their sheets after they wet them because, to the state, that wasn't an emergency. When the parent finally died and the kid was abandoned, when the kid was left completely alone with no one who loved him left to help him understand, when there was no one left to say no when the state dumped the kid into one of the hell holes they funded because they awarded human services contracts with the same low-bidder, highest-donor mindset that left us with collapsing bridges and rotting roadways, *then* it would be an emergency.

The hell holes didn't have donor lists.

"I appreciate that Mark. When will you make an intake decision?"

"In the next week or so. You know we can't afford empty beds, Paul."

I knew. And with the state stiffing them, it's not like they were going to open any new beds, either. It could be years before another slot opened.

In the background, I heard the volume on the TV go up again. I shut the door to the den so I could hear.

"Volume 100?" Adams asked.

"Yeah, he still does that. Look, I'm checking with DCFS today. I'll get back to you ASAP."

"OK.," Adams said. "Good luck."

I was about to go turn down the TV when I heard the doorbell. I looked out the window. The police. Second time this month.

I stuck my head in the den door. Billy gave me his sideways glance. I made a twisting motion with my right hand. He turned the sound down.

"Mr. Markham?" The officer on the left. My age, or close to it, beefy, sergeant's stripes. The other guy looked about twelve.

"Yes?"

"We've had a complaint concerning noise and possible child neglect."

I nodded. "Welfare check, I know the drill. Come on in."

If I'd known the cops were coming, I'd have dressed. I was in my jeans and a wife-beater, just the impression I wanted to make.

The cops took a quick run through the place. I kept it clean. The sergeant stood in the door to the den looking at Billy, who was rocking on the floor, hands flapping, watching an old rerun of Wheel of Fortune.

"Can I talk to your son?"

"You can try," I said. "He's autistic. He doesn't talk much and he doesn't do well with strangers. I'd wait for a commercial."

The guy nodded. Vanna turned some letters, Pat quipped, and they cut to a Ford spot.

"Billy," I said.

He gave me his sideways look.

"Can you come say hello?"

"Oh boy," Billy gave an exasperated sigh. He got up, walked over and held out his arms. He knew the drill, too. They liked to check for bruises.

"Billy," the sergeant asked, "are you OK?"

"I'm Billy."

"I'm Sergeant Harris."

"Blue policeman," Billy said.

"Are you OK, Billy?"

Billy shook his head. "Mommy is done for the day."

The cop looked at me.

"His mother died a couple of years ago," I said.

The cop nodded.

In the kitchen, the cop went through the spiel, how everything looked fine, they were sorry to have bothered me. How somebody had heard a lot of noise coming from the house early in the morning and they were afraid something had happened. How they'd have to file a report. How DCFS would get a copy.

Then the cop nodded toward my left side.

"The shoulder, what happened, if you don't mind my asking."

With me in the wife beater, he could see the linguine bowl of scars.

"Iraq. Caught a couple rounds right in the arm hole."

"Bad luck."

"Bad luck is a body bag. This was just shit that happened."

"I did a hitch over there. Guess my luck was better."

"Yeah, well, you're still playing in the shit, Sarge. Let's hope your luck holds." We shook hands. He held out his card.

"Neighbors," he said. "What can you do? Any more shit comes up, give me a call, maybe I can smooth things out."

I took the card. "Thanks, I will."

As the cops walked out to their car, I saw Mrs. White watching from her porch.

• • •

A milk run. Diplomatic security. Babysitting some Foggy Bottom types for a half-hour sight-seeing cruise outside the Green Zone.

This was after I went private. In 2003, my hitch was up. I had fourteen years in, ten of them in Special Forces, figured to be a lifer. But Billy was thirteen at that point, we'd had the diagnosis since he was three. Leaving Grace home alone with him for months on end, that was one thing, but leaving her to deal with all that shit on an E-8's pay, that was another. So when the guy from Black-thorne made his pitch, go private for way better than six figures, chance to top 200Gs with bonuses, that was a no brainer.

Three years of that, socked away a ton, including more than my share of the under-the-table money floating around. Screwed up war for sure, a bottom-less ocean of blood and misery, but a fuck-ton of cash floating around. Money everywhere, and nobody watching it very closely, either.

Then some haji with an AK got lucky.

We're half a mile from the Green Zone, headed back in, and some locals get into it at a checkpoint—one of them trying to squeeze in past the other, they bump fenders, and now its road rage time, except the Middle East version, what seems like a dozen people spilling out of each car, men, women, a couple of kids, everybody yelling at everybody else, everybody wearing a couple layers of bathrobes, so they all could be packing RPGs for all I can tell. Got a squad of newbie National Guard types on the checkpoint, they aren't helping, scream-ing English at people that don't speak it, waving their guns around, the whole thing turning in to a cluster fuck.

Which means that I'm riding shotgun on some VIPs, and we aren't moving. That's the one thing you don't do, stop moving. It's not like the locals can't tell a Blackthorne crew when they see one, and they know that means a high-value target, so even if they don't have anything set up, somebody somewhere is going to run off and tell his cousin Ahmed and bring some bad shit down on our heads.

So I get my guys out of the Humvees to unfuck things. We all speak enough Haji to get by, we herd the locals back in their cars, get the newbies at the check point calmed down, I put my arm up to wave the first car through, beat to fuck old Peugeot, and some somebody somewhere puts two rounds right into my arm hole.

Don't remember much of it after that. My guys dumped me back in the Hummer. Snatches here and there. Shouting. The pain every time we hit a hole, a corpsman screaming how they needed to get some blood into me right fucking now.

First round went through my upper arm, cracked the humerus, plowed into my left lung. Second one slammed right into the shoulder joint and fragged. First one damn near killed me, but a lung wound, you survive it, it heals up.

Arm's OK now for most part. Shoulder's iffy even for day-to-day shit. Can't lift my left arm more than half way, can't lift anything heavy with it, and it hurts most of the time. Just background noise, usually, like pain static, like I can't quite get the feel-good station to come in all the way. Some days though, some days are bad.

Blackthorne didn't need any one-armed operators, and it turns out the disability pay, that's one of the downsides of this whole private army gig. Good thing Grace died or we wouldn't have had much scratch to throw at The Friends.

• • •

12:30 p.m.

"You're gonna get another report. Cops were here again today." I was on the phone with Shelia, Billy's case manager at DCFS.

"Any findings?"

"Do there have to be? I left the better part of my left arm over in Sandland, I got a twenty-two-year-old who's got twenty pounds and two inches on me, I got a dead wife. I've got a good placement lined up, one with an opening. All you gotta do is put the kid on the list and we're golden."

"I understand your frustration, but we have protocols. The new report from the police might help when I get it. Probably not much, not without findings."

"Would it help more if there was something in it?"

She didn't say anything for a minute.

"You said no findings," she said, finally.

"I might have talked the cops out of something. If it helps, maybe I can talk them back in to it."

"If there are findings, yes, that would help. You understand those findings would be against you, right?"

"I get that."

"That's permanent. If that goes in the record, it stays."

"But that doesn't affect placement, right? I mean if it gets him on the list?"

"It doesn't affect him going on the list. But some facilities have concerns about clients from abusive situations. Especially the good ones. Kids like that tend to have more behavior issues. I know you're angling for The Friends, but they like to cherry pick. If you put a red flag in Billy's file, I don't know."

Abusive situation? So it's gonna come to that, let the state brand me as a child abuser so I can take care of my kid.

"Let me worry about The Friends, OK? Just get him on the damn list."

"As soon as I get the report. That could take weeks."

"Let me worry about that, too."

• • •

"This is Harris." Squad room noises in the background.

"Hey Sarge," I said. "Paul Markham? From your welfare check this morning?"

"Mr. Markham, what can I do for you?"

"Have you filed your report yet?"

"Just starting my paperwork for the shift."

"I was wondering if you could do me a favor..."

• • •

2:00 p.m.

Billy'd been in the den most of the day watching his game shows. A little more screaming than usual when he got excited, when somebody won, a few more episodes of volume 100. A little banging on the floor. Nothing serious yet, but it was like watching someone blow up a balloon, blow it up past where they should have stopped.

"Time for 2:00 pm meds."

I looked up. I hadn't heard Billy come in to the kitchen. The kid was nothing if not on schedule. He knew when each of his shows started, knew when he took his meds. Knew shower time was at 6:00 pm so he'd be in his pajamas and ready to watch Wheel of Fortune at 6:30. You didn't fuck with the kid's schedule.

But the 2:00 pm dose? That's one we were cutting.

"We're not doing 2:00 pm meds today, Billy."

He shook his head. "Time for 2:00 pm meds." Louder this time.

I didn't want to fight him on it. I unlocked the cupboard where we kept the pills, opened a bottle of aspirin, shook one out, got a glass of water and handed it to him.

He looked at the pill, and started shaking his head violently.

"NO NO NO NO NO NO NO NO NO NO NO NO! 2:00 pm is blue pill!"

He dropped the aspirin on the ground and threw the cup at me. I ducked, felt the water splash across my back, heard the plastic cup bounce off the fridge. All our dishes were plastic. Plastic didn't break.

Billy rushed me. I was still bent down, so I got him around the waist and held on. He pounded his fists on my back.

"BLUE PILL BLUE PILL BLUE PILL BLUE PILL!"

I slid up, got my good arm under one of his arm pits, my hand on the back of his neck, spun him around, got behind him, had him in a half-nelson, best I could do. His left arm was still free. He went for my face, but I tucked it in tight to his neck on the right side. He went for my arm, tried to dig his nails in, but I kept his nails short. Then he planted his feet and threw himself back, twisting, driving my left shoulder into the fridge.

The pain exploded down my arm and up into my neck, but I held on. He was off balance now, so I dropped, sliding down the fridge door, pulling him to the floor.

He pounded my leg for a while with his free hand, slowly wearing himself out. He started crying.

"2:00 pm is blue pill. 3:00 pm is snack. 3:30 is Jeopardy. 4:00 is news. 4:30 is other news. 5:00 is dinner. 5:30 is dishes..."

He recited his day's schedule over and over as I held him on the floor. He wasn't fighting me anymore, so I just wrapped my arms around him holding him close to me. My left shoulder throbbed and flamed. As soon as I could let him go, I was going to need the Oxy.

He started rocking in my arms.

"Mommy is done for the day," he said.

· · ·

4:15 p.m.

The phone rang.

"I got the report." Shelia from DCFS. "I don't know how you got it here so quick."

"Doesn't matter. Will it do the trick?"

"It should. You're sure about this?"

I'd told Harris what to put down. Bruising, suspicion of physical abuse. If anybody checked, they'd find bruises. There were always bruises. More on me than him.

"Yeah, I'm sure."

"Somebody could go for charges."

"I'll claim PTSD or some shit. Cop said he'd back me, it comes to that. How about you?"

"I know you're a good dad."

"OK then. Help me be a good dad. Get him on that list."

"Tomorrow, first thing," she said. "You want me to call The Friends, give them the news?"

"Let me call them first, spin the abuse thing."

"OK." One of those pauses, the kind that said she wanted to say something else, then "You're doing the right thing."

"There's no right to any of this," I said.

I called The Friends, told Adams, spun the police report. No problem, Turns out six figures does a lot of spinning. If they got the OK from the state tomorrow, they'd even let me move Billy in the next day. Didn't usually do that. Usually, even after the OK, there was a good month of paperwork before you got a move in date. But the money had been whispering for a while. I told him about the situation with the meds, how the next week was likely to be pretty rough, in case they wanted to wait. But he said it would probably be better for Billy to finish the med switch at The Friends instead of at home. More staff to help. And Billy liked it there. Always lit up when we'd go visit. I think he remembered being happier then.

· · ·

5:00 p.m.

I made cheeseburgers for dinner. Billy loved cheeseburgers. When he asked for a third, I made it for him. Grace would have killed me. Billy was heavier than he should be. She always watched his diet, made him exercise.

When he finished the third cheeseburger he actually smiled.

"All done?" I asked.

"5:30 is dishes," he said. He was done.

• • •

3:17 a.m.

Glass breaking. I shot out of bed. I heard Billy screaming in his room. When I got there, he was banging his head against the wall hard enough to leave dents in the drywall. I could see one of his shoes tangled in the blinds. He'd thrown it, broken the window. Through a gap in the blinds, I saw the lights come on at Mrs. White's house.

Billy turned toward me, his face streaming with tears, the front of his t-shirt splotched with red. His nose was bleeding.

"Mommy is done for the day," he choked out through his weeping.

"I know, buddy. I know."

He crossed the room to me and buried his head in my chest. I held him.

"Mommy is done for the day," he said. He said that over and over.

• • •

I cleaned his face, put him in a fresh t-shirt and took him out to the kitchen for ice cream. A little twinge as I spooned it into the bowl, remembering those last weeks with Grace as she tried to teach me everything she'd learned about raising an autistic son while she was home alone and I was off fighting my country's pointless wars.

"He'll try to make everything about food," she said. "You can't let him. I know it's easier sometimes, but you can't let him."

Easier sometimes, Jesus. Even letting him make everything about food, I was barely hanging on.

I'd just put the ice cream on the table when I saw the cop car pull up. I remembered the light going on over at Mrs. White's. That fucking bitch.

Billy saw the police car, too.

"Blue police," he said. His voice was tight and he held his spoon in a clenched fist.

• • •

I opened the door, met the cops on the porch.

"Look, guys, I know you're going to have to come in, but let me just fill you in on what's going on here, OK?"

"Sir, if you'll just move away from the door, we can talk inside."

Both young guys this time. One moved a little to his right, creating some space, The kind of thing you do if you think there's going to be trouble.

I put my hands up. "You guys aren't going to have any trouble with me, I promise, OK? It's just I've got a autistic son, and we're switching meds, he's pretty volatile right now."

"We're still going to have to come in, sir. We've already had a unit here once today. I've seen the report."

I nodded. "Yeah, OK, I can see where that looks bad. It's just, there's a lot going on here."

Billy shouted in the kitchen and threw his bowl. It bounced into the hallway by the door, leaving a smear of ice cream on the floor.

"I need you to move out of the doorway right now, sir." He'd gone to his cop voice, the one that told you things were going to go south unless you did what he said.

Billy came running from the kitchen, heading full tilt for the door. I turned to stop him, taking a step, when one of the cops grabbed me from behind, grabbed my left shoulder.

I yelled, shook loose and bent down, catching Billy around the waist with my right arm. He was running hard, so I lost my footing and went down on my right side. Billy's head hit the corner of the wall and started gushing blood.

"Let go of the boy, get on your stomach and put your hands behind your back!" The other cop shouting now, Billy bellowing and squirming. I held tight to my son, laying on my right side.

The cop on the right had his baton out now. "On your stomach now!"

"Just cool it a minute, OK?"

He gave me a shot on the left thigh. "Stop it!" I yelled. "Just let the kid calm down!"

Billy jerked his head back, catching me on the nose. It started to bleed. My grip slipped a little.

"Let go of the boy!" the cop again. He gave me a shot on the left shoulder with his baton.

A flare of pain, everything blinking out for just a second, but that was all Billy needed. He was up, running, trying to split the two cops, trying to get out the door. They both grabbed him, his momentum pushing them all out onto the porch, Billy bellowing and writhing.

I shoved myself up with my right arm, my left hanging limp and useless.

"Stay back!" the cop on the right shouted.

He had his arm around Billy's head. Billy bit down hard into the blue sleeve. The cop tried to pull his arm away, but Billy's teeth held tight. Finally, the cop tore it loose, losing a chunk of flesh and shirt in the process. He backed away a couple of steps to the right, Billy scrabbling his feet, pushing the other cop away to the left.

The cop on the right looked at his bleeding arm, and then reached for his belt. Taser. He was going to use it on my son. I jumped forward, between him and Billy, and got my hand on the weapon just before he fired. The darts bit into my stomach, the shock freezing me, dropping me, behind me Billy screaming, the other cop grunting, feet scuffling.

I heard a shot.

I tried to roll over, to get up, but could only turn my head. The other cop's gun was out, both he and Billy both had their hands locked on it, the gun pointed at Billy's chest. Billy's face was frozen, his jaw hanging open.

"Oh God!" the cop said.

Billy sank to his knees, pulling the gun loose from the cop's hands as he fell, the weapon clattering to the porch just in front of my face. Billy collapsed backwards, on top of the gun, blood spreading across the front of his t-shirt, some blood already spurting from his mouth as he fought to breathe.

I dragged myself to him, the shock from the Taser fading, got my right arm under his head, my left draped useless across him. I pressed my face to his, kissing him on the cheek. He was panting, blood spattering out in the shallow breaths I'd seen before, too many times.

"This is a scary show," he said.

"I know, buddy."

"Blue police hurt me."

"It's OK."

Billy arched, a violent cough, a sheet of blood flooding out, flowing down his face.

"Mommy is done for the day," he whispered, and he went slack.

I dug my arm under him, trying to lift him, to hold him. I felt the gun.

"He grabbed the gun," the cop said, his voice sounding vacant and empty. I wasn't sure who he was talking to. I don't think he knew.

Beneath my dead son, I curled my hand around the grip of the weapon.

The other cop was yelling into his radio, calling for an ambulance that he didn't need.

I didn't know what to do, but knew I didn't want to let go of the gun. All my adult life, weapons had been the answer. And I needed an answer.

"Where is your pistol? Radio cop talking to the cop who had shot my son.

"What?" Shooter cop, still stunned.

"Your gun, where is it?"

The cop looked down, looked around.

"Fell off the porch I think."

"Ah Jesus. OK. Crime scene will need to look at it. Oh God, what a mess."

My grip tightened around the gun. It's right here. That's what I should have said. That's what I wanted to say.

Radio cop stepped down off the porch, looking for the gun. With him out of the way, I could see Mrs. White standing in her driveway in her bathrobe, holding a cup of coffee, her face looking just like it always looked. Concern, you'd say, if you didn't know her.

I felt the gun in my hand. I thought of the cop who had killed my son, but that was just a fuck up. I thought of Iraq. All the dead soldiers, all the dead Hajis, all the dead women and children, all of it just a fuck up, the dead never being the ones that caused anything, the dead just being the guys that the mullahs and the politicians had sent out to do their bullet catching for them, nothing changing, the new boss, the old boss, everybody playing the fool, thought of all the blood on my hands from back then, the real blood on my hands now, thought of Grace, thought of how you try all your life just to make something right, to make anything right, and how it ends up like this, my son's blood dripping through the spaces between the wood.

And then Mrs. White raised her coffee cup to her lips, took a sip, standing in her driveway in front of her perfect lawn and her perfect bushes, watching my life come apart like she was watching TV.

I yanked the gun from beneath my dead son's body, rolled to prone and put three in her chest before radio cop could even reach for his piece. He had it out now, leveled at me.

"Drop it!"

I stole one last look at my son, and then rolled toward the cop. The bullets hurt less than the Taser, hurt less than any of this. Shock, I knew. That's OK, I'd be dead before it wore off.

I was done for the day.

String Music

George Pelecanos

TONIO HARRIS

Down around my way, when I'm not in school or lookin out for my moms and little sister, I like to run ball. Pick-up games mostly. That's not the only kind of basketball I do. I been playin organized all my life, the Jelleff League and Urban Coalition, too. Matter of fact, I'm playin for my school team right now, in what used to be called the Interhigh. It's no boast to say that I can hold my own in most any kind of game. But pick-up is where I really get amped.

In organized ball, they expect you to pass a whole bunch, take the percentage shot. Not too much showboatin, nothin like that. In pickup, we ref our own games, and most of the hackin and pushin and stuff, except for the flagrant, it gets allowed. I can deal with that. But in pickup, see, you can pretty much freestyle, try everything out you been practicing on your own. Like those Kobe and Vince moves. What I'm sayin is, out here on the asphalt you can really show your shit.

Where I come from, you've got to understand, most of the time it's rough. I don't have to describe it if you know the area of D.C. I'm talkin about: the 4th District, down around Park View, in Northwest. I got problems at home, I got problems at school, I got problems walkin down the street. I prob'ly got problems with my future, you want the plain truth. When I'm runnin ball, though, I don't think on those problems at all. It's like all the chains are off, you understand what I'm sayin? Maybe you grew up somewheres else, and if you did, it'd be hard for you to see. But I'm just tryin to describe it, is all.

Here's an example: earlier today I got into this beef with this boy James Wallace. We was runnin ball over on the playground where I go to school, Roosevelt High, on 13th Street, just a little bit north of my neighborhood. There's never any chains left on those outdoor buckets, but the rims up at Roosevelt are straight, and the backboards are forgiving. That's like my home court. Those buckets they got, I been playin them since I was kid, and I can shoot the eyes out of those motherfuckers most any day of the week.

We had a four-on-four thing goin on, a pretty good one, too. It was the second game we had played. Wallace and his boys, after we beat 'em the first game, they went over to Wallace's car, a black Maxima with a spoiler and pretty rims, and fired up a blunt. They were gettin their heads up and listenin to the new Nas comin out the speakers from the open doors of the car. I don't like

Nas's new shit much as I did *Illmatic*, but it sounded pretty good.

Wallace and them, they with a dealer in my neighborhood, so they always got good herb, too. I got no problem with that. I might even have hit some of that hydro with 'em if they'd asked. But they didn't ask.

Anyway, they came back pink-eyed, lookin all cooked and shit, debatin over which was better, Phillies or White Owls. We started the second game. Me and mines went up by three or four buckets pretty quick. Right about then I knew we was gonna win this one like we won the first, 'cause I had just caught a little fire.

Wallace decided to cover me. He had switched off with this other dude, Antuane, but Antuane couldn't run with me, not one bit. So Wallace switched, and right away he was all chest-out, talkin shit about how "now we gonna see" and all that. Whateva. I was on my inside game that day and I knew it. I mean, I was crossin motherfuckers *out*, just driving the paint at will. And Wallace, he was slow on me by like, half a step. I had stopped passin to the other fellas at that point, 'cause it was just too easy to take it in on him. I mean, he was givin it to me, so why not?

Bout the third time I drove the lane and kissed one in, Wallace bumped me while I was walkin back up to the foul line to take the check. Then he said somethin about my sneaks, somethin that made his boys laugh. He was crackin on me, is all, tryin to shake me up. I got a nice pair of Jordans, the Penny style, and I keep 'em clean with Fantastik and shit, but they're from, like, last year. And James Wallace is always wearin whatever's new, the Seventeens or whatever it is they got sittin up front at the Foot Locker, just came in. Plus Wallace didn't like me all that much. He had money from his druggin, I mean to tell you that boy had *everything*, but he had dropped out of school back in the tenth grade, and I had stayed put. My moms always says that guys like Wallace resent guys like me who have hung in. Add that to that fact that he never did have my game. I think he was a little jealous of me, you want the truth.

I do know he was frustrated that day. I knew it, and I guess I shouldn't have done what I did. I should've passed off to one of my boys, but you know how it is. When you're proud about somethin you got to show it, 'specially down here. And I was on. I took the check from him and drove to the bucket, just blew right past him as easy as I'd been doin all afternoon. That's when Wallace called me a bitch right in front of everybody there.

There's a way to deal with this kinda shit. You learn it over time. I go six-two and I got some shoulders on me, so it wasn't like I feared Wallace physically or nothin like that. I can go with my hands, too. But in this world we got out here, you don't want to be getting in any kinda beefs, not if you can help it. At the same time, you can't show no fear; you get a rep for weakness like that, it's like bein a bird with a busted wing, sumshit like that. The other thing you can't do, though, you can't let that kind of comment pass. Someone tries to take you for bad like that, you got to respond. It's complicated, I know, but there it is.

"I ain't heard what you said," I said, all ice cool and shit, seein if he would go ahead and repeat it, lookin to measure just how far he wanted to push it. Also, I was tryin to buy a little time.

"Said you's a bitch," said Wallace, lickin his lips and smilin like he was a bitch his *own* self. He'd made a couple steps towards me and now he wasn't all that far away from my face.

I smiled back, halfway friendly. "You know I ain't no faggot," I said. "Shit, James, it hurts me to fart."

A couple of the fellas started laughin then and pretty soon all of em was laughin, I'd heard that line on one of my Uncle's old time comedy albums once, that old Signifyin' Monkey shit or maybe Pryor. But I guess these fellas hadn't heard it, and they laughed like a motherfucker when I said it. Wallace laughed, too. Maybe it was the hydro they'd smoked. Whatever it was, I had broken that shit down, turned it right back on him, you see what I'm sayin? While they was still laughin, I said, "C'mon, check it up top, James, let's play."

I didn't play so proud after that. I passed off and only took a coupla shots myself the rest of the game. I think I even missed one on purpose towards the end. I ain't stupid. We still won, but not by much; I saw to it that it wasn't so one-sided, like it had been before.

When it was over, Wallace wanted to play another game, but the sun was dropping and I said I had to get on home. I needed to pick up my sister at aftercare, and my moms likes both of us to be inside our apartment when she gets home from work. Course, I didn't tell any of the fellas that. It wasn't somethin they needed to know.

Wallace was goin back my way, I knew, but he didn't offer to give me a ride. He just looked at me dead-eyed and smiled a little before him and his boys walked back to the Maxima, parked along the curb. My stomach flipped some, I got to admit, seein that flatline thing in his peeps. I knew from that empty look that it wasn't over between us, but what could I do?

I picked up my ball and headed over to Georgia Avenue. Walked south toward my mother's place as the first shadows of night were crawling onto the streets.

SERGEANT PETERS

It's five a.m. I'm sitting in my cruiser up near the station house, sipping a coffee. My first one of the night. Rolling my head around on these tired shoulders of mine. You get these aches when you're behind the wheel of a car, six hours at a stretch. I oughta buy one of those things the African cabbies all sit on, looks like a rack of wooden balls. You know, for your back. I been doin this for twenty-two years now, so I guess whatever damage I've done to my spine and all, it's too late.

I work midnights in the Fourth District. 4D starts at the Maryland line and runs south to Harvard Street and Georgia. The western border is Rock Creek Park and the eastern line is North Capitol Street. It's what the news people call a "high crime district." For a year or two I tried working the Third, keeping the streets safe for rich white people basically, but I got bored. I guess I'm one of those adrenaline junkies they're always talking about on those cop shows on TV, the shows got female cops who look more beautiful than any female cop I've ever seen. I guess that's what it is. It's not like I've ever examined myself or anything like that. My wife and I don't talk about it, that's for damn sure. A ton of cop marriages don't make it; I suppose mine has survived 'cause I never bring any of this shit home with me. Not that she knows about, anyway.

My shift runs from the stroke of twelve till dawn, though I usually get into the station early so I can nab the cruiser I like. I prefer the Crown Victoria. It's roomier, and once you flood the gas into the cylinders, it really moves. Also, I like to ride alone.

Last night, Friday, wasn't much different than any other. It's summer; more people are outside, trying to stay out of their unairconditioned places as long as possible, so this time of year we put extra cars out on the streets. Also, like I reminded some of the younger guys at the station last night, this was the week welfare checks got mailed out, something they needed to know. Welfare checks mean more drunks, more domestic disturbances, more violence. One of the young cops I said it to, he said, "Thank you, Sergeant Dad," but he didn't do it in a bad way. I know those young guys appreciate it when I mention shit like that.

Soon as I drove south I saw that the Avenue, Georgia Avenue that is, was hot with activity. All those Jap tech bikes the young kids like to ride, curbed outside the all-night Wing n' Things. People spilling out of bars, hanging outside the Korean beer markets, scratching game cards, talking trash, ignoring the crackheads hitting them up for spare change. Drunks lying in the doorways of the closed-down shops, their heads resting against the riot gates. Kids, a lot of kids, standing on corners, grouped around tricked-out cars, rap music and that go-go crap coming from the open windows. The further south you go the worse all of this gets.

The bottom of the barrel is that area between Quebec Street and Irving. The newspapers lump it all in with a section of town called Petworth, but I'm talking about Park View. Poverty, drug activity, crime. They got that Section 8 housing back in there, the Park Morton complex. What we used to call "the projects" back when you could say it. Government assisted hellholes. Gangs like the Park Street and Morton Street Crews. Open air drug markets, I'm talking about blatant transactions right out there on Georgia Avenue. Drugs are Park View's industry; the dealers are the biggest employers in this part of town.

The dealers get the whole neighborhood involved. They recruit kids to be lookouts for 'em. Give these kids beepers and cells to warn them off when the Five-O comes around. Entry level positions. Some of the parents, when there *are* parents, participate, too. Let these drug dealers duck into their apartments when there's heat. Teach their kids not to talk to The Man. So you got kids being raised in a culture that say the drug dealers are the good guys and the cops are bad. I'm not lying. It's exactly how it is.

The trend now is to sell marijuana. Coke, crack and heroin, you can still get it, but the new thing is to deal pot. Here's why: up until recently, in the District, possession or distribution of marijuana up to ten pounds—*ten pounds*—was a misdemeanor. They've changed that law, but still, kid gets popped for selling grass, he knows he's gonna do no time. Even on a distribution beef, black juries won't send a black kid into the prison system for a marijuana charge, that's a proven fact. Prosecutors know this, so they usually no-paper the case. That means most of the time they don't even go to court with it. I'm not bullshitting. Makes you wonder why they even bother having drug laws to begin with. They legalize the stuff, they're gonna take the bottom right out the market, and the violent crimes in this city would go down to, like, nothing. Don't get me started. I know it sounds strange, a cop saying this. But you'd be surprised how many of us feel that way.

Okay, I got off the subject. I was talking about my night.

Early on I got a domestic call, over on Otis Place. When I got there, two cruisers were on the scene, four young guys, two of them with flashlights. A rookie named Buzzy talked to a woman at the front door of her rowhouse, then came back and told me that the object of the complaint was behind the place, in the alley. I walked around back alone and into the alley and right off I recognized the man standing inside the fence of his tiny, brown-grass yard. Harry Lang, sixty-some years old. I'd been to this address a few times in the past ten years.

I said, "Hello, Harry," Harry said, "Officer," and I said, "Wait right here, okay?" Then I went through the open gate. Harry's wife was on her back porch, flanked by her two sons, big strapping guys, all of them standing under a triangle of harsh white light coming from a naked bulb. Mrs. Lang's face and body language told me that the situation had resolved itself. Generally, once we arrive, domestic conflicts tend to calm down on their own.

Mrs. Lang said that Harry had been verbally abusive that night, demanding money from her, even though he'd just got paid. I asked her if Harry had struck her and her response was negative. But she had a job, too, she worked just as hard as him, why should she support his lifestyle and let her speak to her like that... I was listening and not listening, if you know what I mean. I made my sincere face, and nodded every few seconds or so.

I asked her if she wanted me to lock Harry up, and of course she said no. I asked what she did want, and she said she didn't want to see him "for the rest of the night." I told her I thought I could arrange that, and started back to have a talk with Harry. I felt the porch light go off behind me as I hit the bottom of the wooden stairs. Dogs had begun to bark in the neighboring yards.

Harry was short and low-slung, a black black man, nearly featureless in the dark. He wore a porkpie hat and his clothes were pressed and clean. He kept his eyes down as I spoke to him over the barks of the dogs. His reaction-time was very slow when I asked for a response. I could see right away that he was on a nod.

Harry had been a controlled heroin junkie for the last thirty years. During that time, he'd always held a job, lived in this same house, and been there, in one condition or another, for his kids. I'd wager he went to church on Sundays, too. But a junkie was what he was. Heroin was a slow ride down. Some folks could control it to some degree and never hit the bottom.

I asked Harry if he could find a place to sleep that night other than his house, and he told me that he "supposed" he could. I told him I didn't want to see him again any time soon, and he said, "It's mutual." I chuckled at that, giving him some of his pride back, which didn't cost me a thing. He walked down the alley, stopping once to cup his hands around a match as he put fire to a cigarette.

I drove back over to Georgia. A guy flagged me down just to talk. They see my car number and they know its me. Sergeant Peters, the old white cop. You get a history with these people. Some of these kids, I know their parents. I've busted em from time to time. Busted their grandparents, too. Shows you how long I've been doing this.

Down around Morton I saw Tonio Harris, a neighborhood kid walking alone towards The Black Hole. Tonio was wearing those workboots and the baggy pants low, like all the other kids, although he's not like most of them. I took his mother in for drugs a long time ago, back when that Love Boat stuff was popular and making everyone crazy. His father, the one who impregnated his mother I mean, he's doing a stretch for manslaughter, his third fall. Tonio's mother's clean now, at least I think she is; anyway, she's done a fairly good job with him. By that I mean he's got no juvenile priors, from what I know. A minor miracle down here, you ask me.

I rolled down my window. "Hey, Tonio, how's it going?" I slowed down to crawl, took in the sweetish smell of reefer in the air. Tonio was still walking, not looking at me, but he mumbled something about "I'm maintainin," or some shit like that. "You take care of yourself in there," I said, meaning in The Hole, "and get yourself home right after." He didn't respond verbally, just made a half-assed kind of acknowledgement with his chin.

I cruised around for the next couple of hours. Turned my spot on kids hanging in the shadows, told them to break it up and move along. Asked a guy in Columbia Heights why his little boy was out on the stoop, dribbling a basketball, at one in the morning. Raised my voice at a boy, a lookout for a dealer, who was sitting on top of a trashcan, told him to get his ass on home. Most of the time, this is my night. We're just letting the critters know we're out here.

At around two I called in a few cruisers to handle the closing of The Black Hole. You never know what's going to happen at the end of the night there, what kind of beefs got born inside the club, who looked at who a little too hard for one second too long. Hard to believe that an ex-cop from Prince George's County runs the place. That a cop would put all this trouble on us, bring it into our district. He's got D.C. cops moonlighting as bouncers in there, too, working the metal detectors at the door. I talked with one, a young white cop, earlier in the night. I noticed the brightness in his eyes and the sweat beaded across his forehead. He was scared, like I gave a shit. Asked us as a favor to show some kind of presence at closing time. Called me "Sarge." Okay. I didn't answer him. I got no sympathy for the cops who work those go-go joints, especially not since Officer Brian Gibson was shot dead outside the Ibex Club a few years back. But if something goes down around the place, it's on me. So I do my job.

I called in a few cruisers and set up a couple of traffic barriers on Georgia, one at Lamont and one at Park. We diverted the cars like that, kept the kids from congregating on the street. It worked. Nothing too bad was happening that I could see. I was standing outside my cruiser, talking to another cop, Eric Young, who was having a smoke. That's when I saw Tonio Harris running east on Morton, heading for the housing complex. A late model black import was behind him, and there were a couple of YBMs with their heads out the open windows, yelling shit out, laughing at the Harris kid, like that.

"You all right here?" I said to Young.

"Fine, Sarge," he said.

My cruiser was idling. I slid under the wheel and pulled down on the tree.

TONIO HARRIS

Just around midnight, when I was fixin to go out, my moms walked into my room. I was sittin on the edge of my bed, lacing up my Timbs, listening to PGC comin from the box, Flexx doin his shout-outs and then movin right into the new Nelly, which is vicious. The music was so loud that I didn't hear my mother walk in, but when I looked up there she was, one arm crossed over the other like she does when she's tryin to be hard, staring me down.

"Whassup mama?"

"What's up with *you*?"

I shrugged. "Back Yard is playin' tonight. Was thinkin I'd head over to The Hole."

"Did you ask me if you could?"

"Do I *have* to?" I used that tone she hated, knew right away I'd made a mistake.

"You're living in my house, aren't you?"

"Uh-huh."

"You payin rent now?"

"No maam."

"Talkin about, *do I have to*."

"Can I go?"

Momma uncrossed her arms. "Thought you said you'd be studyin up for that test this weekend."

"I will. Gonna do it tomorrow morning, first thing. Just wanted to go out and hear a little music tonight, is all."

I saw her eyes go soft on me then. "You gonna study for that exam, you hear?"

"I promise I will."

"Go on, then. Come right back after the show."

"Yes, maam."

I noticed as he was walkin out the door her shoulders were getting stooped some. Bad posture and a hard life. She wasn't but thirty-six years old.

I spent a few more minutes listening to the radio and checking myself in the mirror. Pattin my natural and shit. I got a nice modified cut, not too short, not blown-out or nothin like that. For awhile now the fellas been wearin braids, tryin to look like The Answer. But I don't think it would look right on me. And I know what the girls like. They look at me, they like what they see. I can tell.

Moms has been ridin me about my college entrance exam. I fucked up the first one I took. I went out and got high on some fierce chronic the night before it, and my head was filled up with cobwebs the next morning when I sat down in the school cafeteria to take that test. I'm gonna take it again, though, and do better next time.

I'm not one of those guys who's got, what do you call that, illusions about my future. No NBA dreams, nothin like that. I'm not good enough or tall enough, I know it. I'm sixth man on my high school team, that ought to tell you somethin right there. My Uncle Gaylen, he's been real good to me, and straight-up with me, too. Told me to have fun with ball and all that, but not to depend on it. To stick with the books. I know I fucked up that test, but next time I'm gonna do better, you can believe that.

I was thinkin, though, I could get me a partial scholarship playin for one of those small schools in Virginia or Maryland, William and Mary or maybe Goucher up in Baltimore. Hold up—Goucher's for women only, I think. Maybe I'm wrong. Have to ask my guidance counselor, soon as I can find one. Ha-ha.

The other thing I should do, for real, is find me a part-time job. I'm tired of havin no money in my pockets. My mother works up at the Dollar Store in the Silver Spring mall, and she told me she could hook me up there. But I don't wanna work with my mother. And I don't want to be workin at no *Mac*-Donalds or sumshit like that. Have the neighborhood slangers come in and make fun of me and shit, standin there in my minimum wage uniform. But I do need some money. I'd like to buy me a nice car soon. I'm not talkin about some hooptie, neither.

I did have an interview for this restaurant downtown, bussin tables. White boy who interviewed kept sayin shit like, "Do you think you can make it into work on time?" and Do you think this and Do you think that? Might as well gone ahead and called me a nigger right to my face. The more he talked the more attitude I gave him with my eyes. After all that, he smiled and sat up straight, like he was gonna make some big announcement, and said he was gonna give me a try. I told him I changed my mind and walked right out of there. Uncle Gaylen said I should've taken that job and showed him he was wrong. But I couldn't. I can't stand how white people talk to you sometimes. Like they're just there to make their own selves feel better. I hired a Negro today, and like that.

I *am* gonna take that test over, though.

I changed my shirt and went out through the living room. My sister was watchin the 106 and Park videos on TV, her mouth around a straw, sippin on one of those big sodas. She's startin to get some titties on her. Some of the slick young niggas in the neighborhood been commentin on it, too. Late for her to be awake, but it was Friday night. She didn't look up as I passed. I yelled goodbye to my moms and heard her say my name from the kitchen. I knew she was back up in there 'cause I smelled the smoke comin off her cigarette. There was a ten-dollar bill sittin in a bowl by the door. I folded it up and slipped it inside my jeans. My mother had left it there for me. I'm tellin you, she is cool people.

Outside the complex, I stepped across this little road and the dark courtyard real quick. We been livin here a long time, and I know most everyone by sight. But in this place here, that don't mean shit.

The Black Hole had a line goin outside the door when I got there. I went through the metal detector and let a white rent-a-cop pat me down while I said hey to a friend going into the hall. I could feel the bass from way out in the lobby.

The hall was crowded and the place was bumpin. I could smell sweat in the damp air. Also chronic, and it was nice. Back Yard was doin "Freestyle," off *Hood Related*, that double CD they got. I kind of made my way towards the stage, careful not to bump nobody, nodding to the ones I did. I knew a lot of young brothers there. Some of 'em run in gangs, some not. I try to know a little bit of everybody, you see what I'm sayin? Spread your friends out in case you run into some trouble. I was smilin at some of the girls, too.

Up near the front I got into the groove. Someone passed me somethin that smelled good, and I hit it. Back Yard was turnin that shit out. I been knowin their music for like ten years now. They had the whole joint up there that night, I'm talkin about a horn section and everything else. I must have been up there close to the stage for about, I don't know, an hour, sumshit like that, just dancing. It seemed like all of us was all movin together. On "Do That Stuff," they went into this extended drum thing, shout-outs for the hoodies and the crews; I was sweatin clean through my shirt, right about then.

I had to pee like a motherfucker, but I didn't want to use the bathroom in that place. All the hard motherfuckers be congregatin in there, too. That's where trouble can start, just 'cause you gave someone the wrong kinda look.

When the set broke I started to talkin to this girl who'd been dancin near me, smilin my way. I'd seen her around. Matter of fact, I ran ball sometimes with her older brother. So we had somethin to talk about straight off. She had that Brandy thing goin on with her hair, and a nice smile.

While we was talkin, someone bumped me from behind. I turned around and it was Antuane, that kid who ran with James Wallace. Wallace was with him, and so were a coupla Wallace's boys. I nodded at Antuane, tryin to communicate to him, like, "Ain't no thing, you bumpin me like that." But Wallace stepped in and said somethin to me. I couldn't even really hear it with all the crowd noise, but I could see by his face that he was tryin to step *to* me. I mean, he was right up in my face.

We stared at each other for a few. I shoulda just walked away, right, but I couldn't let him punk me out like that in front of the girl.

Wallace's hand shot up. Looked like a bird flutterin out of nowhere or somethin. Maybe he was just makin a point with that hand, like some do. But it rattled me, I guess, and I reacted. Didn't even think about it, though I should've. My palms went to his chest and I shoved him back. He stumbled. I saw his eyes flare with anger, but there was that other thing, too, worse than me puttin my hands on him: I had stripped him of his pride.

There was some yellin then from his boys. I just turned and bucked. I saw the bouncers started to move, talkin into their headsets and shit, but I didn't wait. I bucked. I was out on the street pretty quick, runnin towards my place. I didn't know what else to do.

I heard Wallace and them behind me, comin out the Hole. They said my name. I didn't look back. I ran to Morton and turned right. Heard car doors opening and slammin shut. The engine of the car turnin over. Then the cry of tires on the street and Wallace's boys laughin, yellin shit out. I kept runnin towards Park Morton. My heart felt like it was snappin on a rubber string.

There were some youngins out in the complex. They were sittin up on top of a low brick wall like they do, and they watched me run by. It's always dark here, ain't never no good kinda light. They got some dim yellow bulbs back in the stairwells, where the old-school types drink gin and shoot craps. They was back up in there, too, hunched down in the shadows. There was some kind of fog or haze out that night, too, it was kind of rollin around by that old playground equipment, all rusted and shit, they got in the courtyard. I was runnin through there, tryin to get to my place.

I had to cross the little road in the back of the complex to get to my mother's apartment. I stepped into it and that's when I saw the black Maxima swing around the corner. Coupla Wallace's boys jumped out while the car was still moving. I stopped runnin. They knew where I lived. If they didn't, all they had to do was ask one of those youngins on the wall. I wasn't gonna bring none of this home to my moms.

Wallace was out of the driver's side quick, walkin towards me. He was smilin and my stomach shifted. Antuane had walked back by the playground. I knew where he was goin. Wallace and them keep a gun, a nine with a fifteen-round mag, buried in a shoebox back there.

"Junior," said Wallace, "you done fucked up big." He was still smilin.

I didn't move. My knees were shakin some. I figured this was it. I was thinkin about my mother and tryin not to cry. Thinkin about how if I did cry, that's all anyone would remember about me. That I went out like a bitch before I died. Funny me thinkin about stupid shit like that while I was waitin for Antuane to come back with that gun.

I saw Antuane's figure walkin back out through that fog.

And then I saw the spotlight movin across the courtyard, and where it came from. An MPD Crown Vic was comin up the street, kinda slow. The driver turned on the overheads, throwing colors all around. Antuane backpedaled and then he was gone.

The cruiser stopped and driver's door opened. The white cop I'd seen earlier in the night got out. Sergeant Peters. My moms had told me his name. Told me he was all right.

Peters was puttin on his hat as he stepped out. He had pulled his nightstick and his other hand just brushed the Glock on his right hip. Like he was just lettin us all know he had it.

"Evening, gentlemen," he said, easy like. "We got a problem here?"

"Nope," said Wallace, kinda in a white-boy's voice, still smiling.

"Somethin funny?" said Peters.

Wallace didn't say nothin'. Peters looked at me and then back at Wallace.

"You all together?" said Peters.

"We just out here havin a conversation," said Wallace.

Sergeant Peters gave Wallace a look then, like he was disgusted with him, and then he sighed.

"You," said Peters, turnin to me. I was prayin he wasn't gonna say my name, like me and him was friends and shit.

"Yeah?" I said, not too friendly but not, like, impolite.

"You live around here?" He *knew* I did.

I said, "Uh-huh."

"Get on home."

I turned around and walked. Slow but not too slow. I heard the white cop talkin to Wallace and the others, and the crackle of his radio comin from the car. Red and blue was strobin across the bricks of the complex. Under my breath I was sayin, thanks God.

In my apartment, everyone was asleep. I turned off the TV set and covered my sister, who was lyin on the couch. Then I went back to my room and turned the box on so I could listen to my music low. I sat on the edge of the bed. My hand was shaking. I put it together with my other hand and laced my fingers tight.

SERGEANT PETERS

After the Park Morton incident, I answered a domestic call over on First and Kennedy. A young gentleman, built like a fullback, had beat his girl up pretty bad. Her face was already swelling when I arrived and there was blood and spittle bubbling on the side of her mouth. The first cops on the scene had cuffed the perp and had him bent over the hood of their cruiser. At this point the girlfriend, she was screaming at the cops. Some of the neighborhood types, hanging outside of a windowless bar on Kennedy, had begun screaming at the cops, too. I figured they were drunk and high on who-knew-what, so I radioed in for a few more cars.

We made a couple of additional arrests. Like they say in the TV news, the situation had escalated. Not a full-blown riot, but trouble nonetheless. Someone yelled out at me, called me a "cracker-ass motherfucker." I didn't even blink. The county cops don't take an ounce of that kinda shit, but we take it every night. Sticks and stones, like that. Then someone started whistling the theme from the old Andy Griffith show, you know, the one where he played a small town sheriff, and everyone started to laugh. Least they didn't call me Barney Fife. The thing was, when the residents start with the comedy, you know it's over, that things have gotten under control. So I didn't mind. Actually, the guy who was whistling, he was pretty good.

When that was over with, I pulled a car over on 5th and Princeton, back by the Old Soldier's Home. It matched the description of a shooter's car from earlier in the night. I waited for backup, standing behind the left rear quarter panel of the car, my holster unsnapped, the light from my Mag pointed at rear window.

When my backup came, we searched the car and frisked the four YBMs. They had those little-tree deodorizers hangin from the rearview, and one of those plastic, king-crown deodorizers sitting on the back panel, too. A crown. Like they're royalty, right? God, sometimes these people make me laugh. Anyhow, they were clean with no live warrants, and we let them go.

I drove around, and it was quiet. Between three a.m. and dawn, the city gets real still. Beautiful in a way, even for down here.

The last thing I did, I helped some Spanish guy try to get back into his place in Petworth. Said his key didn't work, and it didn't. Someone, his landlord or his woman, had changed the locks on him, I figured. Liquor-stench was pouring out of him. Also, he smelled like he hadn't taken a shower for days. When I left him he was standing on the sidewalk, sort of rocking back and forth, staring at the front of the rowhouse, like if he looked at it long enough the door was gonna open on its own.

So now I'm parked here near the station, sipping coffee. It's my ritual, like. The sky is beginning to lighten. This here is my favorite time of night.

I'm thinking that on my next shift, or the one after, I'll swing by and see Tonio Harris's mother. I haven't talked to her in years, anyway. See how she's been doing. Suggest to her, without acting like I'm telling her what to do, that maybe she ought to have her son lie low some. Stay in the next few weekend nights. Let that beef he's got with those others, whatever it is, die down. Course, I know those kinds of beefs don't go away. I'll make her aware of it, just the same.

The Harris kid, he's lucky he's got someone like his mother, lookin after him. I drive back in there at the housing complex, and I see those young kids sitting on that wall at two in the morning, looking at me with hate in their eyes, and all I can think of is, where are the parents? Yeah, I know, there's a new curfew in effect for minors. Some joke. Like we've got the manpower and facilities to enforce it. Like we're supposed to raise these kids, too.

Anyway, it's not my job to think too hard about that. I'm just lettin these people know that we're out here, watching them. I mean, what else can you do?

My back hurts. I got to get me one of those things you sit on, with the wood balls. Like those African cab drivers do.

TONIO HARRIS

This morning I studied some in my room until my eyes got sleepy. It was hard to keep my mind on the book cause I was playin some Ludacris on the box, and it was fuckin with my concentration. That joint was tight.

I figured I was done for the day, and there wasn't no one around to tell me different. My mother was at work at the Dollar Store, and my sister was over at a friend's. I put my sneaks on and grabbed my ball, and headed up to Roosevelt.

I walked up Georgia, dribblin the sidewalk when I could, usin my left and keeping my right behind my back, like my coach told me to do. I cut down Upshur and walked up 13th, past my school to the court. The court is on the small side and its backboards are square, with bumper stickers and shit stuck on the boards. It's beside a tennis court and all of it is fenced in. There's a baseball field behind it; birds always be sittin on that field.

There was a four-on-four full court thing happenin when I got there. I called next with another guy, Dimitrius Johnson, who I knew could play. I could see who was gonna win this game, cause the one team had this boy named Peter Hawk who could do it all. We'd pick up two off the losers squad. I watched the game and after a minute I'd already had those two picked out.

The game started kind of slow. I was feelin out my players and those on the other side. Someone had set up a box courtside and they had that live Roots thing playin. It was one of those pretty days with the sun out and high clouds, the kind look like pillows, and the weather and that upbeat music comin from the box set the tone. I felt loose and good.

Me and Hawk was coverin each other. He was one of those who could go left or right, dribble or shoot with either hand. He took me to the hole once or twice. Then I noticed he always eye-faked in the opposite direction he was gonna go before he made his move. So it gave me the advantage, knowin which side he was gonna jump to, and I gained position on him like that.

I couldn't shut Hawk down, not all the way, but I forced him to change his game. I made a couple of nice assists on offense and drained one my own self from way downtown. One of Hawk's players tried to claim a charge, doin that Reggie Miller punk shit, his arms windmillin as he went back. That shit don't go in pickup, and even his own people didn't back him. My team went up by one.

We stopped the game for a minute or so, so one of mines could tie up his sneaks. I was lookin across the ballfield at the seagulls and crows, catchin my wind. That's when I saw James Wallace's black Maxima, cruisin slow down Allison, that street that runs alongside the court.

We put the ball back into play. Hawk drove right by me, hit a runner. I fumbled a pass goin back upcourt, and on the turnover they scored again. The Maxima was going south on 13th, just barely moving along. I saw Wallace in the driver's seat, his window down, lookin my way with that smile of his and his dead-ass eyes.

"You playin, Tone?" asked Dimitrius, the kid on my team.

I guess I had lost my concentration and it showed. "I'm playin," I said. "Let's ball."

Dimitrius bricked his next shot. Hawk got the bound and brought the ball up. I watched him do that eye-fake thing again and I stole the ball off him in the lane before he could make his move. I went bucket-to-bucket with it and leaped. I jammed the motherfucker and swung on the rim, comin down and doin one of those Patrick Ewing silent growls at Hawk and the rest of them before shootin downcourt to get back on D. I was all fired up. I felt like we could turn the shit around.

Hawk hit his next shot, a jumper from the top of the key. Dimitrius brought it down, and I motioned for him to dish me the pill. He led me just right. In my side sight I saw a black car rollin down Allison, but I didn't stop to check it out. I drove off a pick, pulled up in front of Hawk, made a head-move and watched him bite. Then I went up. I was way out there but I could tell from how the ball rolled off my fingers that it was gonna go. Ain't no chains on those rims, but I could see the links dance as that rock dropped through. I'm sayin that I could see them dance in my mind.

We was runnin now. The game was full-on and it was fierce. I grabbed one off the rim and made an outlet pass, then beat the defenders myself on the break. I saw black car movin slow on 13th but I didn't even think about it. I was higher than a motherfucker then, my feet and the court and the ball were all one thing. I felt like I could drain it from anywhere, and Hawk, I could see it in his eyes, he knew it, too.

I took the ball and dribbled it up. I knew what I was gonna do, knew exactly where I was gonna go with it, knew wasn't nobody out there could stop me.

I wasn't thinkin about Wallace or the stoop of my mom's shoulders or which nigga was gonna be lookin to fuck my baby sister, and I wasn't thinkin on no job or college test or my future or nothin like that.

I was concentratin on droppin that pill through the hole. Watching myself doin it before I did. Out here in the sunshine, every dark thing far away. Runnin ball like I do. Thinkin that if I kept runnin, that black Maxima and everything else, it would just go away.

Black Shuck
Thomas Pluck

The worst summer I remember was when I turned nine years old, and Blind Joe Death came through the holler, strumming a silver-stringed guitar made from a baby's coffin.

That morning I lit out with Pa's squirrel gun on my shoulder, and Shuck, my blue tick coonhound, by my side. It was a great day to be a boy, with the sun fighting through the leaves, the birds singing their hearts out, and three fox squirrels in my tow sack. Back then I thought any day in the woods with Shuck was great.

I'd met my best friend Red at the swimming hole, and we walked home along the mountain road.

"You want to look for arrowheads before supper?" I asked.

"Sure, long as I get my chores done," he said. "I'd like that fine."

Red was as lanky and freckled as a daddy longlegs with the measles. His left eye had a gray shadow of a goose egg underneath. I didn't ask about it. I knew where he got those from.

We dodged a coal truck barreling down the mountain. The ground trembled long after it passed, like a hungry man's belly. Last year, the mine collapse had swallowed Pa whole. I imagined him still trapped down there sometimes, swinging a pick to dig his way out.

As we neared the crossroads, Shuck whimpered deep in his throat, and wouldn't budge.

"What's got into you, boy?"

Red stared up the road. "You believe in haints, Wade?"

"Never seen one," I told him, "but that don't mean they ain't there."

The woods in Shockey's Hollow are dark and thick, and the old folk tell of ghost Injuns leering through the trees. My Grams told tales of the Wendigo, so hungry and skinny you can only see it from the side, and the Behinder, that no one's ever seen and lived. When I was deep in the woods, the Behinder, or something like it, would make the hairs on my neck raise.

Just then I had that feeling. My feet would neither walk forward, nor run away. I was thinking maybe to panic, when we heard a well-deep voice on top of strings that tingled like a pocketful of silver dimes. I couldn't place where it came from. It sounded deep, like the singer was trapped down in the mine with my Pa.

The sun is on fire, and the moon is a liar
But darling I'll tell you one thing that is true
Wherever I wander and wherever I roam
The smile on your face is what I'll call home

Red and me sat as dumb as two coal buckets as the guitar player rounded the corner. He was skinny as a scarecrow who'd hopped off his cross, looking to eat a few ears of corn himself. He had a shapeless hat mashed on his head, dusty boots and an ice-blue pair of overalls, worn threadbare at the elbows and knees. He picked at a square, black guitar that hung from his shoulder on a leather strap. His fingers danced on the bright silver strings.

"Good afternoon, boys," the singer said. He wore spectacles with smoked lenses, and looked pale as death eating a cracker.

"You play fierce pretty," I said.

"Reckon I've been playing long enough that if I didn't, I should hang myself and be done with it," he replied, and a smile full of small grayed teeth spread across his face. "Name's Joe."

"That's Blind Joe Death," Red whispered.

"That's what they call me," Joe said, and scratched Shuck's ears. "Once, it was just plain Joe. Then Blind Joe, when I lost my sight."

"Why don't you wear an eye patch, like a pirate?" Red asked.

"I'd have to wear two of 'em," Joe said. "I'd look right foolish, don't you think? And I can see some, when the sun's down. I usually walk at night."

"Ain't you scared of haints and such?" Red asked.

Joe held up his guitar by the neck. "My playing must frighten haint and beast alike, for I've never met nothing in the dark that's scarier than what hides in the light."

The thought of him strumming his guitar in the nighttime gave me a shiver. Shuck nudged my side and kept his head low.

"It's all right, boy," I said, and rubbed Shuck's neck.

Joe tilted his head and let the sun hit his face, blue veins showing through the skin. "You young fellas know anyone who might trade the listen of the old music for a little supper?"

"My Ma's making Brunswick stew, Mister uh, Death," Red said.

"Just Joe," he said. "And what should I call my new benefactors?"

"I'm Wade, sir," I said.

"My name's Asa Junior, but everyone calls me Red."

"That's all right, Red." Joe said, strumming up a tune. "My name's Joseph, but everyone calls me Blind Joe Death."

He followed us home and played "Frog, He Went A-Courting," with Shuck howling tenor to his bass. "That's some fine accompaniment," Joe said. "What do you call this pup?"

"That's Shuck, my hound dog."

"Best hunting dog in the holler," Red said.

Joe strummed as he talked, answering the birds that chattered in the pines. "He wouldn't be named after Old Black Shuck, would he?" he said.

"Yup," I said. "My Grams taught me about Old Shuck."

Joe picked low notes, and his dirge shivered my backbone.

Old Black Shuck, you charnel hound,
don't come howling at my door.
I left a plate of meat and bone,
to keep you on the moor.

Shuck whined and tugged at my pants.

"He finds that tune too familiar." Joe laughed, and resumed his livelier picking. "Reckon I could set with your grandma after supper? The old folks remember the old music."

I looked down at my shoes, as we walked. "She's passed."

"Sorry to hear that, Wade. Reckon I'll set with her soon enough."

Grams used to rock her chair and gum her clay pipe, and her eyes would go far away. "Old Shuck, he roams the mist between our world and the next. He's big as a pony, and black as a starless night. With eyes of yellow fire, and a howl that turns a brave man's legs to water." She'd poke my arm with her pipe stem. "Whether your time's come or not, if you hear Black Shuck bark three times, you don't see the sun in the morning."

· · ·

Red slouched as we neared his family's rocky patch of land, which had never seen a plow's blade. Their bony milk cow, Millie, had the roam of it. She left her flops on the path to the door, then stood chewing her cud, waiting for you to step in one.

Mr. Collins liked nothing better than to set on the porch with a jug of shine, and that's how we found him. He stared out at nothing, slumped in his crooked chair with an uncorked jug of lightning dangling from one finger, his eyes as mean as a striped snake's.

"Good afternoon sir," Blind Joe said, and finished the tune with a flourish. "My name's Joe, and I play the old songs, and some new."

"He plays real fine, Pa. I thought maybe he could have some of my stew tonight, so we could hear him play."

Mr. Collins squinted, like he wasn't sure we were real. "You come begging at my door?"

"No, Pa—"

"Quiet, boy," Collins said, and raised his hand.

Red flinched and looked down. "Yessir."

Mr. Collins laughed and slugged back a wallop of shine. "Look around, beggar man. It's hell's half acre. You want something to eat, there's some corn cobs in the outhouse, might be a few kernels left on 'em."

"But Pa, he's blind," Red said.

Mr. Collins wrinkled his nose. "You're that hoodoo man, ain't you?" he said. "Went plumb bereft and clawed out his own peepers when his woman died crapping him out a child."

Joe's face went slack.

"Take your cursed self off my land," Mr. Collins said, and spat at Joe's feet. "You come back, I'll kick that guitar up your hind parts."

"I'll see you after supper, Red," I said.

"Bringing that filthy beggar to our house?" Mr. Collins slipped his belt from its loops, and wrapped it around his hand. "To eat the food I put on your plate?"

Red held out his tow sack. "I caught a mess of frogs," he said. "We can have frog legs."

"Ain't nobody's business what we eat!"

"But you said you like 'em—"

"Don't you sass me, boy!" Mr. Collins struck out with the belt. I winced, but Red didn't flinch. His Ma peered out the window, all sunken eyes and stringy hair. She gave a jagged grin, and set her elbows on the sill.

Mr. Collins took Red by his collar, and lashed the belt buckle back and forth across his face. Snot and blood ran from Red's nose, and his Ma cackled at the show.

Joe's fingers danced over the guitar strings like two white spiders.

Red-haired Mr. Collins, what makes you so cold
whip your boy for being kind, don't that seem strange to you
kick a loyal dog enough, and he'll take a bite of you

Shuck pulled away from me, and bolted up the porch to bark and snap. Mr. Collins kicked him in the ribs, and sent him tumbling into the weeds. Shuck leapt right back and chomped the belt. Shuck pulled hard, and Mr. Collins lost the of tug o' war. He stumbled off the porch, and fell face first into one of Millie's runny cow pies.

Mr. Collins yelped and pushed himself away. Shuck clamped his jaws on the back of his neck, and growled deep and low.

"Easy, boy." I said, and Shuck backed away slow, baring teeth.

Mr. Collins wiped the mess from his face, and Joe laughed. "I can't see, but I can smell what happened."

"No one crosses me, who don't live to regret it," Collins seethed. "You remember that, blind man. And you too, Wade, you fatherless little turd. You and your dog got it coming."

"C'mon, Red. You can sleep at my house."

"Boy, you got to come home sometime," Mr. Collins said. "Ain't no dodging what you deserve. That's how it was for me, and that's how it is for you!"

We hurried to the road, while Mr. Collins cursed and stomped Red's tow sack. I felt bad for the frogs. We heard him cussing a long ways down the road.

• • •

Red sniffled, his jaw set. He wiped his face on his sleeve, and picked up a knotted stick to swat the weeds. "Sorry, Joe."

"Nothing you done," Joe said, tuning a string.

"It's the moonshine does it to him," Red said. "He's almost nice in the morning, some times. If he ain't drank too much the night before."

"Me and Pa built a new hen coop for the preacher last week," Red said. "He didn't sneak no shine or nothing. He said I did a halfway good job, and that felt right fine."

"I heard Preacher say how much he liked your work," I said.

"If I knew where those stills were, I'd blow 'em all to hell," Red said, and whipped the stick at the wind. "We should go looking for them. Bet we'd be the heroes of half the holler."

The Muntz boys ran the shine in our holler, and anyone fool enough to complain had the tendency to disappear. My Pa used to take a sip when offered, but never kept a jug in the house. He said you buy enough jugs of shine, and they'll own you.

"I'm not so sure of that," Joe said, picking out a new tune. "And you boys ought not to mess with the Muntz clan. They've put plenty of men in the ground."

I like beer when it's far or near,
And I like bourbon whiskey

But a man who's wicked in his cups
His kind I find too risky
A happy drunk's a lucky skunk
He has friends in ary holler
But a man who's wicked in his cups
I find him hard to swaller

Ma stepped out on the porch as Joe sang us in. She had her hair tied back, and a wooden spoon in her hand. She stared at us and crossed herself.

"Hi Ma," I said. "Can Joe stay to supper? He plays real fine."

"Ma'am, it would be my honor to play the old music, and break bread with you." Joe jumped into another song before she could respond.

Coffee grows on white oak trees
Rivers flow with brandy
I've got a pretty little blue-eyed gal
Sweet as molasses candy

Joe strummed a flourish and bowed so deep I thought he'd break in half.

"Is that you, Joe Fahey?" Ma said.

"I'm just Blind Joe now, ma'am."

"It's Silphy Gibson," Ma said, and squeezed Joe's hand. "I haven't seen you since my wedding day."

"When you married Jeffrey. Where is the lucky feller?"

Ma winced, and I looked at my feet. "He died in the mine collapse last year," she said. "He always spoke kindly of you."

Joe frowned. "I'm real sorry to hear of his passing," he said. "He was a good man."

I held up my tow sack. "Me and Shuck got three squirrels, Ma."

"Well skin them up, and we'll have a stew."

• • •

After supper, we sat on the porch to hear Joe play. Red and me clapped and sang along to the jaunty tunes, and Ma sang the slow ballads. As the sun's red blaze dipped behind our mountaintop, and the jarflies buzzed their last racket of the day, Joe came to a song that made Ma close her eyes, and sing real sweet. It was one Grams used to hum to herself, and Ma's voice rang high over Joe's mournful tones.

That was the first time I realized how beautiful my mother was. Not just to me, but to other people. The last note faded, and Ma finished the chorus alone.

Slumber, my darling, and I'll keep you warm
Through the chill of the evening, and the blow of the storm
For the child that we cradled, and the love in our hearts
I'll wander these hills 'til we're no longer apart

Ma cleared her throat when she caught us staring. "That's a fine old song," she said.

"Thank you, ma'am," Joe said. "Ain't heard a voice so pretty in a very long time."

"Thank you, but that can't be true, with your travels."

"Upon my honor," Joe said. "Only voice sweeter is one I'll never hear again. And I've roved these mountains north to Maine, and down to Georgia."

"Why'd you do all that wandering?" I asked.

"Looking for someone I lost," Joe said. The moon was reflected in his black lenses.

"How'd you go blind?" Red asked.

"Why Red Collins," Ma said. "You know better."

Joe unhooked his shaded glasses from his ears. His eyes were black as two wet river stones. "I can see some, in the gloaming. I can tell Shuck's a blue tick. And Wade's gonna catch flies, he don't close his mouth."

I shut my mouth, and waited for him to answer Red's question. Joe blinked at the stars, as if getting his bearings, Then he tucked his glasses in his shirt pocket, and stretched with a creak. "Reckon it's time I move along," he said. "Thank you folk, for the best meal I've had in a dog's age."

"Mr. Fahey, let us fix you a pallet," Ma said. "It's almost dark."

"Thank you Miss Silphy, but these old bones sleep under no roof when the ground is dry." Joe adjusted the strap of his guitar.

"But there's haints out there," Red said.

"And the Behinder," I said.

"Who's been putting them tales in your heads?" Joe laughed. "Besides, if any of them try to spook me, I'll play this." He scraped a fingernail down a string, and his guitar gave a tinny shriek that made us wince, and Shuck whimper.

"Maybe I'll see you on my way back through the holler," Joe said, and began picking. We bid him goodnight, and he disappeared down the road, singing to the sky.

Silphy, O Silphy, sing us a song
The sweetest pure voice I've heard in so long
Shuck's a fine coonhound, best in the state,
And you cook the best squirrel I ever ate

His song joined the night sounds of the forest, and soon we couldn't tell what was crickets and owls, and what was Joe.

"That poor, poor man," Ma said, and shook her head.

"Do you know how he went blind, Mrs. Gibson?" Red asked.

"Joe was orphaned by the War between the States, is what I was told," she said. "He'd sing for his supper, and he was the finest guitar player we'd ever heard. When he came of age, he courted Vandy Wellman. Prettiest girl in the holler. Her folk didn't like it, but her father gave in, eventual." Ma smiled. "She was so in love. And back then, Joe was a handsome man."

She rubbed her tired knuckles a while, before going on.

"Way I heard it, when she was with child, a man from Washington came through the hollers, looking to hear the old music. Said he was saving all the old songs in a museum, on his record machine. Joe didn't want to leave her, but Vandy urged him on until he gave in, kissed her goodbye, and hurried down the mountain."

"The other musicians were green with envy," Ma said. "For Joe's talent, and his bride. They sent him on a snipe hunt all over the state, and by the time Joe realized he'd been fooled, the museum man had already gone back to the city, and lugged his machine with him. When Joe made it home, Vandy was sick with fever. He ran for the doctor, but she died giving birth." She shook her head, looking up at the growing moon.

"What about the baby?" I asked.

"Went to heaven with her," Ma said.

"But how'd Joe go blind?" Red said.

"Rumor is, Joe played three days and nights, begging the Lord to bring her back. And when he got no answer, he played to the devils and the haints, any spook that would listen, cursing the clear blue sky. A bolt of lightning struck his guitar, shattered it to flinders. Struck Joe blind, and made him white as death."

Me and Red stared. I counted the times we'd said the Lord's name in vain.

"But that's just talk, boys. Don't y'all be scared now. I'm plumb crazy, telling you that tale before bedtime," she said. "I'm turning into my own mother."

"Do you think that really happened, Ma?"

"No, I don't believe the Lord's so cruel," Ma said. "I think losing Vandy and his child made Joe a mite touched, and he went blind from guilt and grief."

"That can make you go blind?" Red asked.

"A man who hates himself can do a lot of things," Ma said, and tapped her empty coffee cup. "Time you boys turned in."

We fixed Red a pallet, and Shuck curled up on Grams' old blanket by the front door.

When Ma closed her door, Red whispered, "Your Ma's real nice."

"She don't make you scrub the dishes."

"Don't joke like that," Red said. "You know she's the nicest ma in the holler. Just like Shuck's the best hound, and your Pa was the best—"

"My Pa's dead," I said. "At least you got a Pa."

Red scrunched up his nose. "I wish I didn't."

"Don't talk like that," I said. "You'll regret it."

"I don't have a Pa. Or a Ma," Red said. "I got a belt that drinks moonshine, and a witch who likes watching him whup the tar out of me." Red punched his pillow.

"Let's look for the stills tomorrow," I said.

Red nodded, and curled up to sleep. I stared at the rafters, and thought of Joe singing to haints in the woods.

Right before Grams died, I had caught a bad case of fever. Pa lugged buckets from the well, and Ma dipped a cloth in the cool water, and pressed it my brow. Grams prayed over me as I tossed and turned, and I saw things in the corners that couldn't rightly be there.

The room rippled like pond water, and Black Shuck poked his head out of a shadow. He barked once, but no one else could hear. I crawled out of bed, and he licked my hand with his icy tongue. I looked back and saw Grams signing and praying over my body. Old Shuck grabbed my shirt collar with his teeth and flung me to his back. I held on tight as he bounded through the trees.

The wind was cold as mountain water. We chased the Wendigo, and I felt the Behinder nip at our heels, but dared not spy its face. We raced past the stills of the Mad Muntz boys, and Shuck barked at the moon. I felt my grip on his fur weakening, and he leaped through my window and passed through the bed. I woke with my folks clutching me, and my sheets soaked in sweat.

Grams had collapsed, hands gripped in prayer. She never woke up, and passed in her sleep three nights after. That tore me up so bad that Pa brought home a speckled pup to ease my guilt. The black puppy had wriggled so much in Pa's sooty arms that it looked like a living lump of coal.

I named him Black Shuck, because I knew Grams had traded her place for mine. Ma crossed herself, and mumbled a prayer to the rafters. Pa just shook his head.

• • •

In the morning, we ate biscuits with sorghum syrup, and Red helped with my chores. When we were done, I took Pa's cane pole from the rafters and Red ran home to get his own.

"What mischief you boys up to today?" Ma asked.

"Think we'll try fishing up the creek from the swimming hole," I said. "Saw a catfish there, I swear it could swallow the preacher's wife."

"That's not nice, Wade," Ma said, biting back a laugh.

"Aw, you said she uses a doughnut for a life preserver."

"Maybe if she ate it, she wouldn't be so skinny," Ma said.

I set on the porch waiting for Red, and when I got tired of waiting, me and Shuck headed over, walking slow. It hurt Red more when I saw him catching a whupping. He told me his Pa said you had to beat the devil out of a redheaded child and that's why he whupped him so hard. But Mr. Collins was redder than his son.

I didn't hear any belt cracks as I rounded the bend, and let out my breath. Mr. Collins sat in his chair, the jug of shine at his lips, the end of his belt in his hand. Red's cane pole lay snapped in two at his feet, beside a plump tow sack. I squinted, looking for Red, and caught his father's cruel smile.

"Morning, Mr. Collins," I called, and skipped over a cow pie.

"Didn't your dead Pa teach you to call men sir?"

I hadn't cried over Pa in a long time, but Mr. Collins had a way with words that felt like throwing salt in your eyes. I bit my lip, hard.

"Sir," I said, "Is Red home?"

"Damn sure he is," Mr. Collins said. "Come look."

Past the weeds, I saw Red crouched on all fours, with his Pa's belt looped around his neck. His face was red and puffy, and his jaw tight.

"How you like my dog, Wade?"

The words turned to dirt in my mouth.

"Y-you let him go," I croaked.

"Or what?" Mr. Collins laughed. He tied the belt around a post like he was hitching a horse. "You gonna sic your cur on me?"

He poked Red with his crusty boot. "Bark, li'l doggie."

Red's lip trembled, and Mr. Collins kicked him in the ribs. "Bark, dammit, or you'll get worse than you ever seen."

Red obeyed, and bit back tears. His Pa picked up the tow sack with a splintered half of cane pole. Something squirmed inside.

Shuck growled low. I knew I should hold him back, but I didn't want to. I wanted him to tear Mr. Collins up.

Shuck bared his teeth, and Mr. Collins whipped the sack. A mottled ball of hiss and rattle hit me in the chest, and I fell back in the weeds. The snake felt like a rock on my chest, and I froze as it reared up over my face.

Shuck howled and chomped it in the middle. He thrashed it and snarled like I'd never heard him before. The timber rattler struck him again and again. It was six foot if it was an inch, and fatter than a big man's arm. I whacked it with my cane pole until its head was squashed as a rotten plum.

Mr. Collins cackled, holding the belt tight around Red's neck. I swung for him, and he yanked the belt until Red choked. "You think I won't give you a whupping, you try me, boy! That goes for your hussy mama too."

Shuck walked in circles, breathing hard. His front leg crumpled and he felt in the dirt with a whimper. He looked up at me, his mouth slick with drool, his eyes asking what he'd done wrong.

My chest felt like the mine had collapsed on me.

I scooped up Shuck and ran for home, while Mr. Collins hooted and laughed.

"I'm sorry, Wade!" Red cried, before the belt cut him off.

• • •

By the time I got home, Shuck's face had swollen up like half a sugar melon, and he shuddered with every move. Ma wrapped him in blankets, and fired the stove to keep him warm. He breathed real ragged, with strings of spit hanging from his jowls. He'd whimper now and then, and I'd stroke his ears.

"You got to let him rest now," Ma said. "That's his best chance."

I looked up at her, and the hot tears came. She squeezed me tight. "He's made it this far. We've done all we can do."

I went to fill a bowl of well water for Shuck to lap, and when I returned, Ma stuck Pa's rifle up in the rafters, and tucked the box of shells into her apron.

"Just in case you get any crazy ideas in your head," she said. "We'll tell the Sheriff tomorrow, when I bring my sewing into town."

"Can't we do anything? He's got Red hitched up like an animal."

Ma shook her head. "It isn't the first time we tried, Wade. No one crosses Asa Collins, who hasn't regretted it. Look what he did to Shuck. I'd like nothing better than to take my skillet upside his foul head, but folks round here like you to mind your own business. It would be you and me they run out of town, not Mr. Collins."

"That ain't right," I cried.

"No, it isn't. The world isn't right, sometimes. But we can be. We'll get Red some help, that I promise."

• • •

I slept beside Shuck on a pallet on the floor. I dreamt of him, Grams and Pa in the misty woods. Pa waved a bony hand, and Shuck tried to bark, but a mess of black snakes boiled out of his mouth.

I woke with a start, in the chill night air. Shuck groaned and twitched beside me. He had nightmares of his own. Neither of us slept much that night.

In the morning, I surprised Ma by making coffee, and shivering down a cup of the bitter stuff myself. I gave Shuck fresh water, and Ma left him a bowl of squirrel gravy, in case he got hungry. I wanted to stay with him, but Ma said he'd rest better alone, without me fussing over him. We took turns carrying her laundry sack into town. A coal truck rumbled past, and I thought about Pa down there, hammering to be free.

"Ma, why do good men die, when rotten ones like Mr. Collins don't?"

"Bad men die too, Wade."

"But how come they all don't?"

Ma laughed. "Honey, if we knew that, we wouldn't pray, would we."

We hadn't been to church in weeks, which was fine by me. Preacher had sermoned on "spare the rod, spoil the child," and I'd asked Ma if I was spoiled, on the walk home. She said we could pray to the Lord ourselves, from then on.

There wasn't much more to town than the General store, the Sheriff, and the nicer houses like Doctor Hopper's, with shingles hung out front. "I'll bring Mrs. Fox her dress, and you give the doctor his clean shirts," Ma said. "Meet me outside the Sheriff's, and don't say a thing until I get there."

Doc wasn't home, likely out on a house call, so I left the laundry bag inside his door. The medicine smell made me worry for Shuck, and I hurried to the jailhouse before I thought too hard on it. I heard a commotion, and saw a crowd gathered outside. The Sheriff was talking to Mr. Collins, and my heart rose a little, thinking his comeuppance had finally arrived.

Collins waved his arms and shouted. "Course it was him, who done something to my boy. I chased that beggar off my porch, now my boy's disappeared. I don't know what you done, blind man, but I know it's something terrible, and you're gonna pay!"

Blind Joe stood with his hands cuffed, and his nose aimed at the ground. The Sheriff held his guitar. "Settle down now, Asa. We don't know nothing's happened yet."

The crowd murmured, and it was an ugly sound. As I stepped through, I overheard the words "freak," "plain quare," and "hanging."

"Sheriff," I whispered. I raised my hand like in the schoolhouse. "I need to tell you something."

The Sheriff aimed his sunken eyes my way, then looked away.

"Where's your Pa, boy?" a chinless man asked, and held me by the shoulder.

"Pardon me, gentlemen," Ma said, and the men parted for her. "What's going on here?"

"Mr. Collins says Red's disappeared," I told her. "He says Joe took him."

"What nonsense," Ma said, loudly. "Joe Fahey's never hurt a fly. He couldn't see one, even if wanted to."

"He's blind, but his hands work fine," Mr. Collins said. "I know he's done hurt my boy, probably for nothing but the buffalo nickel in his pocket."

"He looks like the kind of creature who'd kill a boy for a nickel," the weak-chinned man said to another.

"Man like that, he needs killin'," the listener replied.

"Mr. Collins, the way you beat on your boy, he's probably run off," Ma said.

"Don't you tell me how to raise my child," Mr. Collins said. "The Lord says you spare the rod, and you spoil the child. I ain't spoiling mine, like you do yours."

The crowd muttered agreement.

"Is that why you threw a rattlesnake at my Wade? If my husband was alive, he'd shoot you where you stand."

Mr. Collins laughed. "Snake flinging? Ma'am, I did no such thing. I'm no Pentecostal."

The Sheriff snickered, and the crowd joined in. "Take your child home, Mrs. Gibson," the Sheriff said. "This here is men's business."

"He had Red tied to the porch like a dog," I told the crowd. "He treats him like an animal."

"Son, you bear false witness against me, and you'll suffer in this world and the next," Mr. Collins said.

Ma tugged me away. "Let's go check on Shuck, honey."

"But Joe didn't do nothing! Red's gone looking for the Muntz boys!"

She walked quick through the crowd. "Come now, there's nothing more we can do for him."

The Sheriff twirled Joe's guitar. "This here's made from a baby's coffin. Ain't seen anything like it."

"Baby didn't need it," Joe said. "Buried him with his mother."

"Who else you bury, Joe?" Sheriff asked. "We're gonna make a search party. If you stuffed that boy down a hole, tell me now. It'll be easier on you."

Joe tapped his foot and sang,

Burn, burn, burn slow for Judas,
Thirty piece of silver, ringing like a bell.
Red-headed Judas, burning deep in—

The Sheriff backhanded Joe in the mouth, and raised his voice. "You men are tasked with searching this holler for Red Collins, until I say otherwise."

The crowd didn't look too pleased.

• • •

When we arrived home, Shuck wasn't in his bed. His blankets were strewn on the floor, and his bowl empty. I ran to the Collins house, before Ma could catch my arm.

Mrs. Collins sat gaunt in her kitchen, cutting the eyes off a pile of shriveled taters. She barely looked up as I rushed in.

"What'd you do to my Shuck?"

"Boy, mind your manners," she said, and pointed her knife at me. "Your dam might spoil you, but no whelp sasses me unless they want their tongue cut."

"Don't you come near me. What did you do with my dog?" I snatched an iron pan from the stove. "I swear I'll pound your head flat!"

She laughed and showed me the teeth her husband had busted. "Ain't seen your dog. If I did, I'd be cooking him. Asa ain't brought home meat in weeks, and dog's just like coon or possum, you stew it enough." She smiled when I recoiled. "Now skedaddle, or I'll geld you like a billy goat, and throw your mountain oysters into the fire."

Ma panted at the door, straightened up, and took my hand. "Come home, Wade. I found him."

"Your boy sasses me again, I'll—"

"You lay a hand on my son, and I'll hack it off and make a back scratcher out of it, you hear me?"

Mrs. Collins dropped her knife on the floor.

I'd never seen Ma so worked up. I set down the pan, and followed her home.

"I told you not to go off half-cocked," she said. "Shuck's crawled under the porch. I can't fit under there."

I got on all fours, and she gripped the seat of my pants.

"Wade," she said, lips tight. "He might try to bite, if he's in pain. Be careful. And if he's gone, I'm sorry."

My hands trembled as I crawled through the dirt, breathing in the thick smell of damp earth and the vinegary scent of sickness. I saw a black lump in the center, and made my way to it. My heart thumped like a miner's hammer.

I saw Shuck's speckled coat in a knife of light through the slats of the porch, and my throat closed. I kicked myself up to him, and his ribs shook with a low growl.

"It's me, boy," I whispered, and held out my hand.

He licked with a clammy tongue. I reached to lift him, and his teeth closed weakly on my hand, barely pinching the skin.

"Wade," Ma called. "Don't move him." She slid me his bowl with fresh water, and Grams' blanket. I pulled the blanket under, and covered him up good.

I stayed beside him until the exhaustion won out.

I dreamt me and Ma prayed for Shuck on top of the porch, like they'd done when I had fever. A bark from the woods hit me like a slap, and when I turned, two fiery eyes met my gaze.

Tall as a draft horse, and gaunt as the Collins' cow, Black Shuck the haint-dog panted icy fog at our door. His coat black as a coal seam, his tail dragging the ground like a burnt straw broom. He barked again, and looked back over his shoulder bone.

Blind Joe walked out of the mist, his fingers wove together like a skeleton's ribcage. His lips moved, but no song came.

Black Shuck's eyes burned mine, like staring at the sun, and I felt his growl through my skin.

My third bark is for the hound who shares my name, unless you free the singer and find the lost child.

Black Shuck stuck his nose under the porch, and took a deep sniff. He licked his chops with a shredded white tongue, and smiled.

I woke with a gasp. I touched Shuck's ribs, and he nipped at my fingers. "Rest, boy," I told him, and hugged him gentle, ignoring the weak bites he gave.

I crept out the back end of the house, and stayed low until I got to the road. I jumped in the trees when a truck packed with men holding unlit torches and lanterns rattled past. I wished for Pa's rifle, even a jack knife, in case I ran into Mr. Collins.

The town was truly deserted, with the posse searching the holler before the sun was gone. It felt right spooky, with no men loitering outside the general store. I ducked behind the jailhouse, and peered in the glass window. It was dark inside. A squat, barred window was cut higher, and I looked for a crate or something else to stand on, when Joe's white hand stuck through the bars, and waved me in.

The Sheriff's office was dusty and stale. Joe's guitar lay on the desk, gleaming silver and black. I poked in the desk drawers for a key ring, and found jugs of shine just about everywhere I looked.

"Wade," Joe called from the cell in back. "The Sheriff took the keys with him. Can you bring my guitar?"

I picked it up carefully, like unhooking a catfish and avoiding the spines. The fretboard was burnt black, and mated to the coffin with silver screws. I picked a string with my fingernail. It mewled like a cat, and I felt like a swallowed a stone.

"Bring it here," Joe said. "Don't play it."

I found Joe in back, leaning against the bars of his cell. His cheeks were scraped red, and half a lens was knocked out of his spectacles.

Joe strummed the strings, and smiled with blood-flecked teeth. "Thank you, Wade. You're a good boy."

He played three notes that seemed to come from far away, and sang,

How I have missed thee, my long lost friend
My only companion, right to the end.

"Are you really a hoodoo man, Joe?"

"I suppose I am," Joe said, and tugged a loose nail from the coffin. He slipped it into the keyhole, and hummed to himself. The lock made a solid click, and he pushed the cell door open.

"If you know hoodoo, why didn't you just witch it open?"

"You came, and now I'm free. That's not magic enough for you?" He strapped the guitar around his neck. "Hoodoo is like ol' Nancy Whiskey. You sip her, you're all right. You let her grab you by the legs, and you ain't your own man no more. Let's get a move on," he said. "When the moon's up, Black Shuck takes what's his."

The sun was an orange haze in the trees. The search party would quit soon. I led Joe back up the mountain, toward our fishing hole.

"I owe you and Miss Silphy for speaking against that mob," Joe said. "That took grit. You know where Red ran off to?"

"To the Muntz boys' hideout," I said. "We were going to smash their stills. To keep his Pa from getting drunk and beating him no more."

"I didn't want to say nothing, but the words of a drunk man are the thoughts of a sober one," Joe said. "Mr. Collins has had evil beaten into him, and it's all he knows. He's hammered the next link in the chain, and for that, there is no redemption."

"What about Red? Is it like a curse, or his red hair?"

"No, but sometimes it feels that way, when folks pass evil down. Red's got a good heart. He'll break the chain, if he gets away."

We slipped into the woods, and Joe removed his lenses. "You know where you're going?"

"Saw it in a dream," I said. "I had a fever, and my Grams saved me from Black Shuck. He took her instead, but not before he gave me a ride all over the holler."

"He'll want another soul tonight, Wade. Your hound's time has come."

"I know," I said, and wondered what he'd ask in trade. Was a dog an even trade for a man? I tried not to think about it, and what I might do, to keep Shuck from joining Grams and my Pa.

We stopped at the swimming hole. A fat raccoon waddled from the water's edge, with a bullfrog burping in its paws. "We got to cross," I said, and began pulling off my shirt.

"Boy, you think I stumble blind into cricks when I wander at night?" Joe picked a few notes that sounded like water drops, and walked right over the water. "Hurry now. It don't last but a moment."

The water felt spongy, like fresh mud until my last step, which sunk in to the knee. Joe pulled me up quick, and looking back, I saw a dark shape swim away. It looked big enough to swallow me whole.

"That enough hoodoo for you?"

"What was that?"

"Catfish," Joe said, and I decided not to swim there no more. We walked up the creek, on the far side, and the branches scratched past our faces.

"How do you think they deliver their liquor?" Joe asked.

The path opened a few minutes later, into a cleared trail. A handmade bridge, like a ladder for an ogre, leaned against a knotted maple. It had ropes on one end, for lowering it across.

"With that," I said, as we passed it.

The path was well beaten now, bedded soft with years of fallen leaves.

"How come no one's found them," I asked, "if a kid and a blind man found their trail?"

Joe chuckled. "When you're older, you'll understand better. But you're sharp as a tack, so I'll try. Folks are good at not seeing what they don't want to, 'specially if seeing it would cause them trouble. Sometimes they're paid not to see, but most times, they seen it so long, it's like it's not even there."

"Thanks, Joe." He reminded me of my Pa a little, how he'd try and explain things, even if I wouldn't understand yet. Pa never made up tales to shoo my questions, like the other kids' folks.

"You're a real hoodoo man."

"Reckon so," Joe said.

"My Grams made charms, but I don't think they ever did anything."

"Trading her life for yours was no mean feat," Joe said. "But it bound Black Shuck to you. There's always a price, and it's always hard to pay. I don't do bad magic no more, so don't ask me to fight against nature."

"Like what?"

"Like making your Pa walk out the mine."

"I don't want that," I said.

"You say you don't," Joe said, "But you're just too afraid to ask. I played with those spells before, and what's gone can never be brought back. Not the same, anyway."

"Ma told me what you done," I said. "You cursed the Lord, and he struck you with lightning."

"So that's what they say? That's not rightly true."

"Then what struck you blind?"

"My own fool heart," Joe whispered, and slowed to a creep. "Hush now. I hear people near."

With my eyes and Joe's ears, we inched up the trail, to where it ended in a hacked down clearing. A rough-hewn cabin squatted on the shore of a shallow bend in the creek. Weak light flickered from the windows. Spread over the flat campground, pairs of fat barrels sat, mated to tall copper still pots by twirls of metal tubing. I didn't hear a sound but the crickets sawing over the trickle of the water.

"Someone's here," Joe whispered. "Bad men. Take care."

Joe stood still as a scarecrow as I circled the cabin, to peer between the boards. I heard men cuss each other inside. I found a knothole, and spied three men around the wood stove. One was fat and bushy bearded, but hard-eyed. He would be Peyton. His brother Kenny looked like he'd been hacked from dried white pine.

The Muntz boys, and no sign of Red.

They had Mr. Collins on his knees, at the end of a single barrel scattergun. Kenny kicked him in the belly, hard. "You damn fool, you brought the whole holler down on us."

"How'd I know they'd mount a search party?" Collins hacked and coughed, covering himself. "I came to warn you, the Sheriff's coming."

Peyton cracked the shotgun barrel on Mr. Collins' balding pate. "The Sheriff we got covered. But we'll have to lizard out and move operations, if every soul knows where to point the revenuers."

Collins cowered and clutched his head. "I done everything I could," he cried. "He was gonna tell, and I stopped him. Haven't I done enough?"

"You ain't died," Kenny said. "You ain't done that yet."

Mr. Collins whimpered, and part of me felt good to see him get beat, but another part felt pity, that he had to walk the earth being lower than a snake's behind.

There were no sheds, so I tried the outhouse. When I opened the door, something lurched and sent me tumbling. I kicked myself away, and Red moaned. He had his hands and feet tied, and a dirty sock stuffed in his mouth, with twine around his head to keep it in.

I tugged the twine down his chin and pulled out the sock. It smelled like its last owner ran ten miles through an onion patch. Red spat, and wiped his mouth on his shoulder. "Thanks, Wade."

"C'mon, let's see if Joe has a jack knife," I said, and led him hopping behind me.

Joe didn't have a knife, but the Muntz boys did. And a shotgun.

"Looky here," Kenny said, picking his teeth with a fingernail. "Just what I said. Everyone knows our spot, now."

"Kill 'em," Mr. Collins sneered. "Kill that blind freak and the Gibson boy, they'll tell for sure!"

Peyton swept us with the scattergun. "I ain't killing no child, nor a hoodoo man. You'll have to do it your own self, and dig the holes."

"They can dig their own holes," Mr. Collins said, and picked up a shovel.

"You'll have to kill me, too," Red said. "I'll tell everyone, you'll rot in jail, and you'll never drink their shine again!"

"Shut up, boy," Collins said, and punched Red in the nose. "You'll do as you're told."

Red fell on his behind, and tears welled in the corners of his eyes. He rolled and pushed himself to one knee. "I said I'll tell, and I mean it. You only beat me when you drink, why you got to drink, Pa?"

"I said, shut up! I drink because I like it. It makes me forget my ugly wife, and my no good son," he said. "And if you don't like it, you'd best jump in front of a coal truck, 'cause you ain't running off again. I'll drag you back and whup you twice as hard. I own you, boy!"

"I get whupped whether I obey you or not," Red said.

"Reminds me of our Pa," Peyton said. "He was a mean old cuss, wasn't he?"

"Hush, Lard Ass," Kenny said.

"Don't call me that," Peyton said. "Only Pa got to call me that, and he's dead, God rest his soul. You gonna kill 'em, or not, Collins? Give him your knife, Kenny. It's nothin' much, just like bleeding a deer, or a sticking a hog."

Joe picked a few notes, and sang.

Black Shuck, O Black Shuck, please hear my call
Dead man are walking, under your pall

"Shut him up," Collins said, and Peyton leveled the shotgun at Joe's chest.

Joe raised his hands, and kept on singing, beneath a fat thumbnail of moon.

Wendigo, wendigo, and all your foul kin,
Come to my aid, and dine on their skin

"Quiet, hoodoo man," Peyton said, and thumbed back the hammer. "Or I'll risk your curse!"

Joe wiggled his fingers high in the air and bared a gray-toothed smile as the notes kept pealing. I stared at the black instrument, and saw a shrunken black hand, like raccoon's paw, reach from the hole in the coffin and pluck at the strings.

"The hell was that?" Collins said, and a hush fell over the woods. The crickets were silent, and the breeze went stale.

Peyton jerked the shotgun at shadows that knifed from the trees, and Collins raised his shovel like an axe. Something tall and spindly stepped into the camp from over the treetops. I only saw it in flashes. I wish I hadn't seen it at all. It was all limbs with a triangular face like a goat's, stretched impossibly thin. Peyton fired at it, but the Wendigo turned sideways, and the buckshot peppered a copper still.

The fat man fumbled for the shells in his overalls pocket, and the Wendigo picked him up like a baby, and sank its chisel jawbone in his head like a hot needle into a swollen tick. Peyton's scream echoed through the trees as the Wendigo carried him away through the branches.

His brother Kenny bolted for the trail. A huge black spider the size of a coal truck rose out of the brush and skittered after him. The Behinder had a dozen legs bent back the wrong way, and eyeless faces poked through its inky skin. It swallowed Kenny like deep, dark water. The last we saw were his eyes getting sucked into his blackening face as he joined the thing. A blink later and the creature sank under the leaves, and left like a ripple in water.

Red and me gawped like sucker fish, and Joe giggled like a child.

A bark cut through the forest, and the air turned to ice in our lungs.

Mr. Collins stood rooted to the spot, with a dark stain spreading across his dungarees.

"Black Shuck's coming, Mister Collins," Joe said. "To take your soul to hell. It don't hurt none, when it's your time. But when it ain't, from the fuss a body makes, I reckon nothing hurts more."

Mr. Collins looked left and right, gripping the shovel's haft. "I didn't mean to hurt him," he screamed to the woods. "He wouldn't obey. A boy's got to obey his Pa!"

A great wind shook the trees, and a second bark echoed from behind.

"It was for his own good," he stammered, trembling now. "My Pa whupped me and didn't hurt me none!"

A ragged panting answered him from the dark. A gaunt black steed leaped into the moonlight, all skin, and bone, and teeth.

"Red, please! Tell it to spare me!"

Red looked from the hound to his father. "No," he said, his lip trembling.

"Do as I say, boy! You stupid sack of—"

Black Shuck howled and snapped his jaws on Mr. Collins' chest. It began tugging and tearing, and pinned his flailing body to the ground with its claws. I don't know if it was Mr. Collins' soul or his innards, but Black Shuck ripped a pulsing, red-black chunk from his body, and held it high.

Black Shuck bounded into the woods, and the rest of Mr. Collins flopped to the ground like a doll made of sack cloth. Of all the horrors I saw that night, his face is what haunts me the most.

Red wiped away his tears, and didn't look at his father's body. He took the lantern from the cabin, and hurled it at the shot-up still. The glass shattered, and the liquor fumes puffed into flame.

Joe led us home in the pitch dark, and we heard the still pots burst and whoomp behind us as the Muntz's camp went up.

• • •

Ma jumped from her seat on the porch, as we came up the road. She ran to meet us and hugged me tight.

"Wade, don't you ever run off like that again," she said, and pressed her lips to the crook of my neck. "I thought I'd lost you."

She hugged Red, next. "I'm glad you're all right, Red Collins." He hugged her real hard, and she let him. I felt jealous, sort of, but also kind of good, like we were brothers now, for real.

"I'd best be going," Joe said. "Sheriff won't take kindly to me escaping."

"Aw, Joe, can't you stay?" Red asked.

"You know I can't," Joe said. Red moved to hug him, but the guitar was in between them, and Red didn't want to touch it. I didn't blame him.

My Shuck limped to us, while we said our goodbyes. His face almost looked how it ought to, and while he was still weak, he was on his feet. I crouched to hug him, and his tongue gave my face a good lick.

"Easy, Wade," Ma said. "He's only just healing up."

"Best dog in the holler," Red said, and patted Shuck's head.

Joe adjusted his guitar strap. "Reckon this is goodbye, but one word of advice. You'll both be looking for good men to be your fathers," Joe said. "Try to be those men, instead of looking for them."

Joe bowed deep, and picked out a song as he disappeared into the dark. Shuck howled and drowned it out, and Ma herded us inside, where it was safe and warm.

In memoriam, Jeff Fahey and Manly Wade Wellman.

Jolly's Boy
Richard Prosch

The Model T truck turned down a dirt lane leading to the Gus Hanson acreage, and Tom Olsen could see Jolly's boy in his mind, could make out the gleaming puffy face in a trick of sunlight on the windshield. Tom had been allowed to join the threshing crew only once before, and he'd felt awkward and inefficient. Like a tagalong kid.

Tom was barely aware of the cold and the deafening rattle of the engine as his father shifted down into first and they climbed over the last water break, the frosty tops of the barn and corn crib appearing through the sunlit fog.

He glanced over his shoulder at the Marlin .22 hanging in the truck's rear window. Tom had saved all his money for a year, and after he bought the little rifle, he was allowed to keep it under Dad's big cowboy gun.

Wouldn't Jolly's boy, with his scuffed denim jeans and fresh scraped face, be impressed. He would be impressed by Tom, too. The last time, Tom had been a baby. He'd grown at least two inches since then and now weighed a great deal more. He would really measure up, show that he could be trusted, even counted on in their farming community. They pulled in beside Walt Schultz, and his black gelding stepped quickly back, though Walt held the reins tight.

"Heya, Walt," said Matt Olsen as the motor sputtered to a stop.

Tom ratcheted back the hand brake for his dad, then stepped out into the cold gray dust of the farmyard.

"Anybody else here?"

Schultz shook his head, and they watched the sun climb from behind the trees and shine across the surface of Jolly's gray threshing machine, crouched on wood spoke wheels, a wonder of technology covered in sprockets and iron aprons. Tom couldn't help but think of the War and the swift and invincible tanks he'd read and marveled about. Tanks, of course, moved by themselves, but Tom knew the threshing machine was powered by Jolly's gas and oil tractor and a heavy rolling belt.

He drew circles in the dust with his foot, and his dad finally said, "Jolly ain't been along yet?"

Shultz cocked his head. "He pulled the machine over here day before yesterday. Told Gus he'd be here this morning." Everyone disliked Jolly, knew that he drank too much, but he owned the only tractor and threshing rig in the county.

"You ready to work today, Tom?" said Schultz.

The boy nodded.

"Big job." Schultz wasn't looking at Tom or his dad when he said it, but was staring out across the tree-rimmed valley into the last remnants of mist. "Yes sir, a big job," he said again, and Matt Olsen nodded.

Nobody spoke for a while.

Tom stepped toward the black horse and placed a gentle hand on its muzzle. "You give Fritter any apples this morning?" he asked. The horse circled its long head down and around Tom's touch.

"Ain't he always the spoiled one?" Walt reached into his thin coat and passed a white apple slice to Tom, who put it within the horse's greedy reach. While they watched the sliver go down, Gus Hanson stomped over from the house.

"The sonna bitch is still half asleep," he spat, then tipping back his hat, he apologized. "Sorry, Tom. Didn't see you there."

"It's okay," said Tom, his eyes flicking up to meet the old man's gaze.

"Evelyn finally got him on the phone about five minutes ago. Says he'll be here when he's damn good and ready. That's a quote."

Shultz and Olsen stood with their hands in their pockets and stared at the threshing machine. "What's he think we're gonna do 'til then?" said Schultz. "I didn't bring a deck of cards. Did you, Tom?"

Tom glanced at his dad, and Matt Olsen smiled back. For just a minute it was like he was grown up and one of them, jawboning over the price of cattle or the latest news from the local Exchange. "I didn't bring a deck of cards," he said.

"Jolly told Evelyn he'd send his boy," said Hanson. "I was hoping this morning he wouldn't."

"It'll be alright," said Schultz. "We're all here. Evelyn can feed him some breakfast."

"I imagine so."

While they stood waiting, Hanson took a dry twist of tobacco from his pocket. When the old man offered Tom some, his dad nodded and he took a small bite. The juice was heavy and bitter and his eyes watered, but he didn't immediately spit, didn't want to show his inexperience. Schultz laughed at him anyway, but it was a good-natured laugh, and his dad clapped him on the shoulder. The tobacco made his head spin, but it was good to be among the men, visiting and chewing and laughing.

He would be right here when Jolly's boy drove up. In the cedar grove to his right, Tom again imagined the face. The wood showed each scar and every badly healed bone. Tom imagined he could see the black eye from earlier in the spring, and the red cheek inflated to twice its normal size. The boy seemed to be accident prone.

Tom knew there was more to it than that.

They all did.

Finally, the sound of a motor: Jolly's Avery tractor turning onto the lane.

"Bastard expects too much outta that boy," said Schultz, and the men nodded. "How old is he, anyway? Tom? You know?"

"I think he's thirteen," said Tom, firing a stream of tobacco juice into the dirt. "He's thirteen." Older than Tom.

"Evelyn found him down at the branch last time we thrashed," said Hanson. "Jolly busted him up pretty good."

"As I recall, the kid was lolly-gaggin' around," said Tom's dad.

"Ain't no reason to beat hell outta him."

"You're right, Gus. We all know it."

"I saw Jolly hit the boy with a wrench once, right across the chest."

"We all seen it."

Tom leaned into the horse and let more chew spill from his mouth. He didn't like to think about his friend getting hit or kicked. That's how he thought about Jolly's boy, as his friend, though they'd never traded more than a handful of words over the water bucket. But weren't they all friends? Weren't they all gathered this morning to do a job? He stood straight as the belching tractor came down the water break.

Jolly had come after all, mounted on the iron behemoth like a greasy, fat possum, ten times larger than life, a sputtering cheroot bobbing around his unshaven face. His son, smaller than Tom recalled and frail looking, clung with both hands to the rear of the bouncing bucket seat, one foot on the tractor's lolling hitch, one foot dangling free. Jolly didn't turn, didn't even glance at them as he clamored past. The boy dropped off into the dust and quietly limped toward them.

"How are you, Adam Wayne?" asked Walt, using the boy's full name, but it wasn't hard to see how the boy was. The black eye was back, but it was on the other side of his face and only a few days old, purple and yellow and green. The side of his neck had several round burns, the size of a nail head. Or a cheroot. Neither did his jaw seem to sit right. Like it had been broken. Then Adam spoke. "Ah'm fine," he said, the sound almost lost in the roar of the tractor.

The men watched as Jolly drove around the thrasher in circles, like he'd never seen it before and wasn't sure where to park or how to lace up the belts. Tom couldn't stop looking at Adam's face.

When Jolly finally found his position and set the tractor's brakes, Gus Hanson reached out a hand. Adam winced slightly, not turning toward the touch on his shoulder.

"You should go in now, son. Mrs. Hanson has a bite of breakfast for you."

For a long time the boy didn't move, just stood beside Tom in the circle of men, staring at his clumsy, blustering drunk father who heaved and swore at the massive canvas belts he pulled from under the threshing machine.

At last, Adam turned and looked straight at Tom.

Tom smiled.

Adam smiled back, and Tom felt such a wash of gratitude and respect, it would take him days to describe it, even to himself.

Adam walked to the house.

Once the other boy was inside, Tom didn't need to look at the three men to know it was time to go to work. He felt it through the cold.

Jolly had stopped worrying the belts and stood watching as Walt Schultz pulled his gun from the black gelding's saddle boot. Gus Hanson drew a Colt revolver from his coat pocket. Tom's dad opened the truck, got his cowboy gun, and Tom carefully took down the Marlin.

Was Adam watching from inside the house? Tom knew he was.

He worked the bolt action and, as they advanced, hoped Jolly's boy would be impressed with his aim.

She Comes With The Rain

Keith Rawson

1

I feel it coming in my shoulders; its heaviness, a weight which slumps me forward to my knees, turning my body into a donut. If it's a particularly bad storm, I can't get out of bed for days before it hits. I wish I could chalk it up as age; as nothing more than arthritis, but it's not. It's an early warning system I developed in my forties after Ella died. The weight is a burden, but yet I welcome it, and some days I pray for it.

2

"Who is she?"

"Your guess is as good as mine? She's been classified a yellow, but the reclassification is imminent. They think she's getting ready to escalate her behavior and move from cats to small children."

"Better to stop her now, then."

"Isn't it always?"

"God be praised."

"God be praised."

3

The day before a storm, I force myself out of bed. Since Ella's passing I haven't always been the cleanest person. It's funny how women change you. When I met Ella, I was a full blown slob. I'd never lived with a woman outside of my mother. When Ella first saw my apartment with the stacks of dishes in the kitchen sink, the brown stained toilet, the piles of unwashed laundry, she pretended to vomit, gagging into her palm. It seemed so real that I looped an arm around her shoulder and asked her if she needed some water. She shoved me back, giggling, calling me a doofus.

"The only way we're going to live with one another is if you learn to clean up after yourself."

It took five years of her constant cajoling to whip me into shape, but after she was gone and it was just me and Sabrina, I slipped a bit, letting the dishes pile up occasionally, the laundry go undone, at least until Sabrina would tell me I was starting to smell after wearing the same shirt three days in a row.

After Sabrina left, I slipped even further.

So when I know she's coming, I work past the pain and focus on tidying up. She's so much like her mother.

4

"Who is he?"

"Does it matter? He's classified as a red. He's run two motorcyclists off the road in the past three days. From the data received he's one step away from walking into his work place with an AK-47 and a thousand rounds of ammunition. He needs to be stopped, now."

"And he will be. God be praised."

"God be praised."

5

I didn't used to believe in the afterlife. My parents were children of the '60s and believed in nothing, yet believed in everything. It was a confusing way to grow up. I was educated in every belief system and told to make up my own mind in what I chose to believe or not believe, so I chose the easiest route.

Ella was raised as a Pentecostal, full blown Smoky Mountains bred, snake handling Pentecostals. She'd shirked most of their teachings, but no matter how much you reject your spiritual upbringing, some of it still hangs tight. Her belief in Christ the Savior was unmovable and she insisted we raise Sabrina with the gospel.

"You don't have to believe, but don't dare mock it in front of her."

I did as I was told, even going so far as attending church with them every other Sunday when I had a full two days off from the plant. I never understood what either them got out of going to church. But after each service, both of them seemed to be filled with a kind of light.

Even when Ella was in stage 4, the sermons would make her shine, at least until the nausea from her meds would turn her inside out, and God abandoned her until the next Sunday.

6

"Who are they?"

"A high school couple too in love with video games and serial killer movies. They killed an entire family in Flagstaff yesterday. Intel has them hiding out in Glendale with the boy's aunt and uncle, both of them are dead."

"Shouldn't we let the police handle this?"

"You know better than that. All the police will do is arrest them. Neither one of them deserves that."

"I know. God be praised."

"God be praised."

7

I fell apart.

No matter how much you steel yourself from the loss, no matter how well you prepare for the moment when death finally comes, it still destroys you, turns you inside out.

She died on a Friday, in my arms, disconnected from all the machinery and pumps her doctors had her hooked up to make her comfortable, to extend her life, and to further bilk our health insurance for every last penny they could. I pulled out all the wires and tubes. I wanted her to be free of any encumbrance, of anything that pulled her away from God's embrace.

The hospital had me arrested and charged with murder, and Sabrina lost both of her parents.

She was 5 years old and I would not see her again until she was ten and I introduced her to God's plan.

8

Prison wasn't as horrible as I was led to believe. Books and movies paint prison as a place of constant, barely contained violence. For me it was nothing of the sort. For me, prison was a monastery, a place of rest. I slept, ate, exercised, read, and furthered my education. I learned computers. I learned to navigate through the system, to hide in it.

I also started writing Ella, an attempt at bringing "closure" to our life together.

I never expected her to write back.

9

Sabrina's life is a normal one.

She's married, has two beautiful children. I haven't met any of them, which is how I prefer it.

We came up with her cover story years ago. She has no family, both of her parents died in a car accident on the Wyoming/Montana border when she was sixteen and left her with a huge insurance settlement; enough to pay for her education as well as a modest home and vehicle.

She received her bachelor's degree in business finance and met her husband in her senior year. They married a year later and had my grandson the year after; they waited a few years before having my granddaughter. The boy's name is Michael, after her husband, the girl is named Ella, after her mother.

I burst into tears when Sabrina told me what she named her.

10

My first e-mail to Ella was a simple one:

I still love you.

Ella had set up an e-mail account so she could keep in contact with her sister, who was serving in Iraq as a nurse for a mobile unit. She died two years before the onset of Ella's cancer, and as far as I know, she never used the account again. But when I set up my own account in the prison library, Ella's account was the only e-mail address I knew, or cared about. So I wrote her every day without fail; sometimes they were nothing more than little notes like the first, but then others would go on for pages, reliving the small moments I wished I could relive with her again and again and forever.

It wasn't one of my long, gushing love letters that Ella responded to, but my first simple note. She wrote:

And I still love you. God has a plan for us, and for Sabrina.

11

On the rainy nights, Sabrina will spike the children's milk at dinner with Benadryl. She gives her husband something stronger which she mixes in his food. Once she's positive they're asleep, she'll make the trip to my house and prepare her weapons cache. She prefers cutting weapons—knives, box cutters, straight razors—because I prefer cutting weapons, and I trained her for her purpose. She is far better with them than I ever was. But for the purposes of most of our missions, it's rare she gets to use them.

Our targets' deaths must look like an accident. Explosions caused by leaking gas mains or car accidents are the most common form of execution. Occasionally she's been able to utilize her skills with a blade.

A pimp who slashed the face of a seventeen-year-old girl who wouldn't trick for him anymore.

A gang member who purposely shot and killed the three-old son of a rival.

A soccer mom who ran over her daughter's coach for not putting her in the game.

She considers these three kills her proudest moments.

12

I served my full term. I did not want a probation officer. I did not want the state to know my every move; I wanted to disappear and prepare my daughter for the next phase of our lives together.

We were strangers, Sabrina and I, but when I picked her up from the group home the state had her living in for the five years of my incarceration, she dived into my arms, smothering my face with kisses, telling me how much she loved me; how much she missed me.

It broke my heart what I was about to do to her, but it was beyond my control. It was entirely in the hands of God and her mother.

13

The innocence of children astounds me.

They so readily accept what grownups have to tell them. They will believe anything.

They will believe in heaven.

They will believe in hell.

They will believe in Santa Claus, the Tooth Fairy, the Easter bunny.

They will believe that their mother is an avenging angel.

They will believe that the avenging angel that was once their mother wants them to be her living hand of vengeance.

14

Sabrina took quickly to her training and our new life together. After several years, she moved far beyond the things I could teach her and sought out new masters, and prepared for the inevitability of beginning the next phase of her life.

When she turned sixteen, there were no tearful goodbyes, she simply asked: "How will I know?"

"When the monsoons come. She told me when the rains come is when we'll strike."

"God be praised."

"God be praised."

And then she left.

15

I know the things I've done to Sabrina are wrong. I should have given her a happy life, one filled with dance lessons, birthday parties, 4th of July fireworks, and camping trips. I know what I turned her into was the act of an angry, lonely man. The act of a man so overcome by his own grief that he convinced himself that his wife was communicating with him beyond the grave.

Ella is not an angel.

There is no Heaven.

There is no God.

They're nothing more than voices, my rage and pain made corporeal.

So this time, when I feel the weather begin to shift, I spend two days cleaning the house, muscling through the dull ache in my bones, making sure everything is in order, and then I write out Sabrina's final assignment:

Michael Rossen

Classification: RED

Directly responsible for the deaths of 75 human beings.

Responsible for the ritual mental abuse of his only daughter, Sabrina.

Finally, I lay out her favorite weapons: A box cutter, a scalpel, a butcher's knife.

I go to bed just as the first drops of rain begin to tap on the windows and pray that my judgment and death will not be a quick one.

The Greatest Generation

James Reasoner

Ed Bristol came home from North Africa with an empty sleeve and the bitter realization that he hadn't done his part in the war effort. Of course, it wasn't his fault that a 20-year-old private from Hackensack, New Jersey, who was drunk on Arab hooch ran over him with a jeep one night while Ed was standing guard duty. The jeep's left front wheel crushed Ed's left elbow. The rear wheel got him, too, finishing off the job by shattering the humerus in the same arm in too many places for the doctors to put it back together. So they cut it off instead, and Ed, who had come ashore in Morocco proudly with General Patton, got shipped home to Texas with an honorable discharge. It didn't feel so honorable to Ed.

His wife Mary Beth met him at the train station in Prescott, the county seat. She'd been notified by the army about Ed's injury, of course, and he'd been able to send her several letters while he was recuperating until he was well enough to travel, so she knew what to expect. She couldn't have been surprised when she saw the pinned-up left sleeve of his uniform. But she winced a little anyway, and the bitterness inside Ed took a firmer grip on him.

"Let's get you home," she told him with a determined smile on her face after she'd kissed him.

"I'd like that," Ed said.

He was glad to see that nobody else was at the station to make a fuss over him, but a half-hour later when they reached the small town of Lockspur—with Mary Beth driving the Packard that had belonged to Ed's late dad, of course—he let out a groan when he saw the banner strung across Main Street between Hammersmith's Furniture and the drugstore.

WELCOME HOME, ED! OUR LOCAL HERO!

LOCKSPUR IS PROUD OF YOU!

Hero, they called him. Because he hadn't been able to move fast enough to get out of the way of a drunken bum from Jersey.

"When we get to the house, there's not going to be a bunch of people waiting there, is there?" he asked his wife.

Mary Beth still wore that brave, resolute smile. She said, "Well, of course your mother and your sisters and the rest of the family all want to welcome you home, Ed. And Skeeziks is there, and Brother Fred and some of the other people from the church, and...well..."

Ed closed his eyes. "The whole damned town."

"Ed! You can't blame people for wanting to see you. You're a—"

"Don't say it. You know what happened over there. You know how I got like this. So don't say it. You know I'm not a hero." He paused, then asked, "For God's sake, you didn't tell people I lost my arm fighting Rommel or some crap like that, did you?"

Now she was a little mad, too, her blue eyes flashing in the way he always thought was so pretty when her ire wasn't directed at him.

"I told them you were injured in North Africa. That's all. I figured it would be up to you to tell them as much or as little about the circumstances as you wanted to."

"Well, there's that to be thankful for, anyway," he said.

"But there's something you should remember, Ed," she went on. "People don't like it when they're expecting one thing and they hear something else. It might be better to just say that you really don't want to talk about it yet. They'll all accept that. Nobody wants to embarrass you. They just want you to know they're glad you're alive, and you're home."

He looked at the house as she pulled up in front of it, and he said, "Yeah, I'm home, all right."

• • •

He had worked in Howard Strickland's garage for several years before the attack at Pearl Harbor. Skeeziks, as everybody called Howard, was a good guy, and he made it clear that Ed's old job was waiting for him now that he was back. Ed told him that he wanted to take a little time before he started working again, and Skeeziks told him to take as long as he wanted. The job would be there.

But Ed was damned if he thought there was much a one-armed mechanic could actually do around a garage. Most jobs took two good hands.

So for several weeks he sat and read the paper and listened to the radio during the day while Mary Beth was at her job as a civilian clerk/typist as the big military camp on the south side of Prescott. Because she worked for the military she could get gas and tires for the Packard.

Ed tried to keep up with the war news until he realized it was just making him feel worse. He hoped all the guys in his outfit came through all right, but there wasn't a blasted thing he could do anymore to help them, so he figured it might be best not to think about it. He wound up looking out the living room window a lot, trying to pass the time that way. It made him feel a little like a busybody old lady, minding everybody else's business.

But he didn't have any business of his own to mind, and if he hadn't been standing at the window, he wouldn't have seen Scooter Larabee come in drunk.

The Larabees had lived across the street as far back as Ed could remember. Scooter and his family now lived in the same house where he had been raised as a kid, just as Ed did. Ed's mother had moved in with one of his sisters after his father died, not wanting to have to take care of the house by herself, and Ed and Mary Beth had moved in. It was sort of the same with Scooter, except both of his folks were dead, killed by the pneumonia ten years earlier. Scooter, who was seven years older than Ed and whose real name was Phil, had married young and he and his wife Brenda had a kid, a little boy named Charles. Charley, they called him.

Ed and Mary Beth wanted kids, too, but so far that hadn't happened. Sometimes Ed had lain awake at night wondering if he was shooting blanks. Now he thought maybe that was a good thing. No kid ought to grow up with an old man who was a cripple.

The streets in Lockspur didn't have curbs, but if they had, Scooter Larabee would have run his car up over the one in front of his house. He brought it to a stop at a slant, the right front wheel up on the grass in the yard. When he got out he had to catch hold of the door for a second to steady himself before he walked into the house. Ed knew that slow, carefully controlled, but still somewhat shaky gait. He had seen it before in other men who'd had too much to drink.

He wondered if that bastard from Hackensack had walked like that when he left the bar in Casablanca that night.

Scooter went on in the house, and a minute later Ed heard yelling. It was warm enough to have the windows up, and Scooter's voice traveled. Ed heard a woman, too. That would be Scooter's wife Brenda. She wasn't yelling, though. She sounded like she was pleading.

Then somebody who wasn't either of them let out a wailing cry, and the only other person over there, as far as Ed knew, was the little boy, Charley.

The ruckus didn't last long. A little later Charley came out into the yard to play. He was five or six, Ed couldn't remember which. Even from across the street, he could tell that Charley's eyes were red from bawling. The kid wiped the back of his hand across his nose like he was sniffling.

And damned if he wasn't limping a little as he went around the side of the house in search of something to do.

• • •

"You talk to Brenda Larabee much these days?" Ed asked Mary Beth while she was fixing supper that night.

"What?" She sounded a little impatient with him. He didn't really blame her. She worked hard at the camp all day, then had to come home and fix him something to eat. That wasn't fair…but there was a hell of a lot in life that wasn't fair.

"I asked if you talked to Brenda Larabee much."

He was in the living room and she was in the kitchen, but he heard the familiar puff of exasperated breath as she blew aside some of the blond hair that had fallen in front of her face. That was something else he liked about her.

"Oh, I don't know," she said. "Sure, I talk to Brenda when I see her at the store or in church. Maybe sometimes when I'm outside and she's watering those rose bushes of hers. Why?"

"I think Scooter was drunk when he came in this afternoon." Scooter worked at the electric plant in Prescott, and his shift brought him home earlier than most men. Producing electricity was considered a vital occupation, so he hadn't been drafted, and he hadn't enlisted after Pearl Harbor, either, which rubbed some people the wrong way because Scooter was a big, strapping fellow who ought to be overseas killing Nazis or Japs.

"What were you doing watching the Larabee house?" Mary Beth asked.

"I wasn't watching the Larabee house," Ed said, although that was exactly what he'd been doing. "I just happened to be looking out the window when Scooter drove up."

He stopped, unsure whether to say anything else. But he'd been thinking a lot about what he'd seen, so he went on, "I could hear Scooter and Brenda arguing, and then the kid started carrying on."

That brought Mary Beth to the door between the kitchen and the living room. "Charley? Was he all right?"

"I don't know. He came outside a little later and he was still crying some. He limped, too, like somebody hurt him. He doesn't normally limp, does he?"

"Not that I've ever noticed," Mary Beth said, frowning. "But who could have hurt him?"

"Well…"

"Scooter? Oh, no, Ed, I don't think so. I mean, I've heard him scolding Charley before, of course, and he probably has to spank him sometimes, but that's going to happen with any child. Scooter wouldn't do anything to actually hurt Charley."

Ed wasn't so sure about that. When they were growing up across the street from each other, Scooter had been, at times, in the words of Ed's dad, "a little jackass". He had bullied the other kids, including Ed, who was not only several years younger but also small, even considering the age difference. Ed still wasn't very big. He'd been tall enough to get in the army, but not by much.

"I wouldn't want to see anything like that happen," he said.

"You and Scooter never got along very well when you were younger, did you?"

"Not really."

"Maybe that has an effect on what you think you saw and heard."

"I don't *think* I saw and heard it," Ed said. "I did see and hear it."

"My cornbread's about to burn." Mary Beth turned back toward the kitchen, then paused to add, "Whatever happened across the street is family business, Ed. It's none of our affair."

"You're right," he said.

But he wasn't completely convinced that she was.

• • •

For the next week, Scooter seemed fine when he came in from work. But then his tires screeched a little as he came to a rather abrupt stop one day, and when Ed looked out the window after seeing that, he saw Scooter going across the yard with that same tell-tale unsteadiness.

A little later, the yelling and the crying started again, and Ed distinctly heard Brenda say, "No, Phil, don't! Please—"

Ed wasn't a hundred per cent certain of what he heard next, but he was pretty sure it was a slap.

And Brenda didn't say anything else.

Five minutes later, Charley came out the front door moving fast, almost like somebody was chasing him. Nobody else came out, though. The little boy sat down on the front steps. He was sort of hunched to one side, like he was trying to curl himself around a stubborn pain.

Ed knew that feeling. Sometimes, even though his left arm was gone, it still seemed to hurt like blazes.

Mary Beth had told him it was none of their business, so he didn't say anything to her. This time she was the one who mentioned something to him, a couple of days later when she'd been to the grocery store.

"I ran into Brenda Larabee at the store. She didn't seem to want to talk to me, Ed, and she sort of kept her face turned away. I can't be sure because it looked like she'd tried to cover it with makeup, but I think she had a bruise on her face."

"That son of a bitch," Ed said.

"Listen," Mary Beth said, and her voice was even more serious than usual. "I'm sorry if what you're thinking about Scooter is right, but even if it is, it's still none of our business. She's his wife and Charley's his son, and he's got a right to...well...it's a free country, after all."

Yeah, and on the other side of the world men were fighting and dying and getting run over by drunken privates to keep it free so jerks like Scooter Larabee could beat up on their wives and kids.

But she was right. You didn't interfere with somebody's personal affairs. You just didn't do it.

"Hey, Jack Benny will be on in a little while," he said. "You want to listen?"

• • •

Mary Beth was getting restless. She thought he ought to go back to work. Skeeziks had been by a couple of times, too, dropping hints about how he had more than he could handle in the garage and could sure use a hand.

Ed had been tempted to say, *Yeah, so could I*, but he didn't because he knew Skeeziks didn't mean anything by it and just hadn't thought about what he was saying.

It was a cool afternoon with a light drizzle falling when Ed heard more commotion from the house across the street. He'd been dozing, probably because of the gray day, and hadn't noticed when Scooter came in. But the car was there, parked at a cock-eyed angle again, and Scooter was inside yelling. Ed watched for a few minutes, then sighed and turned away from the window. None of his business, he repeated to himself.

Then Charley came out onto the front porch and spat something into his hand. Ed had good eyesight. He saw a flash of white and another of bright red.

Blood.

The son of a bitch had knocked one of Charley's teeth loose, and the boy had just spit it out.

Ed was walking across the street, his face damp from the drizzle, before he even knew what he was doing. Charley saw him coming and drew back. The kid was scared. Of course he was. He was probably scared of everybody and everything, flinching at the least little movement or sound. Like a beaten dog.

Charley looked like he was going to say something as Ed came up the steps, but then he scurried off to the far end of the porch, slipped under the railing there, and disappeared around the corner of the house.

Ed knocked on the screen door. The wooden one inside it was open.

Scooter came to the door still wearing his work clothes, khaki trousers and a gray shirt with "Larabee" stitched onto a patch and sewn to it. He said, "What?", then, "Oh, hey, Ed. Good to see you, buddy. Sorry I didn't make it to your welcome home party. I've been meanin' to come over and say hello ever since you got back. Tough luck over there, eh?"

"Yeah," Ed said. He could smell the beer on Scooter's breath through the screen.

Some guys figured that what they did when they were drinking, well, that wasn't really them doing it. It was the beer, or the whiskey, or whatever they'd been pouring down their throats. Ed had a hunch that private over in North Africa felt the same way. He'd probably already forgotten all about what happened to that PFC from Texas because, hell, it was the booze to blame, not him.

Scooter looked confused. "You, uh, want to come in?"

"No. I've been hearing a lot of racket going on over here, Scooter."

"Really? I'm sorry about that. You know how kids are, always yellin' about something. Between that and Brenda's whinin'...Anyway, I'll make sure they keep it down from now on. Didn't mean to disturb you, what with you bein'...well, crippled and all."

"Why don't you try treating them better?"

Ed knew that Scooter had been making an effort to be polite. That vanished in an instant. He glared at Ed through the screen and said, "Why don't you mind your own damn business, Bristol? You got no right to come pokin' your nose into what a man does in his own house."

"Yeah, Hitler probably figured what he was doing was his own business, too."

The screen came open in a hurry, forcing Ed to step back or let it hit him. Scooter bulled out onto the porch and said, "Are you comparin' me to Hitler? Why, I oughta—"

"Don't stop," Ed said. "What, are you worried about hitting a cripple?"

"Yeah, that'd look real good, wouldn't it? Beatin' up the war hero? Hell, if word of that got around, I might even lose my job, and then..."

"And then you might have to go in the army," Ed said. "Fighting the Afrika Corps isn't like hitting a woman and a little boy."

Scooter shook his head. "Just get outta here. You always were a goddamn little pest, and you haven't changed. Go home, Bristol, and leave us alone. Because if you don't...I'll give you what you're askin' for, war hero or no war hero, and you know I can do it, too."

• • •

That was the bad part: Ed knew Scooter was right. He couldn't stand up to the other man in a fight. Even though he'd been through basic training and all the hand-to-hand combat drills, he'd never been particularly good at them. Scooter was big, he was mean, he had a reputation as a brawler, and even if he'd had both arms—and a Louisville Slugger—Ed wasn't sure if he could have handled the guy.

He didn't say anything about the confrontation to Mary Beth when she came in. She'd be a lot nicer about it, of course, but she would tell him the same thing Scooter had, that he was sticking his nose in where it didn't belong. Every man was the king of his own castle, wasn't he? Even if he called the law on Scooter, that was what they would say, too. They didn't get mixed up in family disputes.

So Ed listened to the radio and ate supper with Mary Beth, and after supper they listened to a program of dance music being broadcast from a hotel in Fort Worth. They were Baptists, so they didn't dance, of course, but it was all right for them to listen to the music. What was a secret between the two of them was that before he'd enlisted, sometimes they *had* danced, with the curtains closed so that if the preacher happened to drive by he wouldn't look in and see them sinning. Ed wouldn't have minded doing it again—he'd always loved the way Mary Beth felt in his arms—but it went without saying that that wouldn't be happening. A one-armed man couldn't dance with a girl.

The orchestra was between numbers when Mary Beth asked, "Did you hear something?"

Ed hadn't, but before he could answer Mary Beth stood up and turned off the Philco, and he heard it then, a woman screaming for help. The cries came from across the street, from the Larabee house.

Ed yanked the front door open and ran out onto the porch, pausing to be sure he was really hearing what he thought he heard. There was no doubt about it. Mary Beth came outside behind him and said, "We should call someone."

Ed didn't answer her. He knew there was nobody to call, nobody who would do anything.

"Ed, wait!"

The rain had stopped, but the yard was still a little wet and muddy. Ed went across it in a hurry, across the street, and up to the Larabee house. He took the steps two at a time, crossed the porch, and opened the screen door. The wooden door wasn't locked. He threw it open and came into the living room in time to see Scooter holding the collar of Charley's shirt and slamming open-handed blows back and forth across the little boy's face. Off to the side, Brenda half-sat, half-lay huddled in an armchair, blood trickling from the corner of her mouth where Scooter had caught her with a punch, too.

Scooter was yelling at the boy, chastising him for doing...something, it didn't really matter what. Probably something trivial and meaningless to anybody who wasn't a vicious bastard like Scooter. Busy like that, Scooter didn't hear Ed coming, didn't know he was there until Ed lowered his right shoulder and drove it into the small of Scooter's back, tackling him and driving him away from Charley.

Taken by surprise, Scooter hit the floor hard. But he recovered quickly, coming up and swinging a big arm around as Ed, who had fallen down, too, was trying to get to his feet. Scooter's arm crashed across Ed's chest like a club and knocked him on his rear. For a second his heart and lungs seemed to be paralyzed by the blow. He couldn't breathe, couldn't make his muscles work.

"You son of a bitch!" Scooter roared. He scrambled to his feet. "I told you what you'd get if you interfered with my family."

He tried to kick Ed. Twisting away from Scooter's foot in its heavy work shoe, Ed grabbed his ankle and heaved, trying to upend him. Scooter just pulled loose and took a little hopping step back to catch his balance.

Then he grinned and said, "You want to fight me? All right, Bristol. I'll fight you. Go ahead and get up. I dare you."

Ed climbed to his feet. From the corner of his eye he saw that Charley had run to his mother and climbed into Brenda's lap. Both of them sat there watching, wide-eyed with fear.

"Ed!" Mary Beth said from the doorway. She had followed him across the street. "Ed, stop! Don't—"

He looked at her. He always looked at her when she talked.

And Scooter lunged forward and hit him in the face.

The impact knocked Ed back against the wall, which was covered with a nice rose-patterned wallpaper. Brenda liked roses. Ed leaned on the wall for a second. In the cartoons when a guy got hit like that, sometimes birds flew around his head, chirping. It did sort of sound like that, Ed thought.

He steadied himself and went forward. He tried to hit Scooter, who blocked the punch with his left arm and drove his right fist into Ed's stomach. Ed doubled over in pain, but he was still thinking clearly enough to realize that in this position his head was already pointed at Scooter. So he drove ahead and butted him in the belly. Ed was small compared to a bruiser like Scooter, but he weighed enough that he sent Scooter stumbling backward.

Forcing himself to straighten up, Ed went after Scooter and lifted a punch that actually landed. It caught Scooter under the chin with a reasonable amount of force behind it. That jerked Scooter's head back and made him grunt. It didn't really faze him much, though. He came back with a left that crashed into Ed's shoulder and knocked him sideways, then a right that landed on Ed's jaw and had him hearing those damned birds again.

"Scooter, no!" Mary Beth said. "Please!"

"He asked for it," Scooter said as he got ready to throw another punch.

He asked for it. Ed would have been willing to bet that Scooter had said the same thing about Charley in the past. *She asked for it.* Anything to justify the violence toward his wife and son. With rage fueling him, he charged again, ducking under the blow that Scooter sent at him. He hooked two fast punches to Scooter's belly.

Beer had laid a layer of fat over Scooter's midsection, but underneath it was muscle, and he shrugged off Ed's punches. He grabbed Ed's shoulders and shoved him against the wall again.

"Back off! You're not worth beatin' up. Leave me alone, damn it, before I really have to hurt you."

Ed shook his head. He was breathing hard, and he hurt in several places where Scooter had hit him. But he was able to say, "No. I...I'm not gonna back off. I'm not gonna leave you alone. You're the one who's going to get what's coming to him, Scooter, and the only way you can stop me is to kill me."

Scooter's mouth twisted in a snarl. "If that's the way you want it," he said.

Mary Beth screamed as two more punches crashed into Ed's face and body. He managed to hit Scooter in the nose. Blood spurted under his fist, and Scooter howled in pain.

Ed remembered then how Scooter's nose had bled easily when they were younger. Every time Scooter got bumped on the nose, the blood flowed. So while Scooter was yelling, Ed hit him again.

He wasn't the biggest guy in the world, but he was quick when he needed to be, and even with just one hand he could pepper Scooter's nose with punch after punch, like a boxer working a speed bag. Scooter stumbled backward, trying to get away, but Ed wouldn't let him.

All the aches and pains were still there. They hadn't gone away. But Ed ignored them. He drove Scooter toward the front door and yelled for Mary Beth to get out of the way. He was going to force Scooter right out of the house. Scooter was crying by now, and the entire lower half of his face was red with the blood that had exploded from his nose.

Ed's valiant charge lasted all of five seconds, and in that time he landed seven or eight blows.

Then a wild punch from Scooter landed on his jaw and lifted him off his feet. He landed in a heap on the rug in front of the radio. It was over. For a moment he had thought he might actually win, but then size and strength, those inevitable trump cards, had come into play, and now Scooter was coming toward him, about to stomp the hell out of him.

He might have, too, if a couple of men hadn't appeared behind him at that moment, grabbed his arms, and hauled him backward. Ed recognized their uniforms. They were deputies from the sheriff's department. Lockspur didn't have its own police force, only an elderly constable, but the deputies patrolled the town and somebody must have called them about all the yelling and fighting going on at the Larabee house.

"What the devil are you doing?" one of the deputies asked Scooter. "That's Ed Bristol, you fool. He's a war hero!"

Scooter might have talked his way out of it, claimed that Ed had invaded his home and attacked him, and that would have been true. But in his rage Scooter got an arm free and punched one of the deputies in the face. It didn't take long after that for them to have him handcuffed and dragged out, loudly promising him six months in the county jail for disturbing the peace and assaulting an officer of the law, not to mention assault and battery on a war hero. A crippled war hero, at that.

Mary Beth seemed not to know who to comfort first, her bruised and battered husband or her sobbing neighbor. Ed sat up and waved her toward Brenda. He was all right.

Well, maybe not really...but he would be.

• • •

When he got home from the garage a few days later, Mary Beth was already there. She had taken half a day off at the camp to help Brenda pack up. She and Charley were going to live with her sister in Sweetwater. Ed figured that was a good idea. They would be long gone from Lockspur by the time Scooter got out of jail. Maybe he would find them and try to convince Brenda to come back to him. Maybe he wouldn't. That was up to somebody besides him, Ed thought.

"Brenda and Charley get off okay?" he asked Mary Beth.

"Yes. She said for me to thank you again."

"No need for that," he said with a shake of his head. "I just did what anybody else would have done."

"No," Mary Beth said. "I don't think so."

He noticed that she was closing the curtains on the front windows, even though it wasn't dark yet. "What's that for?" he asked.

"There's a program of dance music coming on in a few minutes." She smiled at him. "I thought we might be sinful."

Ed shook his head and looked down at his empty sleeve. "I can't dance," he told. "You know I can't."

"I don't know any such thing. And you don't, either, until you try."

He supposed she had a point there. He could still put one arm around her, after all, and there was nothing wrong with his left shoulder other than a little soreness from that tussle with Scooter Larabee. It would do for her to rest her head on. She was right, they could give it a try.

While they were swaying together to the music, she said, "What did you tell Charley when he asked you if you were really a war hero?"

"You know what I told him. You were right there."

"What did you tell him?" she insisted.

Ed figured he might as well humor her. "I told him I wasn't a hero. I told him I was just a guy."

"That's right," she said. "My guy."

Baby Boy

Todd Robinson

Wade stands at the long bank of telephones in the airport, the earpiece pressed so hard against his ear it begins to hurt. He uses the pain to tether him to the moment. It feels a little bit like he's hyperventilating, the contours of the airport too sharp, too bright. He closes his eyes tightly, but the colors just swirl under his eyelids. Tears form in the corners, but he doesn't know if it's from the pressure of squeezing them shut or something else.

"What are you doing?" Liana asks.

"I don't know," he murmurs through lips that are numb. A lie. Wade knows exactly what he's doing.

· · ·

The first hour

Wade's confusion quickly turned into fear when he pulled up in front of the building. Ben didn't come running out in the alcove like he always did when Wade pulled up in the Prius.

And then there was the enormous red and yellow tent draped over the building behind St. Matthews that housed Ben's afterschool program, a truck with Numan's Pest Control parked in front.

A fat man in a gray jumpsuit leaned against the truck, a greasy fish sandwich in one hand.

"Excuse me?" Wade asked.

"Yeah?"

"What happened to the afterschool program?"

"Huh?" A small flake of white fish flew out of the man's mouth.

"There's an after-school program in that building. Did they leave?"

The man with 'Ernie' stitched on his chest just shrugged. "I dunno, man. I just set the bug bombs and I wait."

"What happened to the kids? Did they leave already? Did they move to another building?"

'Ernie' sighed with annoyance at having to answer Wade's questions. "Listen, I don't know nothing about nothing about what goes on in the building, I just set the poison and go. The only person who was in there was that Eye-talian janitor, and he skedaddled over two hours ago."

A cold fist squeezed Wade's heart. "Are you sure that the building was empty? Was there a little boy, about three-foot-six?" Wade struggled to remember what

Ben was wearing when he left the house, but couldn't. "Probably wearing a superhero shirt of some kind?"

"I went through every room. Like I said, I didn't see nobody but the janitor."

Wade looked at the front of the building, the tent looking for all the world like the circus was in town, rather than a building full of poison. A glint of reflective green caught Wade's eye under the bushes.

The fist squeezed harder.

Wade ran over to the hedges lining the building.

"Hey, you can't go in there, man."

Wade reached under the hedge, the fumes burning his nostrils even from this side of the tent. His fingers grasped the object and pulled out Ben's Green Lantern backpack with the reflective strip along the opening. If not for that strip, Wade might not have even noticed the bag.

The fist on his heart clenched. Wade dropped the backpack.

Wade remembered how Ben told him the day before how well he'd done playing Hide & Seek with his buddies, hiding at the back of the cloakroom and covering his head with jackets.

"Ben!" Wade screamed, looking up at the tent. "Ben!" Wade lifted up the edge of the tent over the door and rushed inside, screaming for his son.

"Hey, you crazy fuck," yelled 'Ernie.' "You can't go in there! It's full of poison gas, you lunatic!"

The air inside was thick with fumes that stung Wade's nostrils with an acrid scent that reminded him of bitter lemons and transmission fluid. "Ben!" he screamed again, his voice a croak, constricting against the toxic air that filled his lungs each time he inhaled to scream his son's name. Wade pulled the front of his t-shirt over his mouth and nose as he ran towards the room where Ben was supposed to be that day.

Wade tore into the rec room, stumbled towards the cloakroom with stinging eyes. He tried to call his son's name again, but only a strangled croak emerged from his burning throat.

Stumbling, Wade fell into the cloakroom.

Empty.

No coats, no bags, no evidence that anyone had been there at all that day.

A small pile of gym mats strewn haphazardly in the corner was all that was in there.

A good place to hide.

No. Nononononononono.

Wade tore through the mats, flinging them aside, terrified to find his son.

Terrified not to.

There was nothing under the mats.

No Ben.

Wade's knees gave out from under him and he dropped to the floor, vomiting into his shirt.

Something grabbed his shoulder as he lost consciousness. As the room went to black, Wade saw a figure in an oxygen mash looming over him.

He tried to ask for help.

Wade needed this man with 'Ernie' on his lapel to find his son.

Ben.

Benny.

Benny-Boy.

Baby Boy.

• • •

"Please. Just leave. Walk away right now." Wade can hear the tremble in Liana's voice, but what he doesn't hear is conviction behind what she's asking of him. Either that, or he doesn't want to hear it.

Wade doesn't answer her. He opens his eyes again, scans the crowd.

People are hurrying past, getting their luggage off the slowly spinning conveyor.

"Why are you there? Just leave. Just get in a cab and come home." Despite the forced calm in her voice, he can hear panic bleeding into her tone. She's asking questions she knows the answers to.

"I—I just need to see him. I just need to see his face."

Wade knows that what he's saying is only partially true.

She knows it, too.

The weight in the pocket of his blue windbreaker screams the lie behind his words.

• • •

The first week

It wasn't until a full day after Ben went missing that Wade could answer anyone's questions.

His wife's.

The police's.

He floated in and out of a pained consciousness, the world swimming in and out as the hospital worked to purge his system of the toxic levels of pesticide that he'd inhaled.

Even when his senses did return, Wade had to write his answers down with a pen and pad, his voice shredded by the gas.

The police came in and out. Checking his work schedule. Questions to his coworkers. Questions to him.

"Is there anyone who may have had reason to take your son?"

No.

"Is there anyone who might be angry enough with you to want to take or hurt your son?"

I don't know. I don't think so.

Raised eyebrows and suspicions about his worth as a father. Questions about his relationship with Liana. Questions about infidelities that may have led to jilted lovers with a vengeful agenda.

"Did you know about this?" they asked, producing a wrinkled up notice that the after-school program would be closed that day for the exterminator. Liana found it stuffed into the front pocket of Ben's backpack. Ben had forgotten about it, never showing it to either one of his parents.

Nobody could find the janitor that 'Ernie' said was at the building when he arrived.

Nothing but questions with no answers.

Wade knew from all the cop shows he watched that the clock was ticking, how much worse the odds were for a happy resolution as time passed.

With each movement of the clock hands in his hospital room, the dread in Wade's heart grew.

And the fear.

Fear that they never would never find him.

Fear that they would.

• • •

"This isn't you. Whatever you're doing, this isn't you, Wade."

Wade knows this. This is part of the problem.

Wade needs to be somebody different right now.

It's not lost on him that this conversation is the most that Liana has spoken to him in over six months.

"You don't know what I am any more. How would you know?" He says the words to hurt. Her silence shows him that they hit their mark. Wade immediately feels guilty for inflicting any more pain into their lives than the world already has.

That's how Wade knows she's right.

That's why Wade isn't sure he can do this.

Or at least knew that he couldn't six months ago.

• • •

The first month

The silence in the house was thick. Wade waited alone.

Not that it made any difference. The house was quiet when he and Liana were in it together. They had nothing to say any more. All conversation for the past weeks had been halted, frightened. Ben was all-consuming in their minds, their hearts, but words passed between each other couldn't bear the weight of their heartbreak any more.

The need to blame someone, some*thing* rested between the two of them. They had no right, no reason to hold each other in any way accountable.

But they needed something. Someone.

Wade would find his thoughts drifting to why Liana hadn't noticed the paper in Ben's bag. He wouldn't say the words, ashamed at the thoughts, but Liana would see something flit across his eyes, and she knew.

She just knew.

Then she would quietly walk to another room, so Wade wouldn't hear her sobbing.

But he always could.

And then there were the times where Wade would see something in her eyes, something primal, the mother looking at the father with the loss of faith that comes when the safety of the family has been compromised. Who was responsible for their safety, for their protection if not him?

Wade didn't cry, though. He just accepted the look and went to his bottle of gin and shut himself in the den with his thoughts and his self-loathing. His self-awareness that she wasn't wrong with those thoughts.

He didn't protect his family.

He hadn't protected his son.

Liana was at the airport picking up her father, Terrence. Terrence was a retired detective out of Portland. Retired by way of a bullet to the spine from an abusive husband ten years ago.

The idea of Terrence staying with them made Wade uneasy. He'd always had a lessening effect on Wade. Terrence was hard, tough. A man who fished off of piers in a wheelchair, played basketball in a handicapped league at the age of 61.

He was everything Wade wasn't, everything that made Wade feel like less of a man, with his academia and red pens and cocktail parties and literature.

Liana always told Wade that it was precisely for those reasons that she'd married him; his gentle nature, his mind—all of the things that made him not her father.

But when they were in the shit like they were at the moment, Terrence was the kind of man she needed around, not Wade.

Wade sat, rolling Ben's plastic Green Lantern ring through his fingers, swirling a rocks glass of warm gin in the other.

The toy ring slipped from his grasp and bounced under the couch. Wade went to the floor on wobbly knees to find it, but his fingers instead found soft cloth. Covered in dust, Wade pulled out Ben's baseball jersey from his tee-ball squad. It must have been there from the day before he disappeared, his last appearance at Rice Field less than twenty-four hours before the world opened up and swallowed his son.

Before he realized what he was doing, Wade pressed the polyester mesh against his face and inhaled.

He could still smell him on the fabric.

The force of grief that overcame Wade was a physical thing, assaulting him from the inside-out.

When Liana pulled into the driveway, Wade had himself back under control, but the red puffiness of his face belied the emotional collapse only a few minutes before. His wife had concern on her face.

Terrence had disgust.

· · ·

It was towards the end of that first month when the detectives show up at the door, faces grim.

Liana sees them and runs to the kitchen, covering her mouth. Wade feels nettles blossom in his chest, but just grits his teeth against another scream.

The news vans have long departed, moving on to fresher blood, wounds on families that are still fresh enough to smell.

The detective hands Wade a printout from the Interpol website. It takes a second, but Wade recognizes the face in the picture under WANTED.

Below the picture is a list that makes Wade's blood turn to ice.

FORGERY OF TRAVEL DOCUMENTS
TRAFFIC IN HUMAN BEINGS
KIDNAPPING/ILLEGAL IMPRISONMENT
SEXUAL OFFENCES
CRIMES AGAINST CHILDREN
His name is Luca DiStasio.
Known aliases are Luca Marino.
Andreas DiStasio.
And Peter Steffano—which matched the name on the employment form for the janitor at St. Matthews.

It didn't take long, maybe a half an hour before the first news trucks rolled back in.

• • •

The phone goes dead in his hand, the time run out.

Wade reaches in for another quarter, but stops when his fingers sweep over the gun. If he doesn't call his wife back, there will be no turning back. Wade knows she's the last thing keeping him from what he's here to do.

He closes his eyes and inhales deeply.

His fingers brush the change in his pocket.

The gun.

Wade takes out the quarter and dials home.

• • •

Five months later

The phone rang. Wade lets it go most of the time, lets the machine take it. More often than not, it's one of the news agencies trying to get a follow-up piece. A couple of psychics tried to get them to pay for their paranormal skills. One said she could find Ben's whereabouts.

The other said he had a message for them from the other side.

Wade feels like his entire life is the other side; limbo, Purgatory. His life is waiting for the inevitable Hell to come. This life, this hollow day to day existence with nothing but painful mystery from the moment he opens his eyes to the moment he shut them again at night.

Ben stopped answering the phone after a woman screamed at him that God had taken their son as punishment for America's acceptance of homosexuality.

The University graciously gave him a sabbatical. It was possibly the worst thing they could have done to him. The University gave him a semblance of purpose, something to force its way into his mind, anything but the silence between the layers of sorrow that was once his home.

Was once their home.

It's nobody's home now.

It had become a funeral parlor for a wake that had no end, no coffin to close the lid on.

Liana stopped answering the phone weeks ago. She'd lost a lot of weight. The skin on her cheeks is sallow, her color gone to ash. New streaks of gray appeared in her once lustrous chestnut hair, manifesting physically the years that seem to have gone by over the months Ben has been missing.

Terrence tried to talk to her on occasion, to snap her out of her near-catatonia. After a few sentences, he usually gave up, muttering in frustration. He doesn't try to talk to Wade.

Or doesn't bother.

Either way.

She mostly stood at the windows all day, watched the red and orange leaves fall from the trees in the front yard, the tree that Ben fell out of last summer, fracturing his shin. If Wade could bear to follow her gaze, he'd see she was staring at the branch that their son had climbed that warm July day, his fingers sticky with blue popsicle. As though she were waiting for their son to tumble out of the tree and into their lives again.

It was two days before Halloween.

The phone stopped ringing.

The answering machine clicked.

Wade walked towards the kitchen. Terrence has already rolled his wheelchair out of the room that was once Wade's den, now the handicap-accessible guest room.

Terrence lifted the receiver and hit the password onto the keypad. Wade wondered when Liana gave him access to their password, but finds it hard to find offense in this brazen invasion of their privacy. Wade found it hard to find offense anymore. Things that would have started an angry conversation, if not argument with Liana are absorbed into the sick-feeling that was his normal.

Terrence listens to the message on the voicemail. His eyes go wide with shock.

He looks at Wade.

"They found him."

They found him.

Ben.

Benny.

Benny-Boy.

Baby Boy.

$$\bullet \ \bullet \ \bullet$$

Families and friends embrace around him. Happy reunions.

Who would blame you? *A voice whispered in Wade's mind. After what he did.*

Wade knows what he's here to do is supposed to be wrong. A sin.

Isn't it?

An eye for an eye?

Except he didn't take your eye. He took your boy. Gave you back a shell with Ben's face.

On Halloween, you got a little boy to visit your home in a Ben mask.

Benny.

Benny-Boy.

Baby Boy.

A soul for a soul then?

It doesn't feel wrong.

At all.

• • •

It struck Wade as appropriate that Ben was returned to them on Halloween.

Amid the masses of media and police, there he was, walking very straight, an expression of seriousness no six-year-old should ever wear. A young black woman in a dark blue suit walked with him from the plane, had flown with him from Florida where the Apopka police had found him and arrested Luca DiStasio.

Liana screamed his name and ran to him.

Ben didn't react, just held his head down as his mother nearly bowled him over, weeping and peppering his face and head with kisses. An NYPD officer pushed Terrence's wheelchair over, Terrence smiling for the first time since he'd arrived, ruffling his grandson's hair.

Wade just looked at the black woman's face. Wade assumed she was a Federal Marshal of some sort, who had seen and done this sort of thing before.

But her expression was pulled tightly across her pretty features as she looked at Wade.

She knew what had happened to Ben.

Wade could see it was bothering her, almost haunting her eyes as they met his.

Then Wade looked down over his wife's shoulder, looked at his son's face for the first time in over half a year.

Ben's eyes met Wade's.

Ben.

Benny.

Benny-Boy.

Baby Boy.

He didn't say a word.

But Wade heard his voice, heard him asking:

Where were you, Daddy?

Why didn't you save me, Daddy?

Ben didn't utter a sound even after they got him home. He moved where he was directed, ate the food in front of him.

Ben sat on the couch as Liana put on the Batman DVD he used to watch almost every day.

Ben didn't move.

Ben didn't react.

Ben was in the house again.

But Ben wasn't home.

Liana bathed him that night, for the first time since he was a toddler. Then she dressed him for bed.

Credit to his wife's strength, the power she'd found within herself now that her son was back. She waited until he was asleep before she walked down the stairs and looked at Wade, all her color gone again.

"What is it?" Wade asked.

"Ben...his bath. His legs, he... he..." Liana made a choked dry-heave, then collapsed into a dead faint to the floor.

A couple hours later, Ben wakes up screaming.

Wade never asked her to finish that sentence.

• • •

"Your son needs you."

Wade can't answer her, but the first fingers of doubt worm their way into his mind.

Liana senses the hesitation. "Ben has suffered enough already. Don't put him through any more trauma, Wade. He needs his father now more than ever before. More than he might ever again."

Does he? The voice asked. Maybe Ben needs this. Maybe it's exactly what Ben needs.

Wade hadn't realized that the words, the voice had exited his lips before Liana responded with, "Ask yourself this Wade? Is it what Ben needs, or what you need?"

Maybe it's both.

Maybe it's neither.

• • •

A month later

Ben still woke up in the grip of terror, howling in the dark room, but not nightly. He saw a psychiatrist three times a week. One day, Wade swore that he could see tears in the woman's eyes as she walked Ben out of her office.

The phone rang. Wade answered it for a change, almost by mistake.

"Hello?"

"He's coming in on Thursday." said a voice Wade had never heard before.

"Who is this?"

"The 5:15 out of Orlando."

Click.

Wade doesn't tell Liana about the call. He doesn't tell Terrence. He assumed it was some reporter hoping he'd show up at the airport, hoping he'd make some sort of enraged scene to lead with on the eleven o'clock broadcast. Or maybe it was one of Terrence's cop buddies, letting him know because . . . Wade didn't know why.

Then on Thursday evening, Wade found the gun behind the gin in the low cabinet.

It was already loaded.

· · ·

Wade takes a deep breath and sighs, the breath shuddering out of him. He won't cry, though. He can't cry. It feels like if he ever started, he might never stop.

Wade's fingers play gently over the walnut grip of the pistol, his fingernails rattling off the crosshatching.

"Don't do this," another voice says. A voice that sounds like Ben's.

"I'm . . . I'm going to—"

A commotion erupts behind him, illumination bursting around the terminal. Wade turns and sees several people walking backwards, their lightbulbs flashing. A half-dozen policemen are entering the terminal, trying to push the media back, create a path.

The bright lights of a television camera hit Wade right in the face, momentarily blinding him. When his eyes clear, a mob of television cameras are making their way through the terminal. Reporters yelling over one other in the hopes that their question will be answered for the eleven o'clock broadcast.

The policemen all wear faces of weary determination as they make their way through the throngs of newsmen. In the middle of the sea of commotion, Wade sees him, looks at the face that he has dreaded seeing. The face that has haunted his mind alongside that of his son.

Ben.

Benny.

Benny-Boy.

Baby Boy.

The world runs cold, as though a waterfall of ice water has erupted over him. Wade's knuckles go white on the telephone receiver.

"Wade? Wade, what's happening?"

Wade hears her, but from a great distance, her voice echoing in his mind like a long-forgotten memory fighting for remembrance, disconnected from the present.

Luca DiStasio walks with his hands cuffed in front of him, head down, but with a sly smile barely edging his lips, like a child who's been caught being naughty.

The hood of the sweatshirt moves over Wade's head before he even realizes he's putting it on.

Another phone line clicks. "Wade?"

Terrence.

"Dad, get off the line!"

"Wade? You kill that motherfucker!"

"Dad!"

"You shoot that bastard in the fucking head!"

"Dad, stop!"

Wade's fingers go numb, the receiver falls from his hand. He takes a step forward, towards the man who took.

The man who took him.

Ben.

Benny.

Benny-Boy.

Baby Boy.

Luca throws his head back, blowing his long bangs out of his sharp blue eyes. He makes a quick glance to the right and his gaze falls upon Wade.

Wade takes another step.

"Wade! Wade!" he can still hear Liana screaming through the earpiece.

Luca doesn't recognize Wade for a second.

And then he does.

The sly smile curls a little wider.

"Daddy." Wade hears one last soft voice. He's not sure if it came from the phone or not. If he imagined it or not. Whether or not the voice of Ben is real or just part of the maelstrom of his mind.

Benny.

Benny-Boy.

Baby Boy.

Wade's fingers tighten around the barrel of the gun.

Gay Street

Johnny Shaw

By the time they were ten years old, all the boys that lived on Gay Street knew how to fight. What had started as a necessary defense to repel the childish barbs and attacks of not-so-clever bullies, over time grew to become a school-yard institution.

The older kids trained the younger ones. And while it had been a rare recent event for any kid to muster the bravery to shout *Faggot* or *Queer* at a Gay Street Boy, their reputation for ruthlessness was accepted as fact. It usually took a new kid with a smart mouth for one of the Boys to get some rounds in with the quickly overmatched sparring partner. At fight's end, there were never any hard feelings, all animosity contained within the duration of the beatdown. In fact, the Gay Street Boy was often the first to sign the loser's cast with a cheerful *Give me a Break*.

Gay Street was only three blocks long, just over thirty houses ending in a cul-de-sac where the Boys hung out. What they used to call *latchkey kids*, the Boys were used to their independence. All the kids faced challenges at home: single-parent households, parents working back-to-back minimum wage jobs, borderline-fraud-case foster parents, and people that were parents only in name. If you were looking for one of the Boys, you'd have a better chance finding them at the cul-de-sac than at their houses, no matter the time of day.

The houses on the corners that faced intersecting streets didn't warrant official Gay Street status, as their street addresses didn't carry the stigma of the Gay Street name. It had been decided that while the Side Street Kids could hang out, they were auxiliary members at best. The benchwarmers to the Gay Street Boys' starters.

The Gay Street Boys weren't a big group. Currently, there were nine of them, aged from ten to seventeen (the eldest, Bruce Sullivan, their de facto leader), but reputation and intimidation is stronger than numbers. Rumors spread.

Yes, it was true that eleven-year-old Rudy Danford knocked out sixteen-year-old Martin Escobar with one punch to the jaw. And yes, he made a neck-lace out of the teeth that had been dislodged. He wore it whenever he was out of the house, even as the teeth yellowed and chipped.

No, fourteen-year-old Bart Thorsen did not beat Mike Manville with a base-ball bat. The damage to Manville's face was all Bart's fists. Not that the Gay Street Boys were above using weapons. They just rarely needed them.

The Gay Street Boys didn't fight for show. They didn't fight to prove something. They fought to hurt. They fought to win. And like any soldier, they fought so that eventually they wouldn't need to.

They followed a simple set of rules, a few spoken, but the majority unspoken and understood. Nobody remembers who came up with them, but they lived by them as rigidly as a vow.

Hit twice to their one. The fight is over when a Gay Street Boy says it's over. There is no way to cheat in a fight. When you attack one Gay Street Boy, you attack all the Gay Street Boys. And finally, retaliation has no expiration date.

Little Jimmy Little was a Gay Street Boy. At ten, the youngest current member. He hadn't been around the last three days. He had been avoiding the rest of the Boys. He had been embarrassed. But when they finally got a look at his black eye, bruises, and the cast on his arm, they assured him that he had no reason to be ashamed. That he was a Gay Street Boy and they protect their own. That it was time to set things right.

• • •

Len Chapman hated mowing the lawn. It was bullshit. The boy should be doing it. It was his chore, but the kid was still bitching about his arm. The little pussy. Just went to show how much that boy needed a father figure around to toughen him up. If Len's own father hadn't taken the belt to him, he probably would have turned out a pussy like Marcie's boy. The kid would learn soon enough that life didn't hand out free passes and ice cream cones. Sometimes the only way to toughen thin skin was with scar tissue.

With the lawn only half-finished, Len decided fuck it. Let the kid do it later, arm or no arm. He had shit to do. He had been thinking about calling Mort Tanner, see if he wanted to drive down to the car lots down by the highway and look at the new truck models. Neither of them had any money, but it was a laugh. Kick the tires, maybe take a test drive. Leave a turd in the glove box for the rich asshole who could afford a new truck.

He rolled the lawnmower into the back yard and stowed it in the shed. When he turned around, there were nine of the neighborhood kids standing in a tight group right in front of him. Bruce Sullivan, big for seventeen, stood in the center of the group holding a shovel-head. He knew the kid only from a distance, constantly in his garage pounding on a homemade heavy bag that was little more than a gunny sack filled with sand. He would pound on it for hours, the thuds echoing through the neighborhood.

Len nodded at the shovel-head. "You ain't going to be able to do much digging with only the head and no pole." He slapped his thigh. "That's what she said," he said, laughing at his own joke.

"Ain't for digging," Bruce said, not even a smile.

That's when Len noticed that all the kids had something metal in their hands. A big wrench in the tiny hands of Mickey Lonergan. And a cast iron pan held two-fisted by his brother Liam. He saw short stretches of copper pipe. A rusty set of bolt-cutters. Something that looked like calipers. His stepson, Jimmy, held a meat tenderizer.

"What's this?" He tried to sound casual. "Building a tree fort? You boys doing door-to-door handiwork now?"

The boys cold-stared, silent. In a slow surge, they all stepped forward.

"You boys better head home now," Len said, "Nothing needs fixing."

"Plenty needs fixing," Bruce said, "We're here to do some fixing."

"I told you—" But the shovel-head had knocked the rest of the words and several teeth from the side of Len's mouth, leaving a bloody tear up the side of his cheek. It would have hurt like hell if Len had remained conscious.

● ● ●

When Len Chapman woke up, he was in his living room duct-taped to a chair. Thoroughly duct-taped. They must have brought some with them, because it was definitely more duct tape than he had. Three rolls easy. And it was the brightly colored tape. Why anyone used anything but silver or black was beyond him. Red or green duct tape was for queers.

Little Jimmy stood in front of Len, silent. Bruce Sullivan stood just behind Little Jimmy, close enough for Bruce's breath to make Little Jimmy's hair move with each exhale. They didn't say a word. They breathed and stared. Len didn't speak either, but that's because of the duct tape that covered his mouth. He wanted to say all sorts of words. Actually, that's not true. He really only wanted to say two words. Fuck and you.

Len tried to look to his left and right, but his head was taped in place. He could just catch in his peripheral vision the sight of some of the other neighborhood boys.

Bruce put a hand on Little Jimmy's shoulder and spoke to Len. "I'm going to take the tape off your mouth. Don't talk no louder than you would at the dinner table. There's a boy behind you with a hammer."

Len did his best to nod, but his head was held in place. It didn't matter. It hadn't been a question.

Bruce ripped the tape off Len's mouth, taking half his mustache and the scab on his cheek with it. He yelled from the pain and immediately felt and heard the crack of the hammer on his shoulder. He yelled again and got hit in the same exact spot. This time, he held it to a whimper, sure that his collarbone was shattered. Tears rolled down his face.

"What do you want?" Len whispered, more breath than sound.

Bruce ignored him. "Do you have a reason for hurting Little Jimmy? A good reason?"

Len kept his voice steady, talking through his teeth and the pain. "I don't know. I was trying to teach him something. That mistakes have consequences. It's what I know, how I grew up. My father was quick with the belt. Taught me to behave. Else he'll end up soft. Made me a man."

"So you're just trying to make Little Jimmy the man that you are?"

"Yeah."

"And that's a good thing? That every kid should grow up to be as great as you?"

Len didn't answer.

"You think Little Jimmy wants to be like you?" Bruce continued, "He's ten and he's already a better person. A tougher man than you. And we aren't going to let you turn him into you. You're a loser that won't be missed once you're gone. You didn't beat him to toughen him up, to teach him, to make him stronger. You beat him because you wanted to. Because you could."

"I didn't mean to hurt him so bad."

"But you did."

"It was an accident."

"That's the difference. What we're going to do to you ain't going to be no accident."

"Fuck you, you punk!" Len spat, "Soon as I . . ."

"Hammer," Bruce said calmly.

The wet crack of Len's already-shattered collarbone made a dull, sickly sound, much worse than the sharp snap that had preceded it. Like the bone had already been reduced to mush. But even worse was the row of boys that lined up to his left, each of them patting garden tools and kitchen implements in their palms. He would have screamed, but Bruce re-taped his mouth before he had the chance.

Len cried, but he wasn't going to get any sympathy from this audience. He wasn't going to get anything but bruises and broken bones and a whole lot of pain.

• • •

When Marcie Little came home, it took her a minute to figure out what was different about the house. The living room looked clean and organized. It was usually covered with Len's car magazines and beer cans, but now it was cleaner than she'd ever remembered it. It felt strange. Maybe Len wanted to borrow more money and was trying to get on her sweet side. Even the rug had been vacuumed, she could see the parallel lines.

Then she saw the note on the dining room table.

• • •

Dear Marcie,

Things ain't working out, so I left. It wasn't you. It was me. I have some stuff to figure out. I'll call you when I get settled in another place to get my stuff. Sorry I didn't finish mowing the lawn.

Len

• • •

She turned when Little Jimmy walked in the room.

"Len left," Marcie said, more to herself as she reread the short note.

"Yeah. I saw him go," Little Jimmy said, "I think he felt bad about hurting my arm. Real bad."

"That was an accident, honey. We talked about it. He just got carried away. You know how hard it is to find a good man like Len?"

"He really hurt me, mom."

"He didn't mean to. I have to call him. Get him back."

"He's gone, Mom."

But Marcie wasn't listening. She pulled out her phone and punched in a number.

And as Little Jimmy felt the phone vibrate in his pocket, he turned his back on his mother and went out the front door to be with his real family.

Hushed

Gerald So

An only child,
Cousin Lee was
spoiled to the core,
given every toy
you'd think of,
much less ask for.

So, sure,
I hated him,
but would hate
his father more
when I saw
bruises on Lee's arm.

Like they say
you're s'posed to do,
I asked calmly
how he happened
to get bruised.

He didn't say,
so I never could,
or anyone I told
might well believe
I'd done it.

Wooden Bullets

Josh Stallings

Dope smoke hung like a cloud in the White Whale, a '67 Bonneville, a massive pile of white sheet metal, a monster engine, red leather seats, and an 8-track. Doobie Brothers playing softly in the background. We were keeping a low profile, eyes on the house we were going to creep. It was me and my kid brother Tom. This was his first job. So like any other good big brother I was feeding his fear-soaked brain with dark images.

"This old fucker has a shit-pile of old guns and shit, right?"

"Right, so?"

"So I was wondering if he's got any wooden bullets?"

"Wooden bullet, doesn't sound too dangerous, ouch fuck I been hit by a splinter. Fucking get down they're also firing paper cuts." Tom kicked in to a giggling fit.

"Funny? Nope. World War Two, Pacific theater, the Japanese soldiers used wooden bullets 'cause they fragmented on impact splintering into the wound. But they wouldn't show up on an X-ray. They fester. Pus fills the wound, but the doctors can't find them."

"That's fucked up." Tom had stopped laughing.

"Take soldiers days to die, and all that time someone was looking after them. See, kill a guy and the enemy loses one guy, right? Wound him, it takes two maybe more out of action. Some say wooden bullets were a bullshit myth. I don't think so."

"Why the fuck did you tell me that story big bro? Why?"

"To keep you sharp. Hand me the joint."

Junky Bob brought us the gig. For ten percent, he told us about this easy score. "If it's cake, why don't you do it?" I asked Junky Bob, out behind the Seven Eleven off Middlefield Road. He mumbled something about needing to be in the city, and how the old guy would recognize Junky Bob if he saw him. I stopped listening. I knew why Junky Bob wasn't pulling it off himself. He was afraid.

Junky Bob told us the guy would be gone every Wednesday night, but Junky Bob was notorious for getting important shit wrong. He told us the guy had fought in WWII, and in his basement he kept a shit-pile of old guns, pistols, rifles even a grenade launcher. Junky Bob's dad was a plumber. Junky Bob said, he, the dad, said he'd seen the stash. Said the old fucker was weird.

Tom and me leaned back in the deep leather seats of the Bonneville, smoking, watching the house. We were going in, no question. Just being careful.

"Whatcha' think?" Smoke swirled around Tom's words.

"Give it a few more minutes." I chased the pot with a gulp of Mickey's Big Mouth. Fine Malt Liquor, said so on the bottle. Shit beer, cool name, high alcohol count.

Menlo Park was dead. It was after eleven on a Wednesday night in suburbia. No one was moving. The house was a single story ranch job. A big redwood towered over it, making the house seem small. An overgrown hedge covered the front. The man may have been sitting on an arsenal, but he sure couldn't afford a gardener.

The Doobie Brothers played our song, *Taking It To The Streets*. Tom leaned to turn it up, then thought better and left it low. "Big bro?"

"Yeah?"

"You ever hear of a basement in a ranch home?"

"No, except for grandpa Gene's, I don't think I've ever seen a basement, why, oh fuck… Right. Fucking Junky Bob."

"Fucking Junky Bob. Bullshit information, we could get in and there's a little old lady with like a hundred freaky cats?"

"Guess we pray they don't all know kung fu." I told Tom. "Junky Bob heard this from his dad, it sounds true. Right?"

"You call it. We go in or we ride on?" Tom always counted on me. Somehow eighteen months older made me the chief. Big brothers always play Lone Ranger, little bro is always Tonto. That is the way of the world.

"You ever seen a grenade launcher?" Tom shook his head, "Yeah me neither. boo-coo bucks. If he's wrong, we take what we find and get on down the highway. Kick Junky Bob's ass tomorrow."

"Right." Tom took a deep drag off the roach, put it out on his tongue and swallowed. He put his gloves on, leather workman gloves. Me, I was wearing brown cloth gloves from the garden center at Sears.

• • •

I slipped the crowbar into the door jam. With a small crack the wood gave and we were in. Lock picks? Fuck. Nothing is going to draw attention like a teen kneeling down working a lock. Crowbar, quick snap and you were in, leaving nothing but an echo. We stood in the hallway. Listening. Waiting for our eyes to adjust. The place smelled like dust and old man piss and medicine gone bad and more dust. A clock somewhere was ticking out a loud rhythm.

Eyes adjusting, the gloom receded only slightly. The living room was orderly, like I had never seen. Everything, book case, La-Z-Boy, TV Guides on the end table, all seemed to have been laid out on a grid. An ancient television sat dark and silent. Through the back, the tubes glowed orange, slowly fading to black. Somewhere in my dope clouded brain I knew this wasn't a good sign, just couldn't figure why.

"Look," Tom was ashen, trembling, pointing at an old photo on the wall. A group of soldiers stood on a beach. One was holding a Japanese flag.

"So."

"Llllook. Their feet." I did. Damn. At their feet was a stack of Japanese soldiers' bodies, their heads in a separate pile.

"Ffffucked up," Tom said.

It was the very definition of fucked up. Fuck. Taking heads. I had read about this shit, but fuck. I looked away, sounded tougher than I felt. "I won't mind stealing this old guy's stuff. Fucker deserves it."

Around the room were several other pictures of soldiers, but none disturbing, just young guys serving their country.

The bedroom was military tight. Hell, the bed even had hospital corners. On his dresser I found a wallet, thirty-six bucks, some change. Now we had beer money.

"Why did he go out without his wallet, that don't make sense does it?" Tom asked.

"Maybe he forgot, maybe he doesn't need money to play bingo down at the VFW. What the fuck do I know?" I motioned for him to check the closet. The bathroom was my domain. Little bro didn't know a Valium from an Ex-Lax suppository. I swung open the mirrored medicine cabinet. I almost heard a heavenly choir when I looked in. Dexamyl, Nembutol, Percocet, even the holy fucking grail, a box of 36 4 ml Dilaudid injectable ampules. I popped two Dexies and a couple Percs, just to take the edge off, then packed the rest into my backpack. Caught leaving a house with a pillowcase over your shoulder is a sure way to earn a ride to county.

In the closet Tom found a couple of cool looking medals up on a shelf. Had to be worth something, into the pack they went. Down the hall we found a completely empty second bedroom. The kitchen delivered up a partly drunk fifth of Old Crow and nothing else. The fridge smelled of spoiled meat. I closed it without looking too hard.

"Bail?" Tom asked. I motioned to the garage door, just off the kitchen. Garages are not where people kept their most valuable crap, but you never know.

I was up on a chair checking the cabinet over the fridge when I heard his gasp. "Tom?" Nothing. "Tom?" A little louder. Still nothing. I dropped off the chair. I moved to the open door. The garage had no car. Empty space, lit by moonlight coming in a side window. A work bench. Tools all lined up on a pegboard. Nothing else. No little brother. "Tom?"

"Yeah?" His head popped up through a hole in the cement. "Come on down, this is cool shit man."

At the bottom of the ten foot steel ladder was a concrete floor. The dim light from above lit a small circle, beyond it was nothing but shadow.

"I owe Junky Bob an apology, there is a basement." I said turning slowly on my heels.

"It's a bomb-shelter, from the Fifties."

"I know what it is. Close the hatch."

"Why?" I shot him a look. He scurried up the ladder and closed the heavy steel door. Any noise from the outside world was suddenly gone. It was so quiet it was almost loud. I know that makes no sense. But that's what it felt like, loud silence. And dark beyond lack of light.

I scratched a match to life. My hand cast grotesque shadows on the walls. I lit the lantern I found hanging near the ladder. The room filled with the warm glow and stink of kerosene. Deep shadows hid the corners. It was a large room with rounded cement walls. A set of bunk beds lined one side. On the opposite wall was a pegboard. Mounted with military precision a M1 Garand, a BAR, a 1911 .45, a Japanese rifle I couldn't name and one of their pistols. When I was a kid, I was kind of a WWII geek. Used to draw air battles in class. Made maps of Patton's tank battles. Real geek shit. I'd be lying if I said I didn't get a half chub being this close to the war relics.

"No grenade launcher," Tom said.

"What?"

"Not quite an arsenal. Fucking Junky Bob."

"It'll bring a few ducats. That BAR is full-fucking-auto thirty-aught-six." This was some serious bad mother fucker ordinance. We could start a war with all of Palo Alto and win, not counting East Palo Alto of course, they were armed sons of bitches over there.

"Check it out," Tom pointed to a machete, "think this is what they used to cut those heads off?"

"Maybe." I was fucking with little bro, his eyes got wide like when we were kids in a dirt-clod war and I'd tell him the big kids would tie us to a tree and leave us overnight, if we let them take our fort. He'd freak, but fight like a mad-man. Kid was a terror. Thing about not having a Pop is, you learn to take care of yourself. Last time I was really afraid was when the old man was holding Tom down. He was drunk. He was raging. He was pounding on Tom's face. I came at him, fists flailing, he swatted me back. I was eight. I kept coming. Moms was screaming. What a fucking mess. Pops got off Tom and took after me. I took the beating. That's what older brothers do. They take the beating.

"There's something missing." Tom was pointing to an empty set of pegs in the middle of the board.

"Sure as shit is."

"Maybe it's the grenade launcher? That would be so fucking bitchin'."

"Could be. Let's look." I shrugged towards a tall cupboard. A nasty odor leaked from under its door, like rotting flesh, piss and shit. Tom reached for the handle. The door sprang open. Tom let out a scream. I screamed. A 12 gauge trench gun jammed out of the dark, pointed at my little brother's chest. It was held by a spindly old man in a bathrobe and slippers. The old fucker's eyes were pure madness. His breath rattled and wheezed. It was a miracle we hadn't heard him before. His finger on the trigger was trembling. The barrel danced across Tom's chest.

"You Jap bastard, I been waiting for you, oh yes I have." He was jabbing the shotgun at Tom, emphasizing his crazed words, "Think I didn't hear you? Sarge, I got a Jap." He called over his shoulder, into the cabinet. He nodded his head listening. "You heard the man." He shoved the shotgun barrel into Tom's gut, doubling him over. "On your goddamn knees. What, you no speakie no English?"

"Please," I said, moving towards him. Tom was balled up on the floor, coughing.

"Where the hell did you come from? Sarge, they're inside the perimeter. We're overrun." He swung the shotgun wildly from Tom to me and back.

"Please, we didn't mean-"

"To what?" His spit speckled my face as he shouted at me. "Screw you. Dead is dead. See that pile of bones?" I flicked my eyes to the left. The corner was lost in shadow. I remembered the picture of the decapitated soldiers on the beach. I thought after Pops tried to kill me I was past fear. What else could life toss at me after that? This. Life could toss this. My bladder released. Warm piss ran down my leg. Fuck. I didn't want to die here.

"Are you going to, to, to kkkkiiillll us?" Tom stammered from the floor.

The old man swung the barrel down so that it rested on Tom's forehead.

"Please don't." Came out of my mouth.

"Please?" He mimicked a little girl, "Please, pretty please, pretty witty please." He racked the slide on the shotgun. Tom started to sob. I backed away. Hands behind my back. I felt for anything. Then, on the wall I felt the worn handle of the machete.

An animal cry leapt from my throat as I charged across the room. The old man looked up, his milky eyes fighting to understand what was about to happen. I swung like a batter, full force. He turned away or I would have taken his head off. I buried the blade deep into the old man's shoulder, just below where it joined his neck. He screamed. Blood splashed the wall. I pried the machete from his flesh. He still had the shotgun. I swung again. I connected with his leg. He went down. Blood was spurting from his neck. I kicked the shotgun away from him, I didn't need to, he was done.

I helped Tom to his feet. The way we slipped and slid on the blood slick floor would have been comical, if it weren't for the screams of the old man.

"You Jap bastard, you killed me, godless bastard." His cries became whimpers. "No daddy, no I didn't do it... not... nooo." Wherever his mind had taken him, it was filled with pain.

Tom had torn off his Tubes t-shirt.

"Tom?"

"We have to stop the bleeding or he'll die."

"I'm pretty sure he's not going to make it."

"No, he will make it." And there it was. All the bullshit stealing, petty crime, fist fights, drug deals. This was the line. My little brother had to show me the line over which we would not go. Fuck.

The old man was mumbling to his father. The fight had been taken from him. Mercifully the slash on his leg had missed arteries. His neck had not been so lucky. Blood pulsed out. Tom pressed his wadded up t-shirt against the wound. It quickly soaked through.

"One of us needs to go for help." Tom said, keeping the pressure on. It was clear it wasn't helping staunch the flow.

"You want me to go for help?" I asked him.

"Yes. He needs a doctor."

The old man looked suddenly calm. "No daddy, not again, please." He whispered and let out one slow last breath.

The only sound was the flicker and pop from the kerosene lantern. Tom sat on his blood soaked knees, his hands still pressing down on the old man's neck.

• • •

We got two grand and change for the guns. Junky Bob knew a guy in Oakland. We gave Junky Bob his cut. We never told him about the bomb shelter. Money lasted most of that summer. I learned to shoot dope that summer. It didn't help.

Tom only spoke of the old guy once, "You think he would have shot me?"

We were up on Skyline, laying against the windshield of the Bonneville, sitting on the hood, listening to the engine ping as it cooled. Listening to the Doobie Brothers. The carpet of lights along the south bay twinkled below us. I took a toke off the joint. Thought it over. After, in the bomb shelter, I had checked the shotgun. It was empty.

"Hell yes he would have shot, you saw the look in his eye."

Big brothers take the beating. That's what they do.

In Dreams

Charlie Stella

You are eight years old and school is out for summer. You are playing with your WWII Army soldiers in the backyard. They are your favorite toys because of the television series *Combat*. You make believe the soldier with the Thompson 45 machine gun is Sergeant Saunders. The set is complete with Germans (brown), Japanese (yellow), British (gray) and American (green) figures, all in various battle poses. You're creating a battlefield on the edge of the grass close to where your grandmother has planted a rosebush; where the grass ends and the dirt begins is a trench for the Americans to assault. You're just beginning the battle when Joseph yells down to you to from his bedroom window in the apartment building next door to your house. He's sixteen years old, already in high school, but he's played catch with you a few times out in the street. He's showed you how to field ground balls and how to grip a bat.

He tells you to come upstairs, he has army soldiers from when he was young he wants to show you. You're more impressed with him asking you upstairs than you are about the soldiers. Joseph is someone most of the kids your age look up to because he is a good baseball player and he's older. Most of the parents on your block say he's smart; he goes to Aviation high school, not one of the public high schools.

You've never been inside the apartment building next to your house, a brick three family with a narrow driveway. Inside the front door is a vestibule with a glass door at the top of four marble steps. You can see the stairway from behind the glass door. You reach for the doorknob and a buzzer sounds. You take the stairs to the second, then third floor. Joseph is waiting for you just inside the apartment; he's holding the door open.

Once inside you notice how clean the apartment is—immaculately clean. There is a smell you can't identify, but it reminds you of church. Incense maybe? Your hands and clothes are still dirty from setting the soldier figures in the dirt under the rosebush. You stand very still while Joseph explains how he has some toys he needs to get rid of because they take up too much room. He says he might give you his soldiers, the ones he's not saving for his own kid someday.

You're a very shy kid and are afraid to ask any questions or say the wrong thing. You're also afraid to touch anything from fear of getting it dirty and because you've never been in someone else's apartment or house without their parents. Joseph's parents both work. His father is a construction worker. His mother works part-time at the church rectory. Joseph has the run of the apartment to himself on days when his mother works, at least from the time he gets home from school until she gets home from work around five o'clock.

Joseph's room is as neat as the rest of the apartment; nothing is out of place. There are model airplanes hanging on strings from the ceiling and model warships on the window sills. There are baseball cards glued into picture frames hanging on the walls. His room is like a museum and you can't help but stare at everything.

He takes out an A&P grocery bag filled with army soldiers from a trunk near his desk. He says he hasn't played with them in a long time and you can probably have them once he organizes which ones he wants to keep. Your eyes get big. There are tanks and jeeps and other trucks in the bag, plus what looks to be at least one hundred soldiers. He has everything you have plus ten times more. He even has Nazi artillery with swastikas on each tank and truck. You're already dreaming of setting up battlefields in your living room and playing out the war movies you've watched with your father on television; *The Longest Day* is one of your favorites.

Joseph says, "Go ahead and set them up. I'll be right back."

You're still uncomfortable in this neatest of apartments. You live in the house next door and it isn't half as clean. There's always a mess of some kind and there are always people around. Your family isn't big, but they're always there. If not your parents, sister or grandparents, friends of your mother's often stop in and spend an hour or two having coffee and cake. Every other Saturday night there's a card game in the basement. Every Sunday your grandparents visit and you can't wait to go outside and play. It seems you're never alone.

Your room is nothing like Joseph's room. You cheat when you put together models and never use all the pieces. Then when you play with the models you always break them. Even when you're punished and told to clean your room, it never looks half as neat as Joseph's room.

You set the soldiers up and are into the battle you've created before you know it. You make war sounds with your mouth, but you're seeing the explosions in your head. You mimic the soldiers' pain like an actor shot in a war movie; you grimace and arch your back when one of the soldiers is bayoneted. Some American soldiers are killed from a German artillery barrage. You're moving a Nazi tank across the battlefield when Joseph asks if you want something to drink.

You turn around and are confused at what you see. Joseph is standing in the bedroom doorway in his underwear. He holds a glass of milk in one hand. His other hand is inside the front of his underwear. There is a bulge in his underwear. You try not to stare.

"We have chocolate chips and Oreos, if you want," he says.

You follow him to the kitchen, but you don't ask him why he took his pants off. You don't ask about the bulge in his underwear either. You take a chocolate chip instead while he pours you a glass of milk. You notice his right hand is back inside his underwear. As soon as you finish eating one cookie, he pulls down the front of his underwear and says, "Ever see one this big?"

He's smiling so you smile. You're still too shy and naïve to know what's going on. You know what he's doing is bad, but there's nobody there for you to get in trouble. And it's not like you're doing it.

"Have you?" he says.

You giggle and say, "No."

"Not even your Dad's?"

"I don't think so. I don't think I saw his."

"You can make it bigger. Yours, I mean."

You're embarrassed and giggle again, nervously this time.

"I mean it," he says. "You can make yours bigger. I'll show you. Watch, take it out."

• • •

Your visits with Joseph continue over the next few weeks. You don't notice they are on the same two days of the week; days when his mother works and no one else is home. Joseph teaches you how to make yourself feel good. He teaches you some other things that you're not comfortable with and although he tries to make you do them, you tell him, "No."

He gives you a dollar and tells you that putting his thing in your mouth is the same as putting your thumb in your mouth, no big deal. He says he'll give you his bag of soldiers if you just try. He says, "Watch," then gets down on his knees and says, "It's no big deal. It just feels good."

He puts you in his mouth. He goes back and forth, then stops and says, "See? No big deal."

He gives you another dollar and you do what he says. He will give you more money the next few times you're alone with him in the apartment, but he forgets about the soldiers and you're too shy to ask.

He reminds you each time before you go home not to say anything to anybody because you're not supposed to make yourself feel good until you're his age or even older. He tells you that somebody at his school taught him, one of the teachers, and they made him swear an oath of secrecy and that's what everybody has to do when they get older. He tells you to make sure when you make yourself feel good it's only in the bathroom with the door locked and never to do it in the bedroom because you will stain your bed and your mother will know what you're doing.

"Tell them you're sick if they ask why you're in the bathroom so much," he says. "Tell them you don't feel good."

You do exactly as he says when your mother asks what you're doing in the bathroom all day and night? You tell her you don't feel good.

One day you hear your mother talking about Joseph's parents, someone told her they are moving. You forget yourself and mention Joseph's parents have the cleanest apartment you've ever seen. Your mother asks how you know that and you tell her about going up to play with Joseph's soldiers and that he might even give them to you. You believe he will give them to you, especially since your mother said she heard his family is moving.

Her eyebrows furrow and she wants to know why a sixteen-year-old is playing with an eight-year-old. You become nervous when she asks you more questions but you don't tell her about the sex Joseph has taught you. You ask if you can go outside and play sponge ball against the garage door and she frowns and says, "Okay, but I don't want you going up there anymore or I'll tell your father."

The thought of your father questioning you about Joseph scares you. You tell Joseph the next time you see him in the street that you can't go upstairs anymore. Joseph becomes nervous and asks if you said anything to anybody. You swear you didn't and you lie and tell him that one of the other neighbors saw you go into his building and they said something to your mother. You tell him you told her it was to see his soldier collection and she said, "*I don't like that his mother isn't home. Joseph is too old for you. You can't go up there anymore.*"

Joseph is still nervous. "Okay," he says, and then he crosses the street and leaves you on the corner. He doesn't even say goodbye.

A few weeks later you see Joseph in the street again and his right arm is in a cast. You ask him what happened to his arm and he tells you that he broke it playing softball, somebody slid into him at third base and broke his forearm bone. You try to picture it in your head but it doesn't make sense. Joseph is right-handed. Why would his throwing arm be broken from someone sliding into third base? You ask him again how that could happen, but he says he can't talk now, he has something to do for his mother and he runs home.

You stay with your cousins on Long Island the next week while your parents are on vacation. When you come back you learn that Joseph's family has moved. Your mother and father are talking about it over dinner. It doesn't sound as if your parents liked Joseph's parents very much; something about them acting superior to everybody. Your father says he knows somebody who works with Joseph's father and they claim he's a big brown nose, always doing extra work for his boss to keep his job. Your mother says his mother never speaks to anybody in the streets, but that she was always bragging about her son and how smart he was; how he didn't have to go to any of the public schools because he was going to be an engineer someday.

Within a few days you forget about Joseph and his family. You forget about all the neat stuff in his room and the fact he never gave you the soldiers he'd promised. Most of all you forget all the other things he did to and with you.

• • •

Twenty years pass before you see Joseph again. When you do it is during the subway rush hour leaving Manhattan. You see him at the opposite end of the car. There's a thick crowd of passengers between the two of you. He is wearing a suit and tie. You are wearing your work uniform. You haven't thought of him much, except when all the stories about pedophiles in the church were covered in the news. From that point on, every so often you thought about Joseph and what had happened in his room.

You've since wondered if he was a pedophile in the making all those years ago. Is he one now? Has he changed? Is he married? Does he have kids? Does he abuse his kids? Does he abuse other kids?

You want to ask him these questions and more, but you would hate yourself for talking to him. You want to know why his parents moved so suddenly. You want to know why his arm was broken that time right before his family moved. You want to know if his father was a pedophile too. And what about his mother? Did she know what was going on?

You've yet to tell anyone what happened when you were eight years old. It is something you've buried. You don't know if you've done that consciously or if something triggered your lack of recall. You wonder if it is embarrassment; the more time that has passed, the more you understand what happened, the more you want to forget.

You are staring at him, thinking back to the time when he told you how putting it in your mouth was like sucking a thumb, *no big deal*. You're thinking about how he used you, how he tricked you into going upstairs into his room and how he fondled you and then paid you a dollar to let him abuse you.

You have an urge to beat him. Your hands are clenched into fists. You want to hurt him. You want him to pay for what he did. You finally make eye contact and you can see his face blanch. He's scared, the son-of-a-bitch. He begins to fidget. Somehow that's better. Somehow, at that moment, seeing him a victim of fear is enough for you. You continue staring and he looks away, first down at the floor and then up at an advertisement, making believe he's reading, the chicken-shit. He glances your way, then quickly turns his back. It makes you furious that he's turned his back. You lean forward and have to excuse yourself for bumping into another passenger. You're so angry you don't realize the train is slowing down as it pulls into another station. You begin to wade your way through the crowd of passengers but there are too many people in your way. Everyone sways as the squeal of metal against metal fills the car and the train comes to an abrupt stop.

You call his name as the doors open, but he doesn't respond. He hurries off the train instead. By the time you make it to where he was standing, the doors have closed and the train is moving again. You try to find him on the platform but he is gone. You missed your chance. You will never see him again, except in your dreams.

In your dreams you won't let him escape. In your dreams he will answer your questions, all of them.

Placebo

Andrew Vachss

I know how to fix things. I know how they work. When they don't work like they're supposed to, I know how to make them right.

I don't always get it right the first time, but I keep working until I do.

I've been a lot of places. Some of them pretty bad—some of them where I didn't want to be.

I did a lot of things in my life in some of those places. In the bad places, I did some bad things.

I paid a lot for what I know, but I don't talk about it. Talking doesn't get things fixed.

People call me a lot of different things now. Janitor. Custodian. Repairman. Lots of names for the same thing.

I live in the basement. I take care of the whole building. Something gets broke, they call me. I'm always here.

I live by myself. A dog lives with me. A big Doberman. I heard a noise behind my building one night—it sounded like a kid crying. I found the Doberman. He was a puppy then. Some freak was carving him up for the fun of it. Blood all over the place. I took care of the freak, then I brought the puppy down to my basement and fixed him up. I know all about knife wounds.

The freak cut his throat pretty deep. When the stitches came out, he was okay, but he can't bark. He still works, though.

I don't mix much with the people. They pay me to fix things—I fix things. I don't try and fix things for the whole world. I don't care about the whole world. Just what's mine. I just care about doing my work.

People ask me to fix all kinds of things—not just the boiler or a stopped-up toilet. One of the gangs in the neighborhood used to hang out in front of my building, give the people a hard time, scare them, break into the mailboxes, petty stuff like that. I went upstairs and talked to the gang. I had the dog with me. The gang went away. I don't know where they went. It doesn't matter.

Mrs. Barnes lives in the building. She has a kid, Tommy. He's a sweet-natured boy, maybe ten years old. Tommy's a little slow in the head, goes to a special school and all. Other kids in the building used to bother him. I fixed that.

Maybe that's why Mrs. Barnes told me about the monsters. Tommy was waking up in the night screaming. He told his mother monsters lived in the room and they came after him when he went to sleep.

I told her she should talk to someone who knows how to fix what's wrong with the kid. She told me he had somebody. A therapist at his special school—an older guy. Dr. English. Mrs. Barnes couldn't say enough about this guy. He was like a father to the boy, she said. Took him places, bought him stuff. A real distinguished-looking man. She showed me a picture of him standing next to Tommy. He had his hand on the boy's shoulder.

The boy comes down to the basement himself. Mostly after school. The dog likes him. Tommy watches me do my work. Never says much, just pats the dog and hands me a tool once in a while. One day he told me about the monsters himself. Asked me to fix it. I thought about it. Finally I told him I could do it.

I went up to his room. Nice big room, painted a pretty blue color. Faces out the back of the building. Lots of light comes in his window. There's a fire escape right off the window. Tommy tells me he likes to sit out there on nice days and watch the other kids play down below. It's only on the second floor, so he can see them good.

I checked the room for monsters. He told me they only came at night. I told him I could fix it but it would take me a few days. The boy was real happy. You could see it.

I did some reading, and I thought I had it all figured out. The monsters were in his head. I made a machine in the basement—just a metal box with a row of lights on the top and a toggle switch. I showed him how to turn it on. The lights flashed in a random sequence. The boy stared at it for a long time.

I told him this was a machine for monsters. As long as the machine was turned on, monsters couldn't come in his room. I never saw a kid smile like he did.

His mother tried to slip me a few bucks when I was leaving. I didn't take it. I never do. Fixing things is my job.

She winked at me, said she'd tell Dr. English about my machine. Maybe he'd use it for all the kids. I told her I only fixed things in my building.

I saw the boy every day after that. He stopped being scared. His mother told me she had a talk with Dr. English. He told her the machine I made was a placebo, and Tommy would always need therapy.

I go to the library a lot to learn more about how things work. I looked up "placebo" in the big dictionary they have there. It means a fake, but a fake that somebody believes in. Like giving a sugar pill to a guy in a lot of pain and telling him it's morphine. It doesn't really work by itself—it's all in your mind.

One night Tommy woke up screaming and he didn't stop. His mother rang my buzzer and I went up to the apartment. The kid was shaking all over, covered with sweat.

He saw me. He said my machine didn't work anymore.

He wasn't mad at me, but he said he couldn't go back to sleep. Ever.

Some guys in white jackets came in an ambulance. They took the boy away. I saw him in the hospital the next day. They gave him something to sleep the night before and he looked dopey.

The day after that he said he wasn't afraid any more. The pills worked. No monsters came in the night. But he said he could never go home. He asked if I could build him a stronger machine.

I told him I'd work on it.

His mother said she called Dr. English at the special school, but they said he was out for a few days. Hurt himself on a ski trip or something. She couldn't wait to tell Dr. English about the special medicine they were giving the boy and ask if it was all right with him.

I called the school. Said I was with the State Disability Commission. The lady who answered told me Dr. English was at home, recuperating from a broken arm. I got her to tell me his full name, got her to talk. I know how things work.

She told me they were lucky to have Dr. English. He used to work at some school way up north—in Toronto, Canada—but he left because he hated the cold weather.

I thought about it a long time. Broken arm. Ski trip. Cold weather.

The librarian knows me. She says I'm her best customer because I never check books out. I always read them right there. I never write stuff down. I keep it in my head.

I asked the librarian some questions and she showed me how to use the newspaper index. I checked all the Toronto papers until I found it. A big scandal at a special school for slow kids. Some of the staff were indicted. Dr. English was one of the people they questioned, but he was never charged with anything. Four of the staff people went to prison. A few more were acquitted. Dr. English, he resigned.

Dr. English was listed in the phone book. He lives in a real nice neighborhood.

I waited a couple of more days, working it all out in my head.

Mrs. Barnes told me Dr. English was coming back to the school next week. She was going to talk to him about Tommy, maybe get him to do some of his therapy in the hospital until the boy was ready to come home.

I told Tommy I knew how to stop the monsters for sure now. I told him I was building a new machine—I'd have it ready for him next week. I told him when he got home I wanted him to walk the dog for me. Out in the back where the other kids played. I told him I'd teach him how.

Tommy really liked that. He said he'd try and come home if I was sure the new machine would work. I gave him my word.

I'm working on the new machine in my basement now. I put a hard rubber ball into a vise and clamped it tight. I drilled a tiny hole right through the center. Then I threaded it with a strand of piano wire until about six inches poked through the end. I knotted it real carefully and pulled back against the knot with all my strength. It held. I did the same thing with another ball the same way. Now I have a three-foot piece of piano wire anchored with a little rubber ball at each end. The rubber balls fit perfectly, one in each hand.

I know how to fix things.

When it gets dark tonight, I'll show Dr. English a machine that works.

This Too Shall Pass

Steve Weddle

"The stars," she said. "See how close together they are? Almost touching? Look." She took his fingers, pressed them together to hold a star. "You can almost touch one to another. Feel the light, one against the other. The fire."

He said okay. Sure.

She rolled back into the dark field.

"But then you get close," she said, "and it turns out they're millions and millions of miles away. Did you know that?"

He said he didn't.

"The closest star, I mean one to another, the closest one is like a hundred million light years from the next one, like in the whole universe. And the closer you get to a star, like they look close together now, but if you were to fly up there, all that way, the closer you get to the stars, the further away you are from the next one. The further away everything is."

He said he didn't know that. He closed his eyes, thought about the tips of her fingers on his, pressing together. The flat of her thumb against the knuckle of his. The tip of her index finger guiding his. He'd seen a movie, maybe a documentary, and a soldier had stepped on a land mine in the desert darkness. Had both his legs blown off. And he woke up, still feeling the legs. Still feeling the weight. It was called a "phantom" something. Feeling it pressed against you. He wondered how long that could last.

He heard something. Something deep. Something throbbing. Then a little light in the distance. Like stars on the ground. Only not stars. Not stars, at all. He looked across to see wavy shadows moving in and out of the light as people were coming toward them, getting bigger the closer they came.

"Staci," one of the guys said. They were all wearing their red football jerseys, jeans, boots. "You all right?"

"Yeah," she said, wiping her mouth with the back of her hand. "I think—" She swallowed. "I think those Jello shots put me over the edge. Somebody oughta check those."

Rusty sat watching. No one said anything to him.

One of them reached a hand down for Staci. Then they walked away, toward the house, their football jerseys shining in the moonlight, the stars, the house lights. Everything reflecting off them.

Alone in the field, he watched everything move further away.

· · ·

Jake found Rusty sitting on the steps to house, back turned to the party. "Hey, man, you been out here all this time? Thought you were going to take a piss."

Rusty rocked back and forth a little, legs pulled close. "Tripped over Staci out in the field."

"No kidding? What was she doing out there? Taking a piss, too?"

"Yeah," Rusty said. "I guess she was." He stood up, moved his head from side to side, couldn't get his neck to crack. "You see the stars?"

Jake smushed his lips together, raised an eyebrow. "The stars?" He looked up. "Uh, yeah. Stars."

"I wonder who names them all."

"Hell if I know," Jake said, shaking his head. "Imagine they're all named by now. Hey, remember when Boone Crawford said his daddy went to the moon, came back with a moon rock?"

Rusty laughed. "Oh, yeah. What was that? Second grade?"

"No. I didn't move over until third, so it had to be third or fourth, I guess."

"Man, that was some funny shit. He was so damn proud of that. Remember when he brought it to school?"

"And Robbie and Moe and those guys busted it into tiny pieces and Boone goes crying to Coach Womack?"

Rusty laughed along with Jake, but it all seemed less funny than it had at the time. Rusty hadn't thought about that in years. Now he felt a little guilty for laughing. "Still can't believe about him and his mom."

"Who?"

"Boone."

"Oh," Jake said, stopped laughing. "Yeah. Well his daddy was always a crazy fucker, you know?"

"Yeah."

"I mean, what are you gonna do, right?"

Right, Rusty thought. What are you gonna do?

· · ·

When they got back to the house, Jake said he was going to look for some beer. Rusty said fine.

The house had a screened-in porch. Your basic four-room farm house, emptied when the Campbells left a couple of months before. Behind the four rooms, a mud porch and the bathroom, which didn't work. On the door, Rusty had seen before, someone had written "out of order" in marker on the door. Added below, in pen, "so's your momma."

Jake was probably in the mud porch now, where the kegs were. Living room to the right. Dining to the left. Behind those rooms, kitchen and bedroom. Your basic four-room farm house. Only the farm gone, fields given over to weeds and hay and scrub pines and, a half-mile from the house, near the road, a couple of road kill deer he'd noticed when he and Jake had driven up an hour before. Then he'd walked around, wondering when they could leave. Then he saw Staci walking out the back door and he waited for some idiot to follow after her.

After a minute, he told himself he was just worried about her. Nothing weird about that. He wanted to make sure she was all right. She was his friend, after all. They'd grown up together. Same school. Same church. They'd talked a thousand times. Maybe they could be more than friends. Not now, of course. I mean, look at him. But some day. After the awkward stage. He and his mom were watching one of those "Before They Were Stars" shows the other day. He saw how they were when they were his age. He knew. Like his mom said whenever something went wrong, "This too shall pass."

Jake came back with a red plastic cup of foamy beer in each hand. "You just going to stand around here all night?" He handed Rusty a beer, then elbowed him. "We gotta mingle with the chickies."

• • •

Rusty was standing in the doorway, watching Staci McMahen look out the window as though she were waiting for something.

"Nice night," he thought about saying.

Then what would she say? "Yes, it is." Then he'd be stuck, again.

What if he just walked up to her and said something real. Something like, "Don't you ever get tired of all this fake stuff?"

And maybe she'd say "What fake stuff?" and he'd be able to tell her. Or maybe he wouldn't.

Or maybe she'd say she was tired of it, too. Of everyone trying to act like everyone else. Copying the pack leader. He'd seen a movie at school about that. Mimicking behavior. And maybe they could talk about that. How wouldn't it be better just to go out, lie down under the stars, and talk about, well, what? What did he have to talk about with her? He couldn't stand the music she listened to, but maybe she couldn't, either. Maybe if she would just walk out to the field with him again, he could tell her about the songs he liked. About the words. About how real they were. About how real everything could be if they could just have that moment back, let it carry on, staring at the stars until they blurred across the darkness, edging into each other.

He took a deep breath, then a step forward. Then he moved back to the doorway. He took another breath and was waiting to move when Loriella walked across the room, grabbed Staci by the arm and pulled. "C'mon, we're heading out to the spooklight."

• • •

The story had been there before any of them. Long ago, on a night just like this one, the Georgia Southern bound for Texarkana had stopped near the Walkerville Cemetery to let another train pass. The young brakeman, about to be married, walked around the cars, checking the couplings and reading a letter from his sweetheart. The wind kicked up a little, just the thought of a breeze, and blew one of the sheets under the back car. He looked under, but couldn't find it. The day was getting dark quickly, much like today, and he lit a lantern, then looked back under the car for the letter. He found it between the tracks, wedged under part of a tie. He reached across and the car rolled back, slicing through his neck, sending his body down the hill, the letter into the wind. When the night comes up quickly, like tonight, you can see the brakeman, lighting his lantern and walking along the train line down near Walkerville, looking for the lost page of the letter.

When Rusty finished telling the story, Jake cocked an eyebrow. "Shouldn't he be looking for his head? Shit, how's he looking for anything?"

"I think maybe he got his head back," Rusty said.

"You mean like he found it under the train? Or like when he died and shit, like it magically reappeared like in spirit form?"

"Yeah, I guess. Something like that." Rusty looked down the road to where all the tail lights had gone as he and Jake and a handful of others stayed at the house.

"It's just a light, then. Just floating out in the darkness?"

"Yeah."

"And what? People get all scared of it? Like a ghost?"

"Yeah. Like it's just sitting there, then it's moving. And you're just watching the light there at the other end of the tracks."

"I bet it scares the shit outta the chicks, right?"

"I guess," Rusty said. "I don't know."

"So, you want to go or what? We can follow them or whatever."

Rusty walked to the side of the house as Jake followed him. He looked at the darkness where he and Staci McMahen had been. He looked up at the sky, for the stars covered now by cloud film.

He looked back down the dirt road, where it cut through other people's woods. He walked toward the road, toward the tree line, saw the orange-pink moon rising into a hazy darkness and closed his eyes.

Runaway

Dave White

Two days after Austin Parker went missing, Matt Herrick sat in a sticky easy chair across from the boy's mom, Sharona.

Beer cans, some empty, some half full were piled on top of the table. The scent of the old brews hung in the air. If the scene had been in a modern art museum instead of in a dark Jersey City apartment, people would stare at it for hours. To his left, *The Price is Right* played on a flatscreen LCD.

Sharona had been eying him up for five minutes. She shifted on the couch, crossed her arms, and frowned. "What you want?" Her first words to him.

"Is Austin here?" The smell of weed and stagnant beer filled Herrick's nose.

"I ain't seen him." She tilted her head to the right and tapped her foot against the apartment's hardwood floor.

The first time Herrick "met" Sharona was during the team's eighth game last year. St. Paul's was playing Don Bosco, and with his team up ten, Herrick subbed Austin in. Sharona sat about eight rows behind the bench. She'd been yelling at Herrick to put Austin in since the 8 second mark. In the two minutes, Austin played the lead went from 10 to 2. Herrick subbed out.

Sharona'd seen enough. She stood up and starting cursing him out. A second year coach taking *her son* out of a game? He was a star. He was going to the NBA. Who the hell was Matt Herrick?

When she tried to climb over fans in the four rows in front of her to get at him, two security guards escorted her out. Late in the second half, Herrick tried to sub Austin in again, but he refused. Instead, he sat at the end of the bench and buried his face in his hands.

"When was the last time you saw him, Sharona?"

"What do you care? It's not like you play him."

"He's missing. He hasn't been to school in four days. Mrs. Cullen's worried about him. Asked me to look for him."

Sharona rubbed her face and the movement seemed to take effort. She breathed heavily through her nose. The weight on her arms seemed to hold them down, and when she reached for her beer can, the fat folded around her wrist.

"Ain't no problem. That's the Guidance Counselor's job, to worry about him. No need to go looking for him."

"It's my job."

"You're the basketball coach."

"No. My day job," Herrick said.

Sharona sighed, then belched. "He gonna start this year?"

"Where's your son?

"I told you, I ain't seen him. How are you gonna find him? A basketball coach? In this neighborhood? No one gonna talk to you."

Herrick took out a business card and handed it to her. She squinted at it, and he wondered if she could read it.

"I'm a private investigator. You hear anything about Austin, you can call me."

Sharona crumpled the business card and threw it on the floor. Her thick body jiggled with the movement.

"Let's find your son."

"You a cop? You think that's going to help? They're not going to talk to you."

Herrick waited for her to say more.

She folded her arms and looked toward the TV. Drew Carey was being hugged by a college-aged blonde.

"I don't care where he is," Sharona said.

Herrick found his way into a cool November afternoon in Jersey City.

· · ·

The Guidance Counselor, Sarah Cullen, had called a team meeting for him. It was directly after school, in the gym. When Herrick got there, the team was lined up at the foul line. All twelve of them. Austin Parker would be thirteenth.

Sitting in the first row of the bleachers, Sarah watched the team. When she turned toward Herrick, she smiled and pushed a curl of hair over her ear.

Mike Johnson had a ball under his arm, and slouched. Evan Daniels tapped his foot. The rest of the team's eyes were anywhere but on Herrick. To get their attention, Herrick blew the whistle he carried with him. The team snapped their eyes toward him in unison. The posture didn't change, but at least they were looking at him.

By December, the posture would be different too.

"One of yours has gone missing," Herrick said. "I'm sure Ms. Cullen has told you that. I'm going to find Austin."

John Rogers looked at Will Taylor. Said something to him.

"What is it?" Herrick asked.

"One of our what?"

Herrick tilted his head and Will shook his head. "You said 'one of yours.' What does that mean?"

Big East, ACC, PAC-10. Possible scholarships to some of the most prestigious schools in the country to play basketball all could be earned in this gym. Yet, sometimes, Herrick found himself explaining simple phrases.

"I just meant one of your teammates."

"We don't know where Austin is," Will Taylor said. He was a senior, waiting until the spring to decide on a college. Coaches from Pittsburgh, Duke, and Kentucky had come to see him play. He spoke, the team listened. Herrick too.

"When was the last time you guys saw him?"

Taylor sucked his teeth. "Ain't like that. We seen him in the halls and stuff. But not out."

Herrick held up a hand to stop him, ask a question, but Taylor kept going.

"We don't keep track of him. You know how he is. Don't practice hard. Don't call out screens. All that stuff you yelled at him about last season. No change. We can't hang out with him. Slow us down."

Most days, Herrick would have them run suicides for that attitude. They were supposed to be teammates. But practice wasn't official until Friday. Couldn't do that until then.

Sarah stood up and looked at them. "Guys, this isn't—"

"Who says we gotta like the kid?" Mike Johnson said. "He ain't one of us. He's just on the team."

Herrick shot Johnson a look, and he shut up.

"This isn't about basketball," Sarah said. "It's about a teenager missing on the streets. You know what it's like being out there. You see it when you walk home. If you know something, please—"

"Say something," Johnson said. He rolled his eyes.

"You guys are going to run big time on Friday," Herrick said. He took a breath.

"Why do you care so much, coach? He ain't gonna play."

Herrick wanted to grab him and scream. Instead, he silently counted to ten.

Finally, he said, "If I have to explain that to you, John, I'm really worried about you guys. No one knows anything?"

The kids didn't make eye contact with him. Two stared at the floor. Will Taylor looked at the top of the bleachers. John Rogers chewed on his thumb nail. No one said a word.

"Friday, 8 am. Anyone's late, you're running ten extra laps." They would anyway. "Get out of here."

There was a murmur of words, as the team broke up and headed for the door. The basketballs slapped the gym floor in a slow rhythm as they walked.

Herrick turned toward Sarah. Sitting with her hands folded between her legs, she looked his way and gave him a smile—though not big enough to show off her dimples—and a shrug. He walked over and sat next to her. On Friday, he hoped he'd barely be able to hear himself think over the roar of players talking to each other and the bounce of the balls on the floor.

"We tried," she said.

He shook his head. "They gotta know something. Kids hear things."

"You can't push them. Maybe they're scared to say where he is."

"I push them every day in practice. I'm going to keep pushing them one-on-one. I'll visit each one at home tonight if I have to."

Sarah turned toward him, mouth slightly open. She dealt with students in her office. Called them in individually and talked them. She was good at her job. Herrick had to use an iron fist sometimes.

Two different strategies. Same results.

"I care," he said.

Sarah nodded.

"They don't think I do, but I do." He pictured a boy, not much older than ten, on the floor surrounded by people. It hurt. "I'm their coach, I want to look out for all of them."

"Just being their coach isn't enough. They don't know what it's like to be cared about, and you're just another person telling them what to do. To them, you're practically a cop."

Herrick was going to let that one sit, but Sarah continued, "You earned their trust last year because you won. But that was last year, and you haven't spent time with them. You've got to start again."

Herrick shook his head. "I don't need to prove anything to them. I just need to find Austin."

Sarah sighed. "Happy hour soon?"

He felt his pulse quicken. "Yeah. How about next week?"

She nodded. "Once Austin's back."

Herrick was about to respond, when he looked toward the door of the gym. Mike Johnson was standing there, basketball still under his arm. Herrick didn't react, except to wave him over. Mike looked at the floor as he walked the entire length of the gym.

"What's up, Mike?" Sarah asked.

"Can I talk to Coach?" He looked at Sarah and nodded toward the door. Sarah didn't say anything, just stood up. After she was gone, Mike sat down next to Herrick. He stared at the court, and his eyes glassed over.

Herrick waited a minute, then said, "What is it?"

"I don't know where Austin is. But I'm worried about him."

Instead of asking why, Herrick stayed quiet. Sometimes it was better to let kids talk, rather than peppering them with questions.

Mike rubbed his face, and took a breath. "His Facebook. He posted something the other day."

Herrick thought about visiting Austin's mother. He didn't see a computer. He didn't see a woman who could afford a computer and an internet bill. That Austin still found a way to get on Facebook seemed bizarre.

"It was from his phone, like he was out and about. It said something like 'meeting up with T-Rock.'"

Herrick folded his hands in his lap.

"I don't know who T-Rock is," Mike said. "Probably don't want to know. Georgia Tech came and watched me play AAU this summer."

AAU programs were travel basketball teams, which allowed athletes to show off in front of college coaches. Defense was only a rumor during those games.

"How long ago did he post this?"

Mike shrugged. "I saw it last night."

Herrick got up and walked to center court. He put his hands in his pockets and looked toward the basket. Then he turned back toward Mike.

"You could have told me this ten minutes ago."

Mike shook his head. The intercom buzzed and the Vice Principal asked for a janitor to come to his office.

"This happens all the time, Coach. Players are here, then they aren't. Friends are here, then they aren't. That's how it is in Jersey City."

Herrick closed his eyes. "Thanks, Mike. See you Friday."

• • •

Austin was still a teenager, which meant he put little thought into Internet privacy. Herrick logged into Facebook though his Private Investigations page, and searched for Austin's profile.

Once he found it, he clicked on the picture. There was one of Austin shooting a free throw. Another of him with his arm around a girl. That's it. He wasn't very active on the page. Most of his status updates came from a cell phone. And most updates were either mundane or vaguely sad.

Stuff like: "When no one's around, where do you go?"

"Nobody gives a f——, it's true."

"Pizza for dinner. Nice."

And, "Hanging with T-Rock."

Herrick clicked each of the "View Feedbacks" at the bottom of the status updates to see who commented. He didn't recognize any of the names. No one commented on the T-Rock one, except for a "Like"—the way to let someone know the post was enjoyed without actually having to type. The like was from someone named "Terrance Roberts." Herrick followed the link to his page.

It was set to private. He couldn't read anything.

Shaking his head, Herrick shut the computer down and picked up the phone. If all else failed, old fashioned investigating would have to suffice.

• • •

Herrick stared at the Cricket Hill Lager in front of him. The head of the beer started to dissipate, and he could smell the malt. He tapped his fingers on the bar. Henry Logue was supposed to be here already. He was Herrick's lone contact in the Hoboken police force, and as soon as Herrick mentioned Terrance Roberts' name, Henry said he'd meet him at Oakwood Tavern.

The door opened and Henry walked in, scanned the bar and gave Herrick a smile. He walked over and sat on the stool next to Herrick. The bartender sidled over as well, and Henry ordered a Bud Light.

"Can't even try something new?" Herrick said. He pointed toward his own pint. "This is local, at least."

Henry took half the pint in one gulp. "I can have one of these and not worry about the legal limit."

"Why not just drink water, then?"

Henry smiled, and this time took a smaller sip. "Why do you want to know about Terrance Roberts?"

"Missing kid. Last thing he said on Facebook was he was going to hang out with T-Rock." Herrick took a sip of beer, let it linger on his tongue, and then swallowed. He shook his head. "Somebody named Terrance Roberts 'liked' the status. I took a shot."

After draining the Bud Light, Henry shook his head. "Hate the computer."

"Yeah, I know. Stick to the abacus. Suits you better."

Henry smiled. "Terrance Roberts is T-Rock. Not a fun guy to be around."

The back of Herrick's neck tickled. "I was afraid of that."

"He killed two guys here in Hoboken—over on Garden Street. Something about drug money. He put two in the back of both their heads. Jersey City guys don't often venture over here. We have our own problems with the Bloods. Unless there's a war going on, we don't see many Crips. For Roberts to come over here, he must have been pissed."

The beer sat in front of him, untouched. Herrick didn't want it now.

"Where in Jersey City do they hang out?"

"His—" He tapped the bar as he searched for the word. "—faction isn't called Grove Street Nation for nothing."

"The kid I'm looking for. His name's Austin Parker."

Henry shrugged. "I haven't heard anything about him."

"Keep your ears open. He's the kind of kid who gets lost in the crowd. No real friends. Family life stinks."

"T-Rock's favorite. Nobody says no to T-Rock."

Herrick nodded. "I figured as much."

• • •

The Light Rail went from the Hoboken Train Station into Jersey City. It moved slow, was always crowded, but gave Herrick some time to think. The best bet was to head over to Grove Street and start knocking on doors. He at least needed to speak with Austin, or someone who'd seen him.

He felt the ASP—a retractable baton—at his hip. It was illegal to carry one in New Jersey, and he could lose his license over it, but he was willing to risk it. He'd had enough of guns, but he still needed protection.

Shaking, Herrick reached into his pocket and pulled out his iPhone. Pressed the Facebook app, and looked up Austin's profile again. The status had changed.

"Done with my mom. I'm out."

The train stopped and Herrick got off, headed toward the Parkers' home. The air had turned cold, and he could see his breath. The sun was long gone, even though it was barely six.

As he reached the corner of Parker's street, he saw Austin walking the other way. He was hustling, moving fast, but not running. He wore a thick black coat, and had a large bookbag slung over his shoulder.

"Austin," he called.

The boy pivoted on his left foot, and for a moment Herrick thought if he worked on that move, he'd score twenty a game. Maybe add a shot fake.

"Coach?"

"Where have you been?" Herrick asked, closing the ten-yard gap between them at a jog.

"I quit the team," Austin said.

He started to walk away from Herrick, but didn't run away. Herrick kept pace. The boy stared at his feet. He slouched, and seemed small. Just like he always did on the court, not filling out his body.

"No you're not. What's going on?"

"Come on, Coach. I gotta go."

Austin turned left, abruptly, and his first step was quick, like he was going to run. Herrick reached out and grabbed his arm. Austin skidded on the asphalt and flung himself back toward Herrick.

"Yo, man! Get off a me!" He jerked his arms out of Herrick's grasp.

"I'm not letting you go anywhere until you talk to me."

"Ain't nothing to talk about."

Austin rarely spoke in slang in front of Herrick, none of his players did. It wasn't a hard and fast rule in practice, but Herrick often found himself correcting their speech. He knew they knew how to speak, and they proved that once they were sick of listening to him fix their language.

"Everyone's worried about you."

Austin shook his head and took two steps back. "No one worried about me."

"Your teachers are. Your teammates are." Herrick leaned forward. "I am."

"I can't take her no more. Didn't even miss me those last few days when I was gone. Came back to see her and she was passed out. When she's awake, she don't do nothing 'cept drink and yell. Nothing I ever do is right. Play basketball? Should be studying. Going to school? I should get a job. I got no girl. I got no job. I got no friends. I gotta do something. Nobody else gives a sh—" He looked at Herrick and frowned. He arched his eyebrows, and Herrick noticed how much he looked like his mother. "Nobody cares."

"I do."

"Fuck that."

Herrick took a deep breath and felt the years rolling back.

"Eight years ago I was a soldier in Afghanistan. When we were in camp—it was August 12—a boy, no more than nine years old, walked up to us. There were about ten soldiers around. He was talking and crying. We couldn't understand him. People started to get nervous."

Austin didn't respond.

"We used to have to worry about suicide bombers. Men, women, whatever. They'd come in strapped and blow themselves up. Kill a battalion without even blinking. So when this kid came in, crying, everyone started to worry. The kid was wearing this torn green jacket. It was so hot that day. He didn't need the jacket."

Herrick looked over Austin's shoulder and saw two men walking in their direction. They didn't hurry. In fact, it looked like one was limping. The other kept reaching for his nose.

"The boy's eyes went wide, and he raised his hands. The jacket opened and I saw it. He was strapped and I was the first one to react. Pulled my sidearm and shot him. It was him or us." He hadn't told anyone since he'd gotten back. Only talked about it with the military therapist.

After rubbing his face with his hands, Austin said, "So?"

"So? So I don't want to see you get hurt. I've seen enough of it."

Austin shrugged, "Just did what you had to."

"And I'm doing what I have to now, too."

"This ain't about you, Coach."

That stung, but Herrick didn't show it, "Who is it about then? T-Rock?"

Austin looked at his feet. "How—?"

"I know what the Internet is."

Breathing out, Austin looked over his shoulder. The two men were closer now, checking the traffic before crossing the street. Thirty seconds, maybe, and they'd join the party.

"You gotta go, Coach."

"No."

"Please, Coach. They're gonna think you're a cop."

Herrick patted the ASP at his hip. Two movements: grab the handle then flick the wrist and the baton would be extended and ready. Austin didn't notice. He was too focused on the guy with the limp.

"Little man, who you talking to?" he asked as he crossed the street. His friend grabbed at his crotch.

"Nobody, T. Let's go."

T-Rock was tall and thick, and his skin was darker than Austin's. He wore a bright blue sweatshirt. And a royal blue Yankees hat. Herrick thought that was sacrilegious. His huge pal had a blue T-shirt on, tight against his bulging muscles. He had a thin scar at the corner of his lip. They both slouched.

Austin did a complicated handshake with T-Rock, just a fist bump with the other one.

T-Rock stared at Herrick.

"You ain't talkin' to cops, are you little man?"

Herrick spread his legs shoulder width and gripped the handle of the ASP. T-Rock's friend reached for his waist.

"You don't have to do this, Austin," Herrick said.

Austin turned back toward Herrick. He took a deep breath, then said, "Go home, Coach."

T-Rock tilted his head. "Coach? What do you mean 'Coach?' You never said you played ball."

"Yeah, I—"

The big man stepped to Herrick, too close. His bass voice rumbled. "This ain't no coach. I'd a heard of him. I would know who he is. I go to all the football games 'round here."

Herrick didn't say a word. Austin didn't pipe up either. T-Rock rubbed his chin. Looked at Austin, then back at the big man. "No, not a football coach. You think he's a cop, D?"

D leaned in to Herrick's face and frowned. "Yeah, I—"

The ASP was out and extended before D could finish the sentence. Herrick swung it against the big man's knee. It connected with a pop. D screamed and went down in a heap. Herrick brought the ASP down on the back of the big guy's neck hard. The big man stopped screaming.

Herrick turned toward T-Rock, who was reaching for the gun in the waistband of his jeans.

Without hesitation, Herrick stepped forward and snapped the baton off T-Rock's wrist. Then cracked it off T-Rock's forehead. The Yankee hat went flying, and a stream of blood followed. The gang leader flopped backward and hit the sidewalk hard.

Herrick checked that both were breathing. They were, but neither were conscious.

"What the hell are you doing?" Austin screamed.

Herrick grabbed him by the wrist and pulled. They both started running. Hung a right, and headed toward Austin's apartment building. They passed it, then hung a right and turned into an alley, stopping behind a Dumpster.

Herrick didn't respond. Instead, he called Henry Logue and filled him in. Said they finally had a shot to get T-Rock. Henry said he'd get some Jersey City cops down there, and told Herrick to stay where he was.

After hanging up, Herrick focused on his breathing, tried to calm his nerves and let the adrenaline run its course.

Austin didn't worry about that.

"The cops are going to pick T up?" Austin asked.

Herrick nodded. "On their way."

"You're going to get us killed. I didn't want you there, Coach. I told you to leave. I had that. I got this. I know what I'm doing."

Herrick closed his eyes, felt his heart rate slow. He could see the little boy from so many years ago, yelling. Shaking his head. Herrick couldn't understand the boy. No one could, there was too much shouting going on around them. Was the boy saying no? Was it a threat? Herrick snapped his eyes open, felt his hands shaking.

"You don't know what you're doing. You're hanging out with criminals. T-Rock has killed people. I'm sure his friend has too. Don't you listen?"

Austin stepped forward. He stopped slumping, and finally seemed to show his entire six-five frame.

"I want to have money to get my mom help. I can't get a job. No one else will help me. She doesn't even care. But we can't pay rent. T-Rock's already paid one month. And, he says when I'm a full member, I'm gonna get a top of the line job. Dealing, helping with the money. All I had to do was survive initiation." Austin shook his head. "They're gonna think I'm a snitch now."

"I'll help you with money. You should have come to me."

"Why? You don't care. I'm not a kid carrying a bomb. I ball. And never get off the bench. You put me in, you pull me out."

Herrick shook his head. Looked at Austin, who was staring at him. The boy had his mother's eyes, but there was a fire behind them. Herrick hadn't seen that before.

"Don't you get it?" Herrick asked. "I'm trying to teach you. I wanted you to play hard. You didn't. I wanted you to pass the ball, find an open man. You took contested threes. I wanted you to get back on defense. You jogged. I hoped that you'd watch your teammates and see what they would do and pick up on that."

"They never told me that. You never told me that."

"I shouldn't have to!" Herrick's cheeks were hot. "You've been playing basketball all your life. Isn't that what you told me in practice? That you knew what you were doing? You're sixteen years old. You should know what to look for."

Austin leaned back against the Dumpster. The metal creaked as he did so.

"The coach is supposed to tell me, right? You're supposed to have the right answers."

Herrick took a deep breath. He couldn't stop his hands from shaking. "I tried. You didn't listen."

Austin didn't speak.

"What you're doing now is stupid. You should have come to me. Or Miss Cullen. You can still come to me. But getting involved with T-Rock? You're smarter than that."

Austin said, "I want to go home."

"Not until I know you won't go back."

"It's over." Austin sighed. "I need a job."

"The Christmas shopping season starts soon. How about after practice I take you to some of the malls? We'll see if anyone's hiring. At least for the month. We can worry about what's next after that."

Austin nodded. "I gotta make things right."

Herrick reached out and squeezed Austin's shoulder. Together they walked back to Austin's apartment. Herrick shook his hand and told him to lock the door, and he'd check up on Austin tomorrow.

"Friday we start going hard."

Austin didn't speak, just turned and went inside. Herrick took the long way around. He didn't feel like talking to the cops anymore.

An hour later, back in Hoboken, he was asleep as soon as he hit the pillow. For the first time in years, Herrick didn't dream of the heat and the sand. He didn't smell gun oil in his sleep. He didn't dream of the scared little boy.

• • •

The next morning, Herrick called Sarah Cullen to see if Austin made it to school. She said he didn't. Herrick didn't fill her in, but told her he would later. He hung up and headed out to the Light Rail.

When he was half a block from Austin's apartment, he saw the police car pull away from the front of the building. His stomach tightened, and sweat formed at the back of his neck. The trip up to the Parkers' apartment was a blur. He knew as soon as Sharona answered the door.

Her face was wet with tears. In her left hand was an open beer can. For a long moment, she stared at Herrick. Then, like tuning into a radio station, realization crossed her face.

"It's your fault," she screamed. "He came in last night and gave me a hug."

Herrick's stomach cramped. He felt his knees weaken.

"No," he said.

"Then he said he had to make things right. He messed up, he said. And he had to fix it. He hoped T-Rock would understand." Her words slurred and spit flew from her mouth. She took a long chug of the beer. "He said he needed to make things better. He ain't no snitch."

Sharona burst into tears and fell forward into Herrick's arms. The floor creaked under her weight. He almost dropped her. The can of beer fell, and the yellow liquid spilled out on to the hallway carpet. Sobs wracked the mother's body.

"My baby," she said. "My baby. How could you?"

Herrick thought, *Not again.*

• • •

Henry Logue told Herrick the story. They found Austin Parker face down on the corner of Grove and Grand. Two bullets in the back of his head.

T-Rock and D were missing. The Jersey City cops didn't get to the address Herrick had given them in time. No one had seen the two since.

• • •

Matt Herrick stood in front of his basketball team on the Friday morning after Thanksgiving. The team stared at him in silence. No one bounced a ball; no one stared at the scoreboard or the floor. Sarah Cullen sat on the bleachers.

Herrick cleared his throat.

"The last time I saw you, Austin Parker was alive. And now he's gone." He shoved his hands in the pockets of his gym shorts. "He's gone because...Because..."

He looked at Sarah. She nodded once.

"I fucked up. That's all. I fucked up."

Herrick paused and looked at the team. Except for Mike Johnson lightly tapping his thigh, there wasn't a sound. Herrick blinked and tried to chase the images from his mind. The boy in the desert. Austin's face while he listened to the story.

He looked toward Sarah, but couldn't read her face.

Turning back toward his team, he said, "If you want to know why I care about any of you, that's why. The streets here are as dangerous as the streets there. And I want you to be safe. I don't want to see that happen to any of you. And it happened to Austin. I couldn't stop it." Herrick felt his voice crack.

A couple of the sophomores looked at each other. Herrick didn't stop talking.

"No practice today. We're going to start on Monday. We're going to go really hard. We're going to win it this year. Go home. Go see your families." He took a breath. "If you need to talk, Miss Cullen is here. I'm here."

He blew his whistle and the team dispersed. Mike Johnson stayed behind. When everyone was gone, he said, "You couldn't find him?"

He stared at Herrick, looking down at him, like Austin did behind the Dumpster.

"I did everything I could," Herrick said, trying to ignore the icicles forming in his gut.

Mike stood still for a moment, holding Herrick's eyes. Finally, he shook his head, exhaled, and left to catch up with the rest of the team.

Sarah waited until the gym was empty before approaching Herrick. She put her hand on his forearm.

"Matt," she whispered.

He nodded.

"You must—This, Austin, it's not your fault."

"I had him, Sarah. I sent him home, told him I'd come back for him this morning. I screwed up."

Sarah's hands balled into fists.

"He was going to let me help him."

Herrick stared at the parquet floor, tried to imagine the sound of sneakers squeaking on it during a defensive drill.

"I'm going after the guys who did this."

For a moment, Sarah was silent. Her jaw was tight, and the tendons in her neck stood out. Herrick thought she might hit him. She took a breath.

"So they can kill you too?" Her voice was flat.

He shook his head. "They won't."

Tell her about Afghanistan, he thought. Sarah's eyes would tear up, she'd give him a hug. They'd forget about all this. Even if for a moment.

This ain't about you, Coach. Austin's words echoed in his brain. He kept quiet.

"You and I both know you can't just put away one of them. They'll know who you are and come after you. That's what the Crips, the Bloods—it's what they do. Not like you're a cop. Just a nuisance." Sarah said it through clenched teeth.

Herrick looked at her. Her green eyes were glassy.

"Don't be stupid," she said. "This time, think."

Herrick ran a hand through his hair.

"Even if Austin had come with me—to the cops, to my apartment, anywhere—they would have found him," he said. "At some point."

She gave him another short nod. Without speaking, she went and retrieved her jacket and purse.

When she was gone, Herrick walked to the bleachers and sat down. He pictured Austin, behind the Dumpster, listening to him. Promising him he'd be at practice. Herrick shook his head.

He sat for a long time.

Season Pass

Chet Williamson

I didn't know what Mr. and Mrs. Younger were when I first saw them. To me they were just one more older couple who come out to Magicland for a sunny afternoon of watching the dolphin show, the stage act, and maybe taking one of the tamer rides—the carousel, or the Tunnel-of-Chills. I was sure I'd seen them before, for there was an easy familiarity about them. They looked at home, sitting on the bench near the bandshell, under the few oaks the new owners had let stand when they changed the old Rocky Grove Park into Magicland ten years before.

I wasn't here then, at least not as a security guard. But I came as a guest that first summer, as did almost everybody for a hundred miles around, to see what had been done to the Grove. Some had liked the change. I hadn't. The park had been sanitized away, the grotesque, laughing figures in the funhouse alcoves sold to collectors, the old rides like The Whip and The Octopus prettied up with fiberglass shells and cartoon animals. The Penny Arcade became the quarter arcade, and the flip movies that had intrigued my brother and me as boys were gone, replaced by video screens and pinball machines that offered only three balls for two bits. Everything was bright and clean and shiny. I hated it.

I didn't come back after that first visit until this spring, when I answered the ad for security guards. The office where I worked laid me off in March, and though the Magicland stint paid far less, I thought it would be a pleasant way to spend the summer while keeping my eyes open for something better. And I was hungry for something better. I used to think that hunger was a good thing, something that made us grow. Maybe open hunger, honest ambition, still is. But when hunger disguises itself as something else—kindness, maybe—it turns ugly, makes us less than human.

To look at the Youngers, you never would have imagined that hunger in them. When I first looked at them with more than casual interest, I guessed that they were in their early sixties. He was gray at the temples and near the top, but there were still dark brown patches. She too had streaks of gray-white, but the tawny hair around the whiteness made it look almost platinum in contrast. Neither was overweight, and both their complexions were healthily ruddy. The only outward signs of age were that the man limped slightly and carried a cane, and both wore thick bifocals. Their clothing was neat and clean, if a bit out of date. They looked well cared for, as one might make a suit last for years by judicious handling.

The Youngers. God, how that name suits them. So many don't. A potential assassin named Hinckley? A successful one named Oswald? Those are the names of buzzard towns and cartoon rabbits. But *Younger*—that sums up their deeds nicely, while smacking of the outlaw family too, though I doubt a connection. What *my* Youngers have done is soft and subtle, far from gunshots and holdups.

I noticed them, *really* noticed them for the first time, giving candy to a kid. I was twenty yards behind where they were sitting on their bench, and there was one of those sudden hushes that comes to the park once in a while, and I easily heard what they said.

"Young fella?" The man's voice was hearty and friendly. The boy, about ten, stopped but didn't say anything. "Want this?" the man went on, holding out a Hershey bar.

I tensed. I kept hearing my mother and father and teachers and the state trooper who visited the school once a year saying, *"Never take candy from strangers!"* For kids, it replaced the commandment about adultery.

"We just can't eat two," the woman said kindly. "And it'll melt in this hot sun. Won't you take it?"

The kid came closer and smiled a little. He looked cautious, like he'd heard the warnings too, but shrugged and took the candy. I guess he figured there were people all around, and that's what I figured too. "Okay. Thanks a lot," he said, and walked away with the candy. I watched the couple a moment longer, just long enough to see them smile at each other, as if to enjoy a good deed shared. But there was something else in the look, something more than gratification at giving away a 35¢ candy bar.

I started to notice the Youngers every day now, occasionally walking around the park, but mostly just sitting on the bench near the bandshell, whether a show was going on or not. For the life of me, I didn't see how people were able to sit through "Babes on Broadway" once, let alone five times a day, six on weekends. But the Youngers were always there, holding the bench like a fort, watching with interest as our "professional cast" butchered songs from *A Chorus Line* and *Oklahoma!*, or when little kids scrambled up into the bandshell between shows and pretended that they were our music school dropouts who moved their mouths to the canned tunes.

And they kept giving away candy, too. I'd see them do it once or twice a week, and since I spent only a little of my time watching them, they must have done it far more frequently than that. It was the last week of July when I got suspicious. I saw the woman give a Hershey bar to a little girl of six or seven. I smiled, for I'd written the couple off as just nice, generous folks with no grandchildren of their own to spoil, getting their parental kicks by making kids happy with chocolate. But a few hours later, I saw the same little girl, white as a skull, sitting with her worried parents in the nurse's station.

Little kids are always getting sick in the park—the station doles out twenty or thirty doses of Pepto-Bismol a day to deal with the gut-wrenching mixture of rides and junk food. But the little girl didn't look nauseated. She looked drained, as if something were eating at her. I checked back an hour later, but Jeanie, the nurse, told me the girl felt better and that she and her parents had gone.

I'm a suspicious type to begin with—always been a little paranoid—so the combination of candy and illness put me on my toes, and I began thinking about the kind of crazies who put razor blades in apples. Something in the candy? A little rat poison? A shot of Raid? Were these nice old folks retired elementary schoolteachers with a taste for vengeance? I decided to keep a closer eye on the sweet old couple the next day.

I was stationed at the rear of the grove a full hour before they walked in at 9:30 and sat on their usual bench. They talked softly, but from their expressions and the gentle tones that drifted back to me, I knew it was the talk that people make when they've been with each other for a long time and are happy to stay that way. They looked up at the trees, stretched, turned, situated themselves differently. At times he would put an arm around her, or they held hands, and often they didn't touch at all. Finally she took two paperbacks from her big straw purse, handed one to the man, and they both began to read. It looked like a long day.

At 10:45, when the park was beginning to fill up and people were grabbing benches for the 11:00 "Babes on Broadway," the woman got up and went to the nearest snack bar. I followed and watched as she bought two Cokes and four Hershey bars, then returned to the bench, giving a Coke to her husband and setting the candy between them. In five minutes they gave one away to an Asian kid and his younger brother. There was no way they could have doctored it. I saw them all the time, watching their hands and the candy through the slats in the bench. All she did after she made the offer was pick up the Hershey bar and put it in the kid's hand, and watch and wave as the boys scampered away.

I've got to confess that I was a little disappointed at not being able to nab two kiddie-poisoners, but the relief of knowing that if there *were* people like that they weren't in *my* park more than made up for it. I gave the couple a clean bill, and left the grove feeling better about human nature.

But after lunch I saw the Asian boy in the nurse's station, and that cool lump settled in my throat again. With him were the younger boy and a woman, obviously his mother, and I walked over to them. "Tummy ache, huh?" I said, trying not to sound too interested.

The woman smiled and nodded, not saying anything. The boy just looked ahead, his face pale. But the younger child answered. "I told him not to ride that scary ride, but he did it."

"Yeah," I said sympathetically, "that happens, especially when you eat a lot of candy, too. You have any candy today, champ?" I asked the older boy.

"Not him, not him," said the younger one. "*I* had a Hershey bar."

"You...?" I hoped I didn't look as dumb as I felt.

"Sam gave it to me. A lady gave it to him and he gave it to me."

"Uh-huh. You feel okay though, huh?"

"Yeah, I feel okay."

"Is something wrong?" said the woman, understandably curious about my interest in her son's diet.

"No, no," I smiled, and left the station after a nod to Jeanie, who was also looking at me strangely.

I didn't get it, but I wanted to, so I went back to the grove and parked behind the old couple again. This time I didn't have long to wait. They gave a little girl a candy bar in less than fifteen minutes after I'd gotten there, and this time I trailed the kid, who joined some friends, showed them the candy, and broke it up into pieces to share. A half hour later, after only two rides and nothing else to eat, she began to slow down and look a little sick. She sat on a bench with one of her friends, while the others tackled the Sooper-Loop, but in a few minutes she was back on her feet, as though whatever had troubled her had passed quickly, and I let her get lost in the crowd.

Coincidences. It was possible, but I didn't believe it, so I decided to find out a little more about the generous golden-agers who so dependably held down that bench. I figured they'd have to have season passes, so the next morning I asked Pete, the old guy who heads the ticket-takers, to do me a favor. I told him there was a couple I'd seen in the park who I thought I knew, but that I couldn't place their names, and maybe he'd check for me when they showed their passes. I thought it sounded dumb, and the frown he gave me showed that he did too, but he said he would. I stood by his side until I saw the couple walking in from the parking lot. The man's cane was gone, and there was no sign of a limp. I nudged Pete and pointed in their direction. When he saw them he crumpled up his mouth as if he'd tasted vinegar. "Don't need to see their pass," he said softly. "Name's Younger. Carl and Ethel Younger."

"You know them?"

"Never spoke to them. But I've seen their passes enough times that I remember their names."

I felt I had something. "How long have they been coming to the park?"

Old Pete snorted. "They've had season passes ever since this place got civilized. And before that..." He paused.

"What?" He turned and looked at me, his gray eyes stone cold and serious. "They were here when I ran The Whip. In the old days. Used to be over by the grove."

"I remember," I said. And I did, from when I was a kid.

"I remember them from then," he went on. "They used to sit by the bandshell all the time, talking to kids." His eyes narrowed. "What are you really interested in them for?"

"I told you, I..."

He smiled grimly. "Yeah, you told me."

"They must have been a lot younger then," I said with a little smile, trying to get him back on the track.

"They looked pretty much the same as they do now."

"Well then, they age well."

"Damn right they do," Old Pete said. "I ain't run The Whip for twenty-five years, and I saw them a long time before that yet." My smile vanished. "Anything else? Or can I get to my work now?"

I thanked him and went to the nearest water fountain. My throat had gone dry. Pete must have been wrong, I thought. Twenty-five years? Hell, they looked sixtyish now, so if they were sixty back when Pete had seen them first, that meant they must be eighty-five, ninety, even older.

I walked over to the grove again and watched them. When Carl Younger got up, he walked briskly over to the snack bar to buy the candy. When he returned, they sat and talked, then started to read their books. Neither, I noticed, was wearing glasses. I moved closer, so that I stood a couple of yards behind them. The grayness I'd seen in their hair at the start of the summer had nearly vanished, and Carl Younger's hand that lay on his wife's shoulder looked strangely smooth and youthful for a man of his years.

They didn't seem to notice me, and in a while a young girl passed, and Ethel Younger looked up. "Miss," she said, "would you like this candy? I'm afraid I bought too many for just us."

The girl hesitated, then looked at me standing nearby in my uniform, as if asking for permission. I gave a little nod, and just as I did, both Youngers turned around and saw me. Their smiles never faded and, after only a flicker of interest touched their shining eyes, they looked back at the girl. Ethel Younger held out the Hershey bar. The girl smiled back, said "thank you" softly, and took it, her fingers just brushing those of the woman as the exchange was made. She tucked the candy in a red plastic purse, and walked away.

The Youngers looked straight ahead, apparently neither curious nor bothered by my being there. But there was a smugness to the set of their shoulders, a stealthy triumph in the way they held their heads. My heart was beating quickly, and I felt my ears growing hot. They had done something, something while I was standing right there beside them, and it was as if they knew I couldn't stop them, as if they were laughing inside over the great joke they'd played.

I choked down my anger until I thought I could speak clearly. Then I sat down on the bench next to Ethel Younger, looking at her face in profile, her blue eyes staring out across the benches, the crow's feet in their corners only small lines now, almost unnoticeable.

"What?" I said quietly. Her head didn't turn, but her eyes shifted, looking at a spot on the ground a yard in front of my feet. "What are you doing?"

She looked at me then, her head pivoting slowly. "Doing?" Her eyebrows arched in a question.

"To the kids," I said, still almost whispering. "To the children."

Now Carl Younger was looking at me too, leaning forward slightly to see past his wife. "I don't know what you mean," he said calmly.

"I've been watching you," I said. "You give them candy and they get sick."

Carl Younger shrugged. "I'm sorry to hear that." Then he smiled. "I hope they get better?"

"Yeah," I said. "They get better."

"I hope there's nothing wrong with the candy," said Ethel Younger. "We buy it right here at the concession stand."

"I know. I've seen you buy it."

"Oh." Her mouth grew round. Her teeth were very white. "And have you seen us do anything to it afterwards?"

"No," I said. "You don't touch it."

She cocked her head. "Well then . . . ?"

"It's not poison," I said. "It's not the candy."

She looked at her husband, then back at me. "Well then," she repeated.

I nodded. "That's what I want to know. Well then what?" I stood up in front of them, trying to look big, look tall, look like my silly gray and gold uniform meant more than it did. "It's *you*," I said. "I want to know what the hell you're doing here."

Carl Younger gave an exasperated smile. "What does anyone do here? We enjoy the shows, we look at the people, we never had any children of our own, so it's nice to be able to give . . ."

"We take," Ethel Younger said, interrupting her husband, who jerked his head around to look at her, panic in his eyes.

"Ethel..." he warned.

"No," she said, waving her hand as if she were brushing off a fly, her voice suddenly low and cold. "We take."

"Ethel, shut up..."

"It doesn't matter." She kept looking at me, a smirk on her face. "Let him know. He deserves to know. After all these years, he's the *only* one, the only one to notice."

Carl Younger just looked at her in surprise for a moment, then back at me. Then he smiled too, a smile that turned to a smirk just as nasty and self-confident as his wife's. "You're right," he said. "It won't matter. Who'd believe him? What could he do?"

"You want to stop talking about me like I'm not here?" I said harshly. I didn't like the way they were watching me. But it wasn't hunger, just the overwhelming desire to share a secret they'd kept for years, an unknown accomplishment they were proud of.

"Sit down then," Ethel Younger said, patting the bench. "Sit down and we'll talk to you," and she held out a hand as if expecting me to take it.

"I'd rather stand."

"Suit yourself." She shrugged.

"You said you take. What did you mean? *What* do you take?"

"We take a little time," she said. "Is that so much? I mean, certainly people have asked *you* for a little time—'do you have a few minutes?'" She laughed softly, genuinely amused. "That's all they lose. Maybe more than a few minutes, maybe some days, a week or two, perhaps a month, but they never know it. They never miss it."

"You take...time?" I repeated.

"Time is what it boils down to. Actually I suppose you could call it a little strength...a little..."

"Vitality," her husband said.

"Yes," she nodded. "Vitality. And as you so cleverly noticed, it may make them ill for a bit, but children are always getting ill in amusement parks, aren't they? And they recover. They feel fine in an hour or so. They grow up, they grow old—maybe not quite as old as they would have, but what are a few days to an old person? Unless you can take those days...and multiply them."

"You touch them," I said dully. "When you give them the candy, you touch them."

"Yes. Just a touch." She smiled again. "A touch, I do confess!" And then she laughed. "It feels so *good* to confess it, so good for someone to know at last. You've no idea how hard it..."

"How do you do it?"

She shook her head shortly and looked at her husband, who raised his eyebrows. "How do you walk?" she replied. "It's been so long since we've had to think about it that I doubt if we could explain it in words, even to ourselves. It's just something we do."

"Instinctive," said Carl Younger.

"Yes, instinctive. We had to learn at first. Self-taught, I don't quite remember how. But once we knew we could, once we were able to control it, it became quite second nature. One short season of sharing, and we are primed, charged, secured from the grip of Gerontion until the next summer. And then we begin again." She sighed. "Retirement has proven to be a most rewarding time."

I had to ask it. "How old are you?"

She smiled coyly. "What a rude question. One I won't answer, because I doubt you'd believe me. But old enough to have forgotten how we got this old." She shook her head, frowning. "Don't look so sour. What we take is so very slight, never even missed. And there's nothing you can do about it now, is there?" She replaced the frown with a warm smile, the same one she'd used when offering the Hershey bars. "No hard feelings?" she asked, and held out her hand.

I couldn't touch it. Instead I backed off, bumping into the next row of benches. Then I turned and walked away from them, away from the bandshell and the grove, unable to make myself look back at the pair of them sitting there. And the three candy bars on the bench beside them.

I don't know what I thought at first. I *couldn't* think, couldn't accept something so crazy, so implausible, so totally unreal. So I walked my rounds and looked for slug users, and I didn't go past the bandshell to see if the Youngers were still there. I knew they would be. It wasn't until I was in my street clothes and on my way home that I began to try and deal with what they had told me as a reality, even if a reality created from an aging couple's cruel fantasy. At the best, they were crazy. At the worst, they were…far worse. Either way, I had to get them out of the park.

Or did I? What harm had they really done? Assuming that what they had told me was only their own pitiful delusion, they did no harm at all, except for contributing to tooth decay and nausea, and who was I to stop them? I think that was the main reason I didn't want to believe them—I simply didn't know what to do if it were true. It was a lot easier to consider them wacky old coots with a gift for healthy longevity than to believe otherwise.

But I couldn't help myself. I *did* believe them. Ethel Younger had been sane. Her eyes had been as clear and as honest as a child's. And as young.

Well then? she had asked, and I asked myself—well then?—trying to find a path out, to find a way to do nothing and still be able to live with myself. What the hell, I thought, popping open a fourth beer at my kitchen table, what's a week to an eighty-year-old? And how many kids would even live to be seventy or eighty anyway, with the shape the world was in? Would anybody even be around in good old 2060? What did it matter? And I flopped into bed, mind and room both spinning, thankful that tomorrow was my day off. As I fell asleep, I kept seeing Ethel Younger's white teeth smiling confidently at me, her mouth moving, telling me what she'd told me earlier that day, replaying it in my mind to reassure me that I need do nothing, because *they never miss it... nothing you can do about it... what we take is so very slight...*

once we were able to control it...

My eyes snapped open, and the room started to roll again, but it was only my body that had had too much beer. My mind was suddenly clear, remembering those words so vividly—*once we were able to control it*—and remembering everything else too, so that it all fit together like a snap-lock puzzle. There must have been a time, then, when they were learning, when they *couldn't* control the power they had. And it was because of that time, not all that long ago, that I would do what I had to do.

The next day, Sunday, I woke up early and went to Magicland dressed in my street clothes. I showed my pass, got in before opening time, and went to the grove and sat on the Youngers' bench, waiting for them. It was cool, with a hint of rain in the air, and the light jacket I wore felt good. They arrived ten minutes after the park opened. When they saw me, they slowed down, but didn't turn back, just kept coming toward me until they were right next to me.

Ethel Younger smiled. Her husband didn't. "Another visit?" she said.

I nodded. "Your passes," I said. "May I see them?"

She pursed her lips. "You're not in uniform today."

"I'm still a guard. I can show you my I.D."

"That won't be necessary." She dug into her purse and came up with a plastic card that she held out to me.

"Just put it on the bench beside me," I said, not touching it.

"My, aren't we peevish this morning," she said, doing as I asked.

"Now yours," I told Carl Younger. He hesitated, then took his pass from his wallet and placed it next to his wife's. I picked them up and looked at them. The faces in the photos looked ten years older than those of the people standing in front of me. I bent the soft plastic in two and put the passes into my pocket. "Your passes have expired. They're not good any more."

Carl Younger's face got red, and he opened his mouth to speak, but his wife's raised hand stopped him. Though her eyes looked calm, her mouth had drawn down and her nostrils had widened. "I believe you're wrong," she told me. "The expiration date is September 10th. This is only August 5th."

I shook my head.

"Perhaps we should take this up with your superiors."

"That's fine," I said. "But he'll believe me, not you. And when I tell him you've been giving candy to kids..."

"That's not against the law!" Carl Younger burst in.

"...and asking them for certain things in exchange..." I went on.

"That's a *lie*," Ethel Younger cried.

It was my turn to shrug. "Why would I lie about a thing like that? What point would it serve?"

"You'd need witnesses."

"Would you want it to go that far?" I asked her. "You want people to know your date of birth?"

Then she laughed, softly at first, but it grew louder, until tears started to form in the smooth corners of her eyes. "He *believed* us!" she said, clapping her husband on the shoulder. "Carl, he actually believed our story!"

Carl Younger smiled uncomfortably, then started to laugh himself. It was forced and phony, but it didn't matter. I knew she was lying.

"Such a silly story!" she went on, "and..."

"Shut up," I said, my fear lost in anger. "It's too late for that. Just like it's too late for Jimmy."

She stopped laughing. Her husband continued for a few seconds afterward. "Jimmy," she said condescendingly, as though it were all a joke. "And who is Jimmy?"

"*Was* Jimmy. My brother. My younger brother. Died when we were kids. Died fast, just got sick and died in two days. The doctors thought it was leukemia but were never really sure. That was the same summer my hair turned gray. The other kids thought it was funny. Ten years old and gray hair."

The Youngers weren't smiling any more.

"You hadn't quite gotten it down by then, had you? Not quite able to control it, huh?"

Her mouth opened, trembled, and shut.

"And last night I put it all together. After thirty years I remembered, and it all went click. And I knew why you looked so familiar the first time I saw you this summer. I'd seen you before. Hadn't thought about it for years, but it was still back there. Not every day strangers give you candy. One each. You gave us a candy bar each. A long time ago, *you* probably don't remember. But then why would you? Why remember one out of so many?"

I bit the inside of my lip. My words had been coming in a rush, and I didn't want to get upset, emotional. I had a job to do. "It's time to stop now," I said. "You took too much. Get out of this park and don't ever come back. But I'll be watching you, and if you ever try to touch another child, I'll kill you both." I pushed back the front of my jacket just far enough to let them see the butt of the .38 Special I had wedged in my waistband.

Faces pale, they turned without a word and walked away. I followed them to make sure they left the park, and then I followed them to their home, a small house on a quiet residential street in a town fifteen miles from Magicland. Their lights went off at midnight, and I drove to my place, got my bag, woke up the security head with a phone call, and told him I had to go out of town for a week or so. I think a week's about right. To obtain youth with just a touch must be more addictive than any drug, and I can hardly blame them for slipping. In the past few days we've been to two zoos, a library, three museums, and two small town parks with playgrounds. Although they look for me, they haven't seen me. But they will soon.

Today they bought some candy.

ABOUT THE AUTHORS

Patti Abbott is the author of the ebook, *Monkey Justice and Other Stories*. She is the co-editor of *Discount Noir*. She won a Derringer Award in 2009 for her flash fiction story, "My Hero." More than 80 of her stories have appeared in anthologies, print, and online publications. She lives in Detroit.

Ian Ayris is the author of almost forty short stories, published both online and in print. His debut novel, *Abide With Me*, was published by Caffeine Nights Publishing in March 2012. Ian lives in Romford, England, with his wife and three children.

Ray Banks shares his birthday with Chuck Barris and Curtis Mayfield and screeched into the world on the same day that Roberto Rossellini took his leave. He has worked as a wedding singer, double-glazing salesman, croupier, dole monkey, and various degrees of disgruntled temp. He writes novels (like the Cal Innes series) and short stories (like this one) and keeps a fairly clean online abode at The Saturday Boy.

Nigel Bird has been a teacher for twenty-five years and is proud to have been invited to take part in such a wonderful fundraising project as this. As well as teaching, he's managed to bring three children into the world and has given birth to a number of stories including the novel *In Loco Parentis*, the novella *Smoke*, and the collection *Dirty Old Town*. He lives by the sea on the East Coast of Scotland and is a lot happier than his fiction might suggest.

Michael A. Black is the author of 17 books and over 100 short stories and articles. He has a BA in English from Northern Illinois University and a MFA in Fiction Writing from Columbia College Chicago. He was a police officer in the south suburbs of Chicago for over thirty years and worked in various capacities in police work including patrol supervisor, SWAT team leader, investigations, and tactical operations. His Ron Shade series, featuring the Chicago-based kickboxing private eye, has won several awards, as has his police procedural series featuring Frank Leal and Olivia Hart. He has also written two novels with television star Richard Belzer of Law & Order SUV. His hobbies include the martial arts, running, and weight lifting. Black is currently writing novels in a highly popular adventure series under another name.

Tony Black is Irvine Welsh's favourite British crime writer. The author of eight critically acclaimed crime books, his works include the Gus Dury PI series: *Paying For It*, *Gutted*, *Loss* and *Long Time Dead*, the final installment of which will be filmed for the screen by Richard Jobson in 2012. His police inspector series, featuring DI Rob Brennan, includes the titles *Truth Lies Bleeding* and *Murder Mile*; both published by Random House UK. Before turning to the novel, Tony was an award-winning national newspaper journalist covering subjects as diverse as crime and nightclub reviews. He still writes for the press from time to time but most of his non-fiction now turns up on his blog and his website.

R Thomas Brown is the author of *Hill Country*, a crime novel set in Texas. His writing, thoughts on writing, and general musings can be found at Criminal Thoughts.

Ken Bruen has been a finalist for the Edgar, Barry, and Dagger Awards. The Private Eye Writers of America presented him with the Shamus Award for the Best Novel of 2003 for *The Guards*, the book that introduced Jack Taylor. And in 2010, the Mystery Readers International bestowed the Macavity Award on Ken and Reed Farrel Coleman for their crime novel *Tower*. Ken lives in Galway, Ireland. Learn more at his website: Ken Bruen.com.

Bill Cameron is the author of dark, gritty mysteries featuring Skin Kadash: *County Line*, *Day One*, *Chasing Smoke*, and *Lost Dog*. Bill's short stories have appeared in *Portland Noir*,*First Thrills*, *Deadly Treats*, *West Coast Crime Wave*, *Puppy Love Noir*, and *Diaries of Misspent Youth*. His work has been nominated for multiple awards, including the Spotted Owl Award, the Left Coast Crime Rocky Award, and the 2011 CWA Short Story Dagger Award. In 2012, *County Line* won the Spotted Owl for Best Northwest Mystery. He lives in Portland, Oregon. Learn more at Bill Cameron.com

Jen Conley's stories have been published in *Thuglit*, *Needle*, *Beat to a Pulp*, *Shotgun Honey*, *Out of the Gutter*, *Big Pulp*, *Talking River Review*, *SNM Horror*, and others. In 2011, one of her stories was nominated for a *Best of the Web Spinetingler Award* which was really awesome. Born and raised in New Jersey, she lives in Ocean County where she teaches middle school and writes in her spare time. Visit her at Jen Conley.blogspot or follow her on twitter, @jenconley45

Charles de Lint is a full-time writer and musician who presently makes his home in Ottawa, Canada, with his wife MaryAnn Harris. His most recent books are *Under My Skin* (Razorbill Canada, 2012) and *Eyes Like Leaves* (Tachyon Press, 2012). His first album *Old Blue Truck* came out in early 2011.

Wayne Dundee lives in the once-notorious old cowtown of Ogallala, on the hinge of Nebraska's panhandle. A widower, retired from a managerial position in the magnetics industry, Dundee now devotes full time to his writing. To date, Dundee has had fourteen novels, three novellas, and over thirty short stories published. Much of his work has featured his PI protagonist, Joe Hannibal (appearing most recently in *Goshen Hole*- 2011). He also dabbles in fantasy and straight crime, and lately has been gaining notice in the Western genre. His 2010 Western short story, "This Old Star", won a Peacemaker Award from the Western Fictioneers writers' organization. His 2011 novel *Dismal River* won a Peacemaker in the Best First Western Novel category. Titles in the Hannibal series have been translated into several languages and nominated for an Edgar, an Anthony, and six Shamus Awards. Dundee is also the founder and original editor of Hardboiled Magazine. Learn more at his blog: From Dundee's Desk. Follow him on Facebook: facebook.com/wayne.dundee or on Twitter: @wddundee

Chad Eagleton lives in the Midwest with his wife and dog. He is a Spinetingler Award nominee and two-time Watery Grave Invitational finalist with work available in print, e-book, and online. For more info visit his blog, Cathode Angel.

Les Edgerton is an ex-con, matriculating at Pendleton Reformatory in the sixties for burglary (plea-bargained down from multiple counts of burglary, armed robbery, strong-armed robbery and possession with intent). He's since taken a vow of poverty (became a writer) with 14 books in print. After making parole, he went to college and got a B.A. from Indiana University and an MFA from Vermont College. Recent novels of his include *The Bitch* and *Just Like That* and his next novel, *The Rapist* is forthcoming from New Pulp Press. He is the editor-at-large for *Noir Nation*. Stories of his have appeared in *Murdaland, Flatmancrooked, Noir Nation, South Carolina Review,* and *Best American Mystery Stories,* among others. He writes because he hates…a lot…and hard. Injustice and bullying are what he hates the most. He can be found at Les Edgerton Writing.

Andrew Fader has had poetry appear in several literary journals including *Rosebud, The Literary Review, Journal of New Jersey Poets* and *Paterson Review.* His chapbook, *Taking Stock,* was published by Poets Corner Press in 2007. He has previously had poems appear in two anthologies, *The Poetry of Place* and *The American Voice in Poetry.* His poem "I Visit My Father's Grave and We Talk" was a winner in *Passager Press'* poetry contest. He teaches writing and literature at Fairleigh Dickinson University in Madison, New Jersey.

Matthew C. Funk is a social media consultant, professional marketing copywriter and writing mentor. He is an editor of *Needle Magazine* and a staff writer for *Planet Fury* and *Criminal Complex*. Winner of the 2010 Spinetingler Award for Best Short Story on the Web, Funk has online work at numerous sites indexed on his Web domain and printed in *Needle*, *Speedloader*, *Grift*, *Pulp Ink*, *Pulp Modern*, *Off the Record* and *D*CKED*. He is represented by Stacia J. N. Decker of the Donald Maass Literary Agency.

Roxane Gay lives and writes in the Midwest.

Edward A. Grainger aka David Cranmer, was born and raised near Ithaca, New York but now calls Maine his home. His fiction has appeared in *Out of the Gutter*, *Pulp Ink*, *The Western Online*, *Crime Factory*, and *Pulp Modern*. He is editor and publisher of the *BEAT to a PULP* webzine and a member of the Western Fictioneers. He and his wife Denise are the proud parents of a beautiful baby girl, Ava Elyse. He invites you to visit his website at davidcranmer.com and to email him at paladin-1@hotmail.com.

Glenn Gray is a physician specializing in Radiology. He's had numerous stories published both in print and online. He lives in New York.

Jane Hammons teaches writing at UC Berkeley where she is the recipient of a Distinguished Teaching Award. She has a story in *Hint Fiction: An Anthology of Stories in 25 Words or Fewer* (W. W. Norton 2010) and an essay in *The Maternal is Political: Women Writers at the Intersection of Motherhood and Social Change* (Seal Press 2008). She is the recipient of a Derringer Award from the Short Mystery Story Society. Nominated three times for Pushcart Prizes in both fiction and nonfiction, her writing has appeared in a variety of magazines and journals: *Columbia Journalism Review*, *Crimespree Magazine*, *San Francisco Chronicle Magazine*, *Southwestern American Literature*, *A Twist of Noir*, *Shotgun Honey*, *Verbicide Magazine* and *Word Riot*.

Amber Keller is a writer who delves into dark, speculative fiction, particularly horror and suspense/thrillers. She has been fortunate enough to be included in various anthologies, and features many short stories on her site at A Diary of a Writer. A member of the Horror Writers Association, she also contributes to many websites and eMagazines, including providing horror and science fiction movie reviews. You can follow her on Twitter at @akeller9. When not at her laptop, she can be found looking for things that go bump in the night.

Joe R. Lansdale is the author of numerous novels and short stories, screenplays and comic scripts. He has written for Batman the Animated series, and his story Bubba Hotep became a film of the same name. He has won numerous recognitions for his works, among them the Lifetime Achievement Award from the Horror Writers Association, The Edgar Award, and nine Bram Stokers and the Grandmaster Award from HWA. His latest novel is *Edge of Dark Water*.

Frank Larnerd is an undergraduate student at WVSU, where he has received multiple awards for fiction and non-fiction. His first anthology as editor, *Hills of Fire: Bare-Knuckle Yarns of Appalachia*, will be released in the fall of 2012 from Woodland Press. He lives in Putnam County, West Virginia.

Gary Lovisi is a writer, editor, book collector and publisher, not always in that order. He is a Mystery Writers of America Edgar Award nominee for his short fiction, and a Western Writers of America Spur Award winner for his editing of *Hardboiled* magazine. Gary Lovisi is also the publisher of Gryphon Books which publishes new and classic reprint pulp crime and science fiction books. He is the editor of *Paperback Parade*, the world's leading and longest running magazine on collectable paperbacks of all kinds, and *Hardboiled* magazine, the hardest little crime fiction magazine in the world. He is also the sponsor of an annual rare book show, The New York Collectable Paperback & Pulp Fiction Expo, now in its 24th year! You can find out more about Gary Lovisi, his books and various publications, or contact him via email at his website at Gryphon Books.

Dave Marsh edited *Creem Magazine*, coined the term "punk rock," wrote best-selling biographies of Bruce Springsteen and the Who, edited the first two editions of the *Rolling Stone Record Guide* and, from 1975-1978 the *Rolling Stone* record review section, wrote the AmericanGrandstand column for *Rolling Stone*, was a *Playboy* music critic foralmost twenty years, and since 1982, has co-edited *Rock & Rap Confidential* a newsletter about music and politics. Dave currently hosts three shows on SiriusXM satellite radio: *Live from E Street Nation* (E Street channel 20), *Kick Out the Jams* (The Spectrum channel 28) and *Live from the Land of Hope and Dreams* (Left, channel 127). He is a life member of PROTECT and a member of its advisory board. You can reach him at davemarsh.us and rockrap.com.

Mike Miner lives in Connecticut with his wife and two daughters. A mild mannered grocery clerk by day, at night, Mike writes dark, violent stories. Some of which have found homes in: *Pulp Ink 2, Spinetingler, Narrative, PANK, Pulp Metal Magazine, The Flash Fiction Ofensive, Shotgun Honey* and *Solstice: A Magazine of Diverse Voices*.

Zak Mucha, LCSW, is the supervisor of an Assertive Community Treatment (ACT) program, providing services to persons suffering severe psychiatric and substance abuse disorders in Chicago's Uptown neighborhood. He also maintains a private practice for individual therapy and counseling. Mucha is the author of *The Beggars' Shore* (Red 71 Press, 2000), and contributor to *Heart Transplant* by Andrew Vachss and Frank Caruso (Dark Horse Books, 2010). His forthcoming novel is *The Heavyweight Champion of Nothing* (Ten Angry Pitbulls, 2012). He can be found at zakmucha.com.

Dan O'Shea is a Chicago-area writer. His first two thrillers, *Penance* and *Mammon*, will be published by Exhibit A, the crime fiction imprint of Angry Robot, a UK publisher. Drawing on Chicago's settings and history, the novels explore the city's history of corruption, but with a national, even international flair. Dan is also the author of *Old School*, a collection of short fiction published by Snubnose Press. Dan has been a professional business writer for many years. A few decades of having to write about the US tax code drove him to write about killing people. He would be a handsome gent if he could just stop breaking his nose. Dan is represented by Stacia Decker of the Donald Maass Literary Agency. Learn more at Going Ballistic.

George Pelecanos is an independent film producer, the recipient of numerous international writing awards, a producer and an Emmy-nominated writer on the HBO series *The Wire*, and the author of seventeen novels set in and around Washington, D.C.

Thomas Pluck writes unflinching fiction with heart. His stories have appeared in PANK magazine, Crime Factory, Spinetingler, Plots with Guns, Beat to a Pulp, McSweeney's, The Utne Reader and elsewhere. He edits the *Lost Children* charity anthologies to benefit PROTECT: The National Association to Protect Children. He is working on his first novel. He lives in New Jersey with his wife Sarah. You can find him as @tommysalami on Twitter, and on the web at thomaspluck.com.

After growing up on a Nebraska farm, **Richard Prosch** has worked as a professional writer and artist while in Wyoming, South Carolina, and Missouri. His western crime fiction captures the fleeting history and lonely frontier stories of his youth, where characters aren't always what they seem, and the wind-burnt landscape is filled with swift, deadly danger.

Keith Rawson is a little-known pulp writer whose short fiction, poetry, essays, reviews, and interviews have been widely published both online and in print. He is the author of the short story collections *The Chaos We Know* and Laughing at *Dead Men* (SnubNose Press)and Co-Editor of the anthology *Crime Factory: The First Shift*. He's also a regular contributor to *LitReactor* and *Spinetingler Magazine*. He lives in Southern Arizona with his wife and daughter.

A lifelong Texan, **James Reasoner** has been a professional writer for more than thirty-five years. In that time, he has authored several hundred novels and short stories in numerous genres. Best known for his Westerns, historical novels, and war novels, he is also the author of two mystery novels that have achieved cult classic status, *Texas Wind* and *Dust Devils*. His novel Redemption, Kansas recently won the Peacemaker Award, given by Western Fictioneers, for Best Western Novel. Writing under his own name and various pseudonyms, his novels have garnered praise from *Publishers Weekly*, *Booklist*, and the *Los Angeles Times*, as well as appearing on the *New York Times* and *USA Today* bestseller lists. He lives in a small town in Texas with his wife, award-winning fellow author Livia J. Washburn. His blog can be found at Rough Edges.

Todd Robinson is the creator and Chief Editor of the multi-award winning crime fiction webzine THUGLIT.COM. His short fiction has appeared in *Plots With Guns*, *Blood and Tacos*, *Needle Magazine*, *Shotgun Honey*, *Strange, Weird, and Wonderful*, *Out of the Gutter*, *Pulp Pusher*, *Grift*, *Demolition Magazine*, *CrimeFactory* and *Danger City*. His writing has been nominated for a Derringer Award, shortlisted for Best American Mystery Stories, selected for Writers Digest's Year's Best Writing 2003 and won the inaugural Bullet Award in June 2011. His first collection of short stories, *Dirty Words* is now available exclusively on Kindle. His debut novel *The Hard Bounce*, will be released in January 2013 from Tyrus Books.

Johnny Shaw was born and raised in the Desert Southwest on the Calexico/Mexicali border, the setting for his novels, *Dove Season* and *Big Maria*. Johnny is also the creator and editor of the online fiction quarterly BLOOD & TACOS, a loving homage to the men's adventure paperbacks of the 1970's & 1980's. Johnny received his MFA in Screenwriting from UCLA and over the course of his writing career has seen his screenplays optioned, sold and produced. For the last dozen years, Johnny has taught screenwriting, as well. He has lectured at both Santa Barbara City College and UC Santa Barbara. Johnny lives in Portland, Oregon with his wife, artist Roxanne Patruznick. You can find him online at johnnyshawauthor.com or follow him on Twitter @BloodAndTacos

Gerald So edits *The 5-2: Crime Poetry Weekly* at poemsoncrime.blogspot.com. He previously served as fiction editor of Kevin Burton Smith's Thrilling Detective Web Site (2001-'09) and president of the Short Mystery Fiction Society (2008-'10). He lives on Long Island.

Josh Stallings is the author of the Moses McGuire Novels, *Beautiful, Naked & Dead* and *Out There Bad*. To his amazement he found himself on more than fifteen best books of 2011 lists. His memoir, *All The Wild Children*, will be released by Snubnose Press in November 2012. Find out more at joshstallings.net.

Charlie Stella writes hardboiled crime fiction while pursing an MFA degree at Southern New Hampshire University. He's delivered newspapers (back when people read them), unloaded watermelons, been a dish washer, cooked hamburgers at McDonalds, humped sheetrock at the Olympic Tower, buffed hallways and cleaned apartments in Starrett City, cleaned windows atop several high rise Manhattan office buildings, was a bouncer at a few bars, was into street finance and bookmaking, was a word processing operator, supervisor, manager and director of communications. He currently works as a word processing operator for a law firm in New Jersey. His story, "In Dreams," is part of his MFA thesis, a fictional memoir.

Andrew Vachss has been a federal investigator in sexually transmitted diseases, a social-services caseworker, and a labor organizer, and has directed a maximum-security prison for "aggressive-violent" youth. Now a lawyer in private practice, he represents children and youths exclusively. His many works of fiction include the Burke series and two collections of short stories (with a third to be published in 2013). His books have been translated into twenty languages, and his work has appeared in *Parade, Antaeus, Esquire, Playboy, the New York Times*, and many other forums. A native New Yorker, he now divides his time between the city of his birth and the Pacific Northwest. His latest novel, *Blackjack*, is his first featuring Cross. For more information, visit The Zero.

Steve Weddle is one of the originals at DoSomeDamage.com, as well as being the editor of *Needle: A Magazine of Noir*. His website is steveweddle.com.

Dave White is the two-time Shamus Award nominated author of *When One Man Dies, The Evil That Men Do*, and *Witness To Death*. You can find him blogging at Do Some Damage, On The Banks, and Beers N Books.

Chet Williamson has written in the field of suspense and fantasy for over thirty years. Among his novels are *Defenders of the Faith, Second Chance, Ash Wednesday, Soulstorm, Lowland Rider, McKain's Dilemma, Reign, Dreamthorp*, and *The Searchers* series. His books have been translated and published in France, Germany, Russia, Italy, and Japan. Over a hundred of his short stories have appeared in such magazines as *The New Yorker, Playboy, Esquire, Twilight Zone, The Magazine of Fantasy and Science Fiction*, and many other magazines and anthologies. *Figures in Rain*, a collection of his short stories, won the 2002 International Horror Guild Award. He has been short-listed twice for the World Fantasy Award, six times for the Horror Writers Association's Stoker Award, and once for the Mystery Writers of America's Edgar Award.

COPYRIGHT NOTICES

Made in the USA
San Bernardino, CA
05 April 2014